Eunice

A Tale of Reconstruction Times in South Carolina

Eunice

A Tale of Reconstruction Times in South Carolina

A Novel by William James Rivers

Edited by Tara Courtney McKinney

University of South Carolina Press

Published in cooperation with the South Caroliniana Library with the Assistance of the
Caroline McKissick Dial Publication Fund and the University South Caroliniana Society

© 2006 University of South Carolina

Published by the University of South Carolina Press
Columbia, South Carolina 29208

www.sc.edu/uscpress

Manufactured in the United States of America

15 14 13 12 11 10   09 08 07 06   10 9 8 7 6 5 4 3 2 1

Library of Congress Cataloging-in-Publication Data

Rivers, William J. (William James), 1822–1909.
  Eunice : a tale of Reconstruction times in South Carolina : a novel / by William James Rivers;
edited by Tara Courtney McKinney.
        p. cm.
  "Published in cooperation with the South Caroliniana Library with the assistance of the
Caroline McKissick Dial Publication Fund and the University South Caroliniana Society."
  ISBN-13: 978-1-57003-640-8 (alk. paper)
  ISBN-10: 1-57003-640-3 (alk. paper)
  1. Reconstruction (U.S. history, 1865–1877)—Fiction. 2. South Carolina—Fiction. 3. Young
women—Fiction. I. McKinney, Tara Courtney, 1982– II. Title.
PS2718.R49E95 2006
813'.4—dc22   2006008593

This book is printed on Glatfelter Natures Natural, a recycled paper with 50 percent
post-consumer waste content.

Contents

Acknowledgments

The production of this edition of *Eunice: A Tale of Reconstruction Times in South Carolina* would not have been possible without the aid of several individuals at the University of South Carolina, and I gratefully recognize their assistance.

Thomas Brown introduced me to the original manuscript and encouraged my interest. He read and corrected many drafts, provided extensive editorial guidance and information for annotations, and answered numerous questions. Moreover, he connected me to others whose knowledge proved invaluable and continued to serve as a valuable source of advice.

Lacy Ford served as a reader for the work that became this edition. He read drafts and posed thoughtful questions which improved the quality of the introduction.

Ward Briggs provided many of the Latin translations and insight into Rivers's experience as a nineteenth-century classics professor. Joseph B. Tyson provided Greek translations.

Alex Moore of the University of South Carolina Press expressed interest in the production of this edition shortly after I read the original manuscript and patiently guided me through much of the publication process.

The staff of the South Caroliniana Library made the William James Rivers Papers available for my daily use for many months, provided me with copies of the manuscript and other items, and assisted me eagerly.

Finally, many friends and family members supported me and expressed interest in the project; they generously allowed me the time to complete several drafts of this edition and thoughtfully ran errands and performed many other services so that I could spend more time with *Eunice*.

Introduction

The Author

Few members of the South Carolina elite were better positioned to recount the turmoils of the antebellum oligarchy in the wake of the Civil War than William James Rivers. Although not born into the privileged class, Rivers embraced its ideals and secured its respect as a leading authority on state history and as a faculty member at the influential South Carolina College. As fervently as he supported South Carolina's dominant political ideals, however, Rivers never forgot that he had been an outsider. *Eunice,* his fictional account of postwar South Carolina, combines a passionate representation of conservative thought with an undercurrent of ambivalence toward the demise of the antebellum social order.

The William James Rivers Papers at the South Caroliniana Library at the University of South Carolina provide extensive material for an exploration of Rivers's long life and significant scholarship. The Manuscripts Division houses several hundred documents detailing Rivers's personal and professional life from his days as a student at South Carolina College in 1841 to his death in 1909. It is also home to the heavily edited manuscripts of *Eunice* and several unfinished works of poetry and fiction. Two of Rivers's personal scrapbooks complete the collection and provide a glimpse at his lifelong interest in current events and popular culture. The Published Materials (Books Division) also contains material of interest, particularly a copy of Rivers's most important scholarship, *Sketch of the History of South Carolina to the Close of the Proprietary Government by the Revolution of 1719.* No serious study of the life and work of William James Rivers can be undertaken without delving into the resources of the South Caroliniana Library.

William James Rivers was born in Charleston, South Carolina, on July 18, 1822. His father, John David Rivers, was an English immigrant who kept a business on Queen Street; his mother, Eliza Frances Richwood Rivers, had family who lived in South Carolina, but little else is known of her background. Rivers happily remembered his early life. Although the family was not wealthy, John Rivers was a property owner who adequately supported a family of seven, and the children attended school in the city and lessons in private homes. In 1831, however, John Rivers was financially ruined by the failure of a friend for whom he had been a surety. He died on December 29 of the same year,[1] and shortly afterward Eliza Rivers placed her two sons in the Charleston Orphan House.[2] She moved into the facility a year later and served as a nurse until her death in 1843.[3] This arrangement enabled her to keep her children in her own rooms and direct their care and upbringing.[4]

Although Rivers's experience was extraordinary, the Charleston Orphan House was well known in the 1830s for the attention it offered children. The work of slaves owned by the institution freed the inmates from the drudgery required of many in similar situations,[5] and significant private funding and public support enabled residents to receive excellent care and schooling. The institution provided young boys and girls with training for a trade or occupation and steered the most talented boys toward professional careers. Young boys who distinguished themselves had a good chance for special recognition by the influential commissioners of the orphanage. Christopher Memminger, future treasurer of the Confederacy, was essentially adopted into the household of South Carolina governor Thomas Bennett Jr.[6] William Rivers quickly attracted as his patron James Jervey, the chairman of the Board of Commissioners from 1826 to 1838,[7] whom Rivers believed to be a relative of one of his father's friends from the War of 1812.[8] Jervey placed the excellent young pupil at the Grammar School of the College of Charleston, after which Rivers continued private studies for one to two years before entering South Carolina College at Columbia.[9]

South Carolina College, which figures prominently in *Eunice,* had been chartered in 1801 primarily to cultivate generations of state leaders who shared common goals, principles, and social connections. In establishing the school, the legislature sought to relieve tensions between the lowcountry gentry and the growing numbers of upcountry citizens clamoring for adequate representation and services from the state. The institution aimed to instill lowcountry values in upcountry youths, diminishing the likelihood of sectional or class uprisings against the status quo.[10] The school also provided a vehicle for incorporating other young men from nonelite backgrounds into the state leadership group. Shortly after the college opened, the state legislature created a scholarship for one student from the Charleston Orphan House to attend the institution each year.[11] Rivers's college funding may well have come from this source.

The collision of social classes at South Carolina College left a deep imprint on Rivers, who tried as an adult to compile a family genealogy but could not trace his paternal ancestry beyond his father. At the age of eighty he recalled with bitterness that he had "not been free of the disdain of aristocrats . . . for the unpardonable sin of having been a poor boy who received his education through old-time bequests for scholarships."[12] He responded to this humiliation as he had in grammar school in Charleston, where "a mistake in English" once subjected him to "the laughter of my playmates," prompting him to buy a grammar book and study it so intently that he "became an authority among them on the proper use of our language." Similarly, diligent study moved him toward entry into the state elite as he graduated first in his class from South Carolina College in May 1841.

After graduation Rivers returned to Charleston and established a grammar school that soon flourished.[13] By 1850 professors at South Carolina College recommended Rivers's preparatory school for boys as "one of the best in the State for preparing young men to enter the So[uth] Ca[rolina] College."[14] Although the school offered instruction in Greek, Latin, elocution, geometry, history, and geography, Rivers focused his intellectual energy on the study of South Carolina history.[15] In the early 1840s he compiled *A Catechism of the History and Chronology of South Carolina* to help students learn South Carolina history through a set of questions and answers.[16] The book apparently met with considerable approval, and Rivers helped to circulate it further by donating two hundred copies to the parishes of St. Philip's and St. Michael's for use in the free schools.[17]

Rivers began to enter leading Charleston social and intellectual circles after he expanded on the question-and-answer format of the *Catechism* to publish *Topics in the History of South-Carolina* in 1850. The Literary and Philosophical Society—which included among its members businessmen and professionals Christopher Memminger and Mitchell King, ministers Samuel Gilman, Thomas Smith, and John Adger, and the Lutheran minister and natural scientist John Bachman—invited Rivers to its meetings to discuss his work.[18] As a result of his interest in creating a repository for the preservation and study of documents related to the history of South Carolina, Rivers took a lead role in the founding of the South Carolina Historical Society in 1855, a project that associated him with lowcountry luminaries James L. Petigru, William Gilmore Simms, and Frederick A. Porcher. Rivers was elected corresponding secretary of the group and was responsible for obtaining documents for the new collection.[19]

Rivers's *Sketch of the History of South Carolina to the Close of the Proprietary Government by the Revolution of 1719*, published in 1856, cemented his position in the Charleston literary world.[20] Drawing on material he had gathered from the State Paper Office in London, Rivers traced the history of South Carolina from the beginning of European settlement to the displacement of the Lords Proprietors originally granted governance of the colony. He underscored the extent to which his research exceeded existing work on the topic by including a lengthy description of his archival excavations; he also provided a list of 397 documents used to produce the book and copies of 74 of those documents, most of which were communications of the Lords Proprietors dealing with organization of the proprietary government and issues of everyday life in South Carolina. His narrative account of the colonial charters, constitutions, and political parties centered on the settlers' attempts to free themselves from the rule of the Lords Proprietors. Their vigorous support for the triumph of local government strikingly paralleled the South

Carolina assertions of "states' rights" that had been a prominent theme in American politics since Rivers's birth.

Unquestionably Rivers's most important contribution to scholarship, *A Sketch of the History of South Carolina* received warm praise. George Bancroft, a cousin of Rivers's wife, lauded the "beautiful, most interesting, and instructive volume"[21] and promised to revise his own work on South Carolina's history in light of Rivers's new research. William Gilmore Simms was similarly impressed, and he encouraged Rivers to write for a readership that extended beyond South Carolina. "Address yourself to the foreign, though it even be the hostile tribunal," Simms advised, "and you will compel a secondary and reflective sentiment at home in your favour. . . . Your error has been in addressing yourself exclusively to a community which has neither the courage, the independence or the knowledge necessary to create public opinion. Here we are mere provincials."[22] Simms's shrewd advice reflected not only his own experience but also his recognition that Rivers primarily sought to improve his standing within South Carolina.

Rivers returned to the educational base of the state elite as professor of Greek literature at South Carolina College in 1856. The controversy over his appointment exposed the continuing social strains that the school sought to alleviate. Upcountry trustees voted to reduce the number of required classics courses in an effort to eliminate the professorship. But Rivers held on to the position, and he may not have regretted entirely the reduced place of the classics in the curriculum, for he was not very committed to scholarship in that field. His chief intellectual pursuit remained South Carolina history, and he found a way to infuse his teaching of the classics with conservative, elitist political ideals. He especially encouraged study of the Athenian Constitution, "rediscovering in Athens the value of a small group of patricians prospering by slavery."[23] Meanwhile, he participated in South Carolina's cultural politics outside the classroom. His one-thousand-dollar contribution made him the largest donor to the fund for a public monument to John C. Calhoun in Charleston. A few weeks after the bombardment of Fort Sumter, he reprised his *Sketch of the History of South Carolina* in the annual address to the South Carolina Historical Society, declaring that "the people, in their increasing power and progress towards self-government, would hold their rights and liberties in their own keeping, and would establish a sufficient sanction for them with. Thus saith the law of South Carolina!"[24]

Rivers shared from the home front in the disruption brought by the Civil War. By November 1861 a majority of students and several professors had left South Carolina College for Confederate service; to the dismay of Rivers and the other remaining professors, the institution of a draft forced the closing of the school on March 8, 1862. The buildings were turned into hospitals by the Confederate government. With a wife and four young children, Rivers chose not to enlist, though he felt close to the soldiers' experience through his correspondence with his unmarried older brother, David, who had always been the more adventurous sibling. Exempted from the draft because of his profession, Rivers supported the Confederate cause most notably through his diligent work on the Roll of the Dead, a list of South Carolinians who gave their lives in Confederate service. He sent his family to his father-in-law's home in Athens, Georgia, for safety while he remained in Columbia even as Sherman's army approached. During this time Rivers constructed boxes for the storage of the college's collection of rare and valuable books. He later devoted much of the first chapter of *Eunice* to the burning of Columbia, which he witnessed on February 17, 1865.

When South Carolina College reorganized as the University of South Carolina in 1865, Rivers returned to the faculty as professor of ancient languages and literatures. He continued to concentrate, however, on his work on the Roll of the Dead. "The record cannot be complete without the assistance of all who take an interest in this memorial," he pleaded in advertisements to newspapers in search of information about fallen Confederates. "Especially to our returned soldiers do I now make this appeal. If it be but a single name you can furnish, send it at once."[25] Rivers also contributed to the memory of the Confederacy through the local apotheosis of his former student Henry Timrod.[26] In tribute to the stricken poet laureate of Southern independence, Rivers gave a lecture on Timrod's poetry that he published in 1876 as *A Little Book: To obtain means for placing a memorial stone upon the grave of the Poet Henry Timrod.*

The "little book" for Timrod included "Eldred," Rivers's attempt at the epic poem of South Carolina history he had wanted Timrod to write.[27] Like many of Rivers's postwar writings, the poem addresses the situation of the South after the war. Although Rivers's lack of natal connections with the antebellum elite and his own status as a self-made man contributed to a quiet ambivalence about the fall of the old order, he could not accept the equality of African Americans or the rule of the federal government. In Rivers's view the federal government's Reconstruction policy was directly opposed to God's will and morally reprehensible. He declared in an 1876 address to the South Carolina Historical Society that "God has not abandoned us. He still rules the nations of the earth by providences which we may not fully comprehend; but they give us assurance that He will uphold us and strengthen us if we trust in Him." Rivers predicted that providence would "send forth in the fullness of time His righteous vengeance against falsehood, and fraud, and wickedness in high places, and against all who wilfully pervert truth and justice, and betray the rights and freedom of their people."[28]

When the University of South Carolina began to enroll African Americans in 1873, Rivers resigned his position and accepted the presidency of Washington College in Maryland. Washington College then functioned as a sort of preparatory school, and its facilities, faculty, and students left much to be desired. Rivers introduced a collegiate system of study and attempted to improve facilities and the quality of instruction, but he achieved limited overall success. The trustees recognized his meticulous attention to detail and commitment to liberal-arts scholarship but found him aloof. When his failure to increase enrollment led to initiatives to reorganize the college, Rivers offered his resignation.[29] On its acceptance he sighed, "I now regret that I have in some measure wasted 14 years of my life. I say 'in some measure': for I have really done some good."[30]

Even as he began his work at Washington College, Rivers mentally returned to his home state by drafting *Eunice Tale of Reconstruction Times in South Carolina* in 1874–1875. Although he put the manuscript aside for the rest of his presidency, he returned to it several years after his resignation and move to Baltimore, where he spent his remaining years. Although in declining health, he continued to write sporadically, composing memoirs and brief essays addressed to his family. In 1893 he published *Addresses and Other Occasional Pieces,* a collection of essays and poems spanning his entire career. Several passages in his manuscript for *Eunice* indicate that he edited and partially revised the novel during this period. In 1908 he sent the final draft of *Eunice* to South Carolina historian Alexander Salley in Columbia, with jesting instructions to "do what he likes with it—put it in the fire, or any part of it as it may seem best to him."[31] One year later, at the age of eighty-seven, Rivers died in Baltimore on June 22, 1909. Students, faculty, and alumni turned out in Columbia to meet the train bearing his body and attend the burial at Elmwood Cemetery of the last professor to die of the antebellum faculty of South Carolina College.

The Novel

Eunice is an ambitious contribution to the literary reconstruction by which Northerners and Southerners sought to define the meaning of the sectional conflict. Rivers adopted a standard formula by centering his novel on a beautiful, virtuous Southern maiden who infatuates Northern and Southern male characters. The theme of a belle choosing between competing regional representatives of manhood has been explored more fully by Nina Silber and Jane Turner Censer, both of whom focus on the "romance of reunion."[32] Rivers explicitly disdained the intersectional use of the plot device, however, and instead offered a male version of the Southern variant that would later be most fully realized by Margaret Mitchell in *Gone With the Wind* (1936), the drama of a belle choosing between two images of white Southern manhood. This narrative argues that the postwar South must reject some of its old ways and incorporate new values in order to cope with a changing world. Rivers augments the story of Eunice's courtship and marriage with a host of minor characters, most of which embody some message about issues of race, sectionalism, or gender in the Reconstruction South.

At the heart of the novel is the competition for Eunice DeLesline among former Union soldier Benjamin Isaiah Guelty, Confederate veteran Willie Barton, and

Confederate regimental commander Edmund Loyle. Guelty, brought into contact with Eunice as part of Sherman's invading army, returns to South Carolina after the war in the guise of a missionary to the emancipated slaves and attempts to marry Eunice by force in a series of schemes that drive much of the novel's action. The real contest for Eunice is between the two men who seek to protect her from Guelty. Barton, the scion of a prominent old South Carolina family with close ties to the DeLeslines, is understood at the outset to be at least informally betrothed to Eunice. However, she eventually gives her heart to Loyle, a self-made planter identified as the model man of the New South. Through the men's actions and Eunice's feelings about them, Rivers depicted his ideas about the new Southern man and the role of the defeated Confederate.

Rivers's treatment of his characters as social types is illustrated most crudely in his images of African Americans. Predictably, three types of freedmen appear: those who are loyal to their former masters and are therefore admirable, those who are ineffectual to the point of being ridiculous, and those who join forces with the carpetbaggers and become completely degenerate and villainous. Rivers's virulent racism is particularly striking as an expression of the attitude of the Bourbon elite led by Wade Hampton, which presented itself as the defender of a heartfelt racial paternalism. Rivers did indicate some evidence of African American complexity in the character of Epaminondas, or "Old Pam," a lifelong swindler who shrewdly and indiscriminately deceives white Southerners, white Northerners, and freedmen. For the most part, however, the African Americans in the book are simple pejorative stereotypes.

Rivers similarly painted white Northerners with a broad and tendentious brush. Guelty and his carpetbagger cohorts are utterly diabolical. They are immoral, pecuniarily driven, and generally fiendish people whose primary purpose is to exploit the defeated Southerners to the advantage of carpetbaggers. Rivers devoted an entire chapter to a set of diary excerpts in which a Northern schoolteacher named Miss Sallie reveals her hypocrisy and greed. Miss Sallie is brutally businesslike and efficient, but most of the Northerners in the novel are harmless because their plots repeatedly fail as a result of their own stupidity. Federal soldiers, on the other hand, are generally presented as highly competent and sympathetic to the defeated South. Colonel Nickton, the commandant at Columbia, resigns his commission and returns to the North rather than enforce Reconstruction policy against the state; young Corporal Tom Chiltree questions whether or not he fought for the right side in the war; Lieutenant Andrews refuses to attack Colonel Loyle and his friends when ordered to do so by carpetbagger politicians. The friendly feelings between Colonel Loyle and many of the Union soldiers echo the reunionist sentiment that the sectional conflict resulted from artificial political causes rather than the noble impulses revealed by the war.

Despite its respect for Union veterans and endorsement of sectional reconciliation, *Eunice* in a sense offers a parody of the intersectional romances popular in novels of the period. Guelty's obsession with Eunice and his obvious unworthiness stand in stark contrast to novels that depict an admirable Northern hero winning the heart of a Southern maiden and forming a more perfect union. On the contrary Guelty's admiration for Eunice is pathetic and frankly hopeless; he seeks not to win but to abduct her; his motives are far from pure. The only functional intersectional romance is an antebellum one; Eunice's mother is from New York and her father from South Carolina. Rivers indicated that their relationship achieved success because Mrs. DeLesline embraced her husband's South Carolina, eventually placing more emphasis on its preservation than do any of the native South Carolinians.

Rivers discussed his ideals of Southern manhood and his proposed response to the war and Reconstruction most fully through the contrast between Edmund Loyle and Willie Barton. Rivers clearly preferred the self-made planter to the spoiled ne'er-do-well, referring to the former by his surname and the latter by his first name in order to imply that Loyle has achieved manhood while Willie remains a boy. Willie acknowledges openly that Loyle is the better man; he frequently tells stories of the calm and clearheaded Colonel saving him from some scrape or another. Their responses to Reconstruction also reflect their differences in maturity. Loyle takes the political situation seriously, recognizing the grave situation in which the defeated South finds itself. His approach is to ameliorate conditions for himself and his neighbors while working within the law. Willie instead joins the Ku Klux Klan, which he regards as a lark; his carefree nature is incapable of comprehending any consequences. The contrast includes not only their political judgment and respect for the law but also their ideas about race. Colonel Loyle remains distant from his former slaves while providing them with the opportunity to meet their own needs. Willie, having been raised among African Americans, remains close to them—much closer than Rivers considers appropriate. He is so familiar with their culture that he can imitate their speech and several times passes for a black man without detection. Rivers indicated that this sort of close interracial contact cannot be maintained in postemancipation society and that in order to remain dominant, whites must separate themselves from their former slaves.

The different ways in which Loyle and Willie court Eunice illustrate Rivers's ideals for mature romantic relationships. Willie has loved Eunice since childhood, but he neither respects her nor recognizes her superior intelligence. He assumes she will marry him; although there has been no formal betrothal, he can't imagine that it would be otherwise. He has no use for her opinion on other matters, either. Colonel Loyle, in turn, respects Eunice, largely for qualities they share. It is clear that their union would be a partnership of equals.

In addition to her role as the arbiter of exemplary manhood, Eunice also serves as a model of postwar female virtues. She demonstrates traditional feminine benevolence in her care for elderly former slaves and neighbors, her supervision of a boys' Sunday-school class, and her solicitude for her mother. Significantly, however, Rivers presented his most rhapsodic vision of her in a scene in which she and her friend Mamie Avery practice target shooting. Eunice capably hits the bull's-eye, and this cool competence enhances her beauty. Later in the novel she helps Colonel Loyle prevent a rape and again demonstrates her skill with firearms. These scenes are sexually charged with Eunice's beauty in the face of danger. In contrast Mamie Avery is incapable of handling simple firearms and is thoroughly dependent on the men around her for protection and care. Even more helpless is Mamie Avery's cousin Helen Clarens, who has gone out of her mind with grief and inhabits a dreamworld, spending her days heaping violets on what she believes are Confederate graves. Mrs. DeLesline similarly remains trapped in the past, unable to admit that the DeLesline name no longer carries the political weight it once did. Like Eunice, these women have borne great losses, but they respond by withdrawing into the past. Eunice alone seems prepared for the future.

Among the minor characters perhaps the most notable is Timothy Thomleigh, Willie Barton's self-appointed mentor and guardian. "Uncle Tim," as he is nick-named, surely must rank among the most unusual nineteenth-century fictional characters to invite comparison with Harriet Beecher Stowe's *Uncle Tom's Cabin* (1852). Uncle Tim is martyred by a marauding band of freedmen, as Uncle Tom is murdered by a villainous overseer. The sage serves as Rivers's most direct representative in the novel. Rivers even composed two essays in this persona, which are available with the manuscript but are not reproduced in this edition. Uncle Tim's concerned fondness for the impetuous Willie Barton evokes Rivers's appreciation for the spirit of the Old South's elite, notwithstanding the frustrations implied by Barton's limited attention to Uncle Tim's commentaries on natural science, industrialization, the classics, and numerous other topics. Most frustrating for Uncle Tim, however, is the disruption caused by the war; neither a staunch secessionist nor a strong Confederate supporter, he sees the war mostly as an interruption of his multiple research projects. Beloved by other characters in the novel, Uncle Tim suggests an ambivalence toward the Confederacy that Rivers probably did not feel comfortable expressing more openly.

Eunice is essentially a novel about the direction of the South after the war. Rivers realized that the antebellum order would not return, and the characters who cling to it are swept away or gradually change. Colonel Loyle, unhindered by a lengthy genealogy, is most able to adapt; his character shows what the new Southern man must be to win Eunice, whose surely intentional name means "good victory." Like her successful suitor, Eunice retains many of her admirable antebellum qualities while adjusting to the changed society, providing an example of what Rivers believed Southerners must become in order to flourish in the postwar era.

Notes

1. April 11, 1903, William Rivers Papers, South Caroliniana Library (SCL).

2. Susan L. King, *History and Records of the Charleston Orphan House* (Easley: Southern Historical Press, 1984), 111.

3. Ibid., 13.

4. William J. Rivers to "W.," April 11, 1903, SCL.

5. Barbara Bellows, *Benevolence among Slaveholders: Assisting the Poor in Charleston, 1670–1860* (Baton Rouge: Louisiana State University Press, 1993), 136.

6. Ibid., 125, 137.

7. King, *History and Records of the Charleston Orphan House,* 5.

8. Rivers to "W.," April 11, 1903.

9. Ibid.

10. Daniel Hollis, *University of South Carolina,* 2 vols. (Columbia: University of South Carolina Press, 1951), I:16–17.

11. Bellows, *Benevolence among Slaveholders,* 142.

12. Rivers to "W.," April 11, 1903.

13. A. S. Salley Jr., *William J. Rivers: A Sketch Prepared by A. S. Salley, Jr., to Commemorate the Presentation of a Portrait (painted by John Stolle, of Dresden) of Prof. Rivers to the Charleston Library Society by Hon. William A. Courtenay, LL.D.* (Columbia: State Company, 1906), 3.

14. Robert Rogers to Rivers, December 19, 1850, Rivers Papers, SCL.

15. George Rogers, "William James Rivers: An Address Delivered at the Thirtieth Annual Meeting of the University South Caroliniana Society," Columbia, South Carolina, 12 May 1966, George Rogers Papers, SCL.

16. Ibid., 2.

17. Reverend Christian Hanckel to Rivers, October 30, 1846, Rivers Papers, SCL.

18. Rogers, "William James Rivers," 3.

19. Constitution and By-Laws of the South-Carolina Historical Society, 1855, South Carolina Historical Society Collection, SCL.

20. Rivers, *A Sketch of the History of South Carolina to the Close of the Proprietary Government by the Revolution of 1719* (Charleston: McCarter, 1856).

21. George Bancroft to Rivers, January 2, 1857, Rivers Papers, SCL.

22. Rogers, "William James Rivers," 8.

23. Wayne K. Durrill, "The Power of Ancient Words: Classical Teaching and Social Change at South Carolina College, 1804–1860," *Journal of Southern History* 65 (August 1999): 496.

24. Rivers, "On the Development of the Power of the Colonial Assembly as Indicative of Our Early Progress Toward Constitutional Self-Government," in *Addresses and Other Occasional Pieces* (Baltimore: Press of the Friedenwald Co., 1893), 147.

25. Salley, *William J. Rivers,* 7.

26. Rivers, *A Little Book: To obtain means for placing a memorial stone upon the grave of the Poet Henry Timrod* (Charleston: Walker, Evans & Cogswell, 1876.)

27. Rogers, "William James Rivers," 18.

28. Rivers, "Address Before the Historical Society on its Twenty-First Anniversary," in *Addresses and Other Occasional Pieces,* 212.

29. Fred W. Dumschott, *Washington College* (Chestertown: Washington College, 1980), 107.

30. Ibid., 106.

31. Rivers to Alexander Salley, October 1908, Rivers Papers, SCL.

32. Nina Silber, *The Romance of Reunion: Northerners and the South, 1865–1900* (Chapel Hill: University of North Carolina Press, 1993); Jane Turner Censer, "Reimagining the North-South Reunion: Southern Women Novelists and the Intersectional Romance, 1976–1900." *Southern Cultures* 5 (Summer 1999): 64–91.

Eunice

A Tale of Reconstruction
Times in South Carolina

One

Thou bearest a soul that storms have never shaken,
And resolute will to tread the path of right;
And this is still to conquer though we perish.

W. G. Simms

Perhaps but few of us noticed that the skies were serene and beautiful that seventeenth morning of February 1865.[1] The few who did, felt not from that source any inspiration of serenity. The booming of cannon beyond the river had been continuously heard for two days; then the rattling of musketry began to reach our ears in Columbia, indicating that our breastworks on the west side of the Congaree had been abandoned and that the conflict was raging near the city. Some thousands of gray-clad veterans had, for several days, held in check the Federal army of ten times their number. But although Beauregard and Hampton were present to direct and encourage us, and the gallant Butler hurled his cavalry here and there against the line of the enemy—that ever-extending blue line kept unfolding itself, like a huge serpent, till there was no safety from its coils except in retreat. Slowly withdrawing from their positions the Confederate troops had, before dawn, crossed the Congaree bridge and set it on fire. They formed rifle pits on that side of Columbia and sat down to rest, watching the Federal movements and the artillery duel from side to side of the river. Their soiled and dusty garments showed that the bare earth had been their sleeping place for many nights.

The sun had now risen. The bridge by which our troops had crossed was in flames. The baffled enemy were amusing themselves by shelling the city which was crowded

1. Pinned to the title page of the manuscript was a note that stated,

   Author will send this story ("Eunice") to Mr. A. S. Salley, who is living now, I think, in Columbia, S.C. Mr. Salley may do what he pleases with it—put it in the fire, or any part of it as it may seem best to him.
   W. J. R.
   Oct. 1908–

with women and children. I was then on the street leading up from the burning bridge. A shell burst above me and a fragment fell at my feet. Picking it up, still warm, I was looking at it when a second shell, screeching as with infernal glee, buried itself in the ground near by. At this moment a woman with disheveled hair and bearing an infant in her arms, rushed to me exclaiming "In God's name, what shall I do?" On all sides other cries arose and many affrighted women, holding little children by the hand, ran wildly to and fro, not knowing in which direction it would be safest to flee. With the bursting of shells and the shrieks of the women, the war-worn Confederates steadily rose into line and faced the foe with indignant imprecations, though they knew no conflict could then ensue.

The Federal army, making a feint to cross the river lower down, below the city, now succeeded in passing a force over on pontoons a few miles above the city; and our handful of brave defenders unable to guard every point, were withdrawn to do battle elsewhere. It was now left to the Mayor to negotiate in behalf of the defence-less citizens for such protection as might be obtained from the advancing host. Sherman had said to Halleck "the whole army is burning with insatiable desire to wreak vengeance upon South Carolina. . . . We must make old and young, rich and poor, feel the hard hand of war as well as their organized armies." It was known that the enemy had threatened to "play h-ll" when they should reach our state. I must crave indulgence for using these two monosyllables; but I doubt if the reader can substitute for them an expression more truly indicative of what was intended to be done. There had been no conspicuous opportunity for such performance as the words indicate till the troops reached, as they now did, the abandoned Capital—the birth-place, the nest, the hot-bed of all disloyalty and, as they thought, the exact spot for retributive justice by their hands.[2]

It was currently reported, too, that at their coming, although others might be spared, no mercy would be extended to those (if they could be caught) who had signed the Ordinance of Secession, or who had especially influenced the initial movements of the "rebellion," as Northern writers falsely name it. Such reports were generally believed. By various means we often knew what the enemy said and what they intended to do. Many instances could be given of the private information we had; and it is likely the Federals also often had knowledge of our intentions and movements. This was to be expected in a war like ours. In one instance a lady friend of mine, at a distance from Columbia and within a region controlled by the enemy, was approached on the cars by a young man in the uniform of a private of the Federal army and entirely unknown to her, who said in a low tone "Madame, you reside in South Carolina. I know you and your husband. He once did me a great

2. Union troops have often been accused of a particular desire for vengeance against South Carolina; South Carolina was the first state to secede from the Union and the site of the first shots at Fort Sumter. Rivers embraced this view of Sherman's invading troops.

favor. Tell him to seek his safety if we approach your place of residence." He disappeared before she could make him an answer. Two days before the Federal occupation of Columbia, the same person, dressed as a Confederate, appeared in her parlor only to say hurriedly "Tell your husband it's time to quit this city."—A week before this it was said to me by one who, I was confident, had accurate information, "The enemy have left Savannah; they will not go to Charleston; they will come here and will burn or destroy all public buildings and perhaps lay the whole city in ashes; go, while you have the opportunity, and save what you may be able to save." By such premonition the Secretary of State under authority of the Governor had placed the most important public archives forty miles from the Capital before the Federals entered it, and set fire to the building in which they were deposited. The use of the rail-roads at this juncture was appropriated by the State and Confederate authorities. The citizens had to save what they could by other means; and very few indeed, had such means. "Haste-haste-hurry hurry!" was the order of the day.

While the enemy were entering the city in one direction, there could be seen in other directions, on various roads leading out from the suburbs, every style of vehicle bearing away those who were fortunate enough to have the means of escape and of carrying off their most valuable papers or other personal property. On one of these roads, in a promiscuous, hurrying line of carts, buggies, wagons and every species of two-wheel and four-wheel conveyance, there sat in an elegant carriage (of the style one got in and out of by steps let down for the purpose) an old gentleman whose silvery locks and calm and attractive countenance would have arrested attention anywhere. With heavy heart he had left his family. His sons, three in number, had been slain during the war, and his family consisted now only of ladies. These were his daughter-in-law and daughter, (the latter an invalid), and a granddaughter; all delicately nurtured, but naturally brave of spirit. It was due to their urgent entreaties that he had been induced to save himself from indignities, imprisonment, perhaps from violent death at the hands of the enemy. So they all feared and believed; for he had been influential in all measures leading to Secession. His petted grand-daughter Eunice, a girl of seventeen summers, had clung to his neck, and only when the enemy had actually set foot in the city, had reluctantly consented to let him depart alone. "You will be safer," he said, as she accompanied him to the carriage door, "with your mother than with me, as the Federals have assured the Mayor and councilmen who went just now to surrender the city to them that private property will be fully protected and the people as safe as if there was not a Yankee within a thousand miles of them. These words of Colonel Stone relieve me of apprehension in leaving you and I confide in his candor and promised protection."

Perhaps even this assurance of their own safety would have been ineffectual in her fear and anxiety for him and she would still have sought to take her mother and aunt and to go with him, had there not, at this instant approached at rapid speed a young cavalry officer who waving his hand in greeting to Mrs. DeLesline on the portico, had time only to say to the maiden, in a half-whisper "Eunice, good by" and to her grand-father, "Be quick, Sir; take the Winnsboro' road; we will guard the retreat on that route," and then, before Mr. DeLesline could say "thank you, Willie"—dashed away not a moment too soon to avoid the column of the enemy advancing on a line at right angles with the road he had to traverse. They had speedily crossed the pontoons and a large force of them were marching on the city. Did Eunice's lingering look and tearful glance follow the swift steed of the handsome young cavalryman as well as the rapidly rolling carriage wheels that bore her dear grandfather away?

Where were the promises and assurances of protection? That night a bacchanal horde of brutal soldiers were let loose on the doomed city. The historian may fail to find a written order from the commander-in-chief in Virginia to Sheridan, "To make the Shenandoah Valley a desert waste," and in another communication to Halleck "to leave it in such condition that a crow flying over and wanting to live must carry his rations with him." So too the historian may fail to find a written order from the commander of the southward Federal forces to burn the city of Columbia; but all who were there that night saw that he permitted it to be done. A whole street of flaming houses, a mile in length, sent a lurid glare on high lighting the yelling incendiaries on to other houses to be burned. Here and there throughout the city and far off in the suburbs, blaze answered to blaze from the finely built dwellings of eminent citizens and in every direction, wherever there work of pillage had been finished. The roaring of the conflagration, more frightful than the reverberating rush of mighty waters, could not always drown the heart-rending outcries of delicate women, many of whom were driven into the blasts of that stormy February night to shiver in the woods and open parks. Their husbands, fathers, brothers, and sons were battling far away and there were at hand none to protect them. Again let me ask Where were the promises and assurances of protection?

The flames were spreading fearfully near the mansion of Eunice's grandfather.— But first permit me to go back a few hours and tell you some incidents which occurred before this point of time, to elucidate our story; for it is chiefly the story my thoughts are engaged upon.—

The enemy had entered the city in the forenoon, about eleven o'clock. In the afternoon, as stores and dwellings had been broken into and robbed, and lawlessness was rampant everywhere, Mrs. DeLesline had requested the commandant to station a guard at her house and the request had been promptly granted. Similar requests had been unhesitatingly responded to in many other cases, whether made in person or by writing a note to the commandant. But in so many instances did the guards turn out to be wolves in sheep's clothing that either the protection was a sham or there were not honest men enough among the invading troops—at least among those in the city that day- to make up a few dozen conscientious protectors of helpless innocence. The abodes of prominent citizens were well known to the enemy. On the table of an officer in high command lay a map of the city with marginal notes and designations of houses; and the foreigner, a renegade, who had prepared the map, was present to afford any further information which might be required.

About sun-set a sergeant, Benjamin Isaiah Guelty and two men—two genuine army-roughs—were sent as a guard to Mrs. DeLesline's. They paced up and down the piazza; strolled through the garden-walks; lolled on the velvet sofas of the drawing room; questioned the negro servants; peered into the dining room and pantry;—till Mrs. DeLesline, in hope of conciliating their good-will, asked if they had dined, and furnished the inquisitive, eager-eyed trio, the best dinner the confusion of her household permitted her to have prepared for them. From the impudent stare of Sergeant Guelty,—looking at her as wondering where he had seen her before—Mrs. DeLesline shrank with a chilling horror, and yet she asked him, with an impulse which a moment later seemed to her as strange as it was uncontrollable "Were you ever at Sharpsburg?" "Why do you ask, Ma'am? We are from the West" he replied, a little confused. "It is nothing I thought perhaps some New York men were sent to guard us," said Mrs. DeLesline recovering her self-possession; and bidding her faithful old butler attend the table, she returned to the chamber of her invalid sister-in-law, over whom Eunice was keeping watch. This lady, (Eunice's aunt Alicia), losing in quick succession mother and brothers, had been failing in health for several years and demanded now constant attention. She had, after the unusual agitations and alarms of this dreadful day, fallen asleep; and Eunice, closing the bible she had been reading to her, was on her knees at the bed-side when Mrs. DeLesline returned. Perhaps again and again such quiet devotion will be engaged in ere the few hours shall have passed when that home they so dearly loved will be to them a sheltering home no more.

The mansion which was destined so soon to be destroyed, stood—we cannot help saying, unconscious of its doom—for does not home seem to us like a sentient being—so twined about is it with our hallowed recollections?—it stood, in all its simple architectural beauty, amidst a garden of evergreens tastefully arranged and interspersed with beds of rare roses and exotics; which, though not now in fragrant blossom, were budding in the promise of a warmer atmosphere. The arched and airy portico facing the west was sheltered from the sun in summer by a few magnificent magnolias sufficiently far from the house to be innocuous to the flowers. The fluted columns of the portico at the front entrance, I have often seen later in the season, for it was now the second month of the year—half concealed by festoons of jasmines which diffused far off their perfume on the evening breeze. The jasmine vines twining also from baluster to baluster of the marble steps which led to the spacious piazza, seemed to spring on either side from the conservatory of rich geraniums which had luxuriantly shot up and were touching their shelter of glass with a varied and commingling array of blossoms, as if bidding welcome to all who visited the house. All that correct taste aided by wealth could create for the enjoyment of an unostentatious refinement seemed clustered around this peaceful abode. We need not speak of the venerable and accomplished servants, as well known in the city as their master and who were an inseparable portion of the household, as if indeed they were part of the family; we need say nothing of handsome outbuildings or of the interior of the mansion, its wine-cellar, dining room or old style parlor with its wide chimneyplace and carved mantel and silver candelabra; but we must make brief mention of one room—the library—a spacious apartment with a bay-window towards the south. It was filled with valuable books in several languages, and in a corner were folded maps and charts. Its walls were adorned with family portraits, some more than a century old. An inner, smaller room, which formed part of the library and was approached both from the larger library and also by a door from the hall—was more luxuriously furnished and bore evidence that the ladies of the house presided here. This we would readily suppose from the lighter character of its library treasures and from its works of art and its resources for agreeable pastime. On the walls of this boudoir hung exquisite portraits of Eunice and of her father and mother, Colonel and Mrs. DeLesline; that of the Colonel being draped in folds of crepe since the day he had fallen in battle at Sharpsburg. Bravely and generously had he devoted his fortune and his life to secure the independence of his State from a thraldom which he feared would be hers when the Constitution which she helped to frame—largely helped to frame— would be no longer a binding covenant for her safety and protection. So we, many of us, feared; so, he feared. In the toils and dangers of the arduous campaigns through which he passed, he had been to his younger brothers a guide, guardian and tender nurse, and had at last brought their bodies home for burial. When his own death-day came, he consigned his widow and his daughter to the care of his aged father. The bodies of the three noble sons were sleeping side by side (happy their lot!) in the quiet cemetery almost in sight of their father's residence. The fate of the eldest of the family—Richard—who had gone to California, was unknown to them. They supposed him also to be dead. Opposite the small inner library room and on the other side of the hall, was the dining room in which sat Guelty and his men attended by the stately, white-haired, ceremonious butler, Sancho by name. O! by how much the worthiest in that room, wert thou, honest and timid and tender-hearted Sancho! How many long years did I know thee, and never, by gentleman or lady, by colored or white, was aught said of thee save in the kindliest recognition of thy truthfulness and uprightness!

"I say, Sancho, you black dog," cried the sergeant, "where's the wine? Where did your confounded rebel master hide it? Do you see here, you old thief—do you see this pistol?" Click, click! and it was pointed at the shrinking butler. "Bring in the wine then!"—he said as he lowered his aim and lowered his utterance to a less brutal tone in deference to the respectful bow of the butler; who, though in all his long life he had never waited on such as these three at that hospitable board, could not divest himself of his usual faultless demeanor, and replied courteously (he had, however, trembled all over at the sight of the pistol). "Sir, the family are in affliction, and to-day they are in great fear and distress. If you will please excuse mc, I will ask for the keys and procure you a bottle of wine." He retired from the room and went up stairs to consult Mrs. DeLesline.

"I say now, Matt Hawks and Jerry Jailey, we'll have more than one. You stay here and eat away, and I'll reconnoitre. If you hear a crack, it'll be to let out of that woolly head a little of its insulting politeness. And don't you spirit away these silver forks and spoons—New Orleans fashion:—The time for that isn't come just yet."

Stepping from the dining room Guelty kept watch and soon saw Sancho with a bunch of keys in his hand descending the carpeted staircase which led from the chambers above into the hall. So soon as he had unlocked a door under the staircase and descended into the wine cellar in the basement, Guelty slipped after him, first taking the bunch of keys from the lock and thrusting them into his pocket. He reached the wine cellar close upon the footsteps of the butler, and threatening the old man's life, violently dashed him aside and took half a dozen bottles of old Madeira. Indeed he claimed the whole as forfeited property—and under his especial guard for the present. Hurrying the old man up with imprecations and shaking his pistol in his face, he gave him no time to think of his bunch of keys, and drove him out of the house with "Get to the kitchen. We can wait on ourselves now."

As he locked the back door on Sancho, he muttered with a cunning expression on his face, "I'll make these fellows drunk and then see where these keys lead to. It's the first time I have been at home—and with the keys too!—in the house of a stuck-up South Carolina aristocrat!"

"Hello! Jailey and Hawks," cried he re-entering the dining room, "here we are, and more where these came from. Look at the yellow ribbons on the bottles. And look here, 1824! Why, this wine's forty years old!—Hip! hip! Here's to Old Abe and the best government on Earth!—A new toast in these walls, I'll bet."—And punching in with his table knife the cork of a bottle, he poured the gurgling wine down his throat or pretended to do so. "Two bottles for you, Jale and two for Hawks— and never mind to touch tumblers, for they haven't furnished us with wine glasses to day. While I'm drinking this bottle, I'll get the other ready."—With jocose hilarity, he punched in the second cork: and between the two bottles eluded the notice of his men with regard to the quantity he was actually swallowing. They, however, made a dash at theirs like heroes and were soon discomfited and thoroughly fuddled. They had had but little sleep for the past four days and were nodding while vilifying the weakness of wine and calling for brandy and whiskey. Guelty tossed them some cigars (cheaply obtained from a sacked store on Main Street) and told them to stay where they were while he went to the kitchen for the butler to find out where to get the brandy and whiskey for them. He had no intention of doing so. He closed the dining room door, and had quickly changed his assumed staggering walk to the quiet stealthiness of a cat, when whom should he see keeping guard on the staircase leading to the chambers but the calm and respectful Sancho.

"Here you are again, eh!—I say, old white head, take some cigars. No!—well, carry these to the niggers in the kitchen. I'll let you out once more, however you got in—and, I say, stay out there and keep watch. That wine has some strength in it, and my two men are so sewed up, I must go to camp and bring in some sober men. Don't let any one come into this house or the yard till I come back."

Sancho, who had a shuddering dread of Guelty's pistol (in fact, from boyhood he had always shuddered at sight of a pistol), went through the hall once again, knowing that if he were locked out of all the doors commonly in use, he would still be able to find ingress by a private entrance at the rear of the house. So soon as he disappeared, Guelty began to try the keys. The only rooms on this floor which he found locked, were the pantry, store room, and the inner library. In the last, having got hold of a key, to fit it, he found some trunks apparently ready for removal, in case removal should be necessary. He locked himself in, and began to examine them more closely. He first lifted the trunks one by one and shook them. One trunk was especially heavy, and he knew by the jingling sound of the contents that it contained silver ware. He placed it aside; and turning bottom up a trunk which he judged to be a lady's, succeeded in breaking the bottom in by hitting it with another trunk; and then ran his arm into it, and after a little rummaging drew out a beautiful watch and chain and some valuable jewelry. He put them in a pocket which appeared to be somewhere under his arm. "Ladies *will* put these things in the lowest part of their trunks. They think that the safest place. I've learned that much since I came south," he said with a suppressed chuckle. At this moment he heard a noise as of brawling soldiers in the yard, and the angry altercation of the butler. Seating himself in an elegant arm-chair, he awaited results. But lifting his eye casually from the portraits on the dimly lighted wall, he started as if a ball had whizzed by his head. Hastily jerking down the likeness of Eunice, he threw open the shutter of a window, regardless of the disturbance in the yard and kitchen or of his own detection; and placing the portrait in a good light he sat down again in the cushioned arm-chair and "sighed and looked and sighed again."[3] Opening the breast of his military coat and also a vest beneath, he drew forth from some inner pocket about his person a small golden medallion set with pearls and containing two miniatures on ivory. His whole demeanor was changed. His face was flushed—

---

3. John Dryden, "Alexander's Feast."

not with wine alone. The roughness of the reckless soldier gave place to a strange gentleness. He kissed one of the miniature portraits and then held it near the portrait of Eunice. "I took this from the corpse of a rebel South Carolina Colonel on the field at Sharpsburg. Could he have lived here? This girl I have worshipped"— and again he fixed his lips upon the miniature—"And does she live here? What name does she go by, I wonder!—Yes, it must be the same or mighty like her. Look here! The same auburn ringlets, the same hazel eyes, the same cherry lips the same more than perfect loveliness of expression!" Then he took up in his arms the larger portrait of Eunice and gazed fondly upon it. He was completely astounded when looking up again upon the wall, the eyes of Mrs. DeLesline—the same as in the second miniature in the medallion he had so long worn, looked down upon him from her canvas portrait. It was a fitting remembrance of the miniature likeness which had caused him, he scarcely knew why, to gaze at her when first she had spoken to him in the dining room. The deep folds of crepe over the third portrait and the twilight of approaching evening in a room all closed except where he had opened the shutter, prevented him from observing the piercing eyes of Colonel DeLesline which, though only depicted on canvas, would perhaps have chilled the rough lips defiling with their kisses the likeness of his fair daughter.

The miniature the sergeant had so long carried about with him was indeed a beautiful work of art; a Fraser, painted in Charleston; and lovely enough to be kissed. So dainty it was, it might have been loved for its own sake. Many have admired almost to that extent some painting or piece of statuary delineated with a fascinating beauty beyond that which we find in living forms and features. Guelty, notwithstanding his sordid nature, prized very highly this enchanting face in the medallion and wore it in his bosom in a special pocket provided for it. Rather than part with it he would have given up his watch or money or any other portable treasure he had.

The daylight had long faded. Shouts and discordant noises mingled with the fire alarms—alas, useless tocsins!—which were ringing from every steeple, as the first houses set on fire sent their blaring signals to the sky. Sergeant Guelty, putting Eunice's portrait carefully aside, replaced his miniatures where he kept them and buttoned his coat up to the chin. Then he emerged from the smaller or ladies' library and locked the door, thrusting the keys again into his pocket. Rockets from the north western portion of the city scintillated and burst on high. He knew what they meant, and returning to the dining room, drained at a draught one of the bottles of wine which before he had only pretended to drink and then tried to rouse his besotted men. He was elated at the discovery of the trunks and was scheming in his mean soul the robbing of them. Sancho was again on hand lighting a few candles. "Old buck, here you are again, eh! old silver head?" said Guelty in gentler tones than he had used before. "How many ladies are upstairs?" "Three, Sir." "Only three—and the name—did I understand aright that their name is Lesly?

The commandant mentioned some such name. Do they all bear that name?"— "The family name, Sir, is DeLesline."—"It seems to me I've heard that name before; but my head's wool-gathering—like your own; eh, old buck? Is one of the ladies upstairs a young lady?"—"Miss Eunice, Sir, is a young lady."—"Say that name again, if you please." "Miss Eunice," repeated the butler. "Eunice—Eunice—where have I heard that name!—Can I see her, my old buck?"

"That question, it is not in my province to answer, Sir; Shall I present your card, Sir, to the mistress of the house?"

Decency forbids that the reply—which was a string of strong cursing—should be recorded in these pages. Sergeant Guelty was not altogether sober. Sancho thought it prudent to retreat from the room as soon as possible. Tolerably brave otherwise, he had an unaccountable horror—a sort of premonitory one—of Guelty's pistol. The sergeant was now evidently unsteady in his gait and without pretence, as with a lighted candle in hand he carried Hawks and Jailey, whom he had shaken up, to the entrance of the wine cellar and was going with them to search for the whiskey and brandy they desired.

He had determined that he would see the young lady and satisfy himself if she was the original of the miniature he had so long worn; and to satisfy himself of this he would go above to the chambers on some pretext. There was no name on the medallion, and he knew not the name of the officer from whose dead body it had been hurriedly taken. He had reason to know well the name of the family; but he had heard it indistinctly when he was detailed to guard the house, and it had not revived in him, at the moment, any recollections of long past events. He was excited now. What cared he if Hawks and Jailey were sprawling among the wine bottles in the cellar? His instincts were not theirs. In his present mood he cared not if they perished down there.—When sent to this house to guard it, he had managed to tell a cousin of his, who belonged to the same regiment, to come there that night to look for plunder. Plunder enough he was sure was there. But this sudden discovery of the portraits in the library and the confused revival of the DeLesline name, had set him almost beside himself; and in the flurry of his thoughts he was getting Hawks and Jailey away from interference in his own designs and down into the cellar room into which he had at first followed Sancho. He would just put them down there, at any rate, till it suited him to bring them up stairs again. The three had begun to go down the steps.

But they did not all descend. A low whistle from the direction of the piazza reached Guelty's ear, and bidding Hawks and Jailey go down with the candle—or stumble down—and help themselves, he opened the front door and let in the man from whom the whistle had proceeded. "I was late in coming," said this recruit, "but there were too many officers about."

"Some fine paintings are in the parlor here, St. Julian," said Guelty in subdued tones and with a few hiccoughs, "come in and examine. I heard you say you were once a clerk in a picture store. You can make a good sale of these specimens of the old masters. Cut out and make a roll of what you want. You have a candle and matches have you not? You always think of everything needed; or wait a minute and I'll bring you a light from the dining room."

This was done; and St. Julian's pocket knife soon cut out from their frames a half dozen beautiful paintings. "This Annunciation is just the thing for our pious Major," said St. Julian. "And I'm sure he'll give a good price for this martyrdom of a saint. This Venus and Adonis will just suit Ezekiel. You won't get him to carry anything in his wagons unless he shares. Any [illegible word], Isaiah?"

"Ought to be; yet scarce in the South as greenbacks," he replied, "but there's what'll bring it, packed up and put aside for us."—Placing his hand on his cousin's shoulder and looking in his face with glittering eyes, he whispered, "I never had before such a chance as this—and it's confiscated—is it not? And then there's a good wine cellar, too; and some wine 40 yrs. old. (A few hiccoughs). But you carry now what you've got and stow away in camp and hurry back. Too much at a time will be plundered from you; and you may meet some priggish officers of the old Regulars who'll make you put it all down."

"I'll swear they are psalm books and bibles for the chaplain—stolen by his special request. But here's something for myself! No halves, Isaiah!" and he seized from an ebony stand in the corner of the parlor, where it had been forgotten by the family, a curiously wrought small silver vase for flowers.

"No halves! And I not concealing the smallest thing from you," cried Guelty— "no halves, by Hux! (and here his hiccoughs began again)—don't you know I'm guarding this property—all of it? No halves, did you say? Why, Cousin Yarkly, there's plenty more, and God knows I wouldn't hide anything from a partner. All you get is on shares. Quick, now, quick; and come back with a dozen empty ham bags. It'll look as if we're only foraging. We'll fill them all, I tell you with solid gold and silver, if by Hux, I can keep the thievish camp-followers out of this house long enough."

St. Julian, chuckling at his cousin's pleasantry, hurried off with what he had purloined or, as he called it, confiscated.

The night was now well advanced. "Nine o'clock and hell let loose" was the cry. The terrible uproar and revelry on Main Street, which was soon burning from end to end; the trampling and vociferations of irregular bands of the enemy; the clanking of the scabbards of officers riding to and fro; the lamentations of hurrying crowds of women and children; the rumbling of carts and wheelbarrows; and the loud blasphemy of inebriated marauders and exultant negroes; came more and more distinctly to the ears of the helpless inmates of the DeLesline mansion and added to the terror excited by the rapid and awful rush of the roaring conflagration and increasing wind-storm; for such a storm had risen and was coming in wild career upon the devoted city. Nearer and nearer the hissing flames leaped and bounded from house-top to house-top, and towered so high that their red glare in the heavens was visible forty miles away—as far as Winnsboro'. The wind-storm which had set in from the north-west was scattering blazing shingles and rafters upon distant dwellings. The whole city, eastward of the burning Main street houses, was dotted with spurting flames. To help the raging elements, lighted cotton bolls steeped with camphene were thrown into houses and burning brands put under floors and doorsills. Escaped Federal prisoners and revengeful criminals who had been incarcerated in the jail and had broken out or been let out, joined the half drunken vagabond soldiers and negro thieves and helped them in their pandemonious revenge.

The roof of Mrs. DeLesline's house had at last caught fire. At the same time a crowd of marauders burst into the lower rooms for plunder. Sergeant Guelty (helped to his senses by large draughts of cold water) had an interest in ejecting them and virtuously protested against their entrance. But finding the task of keeping them out not an easy one, he had recourse to a diversion by pointing them to the wine cellar.

"Only that; you'll take nothing more or I'll report you." "You don't say so, now!" they jeeringly replied with a mixture of oaths; "haven't we a right to every rebel's house here and this among the special ones? We saw Saint Yarkly come out here with a bundle; why didn't you stop him?"

But they dashed by instinct to the cellar and thoroughly pillaged it, to sell in camp what they could not themselves consume. They left a few bottles for the virtuous and dutiful Guelty, and carried off, at his request, the fuddled Matthias Hawks and Jerome Jailey. They caught on the street several negroes, women as well as men, and lading them with their spoil drove them like beasts of burden to their encampment.

The sergeant, left alone, took a little more old Madeira to stimulate his brain to a plan to get a close look at the ladies up stairs especially the one Sancho named as Miss Eunice. He was becoming uneasy and wondered too why his camp comrade and cousin; St. Julian Yarkly, had not returned. No time, however, could now be lost. He ran up stairs to the chambers, his Madeira bottle still in hand, to beg the ladies to save themselves by instant flight as the house was already on fire and nothing could prevent its burning down. The ladies had shut themselves in their rooms he saw only their maid servant who had come to the chamber door. The glimpse he had, from the stair-case window, of the vast volume of smoke and of the flames and sparks coming—coming—and now in near approach to the house he was in, excited him; and he staggered down stairs again, crying out as he went, "the house is burning down—burning down; the shingles are a-fire! We've smashed every engine and chopped up all the hose in town, by—!—Don't you hear the shower of blazing brands—from quarter a mile off? How they thump and rattle and patter and fizz on the house, clattering over the roof like devil's hoofs?—The very garden trees are aflame! Hurrah—let 'em crackle and sputter, by—!"

At this loud and brutal announcement Miss Alicia fainted in Mrs. DeLesline's arms. The maid servant was dispatched to call the butler to help in the removal to a place of safety. "And run down, my daughter," said Mrs. DeLesline, "and beg the good sergeant to save the black trunk. It contains all our silver and most of our jewelry. His men can move it for us."

Eunice hastened down and approached Guelty, though she observed with some alarm that he was not quite sober. "Will you be so kind as to save a trunk for us, Sir?"—"Certainly, Miss; show me which."

"It is in this room," said Eunice, touching the door of the inner library.

The light from the burning city was now so great that one could have read the finest print in any room of the house. Guelty recognized in the glare of the conflagration the beautiful object of his insane admiration. He was inflamed with wine and no one was nigh. With the thought "will she kiss me" he opened the library door (after fumbling at it with the keys) to have the trunk pointed out. He had scarcely offered to kiss her—she had but half uttered a cry for help, when he was caught by the nape of his neck and hurled spinning along the floor. Tripped by the trunks and striking his head upon the edge of one of them as he fell, he lay stunned and bleeding; while Sancho, supporting his young mistress who was trembling and almost fainting, led her into the hall; and meeting Mrs. DeLesline and the female domestics bearing the pallid form of Miss Alicia from the chamber above, they all hastened from the house to seek shelter in a portion of the city remote from the devouring flames.

The roof of the house was all ablaze when St. Julian returned and helped Guelty to his feet. "What's all this? There's blood on your face! Are you drunk at such a time, Isaiah?"—"Yes, St. Julian, I suppose so. Here's a bottle—have a little for yourself, old man!"

"Why, goodness gracious, you're mad. Business is business. Where's the gold and silver?"—"Here, this trunk is full of it. Where're the bags?"

"No time, a night like this, to hunt for what you can't find. We must be quick the roof of the house is all a-blaze"; and St. Julian wrenched the trunk open.—The glitter of its valuable contents roused Isaiah's confused brains to new activity.

"We can't carry all this, Isaiah," said St. Julian. "We must hide it and trust to tomorrow to get it."—"We can bury it in the cellar," replied Guelty. "I know where a spade is, in the garden."—"Run and get it quick then." Running was a kind of agility his legs were not capable of; but he staggered slowly out for the object of his search.

St. Julian used the few moments of the sergeant's absence to examine more closely the contents of the black trunk, and seizing a small velvet box, forced it open and saw displayed to his eager eyes clusters of sparkling diamonds in rings, eardrops and brooches. He slipped the contents into his capacious breast pocket, saying to himself "Even shares, cousin Isaiah, ha, ha!"—and pretended to be drinking from the bottle Isaiah had left, as the latter entered with the spade.

To carry the trunk below and dig a deep hole in the wine cellar and cover up the treasure securely was a dangerous delay beneath the roaring fire which was eating its way down to the hall ceiling while from the staircase above came, ever and anon, puffs of suffocating smoke. The burying of the trunk could not have been effected except for the calm brain and energy of St. Julian Yarkly. Emerging dirty and begrimed from the basement, they encountered Sancho who had returned for the black trunk, bearing on his head one of the other trunks from the library to the yard to which he had already carried one or two. Guelty, half inebriated and reckless and smarting from the bruises received when Sancho hurled him down, gritted his teeth and with a terrible curse leveled his pistol and fired. But St. Julian struck up his arm and the ball crashed through the trunk near Sancho's head. Before St. Julian could prevent it, another shot was fired just as Sancho reached the threshhold leading into the yard, and the faithful old servant fell.

Did any one beyond the house walls hear that shot fired? The running to and fro, dragging loads over pavements, screams, shouts, prayerful ejaculations, oaths and blasphemy, roaring of flames, collapse and downfall of stores and dwellings, tramping and thumping of soldiers' boots and horses' hoofs, shrill orders of officers, clanging scabbards, pistol shots here and there in the streets, bugle blasts, inexplicable explosions and reverberations, rumbling of wheels, the rush of the increasing and raging wind pattering down blazing brands (showers of them thick as rain), awful sounds of men fighting near by and far off and of death blows given —amid all this din and clamor and the hurry, hurry, hurry of pillagers and those fleeing from them—was it any wonder that the thud of the pistol ball into the brain of the defenceless negro was as unnoticeable as would be the falling of a pin in the deafening burst of a thunder storm? Yet that murderous shot, inaudible beyond the secluded house walls, was distinctly heard where the Record is kept of men's malicious deeds.

Two

"Stack arms!" In faltering accents slow
and sad, it creeps from tongue to tongue,
A broken, murmuring wail of woe,
From manly hearts to anguish wrung;
Like victims of a midnight dream,
We move, we know not how or why;
For life and hope but phantoms seem,
And it were a relief—to die.

J. B. Allston

There is no doubt that a good deal of choice wine and liquor was found in Columbia and that some soldiers and escaped criminals were intoxicated and more than ordinarily bent on deeds of destruction. But there is also no doubt that it was predetermined (by subalterned privates, if not by those highest in authority) to burn the city; and the majority who did it were perfectly sober and not prevented from doing it by those who had the power to prevent it. The committee of citizens subsequently appointed to collect affidavits, base their report on indubitable and cumulative evidence. Before the enemy reached the city (say the committee) "The villages of Hardeesville, Grahamville, Gillisonville, McPhersonville, Barnwell, Blackville, Midway, Orangeburg, and Lexington were successively devoted to the flames. Indignities and outrages were perpetrated upon the persons of the inhabitants; the implements of agriculture were broken; dwellings, barns, mills, ginhouses were consumed; provisions of every description appropriated or destroyed; horses and mules carried away, and sheep, cattle and hogs either taken for actual use or shot down and left behind. The like devastation marked the progress of the invading army from Columbia through the State to its Northern frontier. These facts have been fully and minutely established, and are we then to expect a different method of procedure at the centre of the State? And a different course of action from that exhibited before the centre was reached and after it was left? Columbia—

this centre—the store-house of Confederate supplies, was the richest and most important place on the enemy's line of march. In its fall, the Confederacy was doomed—its last line of supplies cut off. The report, drawn up by Chancellor Carroll from the affidavits informs us that during the afternoon of the day (Friday) on which the enemy entered the city, and before the conflagration began, 'scarcely a single household or family escaped altogether from being plundered. The streets of the town were densely filled with thousands of Federal soldiers drinking, carousing, and robbing the defenceless inhabitants, without reprimand or check from their officers, and this state of things continued until night.'"[1]

Perhaps there is, in every application of it, inherent injustice in the old adage "ex uno disce omnes."[2] A change to "ex milibus" would not pass altogether without exception. We cannot believe that the whole army or the greater part of it were represented by the wicked fellows, many of them unprincipled foreigners, whose appropriate place would have been the Penitentiary for life. For their conduct, however, their superiors must bear the blame for they had power to control; and the opprobrium converges at last upon the commander-in-chief. How many stories of cruelty and oppression are still associated with his name! Perhaps he knew not, for example, of the aged Episcopal clergyman who left all his effects in his burning house, but tried to save one little box containing the Communion plate and his manuscript sermons. He had not gone far, accompanied by his feeble wife, when he was roughly assaulted, a pistol held to his head while his pockets were searched, and his box taken from him. The Communion plate was carried off when the army went away; but the sermons were left scattered about their place of encampment.—A volume could be filled with the sad experiences of that awful day and night and all would not be told. Hundreds of cases were far more pitiful than the following, which is selected because it is told by the Hanoverian consul himself, who, fleeing from Charleston, had taken refuge in Columbia, and endeavored to save his official records and some pecuniarily valuable papers entrusted to his keeping. Though entitled to respect as the representative of a foreign State, he fared no better than others in the hands of the rough plunderers. The poor widow with whom he was staying, begged, on her knees, the officer quartered at her house, for protection to herself, her children and the little property she possessed. She was told her property could not be saved, unless she managed to save it herself. "We hastily gathered up," says the consul, "what we could in bundles, trunks and boxes, took them down stairs to carry them off ourselves if we could, or depending upon

<hr/>

1. Marion Brunson Lucas, *Sherman and the Burning of Columbia* (College Station: Texas A&M University Press, 1976), 119–28. Approximately one-third of Columbia's buildings burned. Most were in the business district; relatively few residences were destroyed.

2. Virgil, *Aeneid* 2.65–66. "You will know all things [about a group or class] from one example."

the assistance of the captain and his men. But no sooner did any article reach the street than the band of robbers greedily fell upon it, dragged it off, or shared its contents before our very eyes; and every further attempt to save anything ended in the same result. The commanding officer declared that he could do nothing to prevent this; we had to submit to the inevitable, and were glad that the officer promised personal protection to the lady now frightened almost to death." The consul left the house with his tin box of archives and such small parcels of valuables as he could carry and sought to reach the dwelling of a friend at the further end of the town. Passing many distressing scenes, he met in a by-street a detachment of soldiers, whom he took for a patrol and as they were going his way he joined them as a fortunate means of protection. But he was halted and asked by the captain what he was carrying. He replied, partly his own property and partly the consular records. "But the captain, who was curious, proposed to convince himself of the truth of my assertion, and took my baggage from me. I had to unlock the box; the whole party handled the scattered contents. One took this and another that, and they left me nothing but the empty box, the consular seal and a few letters and valueless papers. Protests and prayers availed nothing; and my cries of despair at the great loss, the extent of which, in the excitement of the moment, I did not soon realize, were met with the threat that I should be instantly killed if I did not stay quiet. Not satisfied with the result of this robbery, the captain demanded my watch and my port-monnaie."—At last, weary and despoiled, he reached the house of his friends, where there lay a paralytic husband and a grandmother sick in bed. But there too robbers broke in through windows and doors, and the family empty handed, carried forth the helpless ones to seek safety elsewhere—the grandmother barely escaping a horrible death, her bed being wantonly set on fire by a brutal soldier— whom the consul found to be one of his own countrymen!

My own house near the suburbs gave refuge to seventeen whites, mostly ladies, and twenty-two negro women and children, bringing with them what little they could save, and it was very little indeed. There was no surprise in seeing in one's yard or house, strange persons; for soldiers and negro men prowled about premises as they pleased; at times coming over the fences. Four times my roof was on fire from ignited shingles borne from a distance by the fierce wind. A good man-servant of mine sat, with others, upon the ridge of the roof, with buckets of water, and succeeded in quenching the flames. A burly negro whom I knew not passing through my yard, I offered to pay if he too would help; muttering a curse, he went on his way. When at one time the roof appeared so much on fire that it was likely the house would be consumed, some of the ladies, against every remonstrance, ran like affrighted deer into the neighboring woods, where they knew others had already gone.—A servant of my household, a bad-hearted young fellow he proved to be, trudged home from a plundered store—for every store in town had been broken open—with a mighty half-barrel of coffee, as he supposed it to be—(coffee was a precious article at that time) to discover after his sweating labor, that it was castor-oil beans. My neighbor's coachman, fond of drink, trundled a barrel of whiskey a mile or more to his very gate to have it there burst open by a soldier (for fun) and the fragrant contents spilled upon the ground. In the same yard a cunning servant woman who had done no work for years and had gone on crutches, pitied and generously supported by her kind owners, flung her crutches in the air and danced about singing "I'se free, I'se free!"—Every five minutes something new occurred. In the medley of events, trivial or distressful, the heart grew callous. Men and women laughed where, at other times, they would have wept. Unless indeed—ah! unless indeed, a great calamity came and poignant anguish pierced the soul!

After the incendiaries—helped by escaped criminals and revengeful bondmen —began their work at night, an indiscriminate spoilation prevailed till near three o'clock; at which time the results were so glaringly horrible and piteous that the Federal commander sedulously appealed to and obliged to relent at last, summoned a fresh corps—the Second division—men of a better class no doubt—from the camps in the environs of the city, to come in and check the incendiary horde, and stop the conflagration. It was effectually stopped in the space of an hour. Never in my life have I seen fire extinguished after their manner of doing it. An army ordered to stop a burning city from being further consumed—and without the help of engines! Men who had, under musket shots from our troops, bravely waded the Edisto, up to their arm-pits in water—now with beams of wood crushed down the burning houses, literally trampling out the flames, at the command of their officers. This shows what could have been accomplished at any hour. It would have been humane to have issued such commands before nearly three-fourths of the buildings in the city (not blocks of houses only, but separate residences) had been burned; it would have been generous and in keeping with civilized warfare, to have prevented the conflagration altogether; to have forbidden altogether the sack and pillage of dwellings in which none but helpless non-combatants were living.

The next day, Saturday, the Federals amused themselves upon other objects of destruction. A keen search was begun in the unburned portion of the city for all kinds of weapons which, so soon as found, were broken, bent, or otherwise made useless. The Confederate Powder Magazines near the city were rifled, and all the ammunition not serviceable to themselves was thrown into the Congaree river; an effort was made to demolish foundry-stacks, and they were anxious even to blow up the massive granite walls of the unfinished State House, after the burning of the old wooden one with its interesting historic contents. The Arsenal and the Armory were ruined; as were grist mills, the cotton mill, the gas works, the rail-road machine shops. Every tin plate of the roof of the gasometer was slit open with axe cuts. Every wheel of every description of car had a piece of its rim knocked off. Every machine was so smashed in its important part as to be of no further service. There was no time for a complete demolition of the costly machinery at the rail-road shops, but the damage was effectual and wrought by skillful hands. The amusement had been changed from applying torches, as in the night before, and the cry now was "blow it up or knock it to pieces!"

Miscreants, unrestrained by officers, seemed to have a general holiday. Roaming about in squads they stopped and robbed citizens on the streets; snatched from others bags of food or clothing and wantonly destroyed them; entered private dwellings and searched every recess; probed with iron ramrods each spot of ground—not excepting freshly made graves in the cemetery—where they supposed some treasure had been buried; being piloted to such spots by faithless negroes who had been cognizant of their masters' attempts to save some little of their personal property. Often the negroes themselves were compelled to disgorge what they too had stolen; for many of them had joined in the pillage during the conflagration. Within a stone's throw of the place in my house from which I was looking on, a party of soldiers dug up concealed groceries and dry goods of some thieving "wards of the Nation," and forced also a young buck of the said "wards" to strip off a handsome vest he was wearing and to which one of the Federals had taken a fancy.

Even inferior animals were not exempt from molestation. Cattle which could not be conveniently driven off, were killed and left to fester on the streets. Raids were made on every hen-roost and hog-pen. When the Federal army left there were no more pigs to squeal, no cocks to crow, within the limits of the city. The dovecotes were already empty; the poor pigeons had during the conflagration, circled in affright nearer and nearer till they dropped into the fierce flames. Singed cats though not in requisition, seemed to think they might be, as they scurried from one hiding place to another. Whining dogs having lost their masters or those who had petted them, fawned upon any one whose kindly look or tone gave promise of protection. The most handsome ones were tied and taken to the camps.

When sudden orders at an early hour, Sunday morning, hurried away the army and its vagabond camp followers, the spectacle presented by the city was one not easily forgotten. Smoking ruins, hundreds of begrimed chimneys—many tottering to their fall—gloomily looming up where happy houses had stood; pavements piled up with misshapen masses of broken brick walls and charred beams; people walking, some distraught, in the middle of the streets; for in many directions there was nowhere else to walk; groups of families, lately in affluence, raking up from the debris of their dwellings any little remnant of value which they might discover even old iron,—or seeking here and there assistance from the more fortunate who still had some food and a sheltering roof.

For awhile there were no means of conveyance to help away such as wished to leave and seek accommodation in towns or villages beyond the disastrous line of march on which the enemy had come and gone. It was desirable that all should go, who had friends elsewhere. More than ten thousand people had to be cared for, many of them incapable of self-help. The chief resource for food was the "gift" of several hundred lean cattle, taken up on the route by the Federals and too feeble to be driven further—and only given when the mayor asked "Will you leave the people to starve?" These were speedily slaughtered, as they were fast dying, and distributed to the people in rations. Sydney Park was the butcher pen; and what a sight was there! Corn, which the enemy's horses had left upon the campground, was eagerly picked up; and salt was scraped from the cellar floors where grocers had kept it, if there was no danger of the walls of the burned store-houses falling upon the scrapers. In the emergency, an energetic young man, acted as mayor and was everywhere among the destitute, riding the only horse in the city—also a "gift." When the mayor asked for a horse (the aged mayor, Dr. G.)[3] he was told "there is one at the door, saddled and bridled—get on and ride off." Then came to the suffering people the first generous aid; the beneficent citizens of Augusta sending wagons laden with provisions and saying "keep the wagons and the mules, for you may need them." The acting mayor the every-where-present J.G.G.[4] kept these going and coming and supplied the needy with such food as could be procured. A rude ferry had been substituted, over the Congaree, in place of the burned bridge.

In the meanwhile the war came to an end. April had passed, May had passed; June was passing. With the cessation of hostilities foot-sore Confederates daily arrived, walking through the desolate city; no baggage, no arms, no bundles; dusty and way-worn they walked onward to their own desolate homes. Yet with their coming brighter mornings, fairer evenings came. They had stacked arms for the last time. They believed they were in the right; they believe so still. Fathers, brothers, sons—strong, resolute, erect in bearing—exclaimed to the sad-hearted ones "Home once more! Out-numbered, over-powered; but we shall rise in strength again! Courage & patience! To the plough, to the work-shop! Build up your houses—the future may be more glorious than the past!"

Having in fealty to their political principles and in order to repel invasion endured all of toil and privation that man can endure and fought the bloody battles of a four years' war, these veterans brought to the afflicted at home new life and hope. They had gone forth, as the lion and eagle, to rend and destroy; they returned—these buoyant, stalwart men—to build anew the fallen fortune of the State. Would they be permitted to do it?

Thousands of non-combatants who had come to the city for safety, now, as opportunity offered, went back to their old homes. Many refugees from the devastated part of the sea-coast, fascinated with rural scenery and the healthiness of the

---

3. Marion Brunson Lucas, *Sherman and the Burning of Columbia* (College Station: Texas A&M University Press, 1976), 69–70. Mayor Thomas Jefferson Goodwyn surrendered Columbia to advancing Union forces on the morning of February 17, 1865.

4. Marion Brunson Lucas, *Sherman and the Burning of Columbia* (College Station: Texas A&M University Press, 1976), 142. Rivers refers here to James G. Gibbes.

up-country, made their permanent homes there. In coming from their old abodes the rule was Pack Everything. In seeing them unpack we were moved both to smiles and tears. Yes, we helped each other then. Refugees and mountaineers were all one people, united in a common cause. Some of the new-comers remained to live even in despoiled and smouldering Columbia. Many a widow, childless mother, decrepit old man, in mourning habiliments, had, alas, no home to go to. Those whose home was in the city and who had fled from it at Sherman's approach, now came back bringing their much-needed horses and vehicles. Associations began to be formed for gathering and sharing food. Grist mills and saw mills were repaired, rail-road tracks relaid—signal whistles from locomotives were heard anew—how joyous the sound!—a post office was opened in a little one-story house in a by-street; from old bricks on the burnt district temporary stores and dwellings were constructed; strangers from the North came with rolls of greenbacks to buy up old silver and gold. Some that I sold was weighed with bullets trimmed down to the weight of ounces according to standard weights somewhere in town. Farmers from districts unvisited by the enemy began to bring in, from fifty to one hundred miles away, bacon and corn and cowpens to swap for salt. They had never seen "greenbacks"; regarded them with suspicion; preferred to have nothing to do with them. Some gentlemen from a neighboring State, with capital from somewhere, came to open a Bank. Money could be borrowed at 14 to 18 percent; and Northern loans—with plenty of profit—helped to set in motion once more the old wheels of trade.

It was the policy of the conquerors to suppress *emeutes;*[5] to be ready to confront any further hostility; and the city, as a central post, was therefore placed under martial law with U.S. troops in barracks. The State was to be reconstructed before its legislative, judicial, and executive systems could work in harmony with the new *regime* at the National Capital. For the nonce a certain Colonel Nickton, from a mercantile house of Cincinnati, exercised absolute control, judicial and executive, over this part of South Carolina, once a Sovereign State in her own right; now a province in "Military District No. 2."[6] The whims and caprices of the commercial man "clothed in petty, brief authority" were often ludicrous; but his services were at times really commendable. Powerful in frame, he could, while riding by, catch up a delinquent or inebriated private of his command, and drag him (bearing him awhile off his feet) nearly at full speed to the camp to have him soused in the horse-trough, tied up by the thumb, shackled to a forty pound ball or marched around

5. John B. Boles, *The South through Time: A History of an American Region,* vol. 2 (Upper Saddle River, N.J.: Prentice Hall, 1995), 382–84.

6. The Military Reconstruction Act of 1867 marked the end of legal state governments in seceding states. Former Confederate states were divided into five military districts held by military commanders.

for hours with a heavy log upon his shoulder. Lazy negro vagrants, believing free-dom meant idleness, he arrested and put in gangs to clear the burnt district of weeds (for summer had now come again), to covering up exposed wells on house-lots or to removing the unsightly bricks from the side-walks. Keeping hundreds of them under guard, he sent them to work, under the bayonet, wherever their work was needed. It seemed to be fun for him and his blue-coat men. All manner of business engaged his attention; and he dispatched it too in a very off-hand mili-tary manner. On one occasion a negro complained to him of being struck by his old master. "You must not strike a negro," he said. "I am bound to protect him." "Then what shall I do if he is insolent to me" inquired the old master, who had been marched half a mile to the court of the commandant. "Shoot him," was the answer. On another occasion an old ex-slave judging the time had come to rem-edy all grievances applied to Nickton, calling him "My Jesus" and desiring punish-ment on his former owner for an injury—"When did he injure you?"—"About twenty year ago." The Colonel jumped from his judgment seat and kicked the sup-plicant from the room and all the way down stairs, with expressions by no means Christianlike.—Speaking of this man, I cannot refrain from telling of his having before him a young gentleman who came to identify some silver ware as the prop-erty of his father. It had been found at the Lunatic Asylum which was on the out-skirt of the city and had not been molested. "Why don't Mister keep his silver at home!" angrily cried the Colonel. The reply was admirable and would have been suitably made to the incendiaries of the 17th of February, who had burnt the fam-ily mansion, "My father, Sir, General—, has no home."

The Colonel's roughness did not hinder his doing many kindly acts. He particu-larly wished to meet again Colonel Loyle of the S.C. troops who had once wounded and captured him and had treated him tenderly. Colonel Loyle had succeeded to the command of the regiment on the fall of Colonel DeLesline. He happened to come to Columbia at this time in behalf of his neighbor and friend, the sick and infirm old Mr. DeLesline—who could not come to the city—to help in the removal of the ladies of the family to the country seat which was intended for their future abode. Mr. DeLesline had not returned to Columbia after escaping from it on the approach of the enemy; and the ladies had found temporary refuge in the College buildings, as many other families had done; and Nickton's headquarters were there also. The buildings had been spared during the conflagration, because used as a hospital and under the yellow flag. They were crowded with sick and wounded Confederates and many Federal sick and wounded prisoners. Here Nickton met Colonel Loyle; and his cordial greeting was followed by placing every resource he could command at the service of his former captor. Horses and wagons were fur-nished for the removal of such personal and household property as still remained to the DeLeslines—saved by their servants from the burning mansion.

Arrangements for the comfortable conveyance, from the College buildings, of the invalid Aunt Alicia and of Mrs. DeLesline almost as feeble and unnerved, were perfected by Miss Eunice and her nurse, the wife of the murdered Sancho. The old family carriage sent back for them (and drawn by mules) and two capacious army wagons kindly furnished by the Commandant, were soon upon the road. As Colonel Loyle was preparing to set out as their escort, Nickton joined him. "Loyle," said he, "I will ride some miles with you; and I have a horse here I wish you to try and to give your opinion of his qualities."—A soldier forthwith brought Colonel Loyle a handsomely caparisoned, spirited young horse, glossy and black as jet, except the white star on his forehead. "Tom," said Nickton, addressing the soldier, "ride Colonel Loyle's horse and go forward with the wagons."

As the two friends rode on away from the city, Nickton remarked, "We may never meet again. I have resigned my position and shall, in a few days, go home to resume commercial pursuits. My reasons for this course would hardly be tolerated by the authorities at Washington. But I see approaching so much oppression of your people under plea of Reconstruction, so violent an infraction of the old relations between them and the blacks, that I desire no participation in the transaction. A subordinate officer who has a conscience may have, ere long, to execute orders here with tears in his eyes, and this, it is not my disposition to do. Your Legislature is to convene and your wise men are excogitating, as seems best to them, a re-adjustment of the relations of the two races living together. They are thinking of enacting a code. What they shall do will be set at naught by Congress. The negro will be put upon political equality with you. All the prominent men who took part in rebellion—and who of you did not?—will be denied rights of citizenship. And there are plenty of designing, even reckless men, who care nothing for your welfare, who for private gain will come here to carry into effect the iniquitous policy of those who are now in power, and are likely to remain in power. They control the army, long unused to peaceful measures; and they will use it to effect their aims. You will have, for years to come, troubles which I shudder to contemplate. The assassination of Lincoln, the shackling of your late Confederate President indicate a renewal of hostility, or you may call it oppression, not to be checked by the impotence of Andrew Johnson who would withstand the maddened Congressional majority. The under-current of enmity which I see spreading among your former slaves—threatens your peace and security; and God alone knows how all this must terminate. You once saved my life; would to heaven I could do you an equal service."

They had ridden about three miles conversing together, when a courier from the city overtook them with a message from an officer at the barracks, that Nickton's presence was needed to settle a case of maltreatment of a negro by a Mr. Barton. He had been arrested; but a mob of negroes were threatening his life. His friends were also armed and a serious difficulty was apprehended. Colonel Loyle talking to the commandant in a low voice so as not to be overheard by the ladies informed him that an ex-lieutenant of his old regiment of the name just mentioned had been expected by him as an escort for the family then under his own care; and if it were his young friend—Willie—who had been arrested, he would venture to ask that he be dealt with as leniently as the justice of the case would permit; for the young man, though rash and impetuous, was not disposed to evil and would not designedly harm any one.

"I shall," replied Nickton, "attend to the case immediately and, if possible, shall send him on to overtake you and the ladies. Take this note with you, Colonel, and read it when you shall have reached your first resting place"; and Nickton grasping the hand of Colonel Loyle, bade him adieu and in a moment was out of sight on his rapid return to the barracks. When Colonel Loyle as requested opened the note at his first resting place, he read with surprise the sentence "Please accept, in remembrance of me, the horse you are riding.—Selim I call him. May he save your life if while you are on him, it shall ever be imperiled. Farewell. J.D. Nickton."

The commandant soon dashed in among the crowd at his quarters, scattering them right and left in his usual blustering manner and crying out "Who brings this disturbance here? Let every man who cannot justify his presence, be arrested and put in prison. Order in Company B."—In five minutes scarcely half a dozen persons remained; and the complainant, a dull-eyed obtuse young fellow of the fullest Ethiopian type, became completely obfuscated, and made so lame a statement of what had occurred that the counter statement of Willie Barton, ingenious and lucid as it was, was accepted as a disproof of the charges, and the case was dismissed. Nickton, however, detained the defendant, thinking it injudicious to expose him immediately to the still angry colored friends of the complainant—a large crowd of them having gathered nearby.—He sent the said defendant Barton under guard, to the barracks, to remain till he could be safely returned to his home. The negroes, supposing him imprisoned, were satisfied with the impartial justice of the Federal Colonel, and boasted that the "white trash" dare no longer trample on their rights. They went off singing "If you want to see a rebel run O ho! O ho!—Just fire off a Yankee gun—O ho!"—a refrain popular at that day and meant to irritate and insult the ex-Confederates who heard it.

Three

Twine Amaranth for the noble dead,
Nor be the victor leaf forgot,
And, while the parting prayer is said,
Strew Heart's-Ease and Forget-me-not.

J. D. Bruns

At my time of life I am not easily changed; and must confess a lingering of unkindly feelings against those who bitterly wronged us. The warfare, when it came to our doors, came with vindictiveness against us and ours; and therefore it engendered a resentment which is dying out only as a flickering fire dies out.

Although, at the period of our story, we had buried our noble dead who "wrought such deeds and lived such lives / As venal history cannot lie away"—I would fain still linger at their graves without the Heart's-Ease, but strewing, as we then did, the unfading amaranth.

Gather the sacred dust
Of the warriors brave and true,
Who bore the flag of a nation's trust
And fell in a cause, though lost, still just,
And died for me and you.
We care not whence they came,
Dear in their lifeless clay!
Whether unknown or known to fame,
Their cause and country still the same;
They died—and wore the Gray.[1]

---

1. Abram J. Ryan, *Father Ryan's Poems* (Baltimore: John Murphy, 1892), 76–77. Rivers quotes the first and fourth stanzas of "March of the Deathless Dead."

One cannot, however, but admire the generous good-will exhibited by those who had so recently faced each other in hostile array. General Grant, shortly before he died, said to the ex-Confederate General Buckner, "I have always contended that if there had been nobody left but the soldiers we would have had peace in a year." No doubt the friendship between Colonel Nickton and Colonel Loyle was genuine. If it had been left to such men to balance and adjust the issues of the war, there would be, perhaps, less of wounded pride in our hearts when we sorrowfully say "We accept the situation." Such a situation as that foreshadowed by the Federal commandant?—O no—*that* we could not ever willingly accept.—But let us turn to our little history, or romance, if you choose to call it so.

Instead of traveling all night, the carriage and the wagons, under the guidance of Colonel Loyle and the Federal soldier Corporal Tom Chiltree, were halted at the residence of a friend of Mrs. DeLesline—the widow Axtell—just as darkness settled upon the road. It was by the Colonel's arrangement, after he went to Columbia, for he knew the laden wagons would move slowly; and it turned out to be an agreeable surprise to Eunice and her mother and the wearied aunt Alicia; for the Axtell residence could only be reached by deviating a quarter of a mile from the main road; and in the late twilight they had neither expected nor noticed the deviation. Preparations had been made for their reception by the lady of the house and her two maiden sisters who lived with her; and ample accommodation was soon found for the horses and the men in charge of the wagons. The two sons of the lady of the house had been, one an officer and the other a private, in the Colonel's regiment and had come safely through the war. They were not now at home; and their mother, whether lonely or not, in her secluded dwelling would have joyously welcomed the ladies for the sake of Colonel Loyle, whom she admired, as well as for the sake of her own friendly acquaintance with them.

Her sons, the young ex-Confederates, were off on a quest to regain, if possible, their farm mules. A squad of Federals, under a Captain Dunn, were still encamped a short distance off. They had been engaged, evidently with reluctance and mortification, in the ungracious business of seizing all mules and horses branded with the Union letters; which was prima facie evidence that such animals were captured property of the United States. They were to be sent to Columbia to be sold at auction to the highest bidder. Several droves had already been sent down. The cash proceeds went somewhere. The customary labor on the farms had long been disorganized, in many cases utterly broken up, by the emancipation of the colored workmen; and it fell heavily upon the impoverished farmers to be deprived now of their mules. The 4 years of war had used up horses and mules in the Confederacy; and good mules were highly prized by the returning soldiers. Most of them had come fairly by them; and had not really the means to purchase them back again. The young men spoken of, had brought their four (each had the Federal brand) all the way from the Potomac. They were good sound mules and their owners, on the approach of Captain Dunn, had endeavored to conceal them in the depths of a contiguous swamp; but the hiding place had been betrayed by some of their ungrateful former slaves who wished to spite their old masters and were eager to curry favor with the Federal soldiers. The liberated negroes were a little too much in the habit of prowling around. They conveyed news from farm to farm, and were well posted as to what the white people were doing or saying. They knew all the lanes, by-paths and lurking corners in their neighborhood. Hide a mule from them in a swamp?—Why, they could tell, in a circuit of several miles, where every sow had farrowed, where every hen had made her nest. And some wandered, too, not from farm to farm, but far from home, from county to county, in order (as they expressed it) "to feel their freedom." One met them almost everywhere, tramping alone or by twos and threes. Their usual salutation on the road was "Say, boss, you ain't got no terbaccer bout you—is you?" A few sought their relatives who had been sold and sent away in slave-times; and by giving erroneous names of places and by consequent misdirection, had gone even through parts of several states to find at last that they whom they sought were living not very far off, perhaps only in an adjoining county. Tramp they would; and although impecunious and doing no work, they were fat; and contrived to keep so by hook or by crook.

The old perfected system of managing the negroes had fallen into disuse at the close of the war. And up to this time there was no mutual agreement for another system either by their old masters or by those who professed to be the negroes' liberators and best friends. In numerous cases the freedmen, of their own accord, remained with their former owners and were well treated by them. Many instances there were of continued faithful service and warm attachment. In history we read of superior races pressing out inferior ones. With us the goodlooking and intelligent young of the lower race were brought into our homes as domestic servants and became assimilated to us mentally and morally, and in some cases were elevated to important trusts. The property and lives of white families were under their guardianship. Genuine and mutual friendship hallowed the relationship of master and slave.[2] Of course there was another side of the picture. There were vicious negroes; here and there desperate ones. Happily they were scattered; were never

2. "My cook for many years was a good and faithful man, named Campbell. After the war he lingered in his old place with me although in most cases other negroes deserted their masters or compounded with them for wages. I was then unable to give wages and said at last to Campbell, You are free now and I advise you to seek employment elsewhere that you may be paid for your services. He replied, 'I know not that I am free, Sir.' The result of the war has made you free, I told him. 'I look not to what the war has done. I am still your slave till you, Sir, give me freedom.' 'Well, Campbell,' (I said) 'I now pronounce you free.' He bowed and with a touch of sorrow in his tone, replied 'I thank you, Sir. Now indeed I am free.'—When he died a few years later and at a distance from us, my little children made up a purse to buy a tombstone for his grave" (WJR).

united; and on that account were not formidable. Could they have been banded for any hostile purpose? I think not; both from their own inaptitude for organized movement, and from the fact that no alien white man had any personal interest in such a direction. The aliens came to make money, not to kill old Confederate soldiers; and most of them, in their hearts, cared not the snap of a finger for the black population. That population, with the prospective franchise to be bestowed on them by Congress, was to be used for political party purposes. Combinations with that view were beginning to be formed. The process at first seemed to be somewhat experimental. Any capable man might, unmolested by the other aliens, get up a combination for the ostensible or real advantage of the Republican party. He was for the time shepherd of his own flock; and all the flocks could be led to the polls when voting time should come. If an individual leader had a private design to accomplish—well, that didn't interfere with the Party's success, and was a matter not to be inquired into. It could remain a secret locked up in his own breast.— We shall now introduce to you one of these shepherds. The above remarks are presented as preliminary to his introduction.

A bush-meeting of the colored people of "these diggings" (an expression going out of use with them as suggestive of too much labor) was in progress half a mile further on, between the residence at which the ladies stopped and the camp of Captain Dunn. The meeting was in the midst of an extensive pine-barren which stretched between the places mentioned and far away north and south. Though the pines appeared at a glance to be interminable and the whole extent of the forest to be a "barren," yet the surface of the land was undulating and trees of other growth might be seen here and there, indicative of depressions and of bubbling springs. Nigh one of these springs the bush-meeting was in progress. After supper Colonel Loyle, with Tom (who had proved himself, in the day's ride from Columbia, to be a pleasant companion and, in sentiment, more of a Southerner than one would expect to find in a wearer of the blue) strolled out with their cigars and walked towards the collected worshippers—so-called—amidst the trees and bushes of the forest. The Colonel and his companion needed no guide to the spot; the evening breeze was redolent of roasting pigs and poultry; and loud guffaws and snatches of hymn tunes and the glittering of camp fires led them on to the assemblage. So far as could be seen there was but one Caucasian and several hundred colored people, male and female, the latter chiefly employed with gridirons and frying pans. The Caucasian was clean-shaven, wore a white-necktie and had his hair combed back from his forehead and reaching behind to his shoulders. He occupied a rudely constructed stand or platform in a cleared space of ground, and was apparently conducting religious services for some fifty negro men grouped before him on improvised seats of fence-rails. Some of them, however, preferred to squat upon the ground. A blaze of pine knots lighted up the scene.—To the right and left of the stand they had fixed posts and on top of them had nailed barrel ends sawn off with about six inches of the staves remaining on them. These circular boxes they had filled with sand in which they stuck blazing lightwood. A supply of pine knots was at the base of each post to replenish the lights.

"Do you know, Tom, who that preacher is?" asked the Colonel.

"A closer view would make me sure; yet I can hardly be mistaken, Sir, in saying his name is Guelty. He is a sort of land agent to hunt out cheap desirable places for Northern capitalists; so he says. But his prominent calling is preaching to the negroes. I came in contact with him in one of my rambles under orders and don't like him. He's after mischief rather than conversion of souls. If men go by breed, that fellow doesn't come of good stock. To make him better you must scoop out his moral nature and put a new one in. Let us go nearer and hear what he is talking about. He must not see us; it may check him in his language. Stand behind this clump of pines and listen to him."

The preacher's voice was rather low and only some of his expressions reached their ears; but it seemed to them that he certainly was not referring to death when he said impressively, "I tell you your time is coming, and you must be ready for it." —"they have too long muzzled the ox that has been treading out the corn. Under our new blessed dispensation even the ox shall have its rights"—"my dear friends, after the benediction to night there will be a private meeting of the B, R's."

"Tom, who are the B, R's? Black Republicans?" asked Colonel Loyle.

The corporal replied, in a whisper, "No—he means the Marching Band of the Black Rosettes."

Colonel Loyle had heard of the "Junior Rising Sons and Daughters of the Vineyard," the "Benevolent Sons of the Young Army Shining," the "Daughters of the First Star of Jacob," "Daughters of the Harp of David," "The Seven Golden Candlesticks," the "Young Rising Sons of Ham," "The Loving Sons and Daughters of Revelation," "The King Darius Pasture of the Order of Esdras," "The Young Daughters of the Aid of Shiloh," "The United Sons of Adam," "The Sweet Prospects of Paradise," and "Daughters of the Golden Chariot," and various other associations of the black people; and he knew that in the Societies of "Daughters"—the women were often so irrational and vindictive that the "Daughters of the Hornet's Nest" would serve them best; but he was puzzled by the new name of the "Marching Band of Black Rosettes." What could be the object of a "Society" whose name was not even disguised by a single word significant of charitable or peaceful purposes?

Tom Chiltree looked carefully around to see that no one else was nigh, and replied:

"I learned something about them on my last expedition from headquarters. While others hunted specially for mules, it was my instruction to associate on friendly terms with all classes in order to discover latent disaffection or hostility to the existing Federal supremacy; some congressmen seem anxious to propose that there really is such latent hostility; and I suppose my reports were sent forward along with others to the political leaders at Washington. I am from Tennessee, Colonel Loyle; but joined my cousins in an Illinois company, for fellowship. I remember you well; for you rode over me when you charged our line and captured our leader; and I tell you that most of our men bear no ill-will to the defenders of the Lost Cause, and now that the war is over, we agree in praising Andy Johnson for his vetoes of oppressive and revengeful measures against the South, hatched out by non-combatant Congressional wise-acres.—laws akin to such as Mr. Seward himself stated to Judge Campbell[3] 'were the offspring of the most vehement passion in time of war.' These Black Rosette fellows will bear watching, Sir; and so will yonder hypocrite with his hair combed back and white neck-tie. The Rosettes were originated by him and were to be limited to one hundred; but I doubt if he has found twenty-five of the stamp he is seeking for. I have seen one of his Rosette badges, although they conceal them. It is black on top of white, which is emblematic. He says his motto is 'Land for the Landless, Homes for the homeless.' but I judge that to be a deception. The ultimate aim of the league whatever it is—must be bad; for every upright colored man whom he has tampered with, has refused to join him; and one—an assuredly good old man—influential too—who was induced to enter the 'lodge,' soon became alarmed, and was only permitted to withdraw upon swearing a solemn oath to divulge nothing he had heard. If Guelty has a wicked object in contemplation he will have to keep it to himself till the hour of consummation; for even the reckless young freedmen are incapable of steady persistence in a plan and will play traitor for a bribe. I have mingled confidentially with all kinds of colored people and can assure you there is nothing to fear from them as a body. The large majority are content and harmless—at present—and will continue so, if you can get rid of corrupting alien politicians and such sneaking hypocrites as that fellow yonder who would instigate the ignorant freedmen even to criminal acts if he could thereby subserve his own pecuniary advantage." Tom Chiltree paused a while; then said, "Hear him now! Did you not hear him tell them that all who know how to read must come to him to be prepared for the ministry—and that the harvest is plentiful but the reapers are few? He'll get out of them, I dare say, considerable of the kind of harvest he came here for. But he can't cheat everybody. He will meet up with his 'oldest uncle' one of these days."

Hereupon they walked closer to the speaker's stand. His sermon or address was evidently near its close. The peroration was rather of political than religious import. He had just closed his eyes, raised his hands and said "Let us pray"—when with a startling whoop, Lieutenant Barton,—who had escaped from his unenforced detention in Columbia—plunged his horse through the midst of the congregation,

---

3. Rivers refers here to Lincoln's secretary of state, William H. Seward, and to Supreme Court Justice John A. Campbell.

upsetting, as he passed, the pine-knot torches which lighted up the preacher's plat-form. Springing from their knees with screams of fright—and curses too—and ejaculations of "I know him—I know him!" they cried "there he goes!" as they caught a glimpse of him disappearing among the trees. There had, entered into them (if they were not there before) unclean spirits that cried with a loud voice. Twenty or more of the incensed worshippers—members perhaps of the Marching Band of Black Rosettes—rushed after him. Colonel Loyle, who had recognized the rider, felt uneasy at hearing rapid reports of pistols in the distance, and accompanied by Corporal Tom, hastened in the direction of the shots.

By running all the way he overtook the excited crowd of pursuers as they reached the outpost of the detachment of Federals by whom Barton, a few minutes before had been arrested, taken from his horse and led to their captain's tent. Vengeful vociferations echoed through the pines, but the "stand back" from the Federal guard checked the rush of the infuriate negroes. The moment Captain Dunn with an armed squad appeared, his presence calmed the turmoil. In the meanwhile Corporal Tom being recognized by his fellow soldiers, was allowed to conduct Colonel Loyle through the further side of the camp and straight forward to the Captain's tent. Instead of finding Barton shot or otherwise injured they saw him quietly sipping a cup of coffee and heedless of the hubbub he had raised.

"In the name of common sense," was Colonel Loyle's greeting "why have you acted with such rashness?" "Only a little fun, Colonel; I could not resist the impulse to dash through them."

"I fear, Willie, you will die with your boots on," was the only reply, as the Colonel went out with Tom to observe the result of Captain Dunn's attempt at pacification or his order for the arrest of the crowd, as the case might be. Fortunately, before anything was done, and while the Captain was listening to a lying statement by the ringleader of the mob from the bush-meeting a diversion occurred in Barton's favor. Two of the Federal teamsters detailed from headquarters to accompany the army wagons, with the ladies' baggage brought in, with arms tied, a sullen faced, thick-set fellow whom they had caught stealing from the wagons in their charge, and desired the Captain to convey him next day to the barracks for trial in Colonel Nickton's court. Colonel Loyle, at a glance, recognized the culprit as a former slave of the DeLeslines, named Caesar, who still worked for the old family from time to time when he was not out foraging on his own behalf. The party under escort from Columbia were now but a short day's journey from the country seat of the aged Mr. DeLesline; and Caesar, no doubt on one of his single-handed expeditions and unaware whom he was attempting to rob, had stealthily pushed himself, all but his legs, into a wagon, rummaging for coffee and sugar or any portable article that came within his reach, when he was unceremoniously drawn out by the heels. Colonel Loyle said a few words to Tom, who approached Captain Dunn and told him that the young lieutenant in his tent was to be part of the escort of the ladies whom Commandant Nickton was befriending, and had merely indulged in a little fun at the bush-meeting. The Captain's eyes twinkled as the notion of a compromise occurred to him. He stepped forward, saying, "Look here, you colored folks, let's make an end of this. Your cousin Caesar here, with his hands tied, will certainly be lodged in jail or put to hard labor for a month or two, if I send him down to Columbia tomorrow. I'll swap him with you for the young man who rode through your campmeeting. The horse, perhaps, was unmanageable and frightened by your blazing torch lights in the woods. Forget all about it so far as he is concerned, and give him up to me, and I'll untie the thief, as he didn't get anything, and give him up to you, and there'll be no trouble anywhere."

"All right, boss; we 'gree to dat," they cried in chorus; and Caesar, delivered up, went with them rejoicing; and was, we dare say, initiated that night into the Marching Band of the Black Rosettes or put on probation for that honor.

Lieutenant Barton had been very much surprised to see his old friend enter the tent in the camp of the Federals. He did not know that the ladies whom he ought to have met and assisted in Columbia had stopped near by for the night; but supposed they were still journeying homeward, whither he himself was going. He had learned from Colonel Nickton that they had set out from Columbia. He hoped now to make some amends for the neglect of his duty towards them; and was profuse, when soon afterwards he rejoined his old commander, in thanks for his thoughtful attention and service to them and to himself. He and Colonel Loyle and Tom and the genial Captain Dunn sat smoking till near midnight under the rustling pines, and chatting of their campaigns in Virginia.

The theme was by no means exhausted; it could not be; but the conversation at length drifted, by some association of ideas, to Barton's recent escapade and Captain Dunn who had not now for twenty or thirty minutes fallen into his usual vein of merriment, inquired:

"Have you men ever thought of the philosophy of picnics in the woods and such gatherings as the darkies are now enjoying over yonder?—I have; and my conclusion is that it is an outcropping of man's original anthropoid nature. There is an appetency or proclivity along with it—another outcropping of our ancestral barbarism—to slay and devour animals. Whoever of us peeps into a forest thinks 'Where is there something here to kill?' All this proves where we came from; and nearly every man has still a little of his old wild beast nature inside of him; and you who have been in battles have seen it come out of him occasionally and with bloodthirsty fierceness too. Our lieutenant here came pretty nigh seeing something of the kind an hour ago. No one is completely civilized till he eradicates that thing out of him. All of us who are unconverted from the purely human will show at times traits of our own aboriginal progenitors—But—but—all that is philosophical, and my business is action, and plenty of it. Tom, you have a reputation for a special memory of bits of poetry; like a brother of mine who had a separate stomach for pudding; can't you repeat (or sing if you choose) 'Away with melancholy'?"

Tom Chiltree, without hesitation or even clearing his throat repeated it, prettily too; then some additional jocose verses to the same effect, which set them laughing.

Captain Dunn was stout-built, rollicking, good natured, about forty years of age; had seen much service; could laugh heartily; had a peculiar habit of clipping or hitching up his speech, when you least expected it, into short sentences. We cannot detail all they talked about; subjects unconnected with our story. But towards the end of their conversation, he remarked: "Your men, Colonel—for the people about here were with you in goodly numbers—must have been quite active along the Potomac in cutting off supply trains before and after your 'Commissary Banks' came by.[4] I've gathered nearly a hundred mules in the past week with our mark on them. Sorry to do it. Must obey orders. At the last sale I bought in a poor widow's spavined old sore-back mule and sent it to her with proper vouchers for its repurchase. Wish I could have sent her a better one. But she loved that particular mule. Said it reminded her of her husband—complimentary." And he laughed one of his short merry laughs.

"Did you find any on my farm, Captain?" asked Colonel Loyle.

"No—been all through your place. Not a mule there." The Colonel smiled. Captain Dunn continued, lighting a fresh cigar: "I took a fancy to your young man with the velvet cap. I wanted to buy some fowls for dinner. Like Dr. Foster 'he had hens and put them in pens.' None running at large. I pointed out some fine looking ones. 'Why,' he said, 'that's Jennie and Maud and Blacktail and Susannah—members of my family. Can't be sold.' He took me, however, to pens where he kept his nameless hens, and bade me take my pick. So with his geese and turkeys and ducks. His own families knew him well. Flocked to him as around a Robinson Crusoe. His colts were all of the family circle too. He had names to suit their idiosyncrasies, as if they were Indian chiefs.—By the way, your stables and halters and harness are quite extensive for the few horses I found there; and I had a suspicion Mr. Velvet Cap could tell something of a mule or two; but he was as innocent about that as a newborn babe; and your old German, Hennchen, couldn't understand a word of my English.—Found the roads about your place hard to travel. Badly washed into gullies. Deep ruts everywhere. Haven't been worked for years. Glad to get away from there. You agriculturalists in this un-reconstructed state should speedily reconstruct your roads; dirt roads, plank roads, private roads, state roads and build more rail-roads."

"Speaking of repairing our roads, Captain," observed Willie Barton, "it puzzles me to imagine how Sherman's men, on a forced march, could find time to wreck so completely our rail-road tracks; nor can I see the policy of it."

4. Rivers refers here to Union major general Nathaniel Prentiss Banks.

"Easy enough in point of time" Captain Dunn replied; "send forward squads. First, rip rails up; march on. Next, tear apart sleepers and cross-ties; march on. Next, make piles of the timber; march on. Next, put the rails on the piles; next, set piles on fire; next, seize ends of the rails and bend them in the middle where they were red-hot, or twist them round trees where trees were near at hand. Didn't leave you a rail fit for use.—As to policy, it stopped trains and the thoroughness of destruction helped Northern industries. Rather revengeful; but war means destruction all around." "Destruction of things material," said the Lieutenant, "but principles survive."

"Principles of expediency (and methods of government are founded on such) come to an end like other things," said the Captain; "and some of that kind you'll have to abandon, my young friend. They're not everlasting. Cull 'em over. Keep the best. The best are the profitable ones. We are progressing; we are conglomerating Colonial and other elements (discordant at times, as the Northern and Southern ones) into homogenous nationality. In comparison with centuries of unificative conflicts, say English or German, what are our few decades of political unrest and turmoil? By the way—I had almost forgotten to ask and with a view of offering any service I can render—who, Lieutenant, are the ladies you are escorting?—The De-Leslines, eh! I have the honor of being acquainted with them. Miss Eunice is a beauty; so is her mother, whom I used to know in New York in her maiden days. At day-break tomorrow I must move on. Please present my compliments. Maybe, by the time I reach the College Campus, all the ladies will have left their temporary homes there. It did our starved hearts good to see them.—Heigh-ho! Thoughts of maidens far away!" Then he repeated jocosely, but yet with a tinge of serious reminiscence, "One of your own poets sings ''Tis said that absence conquers love, But O! believe it not; I've tried, alas, its power to prove, But thou art'[5]—going to sleep at my tent, to night, my young friend, if you have no other resting place. We'll take care of your horse."

Barton accepted the kind invitation. Colonel Loyle and Corporal Tom bidding adieu to the genial Captain returned to the widow's residence, where they were expected.—As they advanced the stillness around them—a stillness as of the grave —was in solemn contrast with the wild activity and outburst of passionate screams which lately filled the scene—now so still! The perfect quietude around forced upon the mind the reflection that in more than visible resemblance Sleep is the brother of Death. After walking a quarter of a mile or more, Colonel Loyle had to traverse a clump or grove of trees larger in dimension and more densely crowded together than usual, (for he had made a *detour* to avoid the camp fires of the negro bush-meeting). Pausing a moment in a thick grove he looked up to the stars seen

---

5. Frederick William Thomas, "Absence Conquers Love."

dimly, here and there, through the canopy of interlacing leaves and branches. His companion paused too, no less impressed by the solemnity of the hour and the quietude of the spot; and modestly remarked that he was reminded of Bryant's "Forest Hymn," which once he knew by heart; Colonel Loyle, resting his shoulder against a giant pine, with his eyes still fixed upon the stars, said "Please repeat it for me, if you can recall it to memory." Tom Chiltree recited it all, in a soft melodious tone. Perhaps no words of praise uttered that night "among the crowd, and under roofs that our frail hands have raised," found more acceptance at the throne of God.

> Father, thy hand
> Hath reared these venerable columns; Thou
> Didst weave this verdant roof. Thou didst look down
> Upon the naked earth, and forthwith rose
> All these fair ranks of trees. They, in thy, sun,
> Budded, and shook their green leaves in the breeze,
> And shot towards heaven. The century-living crow,
> Whose birth was in their tops, grew old and died
> Among their branches, till, at last, they stood,
> As now they stand, massy, and tall, and dark,
> Fit shrine for humble worshipper to hold
> Communion with his Maker. These dim vaults,
> These winding aisles, of human pomp or pride
> Report not. No fantastic carvings show
> The boast of our vain race to change the form
> Of Thy fair works. But Thou art here—Thou fill'st
> The solitude.[6]

While they walked on Tom Chiltree remarked "I'd like to live in this State. Perhaps it was not wise—my joining the Illinois regiment. I gained nothing by that. I belong to a family whose peculiarity is not to get good common sense till they reach forty-five years of age. I mean by that kind of sense the adapting one's self to circumstances so as to gain advantage from them."

Colonel Loyle: You think, then, you ought not to have fought against the South?

Tom: I'd just as lief have been on your side. I lost friends by not doing so.

Colonel Loyle: You may regain them by sharing your pension with them.

Tom: That may suit their human nature, but not mine.

Colonel Loyle: It seems to me: Tom, you're not far from your forty-fifth year.

6. William Cullen Bryant, "A Forest Hymn."

Then Tom said laughingly, "Your young friend, the Lieutenant—I've met him before."

"If you knew him before," replied the Colonel, "then you were not surprised at what he did to-night."

"No, indeed; he was on a visit to some of his army comrades in the upper part of the State, and got into a difficulty with the squad I was with up there. He played a mischievous trick on one of us and it may have ended seriously, had not an old gentleman carried him off"

"Was the old gentleman," asked the Colonel, "named Thomleigh?"

"Yes, sir, that was his name—wore a broad-brim hat and peered at you through large spectacles. Some said he was searching for a gold mine; others for coal and iron; and others that he was writing an essay about the resources of that mountainous region and investigating the minerals."

"Yes," said the Colonel with a smile, "he is a guardian of Barton; self-appointed, I think; and taken a great interest in him. I have some of his essays at home. If you shall hereafter meet this old Mr. Thomleigh in his wandering explorations, I hope you will help him and befriend him. A kindly old gentleman he is, and full of information on a variety of subjects. He tries to interest the Lieutenant in some of them, and perhaps took him with him in his exploration."

The night was far advanced and they quickened their steps towards the widow Axtell's. But before Colonel Loyle retired to rest a further incident occurred—a pleasant one—a vision ere he slept. On reaching the house, about one o'clock, he noticed the quick moving of a light unusual at such an hour, borne past one window then past another, indicating some disturbance in the quiet mansion. Tom had stepped to the stable to see that all was right with Selim and the Colonel's horse which he himself had ridden. The Colonel, entering the house alone, met Eunice who, alarmed by his sudden appearance, stood still; a candle—raised up—in her left hand, her right closing her wrap across her bosom, her luxuriant tresses falling around her shoulders; a picture whose blushing beauty no painter's art could adequately portray.

"What is the matter," he said, "how can I serve you, Eunice?"

"Aunt Alicia is ill; one of her sudden spells of sickness; and the phial of restorative medicine she brought with her she has left in the carriage. Mamma is obliged to stay with her and I was about to seek some one of the family—for there are no servants here—to help me get the phial."

"Give me the light and I will get it for you."

When he found it and brought it to the house, Eunice was no longer visible. The widow, who had been aroused, received the phial from him. I must tell Eunice, thought the Colonel while he was returning to the house, that her admirer, Willie Barton, will be her special escort in the morning. It was well Colonel Loyle did not meet her on his return with the phial and that he found no occasion to tell her of

Willie's arrival; for when the morrow came, Willie Barton was riding back to Columbia with Captain Dunn. He had indiscreetly informed that officer in his tent, before going to sleep, that he had escaped from Colonel Nickton; and the Captain considered it his duty, under the circumstances, to hold him in arrest till his superior's commands in the matter should be known: A note of explanation from the Captain to Colonel Loyle was not delivered—perhaps intentionally—till four hours after the departure of the cavalcade and mules.

When Aunt Alicia felt sufficiently recovered to resume the journey the day was already on its afternoon course. Tom Chiltree however had set out, after an early breakfast with the wagons on the road pointed out to him by Colonel Loyle, who remained with the ladies. During the journey no mention was made of the Lieutenant by any one except Mrs. DeLesline; who was grieved she said "lest Willie's failure to join them at Columbia had been occasioned by sickness. For I'm sure he must have received my letter. What do you think of it, Colonel Loyle?"

"Perhaps he is on his way to Columbia now," he replied.

"But I told him exactly when he should meet us. Did you not teach your young officers strictness in timely movements?"

"Oh—yes," he answered with a laugh—"but Willie, you know, is under orders of a more indulgent commander at present."

Eunice had turned her face at the mention of Willie Barton and was looking out of the opposite window of the carriage.

When the carriage was almost in sight of its destination it was met by a young clerical gentleman, Reverend John Fairbanks, who came by a cross road from the county town of Bartonborough, so named after Willie's grandfather who had possessed extensive plantations in its vicinity. Mr. Fairbanks having been chaplain to Colonel DeLesline's regiment, afterwards known as "Loyle's" greeted the ladies—old acquaintances of his—and welcomed them as a very important part of his small congregation; for he was rector of the little church whose modest spire could be seen from the elevated point on the road where they stood. He told them of old Mr. DeLesline's increasing feebleness and of his anxiety for their coming. Towards Aunt Alicia he looked with his soft, benevolent blue eyes as another invalid committed to his spiritual ministration.

To Colonel Loyle, as they moved on, he said "I've been to Barton town to the Mission Meeting you take so much interest in and while there it was my good fortune to befriend an old soldier of yours, Jim Perkins who, you may remember, was discharged on account of his wounds. His little son was playing marbles in the street, rolling them into small consecutive holes which he had scooped out—not larger than a thimble—when a self-important negro fellow a new-fledged politician —cuffed him for injuring the side-walk and began to drag him off by the collar. His screams brought his older brother, about 14 yrs of age, to his rescue. He in turn was cuffed and knocked to the ground; and a crowd of colored men and women—

far more women than men—were soon upon the spot. The new politician harangued them and told them what he intended to do to vagrant white boys so soon
as Congress put the military fully in power and he should be appointed by them
as town-marshal. I managed to get the lads away from the crowd and accompanied
them to their mother."

"It is hard to bear," said Colonel Loyle, "but at present we have no redress. The
Mission, I hope, will be one means to help us out of the quagmire. The active work
of you ministers, of all denominations, in the religious welfare of the freedmen,
and in their education, must eventually diminish their distrust and prove to them
that we are their friends."

"I fear, Colonel, their distrust is on the increase—instigated daily by the malicious and spiteful. They are less inclined to be led by us spiritually. They say they
can interpret the Scriptures by the Spirit in their own hearts and by the same Spirit
they can prophecy. They want their separate churches and preachers, and without
any white man's interference. They take all we give, except our advice & guidance.
By 'we,' I mean their old owners. They are led easily, at least for the present, by
Northern philanthropists, so-called, who tell them they helped to give them freedom while we were doing all we could to keep them slaves. Our Mission which you
were so anxious we should inaugurate will, I fear, soon end in utter failure."

"If such be the case," remarked the Colonel sadly, "when shall we find effectual
means to secure good-will and harmony? We must not be discouraged. It is of the
highest importance for their future welfare as well as ours to overcome the subtle
antagonisms which beset us. Let us persevere in efforts we know to be right.—But
yonder is Glyndale and Tom Chiltree unloading the wagons."

While conversing with the Reverend Mr. Fairbanks, there passed by—and Fairbanks, to the surprise of the Colonel, instinctively uncovered his head and bowed
—quite a different character from any who had lately appeared in the State. The
Colonel's attention was so riveted to the electric-like alteration in the Reverend
pastor's countenance that he saw indistinctly the person bowed to, and who passed
quickly among the forest trees. I, the writer of this, hardly wish to introduce a mention of this strange person, this wanderer, at the present point of our story; but
conclude to do so, because he subsequently influenced, in a slight degree, its course
of events. When thus casually seen by Colonel Loyle, and simply glanced at, he had
been engaged in carpenter's work nearby, repairing a widow's cottage and was
going off with his hammer and saw and bag of nails. He was described by those
who had seen him frequently as calm in deportment; and I wondered wherein lay
the power which he was reputed to exercise at the disposition and morals of many
who had talked with him. He had been working in various parts of the State and
bore the name of Noel. But we did not bother ourselves about him, since his
ways were humble and he never mixed in brawls or any act of hostility against our

interests. So he was unmolested by us, and pursued his vocation or his mission in his own quiet way, going from place to place and honestly earning the wages he received—which in many instances was only the food he needed; for the poor for whom he worked, had generally little else to give. Such people—the kindly ones—called him the missionary peace-maker. Some—those inclined to depreciation—called him Mr. Childey, from his habit of talking with children and helping them in their sports, if there was any child in the families for whom he worked. This quiet Mr. Noel was likely to become, after a while, a trouble to some of us; because those who listened to his teaching were indisposed to join us in such retaliatory measures as were judged necessary for our safety and honor. If it had not been that our opponents, the aliens who began to swarm in upon us despised and perse-cuted and ever maltreated him, this Mr. Noel might have been taken in hand by us—at least to make him explain the object of his mission among us. But since he appeared evidently to be a source of irritation to those opponents of ours, we did not molest him. It rather made us inclined to be more friendly towards him.

Let me tack to this chapter a few pictures the meaning whereof may not be far to seek. As in the presentation of the itinerant carpenter, so these four pictures are placed before you for your interpretation:

1. A hurricane devastation. Falling tree-limbs have broken down the farm fences; the dwelling is unroofed; rafters and studding joints confusedly jumbled; and it appears likely that what remains standing may collapse; the farmer and his wife and little ones huddle in a corner of the field under temporary shelter, their faithful watchdogs near them. Prowling aliens are in the adjacent thickets, and with them a few dark-featured and raggedly clothed carpenters whom they have seduced from service to their old friend, the farmer. They are here for the pur-pose of stealing; but fear the sorrowful farmer and his dogs, and are awaiting an opportunity to get surreptitiously from the dilapidated dwelling any valuable which they can lay their hands on.

2. An expanse of prairie overhung with drifting clouds. The sombre sky makes the herds of cattle appear like black masses tramping round in objectless cir-clings. Wherever you look, creeping, insidious ranchmen, with nooses and lariats, are ready to catch whatever they can of the cattle and brand them as belonging to themselves and their children after them.

3. A lion, worsted in fight, has his feet entangled in a snare. A pack of hyaenas at nightfall gather around him. Some leap upon him and tear his skin; others slink about and snarl as if not certain the discomfited forest-lord may not be refreshed in strength, and rise and rend them in pieces.

4. A beach after a prolonged storm. Spars and cargo-driftings and pieces of wreck are scattered over the beach where the receding billows left them. In the offing is seen a noble ship with a palmetto pictured on her drooping flag.[7] She had dragged her anchors, but had not stranded. Her torn sails and snapped and twisted cordage hang about her stately masts which still point heavenward. Her staunch hull is unharmed. The men aboard appear anxious to repair the damage the storm has wrought, but have no means on hand for doing so. Tacking schooners full of wreckers, who ought to be benevolent and ready to help, draw nigh and officiously begin to pick up whatever is afloat and is of any money value. Some of them look rather piratical. They are evidently willing to strip the ship; but are not quite sure the crew on her deck are disabled or all her guns unserviceable.

7. The palmetto tree is a symbol of South Carolina and appears on the state flag.

Four

Can laws avail or philanthropic zeal
To lift a soul like this to virtuous deeds?

(Negro characters being a necessary part of the story, it must be said that it be-comes also necessary to make use, to some extent, of negro dialect; [otherwise I would not touch it]. There are slight varieties of it according to localities; there having been in slave-times very little, if any, intercommunication between distant or even near-by places. A slave would have been "taken up" if he left home with-out his master's written permission.—I was born a decade and a half after the stoppage of the trade,—a trade not carried on by Southern ships—of importing Africans hither for sale; and can remember an aged field-hand with his incisor teeth filed to points, others tattooed or branded with tribal marks, and some whose speech I could only partly comprehend. The original slaves no doubt learned our language, so much of it as they did learn, from illiterate sailors or plantation over-seers; hence, perhaps, some genuine though obsolete old English words still used by their descendants. The terms now clipped, misapplied or conjoined, and the sub-stitutes for moods and tenses and other anomalies, I leave to philologists; begging to remark that my spelling of the words is but an attempt, perhaps an unsuccess-ful one, to indicate the pronunciation of the lower class of our colored people. Many even of this class having been in long contact with us, speak very good En-glish with only a few "negrofied" expressions and with considerable diminution of racial intonation.)

When, in the afternoon, the DeLeslines were superintending the unpacking and arranging of their furniture at Glyndale (which was also, in compliment, the name of the Post Office near their farm)—Willie Barton was far on his return to Columbia with the Federal cavalcade. The night before; the Captain had been lively in conversation and courteous to the youthful ex-Confederate as a guest in his camp. To-day, having him under arrest, there was a perceptible abatement in his tone of sociability while they rode side by side. Willie Barton could not, however, divest himself of the idea that what he was now passing through was only a continuation of a frolic. He was not abashed by the recurring spells of taciturnity or the serious countenance of the officer at his side: who, he noticed, though chary of his own remarks, did not appear to be indisposed to lend an attentive ear to whatever was said about the affair at Columbia, the disturbance at the bush-meeting or the prevailing sentiments of the people of the state. The young ex-Confederate under arrest had never been, even in his own interest, reticent about any matter, and he seemed determined on this special occasion not to allow himself to be irritated by the Federal Captain's deportment nor balked in getting some enjoyment out of his forced return to head-quarters; so he kept on prattling in order to make his captor do likewise. At length, with perfect non-chalance, he turned directly to him and asked:

"Captain, did you ever hear that fellow preach who was at the Bush meeting last night?"

"Yes, once."—Then thinking, since his lips were opened, courtesy required a little further unbending of his reserve, he added: "Has a queer system of ethics."

"Please tell me what he said," Barton asked in a pleasant tone.

"The upshot was this: Wrong is all right so long as it is unknown. Vice in conduct consists in the publicity of it. If concealed it can hurt nobody's morality. It becomes reprehensible only when a man is fool enough to open, as it were, the windows and doors of his house and let other people see what he is doing inside."

A long pause ensued; but Barton set himself again to lead the Captain into conversation, and asked:

"Did he say anything about politics?"

"Well—that's distinct from the subject of morals—at least where he was brought up. No doubt he believes with the majority that in politics, as in war, anything is fair which helps gain the end aimed at."

Hereupon the Lieutenant, who had been brought up on different political principles, maintained that Ethics were the true basis of politics, and expressed unreservedly his detestation of the inimical party influences gathering over the State.

"You must not expect," replied Captain Dunn, "to be allowed, with the spirit now in you, and your divergence from the policy of the party in control—or rather your determined opposition to it—to go back to power throughout the whole South, when there is so ready a means at your own doors to obstruct your doing so."

"What means, Captain?"

"Elevating voters to outvote you; the majority rules."

"Of equals, not of inferiors. But they will never do that; never crush down intelligence beneath a mass of utter ignorance."

"Yes if philanthropy calls for it and party power wills it and swarms come here to see that it is effectually done."

Willie Barton was seldom serious and was unaccustomed to look very far into causes or effects, and in his heart disbelieved that any such thing could ever be accomplished, even if the attempt should be made. He had been taught that Machiavelli was not born in South Carolina; and if he had been, would have written bold satire, instead of what he did write.

"You for one," he said confidently, "would never help bring about such a result." The Captain frowned and said "A soldier obeys orders;—you break them, or you would not be going back to headquarters."

Barton was for a time silenced by this rebuff; and Captain Dunn, as if to render his words less severe, continued in a longer strain than usual with him:

"You said South Carolina was a sovereign State. Years ago the protective tariff did not suit you though you helped make it, and you proclaimed Nullification. You armed yourselves. We would have beaten you out of that indiscretion if a compromise had not cooled you down. You next said that the Federal government had no right to interfere with your State rights; that the Websterian idea, Union and Liberty one and inseparable, was an abstraction, though it is far less so than your indivisibility of sovereignty. You disregarded Northern wealth-power; you disregarded mechanical as well as political development, and believed the Federal government, without constitutional right to coerce a State by force of arms was and could be nothing more than a restricted mutual-benefit compact, and you withdrew from the compact. Even if I admit your view (for the Constitution had not settled the point) and that—at least then—you had a right to withdraw—"

Here Barton interrupted him, saying "it's a pity your wise men had not, in the beginning of the controversy, acknowledged as they do now the Constitutional right of withdrawal—a right your own Massachusetts more than once proclaimed."

"Well," continued the Captain "your action was, at any rate, inexpedient; and in taking up arms again you fired on us. You appealed to the sword. We met you and beat you. That's all.—Now, we don't intend to let you set up a third time against the One and Inseparable doctrine. National Union and Liberty are consolidated—"

"Say National Union only," again interrupted Barton.

Captain Dunn frowned more than ever, but made no immediate reply; and the young Lieutenant was emboldened to say, "It can be proved your side, with statecraft devices, brought on the fighting by menaces and provocations in Charleston Harbor. But let that pass; and let pass the fact that before the fighting began your party in Congress hooted down thirty odd offers of compromise. You now consider us (with your majorities) in the Union for revenue and confiscations, and out of the Union if it suits your purposes. You even go clean outside your own Constitution—which you call inviolable—to bring about the 13th Amendment. You abolish slavery without consulting us as to our vast money investment—"

"You have no right to consultation," said the Captain rather sharply. "You appealed to arms. We conquered. The terms of settlement are at our dictation. We are not yet done dictating. Congress has, despite Lincoln and Johnson, taken up their share of dictating. If it hadn't come to pass that the North recognized a state of war with your section, and your Jeff Davis government became the object to fight against instead of individuals, the law of treason would have come in, and you and many like you would have been treated accordingly. No—we are not done dictating. We shall see to it that the four millions of Africans to whom we have secured freedom, are not left unprotected."

"That means," said the Lieutenant angrily, "your intermeddling with us will never be done. Move your army away; take your unpaid-for National Wards with you; and the trouble effectually! But remember the right to secede is in the Constitution until you annul the name United States. And remember that what you are now doing may return many years hence to plague you people of the North. You are weakening the foundation of your freedom as well as ours."

Captain Dunn, paying no more attention to Barton, separated from him and rode forward to give some orders to the men in the line.—Willie Barton looked at him riding off on his high-stepping horse and remarked "O Gee! sitchen buckra like er dat dere nebber don't care nuttin for nobody. He and his mules! Lookee dar now!"—One of the mounted guard close by heard what he said and laughed; for when Willie worked himself up to an angry mood, it was so uncharacteristic of him that his looks and language were apt to excite merriment.

When they had reached the suburbs of Columbia and the Captain had delivered over to the proper officer his catch of confiscated quadrupeds, he was approached by the two young Axtells who had preceded him to the city and interrogated as to the time of the auction sale.

"Soon as possible," was the reply. "Can't waste our fodder; say tomorrow, ten o'clock."

The young men were not unknown to the Captain. They had met at the farm. Indeed, many of Nickton's and Loyle's men knew each other. For it happened that the regiments had often come in contact, prisoners had been mutually exchanged, and they had been thrown together at the time of the surrender at Appomattox; and some had since seen each other occasionally in Columbia or at various points in the surrounding country. The elder of the brothers, a modest gentleman, answered Captain Dunn's inquiry as to their ability to purchase their farm mules, that they could manage to buy one back, if the price was not run up too high. The brothers were thereupon invited to go with the Captain to headquarters in the Campus to see about it. As they entered Nickton's office, he was chaffing Barton, who had a minute before reported—"Why didn't you clear off home and be done with it? We don't want you here.—Hallo!" said he turning to the new-comers—"Axtell, are you arrested too?"

Axtell restated the circumstances which had brought him to Nickton's office, and the Colonel replied:

"Well—I'll be relieved of command to-morrow; and to assist you in this diffi-culty may be the last of my acts as a military officer here. I shall not forget it."— He appeared delighted with his prospect of returning home; and was disposed to be jocose about young fellows getting into trouble. "Your friend here, (Barton), has a knack at it; and it used to be so with myself. I've been five times captured, and twice escaped—once from a prison-camp in this very state—just to walk straight again into hostile squads. Color blind. Defective vision. Haven't been seeing right all my life. When I get home I shall wear glasses, and hope then to see my way more clearly through the world."

By some mysterious procedure the Axtell mules were the first of the lot put up at auction next morning and were knocked off in a bunch, without opposition, for a comparatively small sum; and the young men were offered by their friends a loan of the money to be paid. So soon as vouchers for the purchase had been secured, the Axtells set out for their farm, and Barton accompanied them. His road to Bar-tonboro' lay nearly all the way in the same line as theirs. When they at last parted company, evening had set in and the Lieutenant had twenty miles to travel alone. About two miles off, on the by-path he had taken, he was suddenly confronted by Caesar who was standing in the road with a well-filled bag over his shoulders. He was evidently awaiting Barton's approach. They looked at each other and smiled; thinking, no doubt, of their "exchange" the night before.

"Whose wagons now?"—enquired Barton, laughingly.

Caesar showed his two rows of white teeth and his eyes twinkled, but he spoke no word.—"I've been riding nearly all day, Caesar, and am hungry. Can't you give me a snack from that bag?"

Without replying directly, Caesar mumbled some words implying that the spot where they stood was not the best place for such a proceeding. He did not refuse the request, but was apparently studying out a method of complying with it. He had known Willie in former days; had seen him often when his mother, the widow Barton, used to bring him to the DeLesline farm; was rather fond of him; helped him to shoot a gun, to catch birds and rabbits; and, perhaps, if he searched the pockets of an old pair of trousers carefully put away in an outbuilding at the farm —which outbuilding he was still permitted to use whenever he fancied to stay there—he could find a silver quarter with a hole in it, which Willie had once given him and which he had kept for luck. Indeed, he had ascribed to Willie and this coin-charm almost all his luck. He kept it at home so as not to lose it. He kept there, too, an old coat—a favorite of his, because each pocket was large enough to hold a full grown hen. Caesar's sullenness and gruffness of speech could be, in large measure, relaxed—if he met with those whom he liked; who, he was sure, were not sly detectives to tell on him and bring him up for correction. His shrewdness was greater than is ordinarily found among his class, the life-time field hands. But he was incorrigible in his cunning, pilfering. When a mere stripling he had often out-witted his elders. His mind was half stupid, the other half filled full with fox-like cunning. Being brought up before his old master on an occasion for pilfering from the pantry, his foster-mother's plea for leniency was, "he too smart, Sir; dat's de matter wid him." His smartness had now increased tenfold and in the same direc-tion. He had, in old times, expected to be flogged if caught in his petty depredations on hen-roosts or in the house-keeper's larder; and always received the punishment submissively, not as for what he had done, but as for not having been sharp enough to elude detection. Success in his operations gave him positive pleasure. Not a scin-tilla of a self-accusing conscience seemed ever to have existed within that swarthy bosom.

I should like to put down his exact language in the conversation which follows. But this cannot be done—at least by me; I "disremember" so much of it. He had seldom associated or conversed with others of his color, except the field laborers; and his words were so intermixed with gibberish—Gullah or home-sprung—that they would be almost incomprehensible if put in print. His set of associates (from the sea-islands) used a dialect which had some peculiarities in it. Willie understood him well enough, having often heard the dialect. His first utterance on this occa-sion was clearer than usual.

"Wurrah tay paht? bimebi-croochy, croochy-click-a-lick," and he pointed his thumb over his shoulder, then stooped and went through the motion of fixing a gun.

Barton replied, "if I took any other path, I wouldn't reach home before morn-ing."

"Cummy yuhh," said Caesar, "bittle nuff, ah you wauh" (i.e. come here, food enough, if you want), and turned at a right angle into the woods, followed by the trustful lieutenant; who soon dismounted to avoid the low-hanging branches. Carefully leading his horse, he kept in view, as a direction for his steps, the capa-cious bag which covered the shoulders of his guide. Caesar had never worn shoes his tread was as noiseless as a cat's. He moved briskly, as one well-acquainted with the forest intricacies. He led Barton, after a long, circuitous tramp, down a gentle declivity, into a steep gully, and pointed out to him where he would best tie his horse. After this was done, he laid down his bag, took his cap from his head and laid it on the bag, stepped a little way from it, spat on the ground, walked three times around the spot he spat on, mumbling heathenishly. Then he came back to Barton and bade him repeat after him an oath in the name of some strange god or spirit and with an outlandish self-imprecation, never to reveal to any one the home in the earth which Caesar was now going to show him. The Lieutenant yielded him-self to the mystery of the proceeding and without his habitual merriment, cross-ing his hands over his heart, as he was bidden to do, took the oath as solemnly as if he had been trained for the ceremony. Caesar then resumed his cap and bag and led him forward. A little further on, in a turn in the gully where a mass of loose stones lay, he stopped, and bent aside a few thick bushes, and removed a large stone. The removal of the mass disclosed an aperture close to the ground. Caesar motioned to his white companion to enter. Willie got down on his hands and knees and scrambled through. The first part of the aperture was zig-zag in its course. Caesar followed, having quickly re-adjusted the bushes and stones and raised a wooden shutter inside as a barricade. In a few seconds a piece of tallow candle was lighted with a lucifer match which he took from his pocket. The tortuous entrance and barricade effectually concealed the lighted interior of the cave from the inquisitive eyes of any one searching the gully or trying to track Caesar to his lair. On a shelf in the cave was a piece of blanket around a tin box in which was a cow's horn with a cover closely fitting it. In the horn was tinder and by the side of it steel and flint and a bundle of lightwood splints tipped with sulphur. These were Caesar's means for kindling a fire in case he should fail to have lucifer matches. The piece of blanket protected the contents of the box from dampness.

On one side of the inclosure was an old, much worn buffalo skin on a bed of leaves. A part of this bed Caesar lifted up and removing a board brought out from a box or other receptacle beneath, a coffee pot; a package of brown sugar, a stolen silver spoon, a tin cup and a large table knife. From the bag which he had placed on the earth floor, he drew out some ash-roasted taters (sweet potatoes) several handfuls of hard-boiled eggs, a roasted fowl, and a folded cloth containing a dozen or more newly baked biscuits. The sight of these eatables spread a smile over his usually sullen face. He looked to his guest and said in words which we modify "You say you hongry. I didn't stay at the bush-meeting and when I come yer last night— I bin off 'bout five miles—I was dat empty, de fust mouthful I swaller I feel it go plum down to my foot."

"You must have been standing up when you swallowed that mouthful" replied the Lieutenant. Caesar chuckled. "Now, Mass Willie, here's a ting to fill a man all ober" and he drew from the bag the last of its contents, a corn-pone with cracklings (bits of fried bacon) in it. The food was placed on a small rough pine bench, the only article of furniture in the cave. He said "Sometimes I'se been wid only a hunk o' hoe-cake. I'se better off to-night." Then he went through a secret and further recess and busied himself in catching in a tinpan some water (which trickled into the cave) and in kindling a little fire for a cup of hot coffee for his guest. What other recesses were excavated or whether there was a back exit for escape in case of alarm, were to Willie matters of conjecture. The dim candle-light showed nothing more than has been described; except over the entrance, on the inside, in a niche, a hideous red-faced, wooden image or idol, about twelve inches high and hung around with threads of various colors—an object no doubt of Caesar's worship— a fetich for the guardianship of his hiding place. Caesar himself may have carved its ugly face; or he may have purloined it from some voodoo conjurer with the design of securing to himself the good luck its possession conferred. Indeed, luck was a ruling idea in much of Caesar's conduct.

The repast being set out and Willie seated on the buffalo skin, the conversation was begun by Caesar in an undertone, as if he feared his place of concealment might yet be discovered, notwithstanding all his precautions. His words, liberally translated for my readers, were somewhat like these:

"Mass Willie, I seed you coming, when I was hiding in de bush, and I stepped out to meet you. What made you come down dis road? You might er got yourself hurt. Your horse, when you knocked de lights over, tother night, tramped a man and mashed his foot. He swears vengeance on you if he ketch you before de next new moon. He and some others are camping out between here and Bartonboro."

"Do you know who they are?"—"I specks I do. But I aint jined de Siety yit. I'se on probatturry. I aint yet took de oath. I'll take dat when de preacher come round nex time. So, till den, I can't be wid dem in ebry ting, and don't know all de members."

"You'd better not join them, Caesar. They are the low down sort."

"What kin a poor nigger do? If I aint jine wid my own, where kin I go? Wedder I jines or not, I reckon I must take things, else I can't lib. Now dey, ober yonder, dey all take, and if I jines I gits my share. We all do dat, but some ain't found out."

"No, all colored people don't do it. Many are honest; and you know they are. Now where, you old coon, did you get this fowl I'm eating? You hooked it; and I wouldn't touch the thing—only I'm over-hungry."

Caesar giggled awhile to himself; not, perhaps, at the moral inconsistency of his guest, but rather in admiration of his don't-care-a-deucedness; a trait of character often exhibited in his boyhood and which Caesar perceived had grown with his growth. All the negro said, when his giggling ceased, was:

"Ah, Mass Willie nebber ax me where I gits a fowl; it aint fair. You always takes up for me; so don't ax too close 'bout sich tings. But I tell you, sir, de day ob Pentecost is coming. Den all de earth'll be for all. De preacher say so."

"You mean that white rascal, with his hair brushed back, who preached the other night?"

"Take some more coffee, Mass Willie"—and not a word more could Willie get from Caesar concerning the Reverend Mr. Guelty's Pentecost, nor about the general unrest of the colored people of the neighborhood.

Whatever was the import of the movement among them, if there was yet such a thing as concerted action even on small scale, Willie was sure Guelty had something to do with it. Nor did he desire any consolation from his recollection of the remarks he had lately heard from Captain Dunn. However, he was not given to serious reflections. He was for the present set upon putting Caesar in a good humor, and handed him a half-dollar for entertaining him. Caesar, being warmed up with coffee (which he drank from the tin pan he had caught the water in) and with corn-pone and chicken, and happy in possession of the half-dollar, began to smile again and appeared so much like himself of old, that Willie Barton asked "Is that a pistol I see hanging up yonder, Caesar?"

"No, Mass Willie, dat's a broken horse-shoe for good luck and something more dan luck. I nebber meddle wid pistol. I kin handle a hoe and a axe—but I don't handle tings like pistol. Dey's wusser dan rank pisen. I knowed a nigger carried one and it gone off in his breeches pocket, of its own self, and 'most kill him."

"What did you nail the half horse-shoe up there for besides luck?"

"Dat's all right; nebber you mind bout dat;—de charm of it aint going for to hurt you nor me needer, if we let it be."

Willie found he was getting again on ticklish ground and thought best to bring the irascible Caesar back to topics of old times when he, the little boy, used to be brought on visits to the DeLesline farm and Caesar had the minding of him.

"Do you remember that young rabbit we chased one day, Caesar?"

"Yaw, yaw! I 'member de teeny rascal. He jump up from under de wood-pile. How he run!—an de closer I git to him de farder off he get from me, till you head him off and cotch him. I 'member, too, you usen to hab at dat time a puppy a gem-man gib you, and I bite off de tip of he tail to take de worrum out, so he wont get mad when he growed up De puppy was more 'fraid ob dat rabbit dan de rabbit was feard of him." They laughed & talked of their exploits with birds and rabbits. At length Barton asked

"Didn't you tell me you once saw the devil?"

"No—I no shum—it was a woman did dat."

"Was her name Eve?"

"No, Sir; she name Lisbeth. It was on a dark night, and she started out for to go to de next house—when, lo and behold, de debbil was coming down de road like a big black dog, just broke loose; big as a horse; and de chain round his neck was a dragging and a rattling on de ground. He shiny eyes was big as saucers. He wasn't linky-lanky like, and hab no thing-a-majig like a arrer point on de end ob he tail. So she say. Well, Sir, she run back quick and shut de door, and watch tru de crack; and she say, says she. O Lawd, ef you ebber saved a nigger, sabe a nigger now! But de debbill nebber took no notice ob her. He bin after somebody else dat time."

"Do you remember," again asked Barton, "how you used to sing for me when I was a boy?—What is that song about the Dust a-rising?"

Caesar obligingly responded in subdued tones:

I looked up de road—I seed de dust a-rising, a-haugh-augh!

(This refrain was in deep gutturals expressive of wonder and awe. the singer looking upward and opening his eyes as wide as he could.)

I looked up de road—I seed de dust a-rising,
a-haugh-augh!
Who should it be but de debbil and his lady,
a-haugh-augh
De debbil & his lady in a four-horse chariot,
a-haugh-augh!

Then came an interlude produced by his thick lips and like a continuous rumbling of a muffled drum, a rubadub monotone. It was a peculiar sound, and Caesar was the only person I knew who could make it. Barton forgot himself, clapped his hands and encored. Caesar sprang up with a "hush-sh-sh!—don't do dat, Mass Willie—fer de Lawd sake! Spose somebody yeddy you and find out dis place!" He was really angry this time and showed it in his countenance. He stood quiet a minute or two; then tip-toed to this point and that, in the recesses of the cave, and listened; then returned to Willie, whispering "I aint gwine sing no more to-night. Now you just fix your eyes 'pon dat projeckshon yonder wot I'se pointing out to you, and dont you look round till I tell you to."—Willie, however, did glance quickly round and saw Caesar place a red string on the neck of the fetish idol near the entrance. (He may have done something also to appease Mingo's frog—which we shall speak of directly—for it was oscillating to and fro). Returning on tip-toe Caesar asked "Did you see anyting where I tell you look?"—"Nare-a-ting," answered the Lieutenant.—"Den nobody bin hear us dis time; and de charm come back agin.—Fore you, come in here, you swear by de oath dat nebber break itself, nebber to tell nobody dat you ebber see such-an-such a cabe as dis yer one; and I trust you, Mass Willie." The Lieutenant having given assurance of his telling nothing to the disadvantage of his host, rose up saying he would now get his horse and resume his journey.

"I don't see, Mass Willie, how you kin stay here all night; so, if you must go and run de risk, I'll go along a bit with you and stand you de safest road to take; for we was always friends."—Willie handed him another piece of money for good luck, he said. The gift of the coin appeared to make him more alert. Willie watched him putting away the remnant of the supper and extinguishing the embers of the fire and setting the place in order as neatly as an old woman would have done, and asked

"Are you married, Cacsar?"

"Not edzackly. I hab three wives, and on' em cook dat fowl for me."

"But you first carried it to her—didn't you now?"

"You see, Mass Willie, there's tame fowl and there's wild fowl. You'd git de wild ones yourself."

"How do you tell the difference?"

"Hard to do dat," Caesar replied seriously, "till dey flutter when de heads is off; den you kin tell. Besides, dis bin a crowing hen and bring bad luck onless you kill um." Willie laughed; and seeing Caesar again in comparatively good humor, ventured to inquire—"Did you make this cave yourself?"

"No, sir, I didn't make any of it. Dis bin a Indian hiding place. Leastways de old man say so wot showed Mingo how to git in here. When I was brought here de fust time, de same ceremony was perform on me as I perform on you to-night. You see dat, hanging up dere?"

Barton raised his eyes and saw suspended directly over his head the dried frog which was still oscillating. "Dat," said Caesar, "dat bin Mingo's charm. It sabe him many a time. It come swimming to him out ob de sea down at Wadmalow onct upon a time when he bin watching de waves. Dat bin before de fambly was brought up here to de new master. I was a baby den I come along wid Mingo fambly."

"What! Black Mingo who was hanged?"

"Yes, Mass Willie, he brought me here to dis cave to stay wid him onct when he bin sick."

"He was hanged, I remember, when I was with the regiment in Virginia. I think it was for setting a house on fire."

"He nebber set fire to dat house. He jump de winder and de light got upset."

"Was he any relation of yours" asked Barton.

"Mass Willie, if he say he bin my fadder, enty dat his bisness not mine? Now muss I make you some more coffee?" That meant, expect no more words on that subject. Willie thought it no harm to try another point. "You said you didn't make this cave. But you made a fire just now and I saw the smoke go right up as in a chimney. How was that? It puzzles me."

"De smoke go through a hollow tree de same wot make fresh air come troo de cabe. But I nebber make fire here in de day time. In de night nobody kin see de smoke come out de top of de tree; and nobody kin smell um so far from de road and way up in de air."

"Are there other rooms besides this one? I mean further on in the cave. I think I see a passage over yonder in the corner."

"Now, I going to kindle up de fire again and make you another cup of coffee."

"Don't do that, Caesar," said Barton, seeing him getting sullen, "I'll ask no more questions about the cave. But, Caesar, suppose you fell sick in here and nobody knew it, you'd die."

"I aint gwine die, dis year."

"How do you know that?"

"Well," replied Caesar, "dis July, aint it?"—"Yes."

"An last month bin June, aint it?"—"Yes."

"Well, I hab always notice if I lib tru June, I lib de balance ob de year."

Willie did not dispute this reasoning, lest he should irritate his sullen and irascible host. There flashed upon his memory other notions among the negroes about months and days—but unlike this one. For instance, that Job had been born on the 30th February and having had so much trouble, asked the Lord to blot out his birthday so the month now never has that day in it; and about the fourth July; for where Caesar came from, near Fort Moultrie, it occurred on the twenty-eighth June as he distinctly remembered.[1] But Willie refrained from further questioning. So Caesar put out the candle, snuffing the wick with his fingers, and they emerged cautiously from the hiding-hole, re-arranging the stone behind the bushes.—When they came to where the horse had been hid, no horse was there. Fierce objurgations bubbled up on Barton's tongue. But Caesar quickly checked him—"hush-hush—for de Lawd sake!—Stop and let me study dis out."—He squatted down against a tree trunk and buried his head in his hands. In a minute he jumped up saying "I tink I know. Some one seen you take dis road; den didn't see you, cause I taken you off; den he tell de camp; den dey scatter round; den dey search; den de horse neigh or he stomp he foot; den dey sneak up to him. You see dat, don't you? Dey know de horse and steal him to spite you. Dey tink you bin asleep near by. Go easy now. Let's spy if 'taint so. Go easy; maybe somebody watching 'long de road."

For the first time that day Lieutenant Barton examined, by feeling, if his pistol was safe in his breast pocket and ready for use. For the first time that night he began to suspect that Caesar might be playing him false and would perhaps lead him to his destruction. The idea "infernal villain" dashed through his mind. His fingers tightened on the handle of his pistol. But he thought it would be better to wait and watch. It was now about ten o'clock and the night so dark in the forest he could hardly see an object ten feet in front of him. He spoke softly to Caesar of the time he was a boy, and of their early acquaintance. He could detect nothing in the negro's responses but a tone of genuine friendliness. Somewhat reassured he followed his guide across the by-path on which he had lately ridden and over into the woods on the other side. Caesar often stopping and listening was leading forward slowly and noiselessly, whither, the Lieutenant knew not. They threaded their way a mile or more among the trees. Then Caesar halted, and in a whisper directed Willie's attention to a glimmering light in the distance. Their steps were then retraced to a spot which Caesar said was well known to him and which he could easily find again. Here he placed his white companion in concealment till he himself should go on alone and reconnoitre. Barton was quite ignorant of his whereabouts and resignedly sat down as he was directed to do. The stillness, his day's fatigue, his

---

1. Walter Edgar, *South Carolina: A History* (Columbia: University of South Carolina Press, 1998), 230. Palmetto Day was celebrated on June 28 in honor of the anniversary of the colonial victory at the Battle of Sullivan's Island.

hearty supper, betrayed him into deep sleep. So had he often slept in his campaigns, in positions when to close one's eyes was mere recklessness. It was a long time—fully two hours—before Caesar's friendly hand shook his shoulder and roused him to consciousness.

"Dey's asleep now," he whispered, "and your horse is in de swamp, over yonder, and some men close by him. The saddle and bridle is gone and He's tied to a tree by a rope. Let's get back now to de big road and you stay dere, Mass Willie, till I try to steal your horse and bring him down de road to you some time before de sun rise up."

What led this cluster of colored men and others throughout the State, to camp out at night, could be nothing else I suppose than their conception of unrestrained freedom—the novel enjoyment of doing as they pleased. The bonds of their servitude were loosed, but their pockets were empty, and this loitering had a tendency to produce a disregard of the *meum et tuum;* for to enjoy a continual pic-nic life, as they were doing, the stomach must be full. But there was at this time so far as we could tell no special object for combination—no movement for any set purpose. If they were let alone, the major part of them would, (perhaps) have become tired of their indolence and returned to their old ways of work. Here and there, individuals of them had wrongs to avenge; here and there, perhaps were some more or less malevolent or bent on mischief. But as a whole they were in an uninimical plastic condition; both those at work and those loitering in the woods; ready to be moulded to some set purpose, if such should be presented to them in a way to excite their enthusiasm. Astute Northern politicians, however, had already elaborated a purpose for them—viz: citizenship in exchange for political allegiance to the Republican party;—and there was now needed only the setting of proper agencies into activity to fix this purpose in their wavering souls. The picture we have here shown of one locality in the State may be applied to a hundred other localities.

The cluster down in the woodlands to-night, whom Caesar had stealthily spied out, had among them confessedly one man with a grudge—the one who would do Barton an injury if he came upon them before the next new moon. The rest, we hazard little in saying, would have thrown impediments in the way of this one's revenge, if it became homicidal in intention.

The half-awake Lieutenant submitted himself again to Caesar's guidance and was led off westwardly in a direction away from the negro camp, and placed in some sheltering bushes by the side of the big road, and where he was probably safe from molestation and was soon asleep again. In the meanwhile his sable ally retraced his steps to the smouldering camp-fires. It took him long to do this; for he frequently stopped to peer into the darkness and listen. At length he had reached the horse in the swamp and had partly untied the rope from the tree when the movement of the horse awakened one of the guard, who rose up—gazed a minute or two at the horse—then lay down again. Caesar had crouched behind the tree and remained there motionless a little while. Then he made a second attempt to loosen the rope, only to cause a repeated movement of the horse's iron-shod hoofs; the noise of which aroused another of the guard, who got up, raked together the expiring faggots of their fire, yawned once or twice, and then laid himself down again. "This will never do," thought Caesar "their ears on the ground hear too much."—So he lay flat down and, like a snake, worked his way gently toward a sleeper among the guard, whose blanket he stole, partly from under him, and gliding as gently away again, till at a safe distance, he rose to his feet and disappeared deeper in the gloom of the swamp. There he sat down and cut the blanket up and prepared four rude coverings for the horse's feet and long strips with which to tie them on. Furnished with these he returned and succeeded by patient and skillful manoeuvres in placing them on the hoofs of the horse. It was now two o'clock—and the deep snoring of the guards attested that their wakefulness was lost to them completely.

But a new difficulty presented itself. The swamp from which he had come, he saw, was to-night unusually full of water. It was also, just at this place, so thick set that he would not be able, without splashing and other noises, to lead the horse off in that direction, as he had intended to do. He must go the other way, straight past the main encampment, with a hundred more chances of being discovered.—Should he mount the horse and dash through? That would spoil his whole design; and his detected interference in behalf of the Lieutenant would no doubt cause his rejection from membership in their Society. But there was no time to lose now. He must venture to carry the horse that way. The alternative was to abandon his attempt altogether. So he assumed courage, walked erect, and led the horse—whose shoes now made but a faint muffled sound—directly towards the cluster of sleepers and then along the margin of their camp. He had nearly passed all danger when one of the men raised himself to a sitting position, rubbed his eyes, and in a tone as if he had been drunk, inquired: "Billups, where you carrying that horse?"—

The name suggested to Caesar that Billups was one of the special guard for the horse. He knew Billups—a limping old fellow. So limping in imitation, he responded, and pretty well in Billups manner of speech, "Taking him to a safer spot." —"All right," said the inquirer, and lay down again. Caesar could easily imitate Billups, for he himself walked (as some of his colored friends said of him) like the hind legs of a dog.

There were incipient streaks of dawn in the east when Caesar reached Willie Barton and restored the horse to him, putting in his hand the rope which was tied around the horse's neck. "Now, Mass Willie," he said, "git on and ride right off to the Axtell farm and go home from there—I couldn't git de bridle and de saddle— Now, you sure and mind now,—if any ting happen bout dis, you got to swear you seen me in Bartonboro' dis very night, and I bin dere to your own knowledge, dese three days.—You know I'm 'bliged to keep on de good side of de crowd down yonder so dey'll make me member in de Siety. I'm going back now to my hole to sleep and eat and sleep and eat till de preacher come round and 'nitiate me; den I do what he say; come life, come death!—I care for you, Mass Willie, more'n for any white pusson dis side o' hell; and so I help you to-night."—

This was the man whom Guelty (so soon as he learned that he had been a slave of the DeLeslines') resolved to win to his service, as one knowing their household and every road around their premises. In securing his fealty, whatsoever was the ultimate purpose of the astute preacher he kept it to himself. Perhaps an inkling of it might have been guessed at, could we have heard him saying to himself as he rode alone in the woods towards this same negro encampment at which Caesar was to be initiated:

"It was his last; he had no chance to make another; for I was with him till he died. The name and the identity I've made sure of. The net will soon be set."—He had no scruple in employing a conscienceless negro like Caesar to help him set that net, whomsoever he designed to entangle in its meshes. The scheme he desired to accomplish he durst not impart to any of his own class of adventurers. He knew them too well and did not trust them. They were villainously bent each on his own interests, and their help could be gained—if gained at all—only for more money than he could well afford to pay. But a negro band, whilst managed as for their own good and swearing allegiance to him, might be used without immediate pay and without suspicion on their part to help him accomplish his secret purpose.

Instantaneously as he had spoken, Caesar turned, resuming his usual sullen, half stupid countenance, and walked away up the by-path. "That fellow," said Barton to himself, as he rode off in the opposite direction, "if he had been an enemy to me could have disposed of me where no earthly eye would ever have seen me again. Say what you please about his race, some of them have as admirable qualities as can be found in any people. We could get along well enough together if we could be let alone in managing our own affairs.

"But I mayn't have to swear an *alibi* for Caesar. I've only to let out the idea that a Confederate war-horse is not like other horses. Carry him where you will, he'll find his way again to his master; or else Confederate spirits will rise from their graves and ride him back at night so soon as the clock strikes twelve. They'll believe it."

The Axtells received Willie very cordially, and he rested with them two weeks. He then borrowed a saddle and bridle and went to visit his aunt near the DeLeslines' and to see Eunice. Before he reached his aunt's, he stopped over with a friend and recovered his own saddle and bridle. After a month at his aunt's he stayed several weeks at Colonel Loyle's; then drifted down to his mother's kin-folks at Bartonboro', where he was at home—for a while.

Wherever he went he saw impoverished farmers industriously at work, repairing fences, tending stock, turning the soil, directing the laborers. Even the young

Axtells, who were better off than many of their neighbors, and with whom he had
first taken refuge, were in the fields ploughing along with their hired freedmen; for
some of these were sensible enough to work honestly, if not for money which was
scarce, for what they could get from a share of the crop.

Political events had, at this time, hurried on with rapid pace. The provisional
governor, appointed by Andy Johnson and the governor who succeeded him (the
last one elected only by white voters) did what they could to bring order out of
chaos and maintain justice among all the people; but the Federal military com-
mandants were insurmountable obstructions to the official authority of the State
functionaries whose tenure of position did not appear very firmly established. And
as between the two powers, the negroes of all ages and grades soon learned to give
heed to the wearers of the blue uniform. The martial strut of a popinjay lieutenant
or sergeant was their model to walk by. A captain or major or colonel, with dangling sword, aroused still higher admiration. A general, they looked upon as a god.
The shabby grey of a poor Confederate was a mark for derision. He had no roll of
greenback, no gold and silver, no voice in making laws or undisputed power to execute them—no Bureau—no piles of bacon and bags of flour, ceiling high, to distribute to the lazy and impecunious.

State authority was in abeyance. The State was still out of the Union said Congress; still voiceless in the National councils; still held off for newer and more
humiliating terms of re-admission. The negroes were being industriously taught
that to the Republican party at Washington and to its army representatives, its im-
perious generals and its host of brass-button demigods around them, their allegiance was due, and not to the "buckra" whose lordship over them appeared broken
down into the dust forever. Now (said they) we know, face to face, our friends and
deliverers from bondage, whose word shall be our law.

In the meanwhile, governmental confusion continued throughout the State till
Congress "camping outside the Constitution" completed their plans of Reconstruction, which gave in effect to the freed negroes (their freedom guaranteed by
State Conventions so they could not be paid for)—gave, I say, to this ignorant mass
complete control over their former owners. And what did the Carolinians do under
such circumstances? They were silent; but stripped off their coats, tucked up their
shirt sleeves, and went to work.

There is no doubt that in a democracy, such as ours, money is power. It commands labor; and 99 percent of the people need the pay it gives. Wisdom, as well
as necessity turned the whites, shut out as they were from immediate political
activity, to recuperate their broken pecuniary fortunes. Success in this respect might
bring back with it, some day, the resuscitation of their governing power. They were
still owners of all the land in the State. An idle young man was an incumbrance at
home and a nuisance too, if he added to his laziness, a dictatorial ill-treatment of
the negroes about him. It was a pity Willie Barton, and others like him, had not

followed the example of the Axtells, instead of roaming about, and hoping vaguely for a restoration of good old ante-bellum days of prosperity. While he was visiting at Glyndale—just after leaving the Axtells—the revengeful fellow whom he had hurt in riding through the bush-meeting, followed him up to waylay him—to kill him, if he could. He skulked and watched for his chance of attack; and at length had the affrontery to go into Mrs. DeLesline's kitchen, being acquainted with the servants there, and uttered his threats. He had become bold now and insolent.

Eunice was told of this, and instantly sent for the threatening Cassius or Cassy, as he was generally called. Her condescension, her winning beauty and pleasantness of manner, her soft voice, her superior wisdom—disarmed at once the aggressive and malevolent spirit of the stolid field-laborer; whose powerful paws could have pulled Barton to pieces or crushed him with a single blow.—"Cassy," she said, "why would you injure him for a mere accident? Did he intend to hurt you? Did he even know that you were there?"

"Yes, but for all dat, Miss, he had no right dere in our prayer-meeting. He had no right coming dere wid his horse's hoofs plunging right troo de pine-lights. I sweared to git eben wid him, if I ketched him before de next new moon—an I bound to do it. He hurt me jest as I was on my knees praying to de Lawd."

"But don't you know, Cassy, the new moon was night before last? It is past the time, and your oath can't hold good now?"

"Is dat so! Well den, of course, de oath done run out. But he got to pay for de hurt, for all dat," and Cassy began to scowl and work himself into an angry mood again; as if the new moon had no business to come so soon—"He got to pay for it," he muttered.

"What pay do you require?" asked Eunice.

"Well, one dollar aint too much. If I had been gone for a Doctor to cure my foot he would er charge dat much; I sure he would."

"If I give you one dollar—a silver dollar—will you consider the case settled, and settled forever?"

"All right, Miss, I 'gree to dat," said Cassy, eager for so large a sum, in shining silver too. Joyous in his triumph he could now boast to his comrades of the Marching Band of Black Rosettes of his following up the matter and getting well paid for the relinquishment of his revenge even after the new moon had come and his oath had "done run out."

Thereupon Eunice summoned all the negroes from the kitchen, and with them as witnesses the treaty of peace was ratified. Willie Barton knew nothing of it. Never a cent would Cassy have gotten from him; but, rather, a settlement of hard thumps, without regard to detriment to himself from ambush or otherwise.

Nor did he, or Eunice either, ever know that he had, indeed, been ambushed the preceding evening by Cassy and a more stupid, and therefore more blindly vindictive comrade (who had been knocked over at the Bush Meeting) and that he had been only saved from assault by the fact that Eunice was walking with him. And, it may be told, she was taking that walk with him along the adjacent road, to urge him, in her gentle way, to a more active and manly career; and with a poor return for her effort in that direction, and a mortifying conviction that the spirit within him was not prone to persistent and heroic achievement, or to put it in plainer phrase, to work for his living, as all manly men were then doing.

We stated that our young lieutenant before he went to his aunt Avery's, stayed a while with a friend. We append his account of getting back what was stolen from him while he was supping with Caesar in the cave.

Letter from Willie Barton to Captain Axtell—dated from DuVose's farm.

"Dear Charlie—I leave your saddle and bridle with Steve Duvose and he will see that you get them. Many thanks. You wouldn't let me run any risk to hunt my own up while I was under your friendly roof. But the evening after leaving you I stopped over at Steve's to talk of army times, and mentioning my determination to hunt up my trappings, he was as full of the fun of it as I was. You remember Steve's negro Sempronius Bantum, who was a year or more in camp with us—cooked for our mess?—He's all for the Yanks now, and a member of the Lig, the one in this neighborhood. Knowing his old failing, I invited him, sub rosa, to join me in Steve's barn for a rollicking high time, such as he and I and some others (dead and gone now) once had near the Pennsylvania line on a 'find' of peach brandy.

"'Golly, Mass Bill,' he exclaimed, 'wasn't dat a good time! It seem like only yisterday! 'member dat time? 'Course I do; in dat catticornered hollow by de spring; when de old man turn de demjohn up. Neex (says he)—by toonder and blitsen, gedrorken dry.—It was halb full. Vat pays, vat pays!—I heard him. None o' you did; you was too far gone. I stay wake to keep guard ober you all. And many a time I keep guard, Mass Bill, and sabe you out o' trouble.'

"According to my recollections of Sempy it was just the other way and it was he who 'found' the Dutch farmer's demijohn. However, to the barn we went and as Semp was my invited guest, I gave him the big tin cup and took the little one; so most of the quart of mean whiskey fell to his share. He didn't object. We 'fought our battles o'er again, and thrice we routed all our foes, and thrice we slew the slain.'[2] Semp himself became triple-slewed before long. But while he was not so fuddled as to be unintelligible, I wormed out of him—in strict confidence,—when and where the Lig was to meet last night and who were the leaders and what the late camping out in the swamp was for, and who accidentally met with the horse and who had the trappings. He said Ephraim Johnson and another (he had forgotten who) came across a stray horse and Ephraim claimed the saddle and the other one the bridle. The horse, so he said, had somehow broken loose and run away.

2. John Dryden, "Alexander's Feast."

"When Semp was keeled over in a drunken sleep, I took his hat—a peculiarly battered beaver—and stripped off his coat, which was an old blue one—a Union-soldier's, with a few brass buttons left on it; his Confederate one, if not entirely worn out, would not be in keeping with his present set of 'principles.'—I then locked him up in the barn and carried the key into the house to Steve. Steve blacked my face, fixed my wool, and dressed me up like Semp. I knew Semp's lingo and how he walked, and Steve told me all about Ephraim Johnson's family and other negroes in the neighborhood, and was quite amused at my setting out on a friendly visit to brudder Johnson's, about half a mile off. I judged from what Semp told me that Ephraim and other negro men around would be gone to the Lig meeting, and it turned out so. The meeting was a special one. Delegates from other Ligs were to be present. When, I rattled at Ephraim's gate, his wife came to the house door, fifteen feet from the front fence and cried out:

"'Who dat?—O, it's you! Huddy, Mr. Bantum—How's all? You on your way to de Lig?'

"'Huddy, Sabina,' I replied. 'Yes, I'se gwine to de Lig, where Ephraim done gone wid brudder Mumbles and brudder Riddick. And how's George and Queeny and little Sabby? I heared George hab a bad fall outen a tree.'

"'Dey's all right peart, Mr. Bantum, tank you; leastways, dey kin eat deir bittle, ebry scrap. You see George only fall 'bout twenty feet and plum on he head. Dat sabed him. His aunty bin dream on a Friday night she seen a white hoss. So I knowed something would happen. Being it was only his aunty, de chile 'scaped. If I my berry self hadder dreamed sich a ting, de ground might er hit him so's to broke he arm or he leg.' 'He aint bin play 'bout when I passed do house dis mawning.' 'You see, he sleep so hard all night he bliege to rest when mawning come.'

"'Dat's so, sure 'nough. I hear say you gwine name your baby Tad Stevens?'[3]

"'You yeddy right, brudder Bantum. You tink he'll send he's namesake a chrissen giff?'

"'Sister Sabina, he aint dat sort; dough you do him sich a honor. Enty more'n a dozen done name deir chillun Isaiah, after de preacher; an dey aint got from him a red cent! an dey nebber will get it. If you had a named him for brudder Morton, mebbe he'd er gib you something.—How many head of chillun you hab now, Sister Sabby?'

---

3. John B. Boles, *The South through Time: A History of an American Region*, vol. 2 (Upper Saddle River, N.J.: Prentice Hall, 1995), 404. Rivers refers here to Thaddeus Stevens, the outspoken Pennsylvania congressman who proposed granting forty acres of land to former slaves. This speech gave rise to the phrase "forty acres and a mule" and convinced many white southerners that the Federal government intended to confiscate their property and divide it among the freedmen.

"'Only seben, counting in de two wot drounded last summer.'

"'Go 'long! Hush it now; hush it; I ought ter known dat. But brudder Johnson, he 'spute 'bout it. He say you hab eight.'

"'Den he must ter counted de twins for two. But wont you come in, brudder Bantum? Your voice show you'se kitching cold.'

"'I done ketch it in my trote and dat make de voice don't sound square like.' (I thought she was beginning to find out I was not the genuine Bantum; so to turn the current of her thoughts I said at random), 'de moonshine is bright when de full moon come; aint it?'

"'Yes,' she said, 'but dese aint de nights we want de moon. We want it on de dark nights.'

"'Dat's so, sister Sabby; I'se heard de complaint an dat's what I says too offen as I tink 'bout it. De Lawd, he kin fix dat, jiss as he fix Sunday at de end ob de week 'stead ob in de middle so we colored folks kin git troo wid our work.—Anybody in dere wid you,' I asked.

"'My aunt and two cousins is here till Ephraim come back.'

"'Well, den, I won't come in, Sabina; but you just step out here a minute; I hab a message for you.'

"When she came I said in a whisper, 'Ephraim say till you he got a horse, anodder stray one, and he want he saddle and he say "Don't go to bed to-night till he ride up here wid a load and bring you something; and don't let any body know nuttin about it."'

"Sabina was excited and delighted to hear this and dropped instantly to whispers 'I wonder now what he going to bring home dis time! You wait down yonder at de dark corner of de fence by de fodder house, Mr. Bantum, till I bring you de saddle.'

"Some time passed before she brought the saddle; perhaps she had some difficulty in eluding the notice of her aunt and cousins. When I whispered 'Where de bridle?'

"She replied, 'dat hobbling old Billups got dat ober dere in he house. He claim it. But he done gone to de meeting and mebbe I kin borrow it from Kitty jist for dis night. Ephraim aint much in friends wid dat Billups. But Kitty, she and me git 'long berry well—so you jist stay here Mr. Bantum, till I step ober and try how de cat jump.'

"Billup's house was not far; it was near enough for me to hear Sabina and Kitty wrangling at the fence gate about the bridle. At last Sabina succeeded in borrowing it 'unbeknown to Billups,' and Kitty was promised some of whatever Ephraim should bring home on the horse, and both women were pledged to secrecy against their respective husbands. I knew Sabina was coming, from hearing her say to Kitty 'I'se coming to sit wid you, friend-like some of dese odd-cum-shorts. Good-bye now, honey, till de horse come home.' And Kitty's response 'So long, den; I'll stay wake for you.'

"I took the saddle and bridle immediately back to Steve's and then determined to go to the Lig meeting in the character of Sempronius Bantum, Esquire; or if I could not get in, not knowing the secret grips and all the pass-words, I could do a little eavesdropping. And well I went; for things happened which the Colonel ought to be made acquainted with; and a few things too which a certain organization may find it interesting to take notice of by and by.

"I can tell you, Charlie, I was nearly discovered and had a narrow margin for getting out of the scrape. It's too much to write about in a letter. That white scoundrel, the Reverend Isaiah was there, initiating, praying, exhorting, and in general leading his black sheep to the Devil.

"I put Semp's coat and hat near him in the barn and left the door open. He opened his eyes pretty wide this morning when Steve rated him soundly for coming from the Lig last night intoxicated and going into the barn and sleeping there, leaving the door unfastened. He will leave Semp to explain to his colored friends about the saddle and bridle.

"Yours truly W. B.
"P.S.

"My last page being filled up, I'll take another piece of paper to tell you how I came nigh detection. I had heard the pass-word others gave the sentinel and slipped in while they were calling the roll of members and delegates, and answered to that of Mr. Sempronius Bantum. Our old friend Catfish Dick from Columbia was present as a delegate; and when the secretary called the biggity names, Mr. Bubsy Pinckney, Mr. Ellick Rutledge, Mr. DeSausure Dunks, Mr. Tunny Singleton, and the like, and came to Mr. Richard Richardson (Dick used to belong to that family), there was no response. He hadn't yet lost the old time negro usage of having a single name 'like de Bible people.'—He was called again, the Honorable Secretary looking straight at him; 'Mr. Richard Richardson?'—No response.—I hollowed out in the tone of the Hon. Secretary, 'Catfish Dick?'—'Yer me,' was his quick reply. Many eyes turned in my direction; and had it not been for a burst of laughter in which I joined and pretended to be so convulsed with merriment as to hang my head down to my knees, they might have found me out. And luckily Dick's vociferous yaw-yaw diverted attention from me to him. 'Sic me servavit Apollo,' as you used to say in Virginia. Being a late comer I sat behind the rest near the door. I didn't stay long in the meeting, thinking it prudent to slip out and listen from the outside.—Good-bye."————

Five

These use the negro, a convenient tool
That quick yields substantial gain or party rule

W. J. Grayson

The Reverend Isaiah had for some months been devoting his attention to mission-ary work in the neighborhood of Glyndale. Yet he never entered the village. Many of the colored people knew him personally; but if the white villagers had been asked to describe his face, they would have been unable to do so. His keeping away was strange, for there was no more convenient spot for a congregation, and the white inhabitants would willingly have helped in the religious instruction of the negroes. Did he fear the DeLeslines might recognize him as the sergeant once in their house in Columbia?

Often he had come to stay overnight at a small farm not far from Glyndale. On many occasions he pleaded weariness and sent for members of his congregation to come to him. After religious services he interrogated them about the families of the planters, especially about the DeLeslines. He asked questions the drift of which his dupes did not perceive. One point he became assured of, that all the people there, white and black, were cordially attached to Mrs. and Miss DeLesline. Their affec-tion for Miss Eunice was so genuine that he believed they would even imperil their lives for her sake. If he aimed by his shrewd interrogations to find any disaffected negro or anyone spitefully inclined towards the DeLeslines, he discovered that he must abandon any such expectation. One, however, who had been connected with that family, he found he could secure to his interest; and that one had no idea of the purpose which the Reverend hypocrite was aiming at. Caesar (Bowlegs was his other name) had been initiated into the "Lig" of Black Rosettes, and selected by Guelty to be his personal attendant and to live with him at Columbia. Caesar blacked his new master's boots, swept his room and went on errands for him; was dressed as a body servant and was given a weekly stipend. Guelty laughed and worked with him and drank whiskey with him and let him smoke in his presence and brought the unscrupulous fellow completely under his influence. And besides, had not Caesar solemnly sworn to do the bidding of this master, the secret leader of a League, membership in which was considered by many of his colored friends to be an enviable honor?

More than a twelvemonth had passed since the DeLeslines had taken up their residence at Glyndale. The changes in that interval had not been favorable to our peaceful political re-establishment nor to the abatement of the alienation—almost hostility—against us growing up in the minds of the colored people, who under the mental as well as the corporeal feeding of the Freedman's Bureau had "grown feet and kicked"—kicked against their former owners. Such moulders as Guelty, with such material as Caesar to transmogrify into peripheral bondmen to the Republican party, had had every facility for furthering their schemes, public or private.

Oh, what a time for true statesmanship! And what a lack of it where it ought to have been!

The Thirteenth Amendment, abolishing slavery, was passed by Congress February 1865, before the war ended, and was ratified at the close of that year by counting five of the seceding and late warring states as full members of the Union according to the Lincoln and Johnson method of restoration. The Proclamation of the ratification of that Amendment was on December eighteenth. That very day the "patriotic" Mr. Thad,[1] leading the opposition to the Presidential method of rehabilitation, pronounced the late seceding States out of the Union; "dead States," incapable of restoring their own existence or autonomy. And in that same debate the patriot said the doctrine that this is "a white man's government, is as atrocious as that infamous sentiment that damned the late Chief Justice to everlasting fame, and, I fear, to everlasting fire" (Hon. H. Wilson's History of Reconstruction).—The thought forms itself upon us, where is Thad himself at this present moment?—And another thought forces itself upon us with respect to hocus-pocus ratifications.

However, we had no fight to make against the Thirteenth Amendment. But the next one (for civil rights of the former slaves) came on, and South Carolina and other Southern States, re-organized under the Presidential plan and believing themselves in the Union, refused to ratify it. Congress then got on its high horse, upset the Provisional governments and established Military governments (March 23, 1867), and a few months later a further Act was passed for registering the blacks, for making a new State Constitution by their votes and requiring the adoption of the Fourteenth Amendment before a seceding State could become again a full member of the Union. Until then the Military should be supreme, and hold down—

---

1. Rivers refers again to Thaddeus Stevens.

as it were, by the throat—the disfranchised whites to the level of their enforced degradation.[2]

The State, now for several seasons held down by such Congressional military power, began to be overrun by a new set of incomers, who could venture to it without fear of molestation. They came from a region called "the land of Great Moral Ideas." They were not military, but peaceful and, in their own estimation, saintly. They were preachers, teachers, political guides and—impecunious. They came to help reconstruct us and to make our new Constitution for us; since so many of us had no right to vote. Each had his carpet-bag containing his other shirt and his other pair of socks. Many of them were consanguineous, no doubt, to those who in former times had bought for a mere trifle the men, women and children of African tribes and sold them at profitable rates to the Carolina colonists. The money so gained had been safely invested "to home" before the beginning of the recent Great Moral Ideas crusade to abolish the right of such property and without compensation. The Crusade was at last successful, under the banner-cry Fiat Justitia! It opened a new field for profitable adventure; and the saints entered in, reaping—pecuniarily—where they had not sown and gathering where they had not strewed.

Whenever the pious new-comers called together the bewildered colored people; they spoke on this wise: "Men and Brothers! Friends and dear Fellow Citizens! We come to you to teach you true virtue and religion, and what is a great deal more, to secure to you the right to vote. We promise each of you, out of your old master's property, forty acres and a mule. To get these you must vote us into office. You can't get the mule without voting, and voting the right way. We come to teach you and your children what is right. Didn't your hands till these lands and make the crops that built up these fine houses about here? And what you worked for, isn't it your own? Yes, brothers, all these things are yours and ours; for a share comes to us for showing you your rights. Now to secure your rights the first thing is to go up to-morrow for registration. All must be done fairly. Go up, every man; carry in carts or on sledges or wheelbarrows or on your shoulders, the old, and the sick and the lame; remember that you are all twenty-one years of age, where no record has been kept. A boy big enough to hoe is old enough to vote; that's the rule to go by. And when you go by rule, you're sure to go right."

So the wool was pulled over their eyes and they went up in each County to the Registrars (who, everywhere, happened to be, by special appointment, Great Moral

2. The Thirteenth Amendment abolished slavery, and the Fourteenth Amendment provided civil rights and citizenship to former slaves. Under Lincoln and Johnson's Presidential Reconstruction, former Confederate states had been readmitted to the Union. However, the passage of the Military Reconstruction Act of 1867 signaled the beginning of Congressional, or Radical, Reconstruction. Many southerners found the stipulations of this act unpalatable to say the least.

Ideans); and some carried baskets to put the registration in, thinking it was a tangible article belonging to the forty acres; and some carried halters to get their mules; and all the roads resounded with "the soul of John Brown marching on"—and "rally round the flag, boys"—and every song ended with exultant hallelujahs!

The carpet-bag ringleaders among The Great Moral Ideans, soon finding the intellects of their dupes not so impressible by political abstractions as their hearts were by religious excitement, turned their attention to religion as the most serviceable basis for politics. Classes, Societies, Revivals, Bush-meetings, Sittings-up till sunrise, shoutings and hysterical ferments became the order of the day, or rather of the night; and while the more serviceable were "getting stiff"—or tranced—in doors, others,—some of the masculine members, of vague political aspirations, were engaged in whiskey drinking and land confabulation in the darkness without.

The Reverend Benjamin Isaiah Guelty, as for the time being he styled himself, was there of course; he had been a pioneer in this kind of work; and another large-hearted Moral Idean arrived. He also wore a white necktie and combed his hair back. He came with a specialty of unmarrying and marrying for two dollars each way. He brought, too, for the cabins of the national wards colored prints (at fifty cents apiece) of the signing of the Emancipation Proclamation. He did a thriving business and soon had money enough to buy a farm "to home." We all know that oaks grow slowly and that the corroding effect of waves against a rocky coast is almost imperceptible. But regarding human activities, did you ever reflect how much may be begun, developed and brought to an end in the course of twelve months? We said that more than a twelvemonth had passed since the DeLeslines had taken up their residence at Glyndale. It has fallen to us to notice and record only a few of the recent developments, such as are connected with our story. And now the progress of the saints in politics on a religious basis began to be very remarkable. Versatile, active, unscrupulous, incessant in labor of every kind in every nook and corner; knowing that to kiss the little ones, dance with mademoisselle, drink or smoke with the old, was worth a vote every time; the saints, as their subtlety prevailed, soon added recruit to recruit, then thousands to thousands; each muddy stream of them moving in the direction in which the others rolled. There was but one potent argument on the part of the deluded plantation "hands," when it came to discussion; "enty de old buckra kin change de fifteenth commandment, ef you vote for um? How you gwine be free den?"—But to make assurance doubly sure, oath-bound secret Leagues were formed and "all present or accounted for" was the answer at midnight in every town and village and on many a farm. Persecution, ejection from Church membership, sometimes severe beating by the hands of their own race, was the penalty for refusing to join the League or, as they called it, the "Lig." Flattery, promises, threats, proscription—and the rolls were completed; the easy distinction drawn of black and white, with a line of separation of interests that seemed indelible. The mission work of the Reverend Fairbanks and his colleagues was, indeed, an utter failure. The artful combination of religion and politics effected by the Moral Ideans had become irresistible, had spread over the whole State and must needs be left to run its destined course.

One change of disposition comes vividly to my mind and represents the change in numerous other cases. Epaminondas or Old Pam was now about seventy years of age; toothless, except a few snags which protruded from his thick lips like the teeth of a rat; small restless eyes; a vehement sputtering utterance, one word tumbling out on top of the other when he became excited; his whole outward appearance, when he was so excited, fantastically like a human being changing to something anthropoid and rapidly changing back to his human self. I had known him long before as an humble, peaceable field-hand, industrious and reliable in whatever his master set him to do. He was known too as funny, and a contriver of practical jokes. He had been inveigled into joining the Black Rosettes. But their leader, Guelty, had found him, in his conversion to politics, rather impetuous and crazy-headed, and had induced him to transfer his activity to a newly formed branch or subdivision of the Rising Sons of Ham, which was in alliance with the Daughters of the Golden Chariot. As Old Pam (paying the two-dollar fee already spoken of) had just taken to himself a fresh wife about fourteen years of age, this association with the Daughters of the Golden Chariot was acceptable to him; and he felt elated by being made head-man in the division of the Sons of Ham. It appeared as if he had been promoted by Guelty who, in reality, had become dissatisfied with him and doubtful whither he might be led by his claim to a controlling power over witches and curing those who were bewitched. Guelty therefore thought it best to turn him in this new direction as the least offensive way of getting him out of the councils of his select band of Black Rosettes. Old Pam had charge of a horse and buggy of Guelty's some two or three miles from Glyndale, on a little piece of worn out farm land with a ramshackle log house and stable upon it, which Guelty had purchased for fifty dollars. Here he placed Old Pam, whose first private business there was to nail up horse-shoes over the door and window in the stable. "I bound to keep Mass Guelty horse safe," he said; "I'se paid to do it. Let de witch meet me on de outside."—After attending to the horse he was accustomed to stand in the corner of the stable and rehearse his next speech to his followers of the Rising Sons of Ham. His mind seemed to be slightly unbalanced by the new excitement he had been led into and one would have supposed, from the sounds of his voice when he was practicing that an uproarious conclave were in the stable with him. "I tell you dat—and I tell you dis—hallelujah!—De Lawd, he know!—Wen de 'lennium come, all be your own; de cawn, de pig, all de ebbryting. Dis de beginnin. Take if you muss take; bun if you muss bun.—We gwine troo de briar patch; we gwine troo de coal of fire; we gwine troo de stickry bush; but we git dere! Yah-yah! stomp de water-snake; quelch de rabbit and de possum; sling de coon to de right, sling de coon to de leff; Yah-yah! but we git dere, we git dere—

and ebbryting your own. Old Pentecost is a coming wid fedders in his hair! De new boss larn me all 'bout it. Who kin stand agin you says he? Drink, says I de red mixter and de bitter juice and no sword kin hutt you; carry de biled crab-claw says I and no bullet kin tech you. Whoop-ee! O Lawd—O Lawd!"

And so Old Pam, like an ugly wizard, continued his raving till the foam splattered from his jabbering mouth. Then he twirled the pitchfork above his head and punched it at the logs of the stable till Guelty's horse became frantic and reared and pawed so much that the enthused orator had to desist from his impassioned harangue. To-day, however, the horse and buggy had been sent for by Guelty. Pam's harangue was a shorter one than usual. It was a sad change in Epaminondas. Compared with his former self, one could hardly believe he was the same man. And similar changed had come over many a deluded negro, male and female. It was especially to be regretted in the case of the elder ones who, if let alone, would have gone on peacefully and happily to the close of their lives.

But what means that red glare on the horizon? Two barns were burnt over there last night! Are the incendiaries again prowling around our undefended haystacks?

"We work for um long 'nuff. An now you 'splain to me dat dey only gib one-fourth de crop, when our new frens from de North gib as high as one-tenth. We gwine bun de barn and de stable for um as you tell us for to do ef we hab a old grudge agin um. We got de power and we gwine to use um."

"Hush, Caesar—somebody might hear you."

"No, Massa Guelty; nobody in dis swamp 'cep us two.—De patrol ketch me more'n once and use de stick on me, and say 'What you doing so far from de Quarters?—don't you dare wander 'bout at night widout a ticket.' Who care for patrol now? Who care for ticket?—To h-l wid de patrol and de ticket too! And den, sah dey make de oberseer lash and lash—I beg um for de Lawd sake. But dey say, weh de money and de pig and de cawn you steal? Enty what massa hab bin mine? Aint you teach me dat? I nebber done more'n to take what I want. I didn't use to; but I does now. Aint I jine wid you, my new massa, and larn what my rights is? I'se full member of de Siety since you 'nitiate me. Well den, I say, nebber mind! My day come yet. He come now!"

"But you'd better talk lower, Caesar. Talk in whispers if you can. That half tumbler of whiskey I gave you—and your whole black skin smells of it—makes you too glib with your tongue.—How many were in the house when you came away?"

"Only old Miss Kernal Lesline and Miss Eunik. Ent you bin send for all de cullard folks to de prayer meeting? Ent you tell um to sing pray till middle night and dat would fetch a blessing? Dey all gone dere to pray for I sot de fire. I done trow bricks tru de winder to rouse um as you tell me, an I see old Miss and Miss Eunik jump from de room 'fore cum here. 'Clare to Gracious I seen um. I couldn't done dis ef Sancho bin alive. He always guard old Miss right close. But he bun up in de big Shumman fire in Columby." (At this the Reverend Isaiah winced a little). "Dey muss pass dis road. I bin raise here and know all 'bout dese roads. You knows I does, don't you? Dis de road to de nex house and dey'll run by here soon. De nex hous is Miss Abery's house. You know dat too, don't you?—Yonder dey cum! All in dey shawls and de long hair flapping in de wind. I most feel sorry for um. Here dey cum! Gee-mun-netty, how dey kin run!"

"Hush, I tell you! Hide behind this tree. Pull your mask over your face. So— that's right! Now, as soon as they come, catch old Mrs. DeLesline and hurry her off over yonder into the swamp, and I'll take the other. Be sure now. I'll give you another two silver dollars tomorrow. Quick's the word.—Can you see my face, Caesar?"

"No, Massa Guilty—it blacker den mine my dilly, dilly massa. De night dark 'nuff, but dat mask make you nigger all ober—just like dey say de debbil is," and he began to chuckle.

"Hush, now—you drunken old fool!—Here they are!"

The ladies not finding a single servant at home, had snatched up shawls and side by side were hurrying in fright to reach their nearest neighbors for protection. Guelty and Caesar had hidden in the dense foliage where the road crossed the margin of the swamp. The part of the plot assigned to the deluded Caesar made him a little nervous notwithstanding the whiskey in him. He had never before been guilty of such an act as to touch a lady and was not in heart—at least at that time— the consummate rogue his counsellor and corrupter was. When, in the indistinct light from the distant blazing dwelling, and the slipping of the mask over his eyes, Caesar dashed from his covert, he snatched up Eunice instead of her mother, and uttering no word (as Guelty had cautioned him that the mere sound of his voice would betray him) he rushed into the swamp and away from Guelty; as he had been directed to do; while the latter seized upon Mrs. DeLesline, and being the calmer villain of the two, soon became aware of the mistake. But before he could let her go, with the words "unhand me, brute!," she smote with a dagger his cheek from ear to chin, and had it not been for the thick black mask he wore, and had he not sprung back, the stroke might have been more serious. To flee in the direction in which she had seen Eunice disappear, and following her screams, was the work of a second for the courageous mother.

The blaze of the DeLesline dwelling had been quickly seen by some gentlemen of the neighborhood who hastened to render assistance, and first of all by the two young men in Mrs. Avery's piazza—sitting there smoking cigars and talking of army times. Luckily they sat there at that late hour, and with their faces towards the DeLesline house. The report of a pistol on the road nearby, then another and another, made Mrs. DeLesline pause to look back; and recognizing the approaching gentlemen she cried "This way, Willie—this way, Mr. Dupont! They've carried Eunice off! For God's sake, this way—this way!"

They sprang to her side. "Where?" was all that escaped from the clenched teeth of Lieutenant Barton and, in the direction to which Mrs. DeLesline pointed, he leaped into the swamp.—Caesar who had safe in his pocket the piece paid for his help by the Reverend Moral Idean, had a sudden fear of losing it and his life besides, and had dropped Eunice when the first pistol shot was fired. He even tore off his disguise, which had all along obstructed his vision (indeed it had caused his mistake in seizing her instead of her mother) and flung it into the swamp. Eunice, almost in a swoon, was found crouching upon the miry ground. Barton stood beside her, peering after the jumping, dodging form of the runaway; who it was, of course he had not even a suspicion. He could see only that the man was escaping into the almost inpenetrable recess of the swamp, and did not restrain his hand from sending a few whizzing bullets after him; but without effect.

Guelty had not escaped so well. When running along the road a minute before, he had been seen; and while adjusting his hat, which was rather loose, upon his head, the first ball fired at him had badly cut a finger of his left hand and passed through the hat. By darting down a foot-path he was shielded by intervening trees from the other shots; and without further harm reached his place of abode. He correctly surmised from whose hand the shots had come. The presence to-night of Lieutenant Barton and his friend Dupont Gillespie in the neighborhood was unforeseen by him. Yet he knew they were the only gentlemen likely to be close at hand and it was from the direction of Mrs. Avery's where they usually stayed that the rescuers so quickly burst upon him. He knew Barton, and no good will existed between the out-spoken young gentleman and the hypocritical intriguer—from the time the former disturbed his services at the bush-meeting. The command to halt before the shots came, he was pretty sure was spoken by the voice whose denunciation he had lately listened to more than once. The affectionate regard which the young officer was boastful in expressing for Eunice and which he had heard about from Caesar was cause enough for Guelty's observance of him. From one whom he would have hated or held in espionage for this alone, he had also received insult and now bodily injury. Smarting with the pain of his wound he reached his abode (not his farm shanty but one he had in another direction), a small house with two rooms and two adjoining shed-rooms, kept in order for him by a colored woman who cooked for him whenever he remained here in missionary work. Removing the black cloth from his face before he entered the house, he hurried in, saying "Hannah, I've had a bad fall into a ditch and briars and hurt my hand and face. Bring me some water; and if any one comes say I'm not at home and send them on to the sitting up prayer meeting at the little church in the woods. But let Caesar in if he comes."

The rain, which had threatened all the evening, had come down in a torrent before he reached his house, and he was completely drenched. To cleanse his wound and bind his hand up and change his clothes and slip the blood-stained ones into his capacious carpet-bag, occupied him but ten or fifteen minutes notwithstanding the pain from his wounded cheek and finger; Then a tap, five times slowly repeated on his chamber window was heard, and in came Caesar pretty well bedraggled and out of humor, and sorely needing another glass of grog.

"Are the buggy and horse tied where we left them?" inquired Guelty.

"I shum as I come long. Dey in de same place Pam tie um, But I tell you now I didn't 'gree to be shot at, Massa Guilty. It's worth more'n you give—a dern sight more. So now!" grumbled the saint's sullen hench-man, adding "I'se dead sure I aint gwine run no sitch risk ebbry whip-stitch, for no man; so, now!"—He (Caesar) had tried to bargain for five dollars, but Guelty made a poor mouth and beat him down to three dollars, then to two dollars in real silver.

"Caesar, I'll make that all right. But we must both go away immediately. You go and stay near the horse as if you had been minding him and keep watch till I come, and don't say a word to a soul about what has happened to-night. Say, if you must speak, I have gone to pray with a sick man and you are waiting till I come back."

So soon as Caesar with reluctant steps disappeared, Guelty wrote the following note to an associate in his pastoral work, dating it at six o'clock the evening before, though it was now past midnight:

"Dear brother Hezekiah—The sudden illness of one very dear to me calls me to home a short time. I shall take the oportunety to carry Caesar Bole, to place him at a theological Seminar. Please have charge of my prayer meetings and raise collections for traveling expenses of Caesar and for

"Yours in the faith, Isaiah.

"P.S. We start immediately. Remit as before."

Having written this, he drew from beneath a bed in the room a leather trunk from which he took a roll of greenbacks and stowed it carefully in his inner vest pocket. He hadn't time to put this roll with what he wore in a belt around his body. Indeed his wounded hand disabled him from doing so. He had in all more than a thousand dollars about him. Then he called Hannah and gave her the note for delivery and also a one dollar bill and said with pretended whimpering "Say that my mother was dying and I left on the six o'clock train. I'm afraid, Hannah, she'll be dead before I reach her." (The truth is, his mother had died before the War Between the States) He fumbled, with his injured hand, for his pocket handkerchief, as if briny tears were welling up to his eyelids and required instant wiping. "I would not have it said I delayed one hour after hearing of her illness. Tell anyone who comes here; and tell my people so. Be faithful in this and I'll bring you a new calico dress when I come back"

Her tears were genuine ones as she said "but won't you let me send for the root-doctor to fix your bruises before you go?"

"No, Hannah, there's not time—I'll have them attended to on the road—Good bye" (and would you believe it, Sir—he actually kissed her!)—"But stop—come with us, and when we've got nearly to the station, we'll give you the horse and buggy to bring back till Pam comes for them; and mind you tell every one I went at six o'clock. Tell Pam to try not to let any one see him carry the horse and buggy to the stable."

The three were soon on their way to the station a few miles off. Guelty and Caesar walked the latter part of the way, and having avoided observation as much as possible, approached and boarded the two o'clock night train just as it started. The purpose of Guelty in having his buggy secreted in the woods was evidently to take Eunice away; and his design, for the success of which he had accomplices awaiting elsewhere, was not known to Caesar nor to the accomplices he had, except that he was going to be married and it had to be a runaway match for which he needed their assistance. This intimation was strictly confidential. If there was to them a mystery in his clandestine preparations for such an event as he indicated— it would have been a mystery past finding out to Eunice, had she been told that one entirely unknown to her, whom—if she were confronted with him—she could not have testified that she had ever seen, unless in that moment in her grandfather's library and in the uncertain light of the conflagration his features were noticed by her—should be pursuing her and yet studiously keeping himself unknown to her even by sight. He feared she would recognize him so soon as her eyes rested on him. Can a mind so evenly balanced as his in all schemes of self-aggrandizement, be subject to mania in the one respect of love? Was it really love on his part, and was this the way to show it—this sudden, unexpected seizure of her? Or was there a hidden ulterior motive for his insidious snares to gain the relationship he sought under sanction of a legal title?—Eunice was wholly unaware that she was the object of any nefarious design. Since she had left the city her life had been spent in quiet rural scenes and she was as free from suspicion of evil as though she moved in Eden amidst "flowers of all hues and without thorn the rose"[3]—Lieutenant Barton and Mr. Gillespie (who had unexpectedly arrived on the eight P.M. train to spend a week at Glyndale) had protected Mrs. DeLesline and Eunice, enveloped in their shawls, to Mrs. Avery's, and immediately taking up axes had run to the burning house. Their exertions aided by the pouring rain arrested the progress of the flames; which consumed only the store-room and pantry below and a dressing room above, which together abutted on the rear of the main building. Many gentlemen from the neighborhood soon arrived on horseback. There was a certain military precision in their appearance; but they were unarmed, except that revolvers were

3. John Milton, *Paradise Lost.*

belted to the waist of each. Browned by their exposure in war, erect in their saddles, stern and silent, they instinctively halted while Colonel Loyle, who was one of them, rode up to Barton and asked, "How did this happen, Willie?"

"Some more deviltry, Colonel," was the reply, as Barton, throwing his axe into the yard, leapt from the low roof of the piazza.

The party dismounted and conversed awhile. The Colonel and Barton then rode off to Mrs. Avery's to relieve the mind of Mrs. DeLesline with the good news that her dwelling was not wholly consumed, and to ask a few questions, necessary to be asked without delay, relative to the persons who had waylaid her and her daughter. All the information to be gleaned from Mrs. DeLesline (Eunice was upstairs prostrated by the excitement through which she had passed) was that they were two negroes. Leaving Lieutenant Barton with the ladies, Colonel Loyle rode slowly back leading the horse the Lieutenant had used. He pondered as he went the events of the night and the strange condition of his fellow citizens who had no power to punish by the law and were obliged to protect their property, watching like sentinels. The necessary delay of Barton and Gillespie in attending the ladies and trying to put the fire out, had given Guelty and Caesar full time to escape; and Pam met no one on the road when he drove the horse and buggy back to Guelty's stable. He was puzzled by the directions he had received and for a long time ruminated about them. The female domestics of Mrs. DeLesline had in the meanwhile returned from the prayer meeting and had met Hannah who told them about Reverend Isaiah as she had been instructed to do. They were interrogated by Colonel Loyle. Was your parson at the meeting?—No!—Gone to see his sick mother!—When did he go? At six o'clock last evening!—The Colonel knew that the parson had been near Glyndale later than six o'clock. Consulting his watch which indicated the time to be a few minutes before two, Colonel Loyle thought of the two miles to the station, the dark road and the rain, and then taking one of his companions aside he said "Find out who is conductor on the two o'clock train to-night and ascertain if any passengers went out from the Station and who they were and let me know as soon as you find out." Dupont Gillespie and one of the gentlemen from the neighborhood remained to guard the house; the rest dispersed to their homes.

Glyndale, the country seat of Mr. DeLesline, was near that of the widow Avery, Lieutenant Barton's aunt. It was situated about two days carriage journey from Columbia, in an adjacent county. Gently rolling hills, cool springs, a meandering rivulet, towering pines within view, shady oaks and fragrant bays; and nearer the villa, evergreen hedges, fantastic arbors, and over all a sky as fair as that of Italy, at least during most of the year—were to the young and romantic its chief attractions. But to the farmer there was a greater charm in the productive soil and security from noxious beasts and birds. In former days an elegant hospitality was dispensed to numerous guests when Spring clothed the delightful vicinity of the villa with fresh foliage and flowers; and an invitation to spend a few days in rural enjoyment at Glyndale often brought together sedate lawyers and statesmen as well as the young and gay. All such entertainments had now passed away forever. Poverty and neglect had in some measure led to the sad change which made Glyndale a comparatively lonely place; The old gentleman, his wife and all his children were now dead. But though mournful recollections in the hearts of the family tinged for them every scene with a melancholy hue, yet a stranger would still have called the scenery picturesque and charming.

Old Mr. DeLesline had retired to this country seat, saddened by his irreparable losses. His daughter Alicia did not long survive the terrible night of the sack of Columbia and her removal to Glyndale; and he himself, having been severely beaten over the head by a straggling party of marauding Federal soldiers, had become after awhile paralyzed, and lingered a helpless invalid for many months. The soldiers or camp-followers had met him at a friend's house near Glyndale (two days after he had fled from Columbia) and supposing him to be the master of the house and not heeding his denial, had ill-treated him to force him to show "where the treasure was hid." Mrs. (Colonel) DeLesline (his daughter-in-law), and his granddaughter Eunice were all of the family now left, and were comfortably dwelling on the farm where the saintly Mr. Guelty had discovered them in his missionary wanderings. He now knew much about them through information derived from Caesar, the new recruit among the Black Rosettes and whom he had attached to himself for personal and intimate services.

On first returning after the war from his farms in a distant State—farms fraudulently acquired and recorded in his father's name—to the interior of Little Africa, as he was pleased to call the Prostrate State,[4] Guelty had no "Reverend" prefixed to his name. He came for that black trunk and for another and more important scheme which his last Manoeuvres, happily a bungling one, had shown his unabated determination to effect. There had been no opportunity to exhume the trunk the Saturday night after the burning of Columbia. He and his cousin St. Julian had to march northward early on Sunday morning and without delay; for all the Confederate troops that could be collected from scattered commands began to be massed under General Joe Johnston in the path which the Federals had to traverse in their swing around from their ships at Savannah to their ships at Wilmington; and Johnston was a strategist whom they feared. The city was hurriedly evacuated.—St. Julian at the close of hostilities a few months later, came back alas in a hurry. He knew his cousin Isaiah would, if he could, get ahead of him. He came as a pretended agent of a grocery firm, bringing with him a few samples of goods and accompanied by an accomplice on whom he could rely; who was to vouch for him in his ostensible business, but in reality to help him in securing the

---

4. This was a popular nickname for Reconstruction-era South Carolina.

trunk. His return to Columbia was soon found out by Isaiah; and although St. Julian swore by all the patriarchs and prophets that the trunk could not be found, yet Isaiah had reason to believe that he had "lifted" it; as indeed he had. But of this at another time.

Eunice, after her rescue, recollected a circumstance which occurred the week before and which appeared, now, to be connected with this bold attempt to seize her and her mother; or to have been another scheme frustrated at the time or abandoned for this more desperate one. An old aunt of Caesar's, once belonging to the DeLeslines, lived about a quarter of a mile away and was an object of Eunice's charity, and visited by her on Saturday afternoons if the weather permitted. A week before the attempt against her and her mother, she had put up a basket of provisions and was preparing herself to carry them to the old woman, when the grandson of the invalid was brought to her by her maid Caroline, saying, "Miss, this Sammy here says he wants to tell you something by yourself."—"Well, Sam," Eunice said, taking him to one side, "what is it you wish to tell me?"

The little negro stood a while blinking and looking through the corners of his eyes. He was twelve years old, but quite small for his age, a bright urchin, a cunning trapper of rabbits and birds; the best of which he was accustomed to fetch to the DeLeslines for sale; and was well known to Eunice.

"Mammy say, says she tell you de owl bin a-hooting and some bad things bin at her house on de outside and crow eggs bin a-hatching."

Eunice, unable to interpret so enigmatical a message, began to think the old woman was losing her senses; but she looked at Sam and said "Well!" Then, fumbling at the rimless hat he held in his two hands he proceeded; looking through the corners of his eyes:

"De carpenter name Noel, de white man what fix de roof for Mammy say, says he we muss nebber do bad and spec good for to come on it. Den I say dat's so. We can't plant gourd seed and spec watermillion to come up 'stead ob calabashes. When I tell Mammy dis, she study bout it and nebber forget. So when she cripple wid pains and can't e'en git up, you bring her all she want. Mammy hear something bout you. Dey didn't think she was any account to hear anything, lying dere in de bed inside de house. But I tell you, Miss Eunik, she hab sharp ears. She seem to hear me half a mile off. So she call me and she say, 'Sammy, watermillion can't grow out ob calabash seed, nor de good out ob de bad; and what I hear somebody say, is bad all over. Now, I kin trust you?'—I say, 'Mammy, you kin.' So she say, says she 'Go, soon as nobody kin see you, and tell Miss Eunik all by herself, Don't come from home to-day, dis Saturday, nor tomorrow needer. Don't come here nebber again, less something might harm you. But send whatever de good God give you to send: And Sammy,' says she, 'tell Miss Eunik, de Lord bless you'—Dese her berry words or hope I may die."

"Who were those your grandmother heard talking outside her house?" inquired Eunice. "Mammy say dey're spies; so she call um; come to find if you at home. But I dunno ma'am; if it was de day time, I bin at de rabbits. If it bin de night time, I bin sleep fast and nebber hear nobody nor see nobody. but yisterday I seed boo-daddies in de bushes."

"Nonsense, Sammy,—don't be baby-fied—there's no such things as boo-daddies."

"Yes, Miss, please ma'am, I seed two, and dey make face at me."

Eunice considered what she had heard to be an old woman's fancy. But to please the poor cripple rather than through any apprehension of harm to herself, she sent the basket of provisions by Sam and with them her thanks for the message. She recalled those circumstances now; yet, rack her thoughts as she would, she could form no conception why or wherefore any one should form a plot against her.

We should not pass from this point of our narrative without mentioning an incident at the close of her interview with Sammy. Her face had a charm even for him. He had gone to the garden gate, the basket in hand, and returned to say,

"Miss Eunik, please ma'am, when de cold wedder come does you want a fat possum? I'll bring you one for nothing, Miss Eunik."

"It's kind in you, Sammy; and when you bring it, I'll give you a new hat. And suppose I wanted not only a possum, but a coon and a rabbit; could you bring them?"

"I kin help to tote um, Miss Eunik."

"Very well, Sammy; but don't stay longer now," and she called Caroline to go with the grateful little fellow to the end of the garden fence and start him off homeward.

The next day, in the afternoon, the ladies wisely thought it would be best to shake off the depressing effect of their calamity and take a walk to their partly consumed country house in order to give directions for its repair. Left alone in the world, they had learned to throw aside weak indulgence in lassitude and repining, and with unswerving trust in God's providence, to cultivate in themselves self-reliance, endurance, even an intrepidity akin to the exalting spirit of heroism; such, indeed as was exhibited by many a delicately nurtured Southern lady in hospitals and wherever else, during the war, their helpful ministration was needed.

Joined in their walk by Mrs. Avery and her daughter Mamie and by Lieutenant Barton and Mr. Gillespie, they strolled, after their visit to the house, through the adjoining woodlands. They had reached a sward at the edge of a grove of oaks— one of those sylvan "openings" of level green which seem to be specially cleared for picnic festivals—when Lieutenant Barton observed a rustic bench beneath the oaks and said, "Ladies, here is a fair resting place; a fine spot too for pistol practice. But your ear, Euny, dreads no doubt the sound of fire-arms. Cousin Mamie I know would flee back to the house if it were not as dreadful for her to return alone as to stay and hear a pistol fired. Yet, in these insecure times our ladies ought to learn a little of the art of self-defence. In a country place like this our lives our property may be saved simply by the knowledge on the part of others that we have the means of self-protection."

Eunice did not like to be called now by her baby name, Euny; yet without showing offense at it remained reticent while her mother, to whom the Lieutenant had turned in concluding his remarks, replied: "I agree with you, Willie and Eunice's grandfather often made the same remark and insisted upon our attention to it. The events of last night may have had I know not what fearful termination had I not providentially taken in my hand as I left my chamber the little ivory-handle stiletto that was lying on the escritoire by my window. Eunice dear, are your nerves steady enough to pull the trigger?"

"I will try, Mamma, if Mr. Barton will place the mark for us, and will bear in mind that we are not regulars nor even volunteers, and should not fall in his strict estimation by our awkwardness or unskilfulness."

The answer was the kindliest of kindly smiles as the Lieutenant (although he noticed that she had said Mr. Barton instead of Willie—perhaps in return for his calling her "Euny") placed his revolver—and it was not a light one—in her delicate hand, and Dupont Gillespie set up the white paper mark on an oak forty feet distant. Slightly blushing and shaking her clustering curls from her cheek she stood with extended arm and eyes riveted in steady aim, a perfect picture. And while the bullet sped to the mark, a wreath of white smoke rose over her head like a halo above some saintly brow. The symmetry of her form, the translucent clearness of her complexion, the softness of her love-inspiring hazel eyes, her faultless features, and pretty lips on which appeared ever lingering the ripple of a smile (all these excellences she inherited from her mother, of Northern birth, in soul a pure De-Lesline)—did not so much impress one as did that perceptible gleam of a spirit not to be trifled with, that reverence-awakening gleam of the hazel eyes. If one half of her soul was like her handsome soft-hearted mother's, the other half was like her military father's, and it looked through the dark lashes and appeared to say To-day I feel only tender affection and may be led captive by a silken thread; to-morrow I may break through heavy bonds and haste wherever duty calls;—to-day, I may tremble and dissolve in tears; to-morrow I may be a stranger to fear and nerved to dare and do whatever duty bids me do;—to weep and to endure is mine; yet mine it may be to subdue and to control if Heaven wills it!

But she, as other young Southern maidens of her age, had been reared in retirement. War-ruin, mourning for the dead, depression everywhere in the State, had precluded social amusements. She had never "come into Society" and never been necessitated to any independent activity. She knew not what she was capable of.

Eunice hit the mark every time she fired. "She has not forgotten, Willie, the lessons her grandfather taught her," said her mother. "And who used to tell her he knew no other girl as good a shot as she was. But to avoid accidents the little silver-mounted pistol he gave her has been always locked up in her trunk. We must venture, however, to keep it nearer at hand in future. Now, Dupont, show Mamie her lesson in fire-arms."

Mamie Avery was escorted to her position half way nearer to the target that Eunice had stood, by the ex-cavalry-man, whose heart unaccustomed to be close a feminine heart, felt now such an additional throbbing as it had never experienced when he used to face the enemy or rush to the clash of sabres. Holding the pistol as he directed her, but with trembling hand, Mamie shut both her eyes and fired into the top of the tree—"O! Mr. Gillespie," she exclaimed, "I am afraid to shoot again—I may by chance kill somebody!"

"Dupont," exclaimed Mrs. Avery, "I will not sit here though we are behind her, if Mamie fires another ball. Who can tell where the next one will go, if she shuts her eyes and trembles so! Mamie dear, you must practice first without cartridges. Run now to the spring yonder with Eunice and wash the powder stains from your hands."

"Come, Miss Mamie," said the smiling Dupont, "this is our first lesson;—and now if Miss Eunice and Willie will come, I will show you near the spring where the first violets are blooming."

A few moments later a horseman entered the further edge of the enclosure, and alighting tied his bridle to a pendent bough. The martial form of Colonel Loyle, as he approached and stood gracefully saluting Mrs. DeLesline and Mrs. Avery in the centre of the green fairy-sward where Eunice had lately stood—presented as in tableau another picture with which the eye of an artist would have been enraptured. He was about 27 years of age, with dark wavy brown hair, calm brow, regular features and benignant eyes of bluish grey. Was it—while Time and Fate looked on—no more than a coincidence that he stood as a picture where the other fair picture had so lately stood? He had called at Mrs. Avery's cottage expecting to find Mrs. DeLesline and Eunice confined to the house unnerved and invalid from the exciting occurrences of the preceding night. There was also a further purpose in his visit; for in the course of their conversation he enquired, "Are you sure, Mrs. DeLesline, that both were negroes whom you met upon the road? May not one of them have worn a mask?"

"I have no reason, Colonel, to suspect any one; yet I will not positively say it may not be as you suppose. I have concluded their purpose was to rob our house and to hold us in the swamp while others effected the robbery. Does suspicion attach to any white person in this neighborhood?"

"No, my dear Madame—no one at present in this neighborhood or likely to be for a long time, has been guilty of the outrage. You must not be alarmed. Those who did it may never be in this neighborhood again. I came to assure you ladies that means shall be adopted to protect you and all with you. With God's help you shall be unmolested and our lives and property safe, although we have at present no voice in framing or administering our laws. It would be well, however, that ladies living apart as you do, should have, if possible the more immediate guardianship of some gentleman of their family. If your nephew, Willie, Mrs. Avery could be induced to remain with you, and could Mr. Gillespie whom Mrs. DeLesline knew in Columbia and whom I know well and appreciate very highly, be induced to superintend your farm, Mrs. DeLesline,—they would be quite a valuable accession to our neighborhood."

"Would it not be well, Colonel," interposed the good-hearted but inconsiderate widow Avery, "to have an organization such as I lately read of—I think they call it something like Ku Klux?"[5]

"By no means, my good Madame," replied Colonel Loyle, "could I approve of lawlessness, nor of doing in disguise or in darkness what I could not rightfully do at midday. Yet," he added with a shade of sternness, "self-preservation is the law of our being.—But here come our young ladies," and he gallantly advanced to meet them. And taking the proferred hand of Eunice he gazed with tender interest upon her beauty flushed as she was by her rapid walk to the spring with Mamie and hastening back. "My brave Miss Eunice, I am rejoiced to see you so well to-day. And who has decked your curls with these fragrant violets? Some fairy who met you at the spring?"—Why did her little hand tremble in his—as with an irrepressible spirit thrill—that hand so steady when it aimed at the mark awhile ago? But checking himself as though expressions of admiration should not have escaped his lips, he turned to the ladies and bade them adieu.—Beckoning to the young men to follow him, he paused and spoke a few words to them, and rode away in a direction different from that which led to his own home.

Edmund Loyle's ability and merit, his courage and manliness,—had made him the foremost man in Glyndale since the death of old Mr. DeLesline. There had always been a slight restraint in the intercourse of the families; but only such as may exist even between good friends, where one appears ever conscious of the distinctions of birth and riches—neither of which distinctions it is the good fortune of the

---

5. John B. Boles, *The South through Time: A History of an American Region*, vol. 2 (Upper Saddle River, N.J.: Prentice Hall, 1995), 396. The infamous Ku Klux Klan is the best known of several white-supremacist terror organizations. Formed in Tennessee in 1866, it quickly spread throughout the South. The Ku Klux Klan waged a guerrilla war on Republicans and African Americans and eventually was responsible for hundreds of murders. Forced underground by congressional legislation and the imposition of martial law in the South, the Ku Klux Klan never was crushed entirely and reinvented itself throughout the century following the Civil War.

other to possess. The present Mrs. DeLesline, too, had been—once—for a little while—chagrined that one so young had eclipsed the reputation of her husband by his brave deeds in war. The recollection, however, of that husband's undeviating reliance on his youthful Lieutenant Colonel, who had extricated him and the regiment from more than one overhanging disaster—and his praise of him in many a letter to her, had forced her to esteem and admire him; and now she knew no living person to whom she would more readily turn for advice and, if need be, for protection. As for Mrs. Avery—she never had had any hesitancy in doing whatever Colonel Loyle thought should be done. His name was a household word in both families;—in many other families also. Even grey-haired men had got into a habit of asking, in emergencies, "What does the Colonel think about it?"

The Colonel's ability to advise and his efficient readiness to do good to others were due, in great measure, to his attention to little matters. And then, he did not put off for tomorrow what should be done to-day. He quickly mastered details; and his inferences from apparent trifles, which others would pass by without notice, led him often to conclusions which seemed to be the wisest intuitions.

On riding off from the Averys' and DeLeslines', there passed the road far ahead of him a person whom he supposed to be the carpenter Noel. It was not he, though the person bore a saw and hammer as Noel usually did. It was a workman whom the Reverend Mr. Fairbanks had engaged to do some repairs at the parsonage. And shortly afterwards the Colonel met preacher Fairbanks himself ambling along on his pony. After greeting him he asked who the workman was; then about other individuals of the surrounding farm houses, and especially about the Reverend Mr. Guelty, and where and when he had seen him last, and what he knew of his discourses to negro assemblages. To this questioning, one answer, apparently trivial, was to the questioner a piece of most important information.

Not to disclose the suspicions in his mind concerning Guelty, the Colonel led the thoughts of Mr. Fairbanks to a more general view of good men's efforts to ameliorate the condition of the numerous needy people throughout the State.

The Reverend gentleman, conversing about this matter, mentioned the efforts of the late Mr. DeLesline; and taking from his memorandum book a manuscript said (with a blush), "I had been thinking of an Epitaph for him. After I shall have decided on a suitable one, I shall offer it to the family for their consideration. Will you kindly read this attempt and give me your opinion of it? I have written it in four sections, in case a square monument shall be put on his grave."

In memory of

—————————

Born _____ Died_____.
His inherited wealth and his political
eminence, ever subservient to the welfare of his people.

At home affectionate, exemplary;
in neighborly intercourse, generous and affable, courteous.

Of integrity unswerving; sensitive to honor; quick to glow
with indignation, yet firm in self-control; through youth
and manhood his sword untarnished.

Prompt in maintenance of State sovereignty; prompt to his
Church's call; in beneficence unwearied; uplifting the impoverished,
comforting the bereaved, ministering to the suffering, protecting
fatherless children, whose voice of blessing, as of angels, hath hallowed
this grave wherein he waits his summons to the skies.

When Colonel Loyle had carefully read the manuscript he remarked "truthful in all points; and appropriate for many a Carolinian of the old school. Noble they were, and the generation of them has not yet died out. It will be an unpropitious day for our State pride when the people become intolerant of such men."

The gentle parson was much pleased with the Colonel's approval of the epitaph; and the conversation reverted to the carpenter Noel.

"I thought at first," said Loyle, "that the workman I saw crossing the road was the one so much talked about. I should like to meet him. I had a glimpse of him once, but no more than a glimpse. He must know the secrets of a good many of the white and black population; for he wanders into every town and hamlet and among the farm houses, seldom abiding long in any one place; and giving good counsel, they say, wherever he goes. I tell you, Fairbanks, if we had half a dozen such men as Noel, there would be quite a change in the disposition of the people. With many of us, however, he has a hard task before him; for one does not like to be offering the right hand of peace to men whose right hands are ready to strike. I'm sure I don't and I shan't.—Pardon me, if my expression sounds unchristianlike.—But some kind of good Noel does effect. When I was lately in Greenville and Spartanburg, in the country places, I found here and there flourishing spots, cheerful, prosperous, while all around looked poor and neglected. I stopped a negro on the road and inquired about the improvements. 'Mr. Noel been here,' he replied, 'fix house, fix school.' I asked 'Does he fix your houses too, you colored people's?'—'If we been lame or sick,' he said. 'But he does not,' I continued, 'fix schools for your little black children, does he?'—'O yes,' he said, 'just the same, if we ask him, and we can find some one of our own color who can teach the children to read the Bible'"—

"I began to think Noel was not only a peripatetic philanthropist, but a sagacious practical philosopher. What do you think of him, Fairbanks, for you tell me he was once working in your immediate neighborhood?"

"He surely," replied Mr. Fairbanks, "sows good seed. He reminds me, when I re-call his face, of a picture of one of the saints in an old book I read when a boy. But what can he accomplish single-handed? Home comforts for us all and our reconciliation with our opponents would take him a score of years to bring about. But I must remember there is not arithmetic in moral work, as to what one may accomplish. When he was here," continued Mr. Fairbanks, humbly bending his head and looking on the ground, "and was repairing a widow's house and fence for her, I requested him to stay and put up a school house in the neighborhood. He said I was called to that task. Without delay I set about the work."

"Then you think, as I do, there is no mischief in his mission?"

"Not the least; his reticence and caution are indicative to me of a divine prudence amidst our political antagonisms. Wherever I hear of him, his influence is surely tending to harmonize the disturbed relations between our two races here, even if it cannot allay the animosity of the people against our white oppressors; and even that may yet be hoped for—"

"Yes, in crushing out the oppressor," interposed Colonel Loyle, "in removing the cause of irritation and letting the fever in the hearts of our people gradually die away. Crush out the corrupting and oppressive carpet-baggers; and the quicker the better. We are God's agent in this work."

Without saying more they parted; the one thinking as he rode off "This Fairbanks is really a good fellow"; the other thinking "This Loyle, if he were God's agent for crushing evil-doers, would crush them mightily."

Six

But here, where sunshine and coy shadows meet,
Out gleam the tender eyes of violets sweet

All woodland sounds—the pheasant's gusty drum,
The mock-bird's fugue, the droning insects hum,
Scarce heard for that strange sorrowful voice forlorn.

P. H. Hayne

There were more violets to gather the next afternoon; and several afternoons. On the last day of Mrs. DeLesline's sojourn with her friend Mrs. Avery, these ladies were accompanied to the repaired dwelling of the former by Mr. Gillespie who having no regular occupation and living at present with relatives a short distance off had consented to superintend the farm for the season and to reside with Mrs. DeLesline. Perhaps he wished to remain near Miss Avery during the delightful new months of the year. But this we only surmise, of course. While he was engaged in conversation with Mrs. DeLesline about the farm work Eunice and Mamie were escorted to the spring by Lieutenant Barton.

On their way thither cousin Mamie took him to task for his conduct the preceding Sunday afternoon. "Yes, indeed," said she, "just as Eunice has formed a promising class of country lads, you nearly broke it up."

"How could such a thing happen, Mamie?" interposed Eunice.

"I persuaded him to go with me, since you were unwell and could not attend church, and begged him to teach your class for you. He asked them unscriptural questions; and, among other things, who was your favorite scholar. A dispute arose about it between George Hutty and Billy Beggs. 'Never mind,' said cousin Willie, 'after we sing the hymn I'll show you how to settle it.'—To my surprise, when the Reverend Mr. Fairbanks and I had left the chapel, we saw your whole class behind the trees; and there was Willie calling out 'Hit him, George! Stand up to him, Bill!' —and to Mr. Fairbanks' remonstrance he replied that fisticuffs was the natural way of settling disputes, and that religion was not designed to eradicate human nature. —Since it was my fault, to begin with, I have been several days explaining to the boys' parents that it should not occur again."

The Lieutenant laughed at Mamie's demure recital. Eunice, however, was evidently mortified; for she had just begun her efforts to assist in educating the little children of the poverty-stricken widows of the neighborhood.—It was a pretty sight—the children clustered around her. She had a kindly word for the roughest of them. They gathered flowers to bring to her. If any one of them was sick, a visit from her was like the coming of an angel. She was grieved at the way Willie Barton had conducted the Sunday School exercises for her. But she made no remark; and they continued their way to the spring.

Violets had grown there ever since the DeLeslines could remember the spot, and they called it Violet Spring. It was in view of the dwelling only in one direction, (through a vista of an avenue of trees), and had been adorned with rustic seats and evergreens whose boughs, arched overhead, were interlaced with clambering vines of woodbine and running roses. Art had not driven nature from the secluded spot, but had only heightened her charms. The seats were so arranged with reference to the adjoining woodlands, that while sitting on them at the spring one could see before him nothing of mansion or fences or improved grounds, but seemed to be sitting far off and alone, as if in the midst of a forest, where all was still except the trickling fountain, the twittering birds and the rustling trees. Seated here with Eunice and his cousin Miss Avery, the Lieutenant fell upon a favorite theme of his, the exploits of his regiment and the brave deeds of his old commander and friend Colonel Loyle.

The young ladies were not averse to such stories, when narrated of their kinsmen and acquaintances. Otherwise Eunice would have preferred a conversation on any of the numerous subjects literary, historical, botanical, in which her grandfather had educated her, or on music which she had learned from competent instructors; and, in which she and her mother were proficient, and on harp, piano, or organ, with Beethoven, Mozart, Handel, Chopin, and other classic masters, used to beguile the occasional *ennui* of their country life. But fortunately for the Lieutenant, for whom hunting and fishing and tournaments and races had from boyhood, had stronger charms than books.—This theme of Colonel Loyle's regiment was one on which he could be eloquent and which Eunice was always pleased to listen to. And then, too, (though the Colonel may have forgotten) she had never forgotten how Edmund Loyle had saved her when she was a girl and Willie had sportingly shoved her off in a bateau on the Congaree River.

"You can hardly conceive, Cousin Mamie," he said, addressing her particularly, (for Eunice generally turned her eyes upon the ground or towards the far off clouds when this topic was introduced)—"the influence our Colonel had over his men and their veneration for him. I believe even the enemy sometimes felt this influence.

It's a mystery to me—I can't comprehend it. Once he sent me out as scout about sunset—and he rode out to recall me thinking, as I afterwards learned, that I would be in danger from some new movements the enemy began to make. I had just hidden my horse and had crept forward on hands and knees to some high rocks nigh the road to reconnoitre. The road led directly from the position of the enemy some mile or two away, and turned abruptly around these rocks. As I raised my head to look around, whom should I see approaching in the path leading around the rocks but Colonel Loyle, riding alone and faster than he would have been riding out there had he not been hunting me; and at the same glance I saw standing behind the rock a large-bodied Federal scout on horseback with pistol in hand. Before I could possibly make ready to defend him the Colonel came suddenly almost against the presented pistol of the scout, who had been sent out, no doubt, to reconnoitre as I had been sent. My heart leapt to my mouth; I thought it was all over with our Colonel. But raising his head loftily and extending his right hand—without an attempt to draw his sword or reach for his own weapon—he cried 'Give me that pistol!,' and the Federal horseman respectfully handed it over. The Colonel gazed in his eye a moment and asked 'Why didn't you shoot me?'—'I intended to do so, Sir' he sad sadly in his discomfiture, 'but something in your eye and tone of voice somehow made me obey you.' And that, Euny, is just the mystery about him I don't understand.—Well, by this time I had appeared and was told to get my horse and take the prisoner into camp; while the Colonel coolly rode on. And what he found out by that ride had its effect, I tell you; for we made a beautiful surprise on a part of the enemy's camp before the night passed and captured most valuable stores.

"And let me tell you, Euny,—for I see you are listening now—how once he saved my life."—Did Willie Barton notice a little brightening of her cheeks while with downcast eyes she arranged that bunch of violets? And did the scarcely perceptible start just now when he called her name, indicated that she had been lost for a moment in reverie? And in the reverie, was Willie himself the central figure?

My amiable Lieutenant! did you not know that as a friend of her father and her grandfather Eunice's recollections of him extended through her life as well as her recollections of yourself? Would her admiration of him, think you, be precisely like your own and nothing more? And when he returned home, at the beginning of the war, from his long tour in the West and found her in her budding beauty, and you a constant visitor and suitor, and she appeared not to be averse to your attentions; were you aware that he became, in his generous nature, more fondly drawn towards yourself for her sake? And could you read his heart when in the perils of battle he watched for your safety for her sake; and in sickness carefully nursed you as with her own gentleness; and brought you back promoted and honored and more worthy of her by whose side you are now sitting?

"Let me tell you, Euny, how once he saved my life—indeed he saved me three or four times. The enemy, under Burnside, were in force on the north bank of the Rappahannock, and General Lee hurrying up his troops, was taking up a strong position on the south side. He divined their purpose of crossing so as to bring him to engagement in a different line of battle. He had been riding over the ground and placing new batteries during the afternoon; and our Colonel came from headquarters about ten o'clock at night and selected twelve of his men, myself among them —I was a private then—and rode with us several miles eastward of our position, and made us dismount in a thick grove, and sent us out in different directions towards the Rappahannock. Well—he gave us thirty minutes to return and report. All returned in the given time except poor me; for I was always getting into scrapes. He waited for me ten minutes, then rode out after me. It was a cold, rainy night in December. The Colonel had a handsome new military cloak of some high Federal officer, which a party of our men had captured a short while before and presented to him. He buttoned it up to the chin and slouched his felt hat over his face and saying to the men 'You see how I am dressed. Let no one fire on me on my return. Let no one fire, unless absolutely necessary, on any one approaching. Remain exactly where you are one hour. At the end of that time, if I do not return, go and report to the Lieutenant Colonel.' With these words he rode into the darkness after me. Euny, I had been captured and disarmed. Having gone to a farm house nigh the river bank and on a winding road which led to the river, I had ventured to make some inquiries, thinking the enemy were surely on the other side of the river, and none of them, at any rate, so far down as this; but I walked right into a party of them. They seized me, made a good deal of fun of me, and under threats forced me to confess who I was. One brutal fellow said 'Let's shoot him for good luck on this side the river.' I think they were really in earnest. They had got some liquor by rummaging in the farm house, and didn't care what they did. Soon all but the sergeant joined in the game. They tied my hands behind me and led me into the yard back of the house. Lighted chips were stuck in the ground in front of me to make me visible as their mark. The sergeant protested and refused to take part in their irregular proceedings, and had sauntered away from them to the front of the farm house and towards the road.—They pointed their guns and gave me one minute to say my prayers. I said 'O Lord, bless Jeff Davis. Give victory to the Confederates and confound all their enemies'—one of the men laughed and said 'Let the young Reb go!'—At this moment the gate flew open at the front entrance on the road and in sprang Colonel Loyle in his blue cloak.

"'Sergeant,' he said, guessing at the man's rank 'whereabout is General Franklin?'

"'Over yonder, General,' he replied, recognizing the cloak or something about Loyle which looked like his Adjutant General's (it may have been in truth the Adjutant's cloak)—'over yonder.' said he—'All his men safe over?'—'Yes, Sir. The pontoons are laid at last.'—'What are you men doing near the barn with that light? How dare you allow a light contrary to orders?'—'General,' said the sergeant, 'they have had some liquor they found here and I can't well control them. They are going to shoot a Reb.'—'Fools!' shouted the Colonel—'run and stop that, put out the light, and bring the prisoner here; he may give us important information.'—The loud tone of his voice had arrested the attention of the fellows just as they were going to fire on me; at least so I thought; and the sergeant running up said 'Boys, the Adjutant is here from the centre hunting up Franklin, and says put out this light instantly,' and he tramped it out with his boots. 'Some of you will get shot yourselves for breaking orders; do you want to show we're crossing—if they don't know it already!' Taking out his knife he cut the cords which bound my hands behind me and hurried me towards the Adjutant, as he supposed. Colonel Loyle, seated on his horse, had placed himself outside the gate. As we approached him there, he leaned forward quickly and touched with his pistol the face of the sergeant, saying in a low voice 'Surrender! one word and I'll blow your brains out!'

"I never saw a man more completely taken aback. 'Now mount him behind me,' he said to me almost in a whisper, 'and get on yourself and hold him.' His horse was a powerful one and equal to the burden. We moved rapidly down the road a while, then turned off in a by-path among the trees. There the Colonel made us get down and walk in front of him quickly and silently. I held the prisoner by the arm as we walked along; for it was so dark he might otherwise have easily slipped from us. It appeared to me the Colonel could make that horse of his walk almost as quietly as a cat. Near the river and on the road which we had just left, more Federal troops, who had crossed a little by Fredericksburg were now moving towards the farm house. They were doing it as secretly as possible. Not a word was spoken: We at last reached the grove where our men were posted. All was still as a graveyard. We halted and at Colonel Loyle's call our men were soon around us. As some compensation, perhaps, for my nearly disastrous scouting, he ordered me, in company with another of our men, to take the prisoner immediately over the hills to head-quarters. With the rest of his little band he rode back towards the river to find out more about these pontoons. I had no time to thank him. I did not see him again till in battle line next day when his sword was flashing among the foremost—.

"Eunice, you see him only calm and smiling; but he is quite another sort of man when the bugle blows to the charge. I suppose the ancient heroes we read of, used to look as he looked in battle."

Eunice's face was flushed and her eye sparkled as she listened to this story. But Mamie, less impressive, had thought all the while only of her cousin Willie's escape, and remarked, "I suppose you didn't mind those wicked soldiers aiming at you. You had got quite accustomed to having guns pointed at you, had you not?"

"Yes, cousin Mamie, I did mind it; for there was an extra chance of being hit that time if they had fired. Anyhow, my prayer was spoken of by the captive and it led to my promotion."

"Did you think that moment of yourself, or of Eunice, or of me or your old Uncle Tim who wants you to become a manufacturer?"

"Why, really, to speak truth, cousin, I was thinking altogether of myself and whether I could kick the light over and then run and jump the fence with my hands tied behind my back."

"It was your duty to have thought of Eunice, I think; and while I pick that pretty flower I see yonder, you must defend yourself on that point as well as you can," she said with a laugh and disappeared.

Willie Barton could not tell when he began to be fond of Eunice. They had been a good deal together, being the only children of their parents who yearly visited each other. Their nurses used to say they were born for each other, and made them sit side by side. A spoilt boy, with flaxen hair and light blue eyes, he was allowed, as he grew up, to do pretty much as he pleased. Expecting considerable wealth, it was not his habit to look ahead with steady purpose to any great duty of life. He had had every wish gratified in boyhood, even when he wished his mother to journey to the city "to see Euny." He had always claimed her as his own; though she had never exhibited any especial affection for him. In her girlhood she had merely "supposed it was to be so." And as she grew up she still supposed it was to be so, though many a suitor flitted about her like butterflies about a rose-bud.

When his cousin Mamie had now gone step by step further and further from the spring as wild flower after wild flower, in their earliest bloom, invited her soft hand to come and gather them; and he moved nearer to Eunice and began to breathe words of love; why turned she so pale, and why did there flit across her face —as an evanescent shadow—an expression as from a heart not altogether placidly at rest—not altogether responsive to the demonstration of his love? He who had been so constantly nigh her and encouraged to be there by her mother, who had never dreamed that any rival for her favor would or could step forth upon the rosy path that led from him to her—he saw not that evanescent shadow or could not interpret it if he did perceive it. The character of his mind was rather trivial or at least not prone to any sort of absorbing passion. Placing some more violets in her beautiful hair, he took her hand in his, and they were about to rise and go in quest of Mamie, when the evergreens over the spring were parted and a soft "voice forlorn" was heard and a sad sweet face appeared among the leaves and its mournful eyes rested upon them. Parting the bushes still more the figure, like an apparition, emerged and stood at the margin of the bubbling spring. She was clad altogether in white. Her streaming black hair reached nearly to her feet. Poor girl! Poor cousin Helen! Willie Barton and Eunice moved towards her as she approached the spring and received her with kindly smiles, but without speaking to her. They knew her purpose and wished her to speak first that they might accommodate their words to her mood of thought. They supposed she had come, as was her wont, to gather twigs and green leaves and flowers to twine into wreaths for the tombs in the neighboring graveyard. This had been her chief occupation for several years. In the winter months her wreaths were only of somber hue and hard to make. But she heeded not the blood which trickled from her frail fingers when in the cold blasts of January she found only the harsh cedar to form her garlands with. Her mother died before the war and she had taken charge of the household in Alabama. Her father, killed in battle, she had laid in his grave. Her brothers, killed in battle, she had, one after another, laid in their graves. Her two cousins, part of the same household, were also killed in battle and she had laid them by the side of her brothers. But when her lover's bloody corpse was brought home, her wild shrieks betokened too sadly that her accumulated grief was more than her heart could bear. Yet no shriek ever came again to her lips. Drooping and melancholy, she lost all relish in life's joys, and for months at a time remained in the seclusion of her chamber. Bereft of her nearest relations and needing kindly attention, she was at last brought to her aunt Mrs. Avery, whose benevolent heart received her brother's sole remaining child as her own, and gently guarded her in the constant hope that her reason would be restored, and again the beautiful, the accomplished, Helen Clarens would be newly admired as an exemplar of filial and sisterly affection, if not again as the belle she had been through all the neighborhood of Glyndale as well as of the distant city in another state where she had lived before she was brought to her aunt. When the first Memorial Day[1] arrived for decking the soldiers' graves, she had been induced to accompany the Averys and DeLeslines to the ceremonies of placing flowers on the graves in the quiet cemetery near the little Gothic Episcopal Church at Glyndale. The sight of the graves and the strewing of flowers on them revived a recollection, a clouded one, of her putting flowers on graves in the cemetery at her home. She conceived the idea that these were the graves of those she loved. She had strangely selected in this cemetery a little grave beneath a drooping willow—the grave of a little child—as "her Robert's" grave; and here they were accustomed to look for her when at late hours or through the rain or snow she roamed away from the dwelling.

---

1. Gaines M. Foster, *Ghosts of the Confederacy: Defeat, the Lost Cause, and the Emergence of the New South* (New York: Oxford University Press, 1987), 42. Confederate Memorial Day probably grew from the custom of placing flowers on the graves of Confederate war dead. Various parts of the South chose different dates for the celebration. South Carolina celebrated on May 10, the anniversary of Stonewall Jackson's death.

Her black eyes, with the strange gleam of lunacy in their still tender expression, sparkled with unusual pleasure at the handful of violets which Eunice and her companions had gathered. These were affectionately given to her while she pleadingly begged "Some for papa—some for brother Will—some for brother Charlie —some for little brother Ned—some for cousin Georgie—some for cousin Ben— and oh! a heap for my Robert!" And pointing at last to those in Eunice's hair, she said "And these too, pretty lady, to place at the head of my Robert's grave." And these too were given. Then she quickly hastened away with her prize to the humble graves in the churchyard, fancying that she was decorating the graves of her loved ones. They, indeed, were reposing far away; but, valiant soldiers they had been, and their tombs were not neglected by their friends in Alabama though not so often replenished with fresh flowers, poor Helen, as those humble ones thy gentle hands attended!

Eunice now covered her face with her handkerchief and for a moment silently wept as recollections of her own father and the bereavements of her grandfather filled her memory. Meanwhile Lieutenant Barton sat musing by the spring, till seeing Eunice rising and about to leave the rustic bowers, he said,

"See yonder, Euny, cousin Mamie is half way to the house, sitting under the red oak and binding together her wild flowers. Let us linger here awhile, for we must soon say goodbye. I do not mean, Euny, when you reach home this evening; and which I hope will be a home never again disturbed by such an alarm as drove you to my aunt's for safety. She says I need not stay with her for her protection when duty calls me elsewhere. Indeed she is perfectly satisfied, even to be alone; because Colonel Loyle has assured her and your mother that no such disturbance as we have had may occur again. Since the war closed and all our fortunes have been shattered, I have thought it my duty to seek a profession; and I shall go very soon to Columbia to study law at the University with my esteemed friend the Professor— whom I knew well in Virginia. My Uncle Tim's plans for my manufacturing and finding mineral deposits and for stock-farming and writing essays (as he is always doing) I cannot consent to. They don't suit my lineage.—Dear Euny, we have always been like brother and sister and more than that, and I feel that your heart is securely mine,—do not withdraw your hand from mine, Euny"—and he seized again her reluctant hand and looked pleadingly to the downcast face. "We have grown up together and you know that I expect you to be my wife"—

With a sudden energy she raised her head, while a pearly teardrop glistened in her eye—and said, "Do not speak so—pray, do not. Come Let us join, brother Willie"—with an emphasis on the new epithet,—"our cousin Mamie, for see yonder on the piazza your aunt is waiting for you to escort her home before the night sets in. And when will you begin to trim your midnight lamp over those musty old law books? Grandfather used to say that it required the full twenty years of lucubrations to make him a lawyer. And I have heard him say too law is a jealous mistress and demands all one's devotion. But I hope your cheeks will not become too pale with study before you visit Glyndale again, to see your sister." A slight emphasis was on this last word.

Miss Avery now came bounding towards them in girlish delight with her pretty array of wild flowers, the first of the season. Her mother waved her handkerchief from the piazza for the loitering ones to hasten on. We need not tell of the various heart-conditions of the assembled group, how they met and how they parted; how Mamie presented her bouquet to Mr. Gillespie, telling him she had selected it especially for him "to reward him in advance" she said, "for guarding Eunice day and night and not letting any more fires break out"; and how silently the Lieutenant with a five-minutes chilliness in his heart walked home with his aunt and cousin; and how Eunice went swiftly to her favorite little study or book-room (as she called it) and closing the door, threw herself on the sofa and burst into tears; and how a half hour later when her mother came to seek her and consolingly and laughingly said, "Why, Eunice, do not fret so because Willie is going away!" she buried her face on her mother's bosom and sighed and answered nothing.

"Come, my child, it will all be well," and kissing her daughter's cheek and placing her arm around her waist she said "we must be thankful to our Heavenly Father, Eunice, for restoring us safely to our home once more; and let us make this evening pleasant to Mr. Gillespie. Come and see how he has adorned the parlor with feasting garlands to welcome us home; and your good old nurse Patty has prepared quite a banquet for us. Had not all this been kept a secret to surprise us, I would have insisted upon our kind neighbors and friends remaining to spend the evening with us. We will go down to the parlor and select our music for this evening; And don't you fret about Willie; he will soon come to see you, I am sure."

About eleven o'clock that night, as Lieutenant Barton nearly a quarter of a mile away—sat on the porch of Mrs. Avery's cottage smoking his cigar and dreaming of the future, a horseman stopped at the garden gate which opened upon the gravel walk leading to the porch. Calling out "Willie, come here," the late rider was instantly recognized as Colonel Loyle. "Willie" said he with his quiet laugh "I have traced them out. I am just from North Carolina. I came on the train an hour ago having (when I went away) left my horse at a friend's near the depot."

"Will you not dismount, Colonel, and come under the porch?"

"No, thank you, it is late, and I have but a few words to say. When I learned that two persons left on the night train and that one had his face bound up, and that they had paid their fare only to Charlotte, I concluded they would stop there if the wound—I supposed he had one from what Mrs DeLesline told me—was such as to require dressing; for they would reach there at daylight. I did not expect to find any trace of them at the hotels. With the help of some Charlotte friends I sought out such 'underground' places as the men whom I suspected would be likely to go to. They had stopped at a colored man's house and sent for a surgeon to whom the chief villain, our delectable parson, gave his name as the Reverend Paul Niggle of the Methodist Union—and by the by, he had a finger badly hurt as by a ball; you must have hit him when you fired at him. And besides belying himself, he was shrewd enough to change Caesar to the peaceful Cicero; and advised him to alter his name Bole to Boley as that would sound more respectable. He told some cunning lies about getting hurt by slipping from the platform of the cars and being saved by Cicero's catching hold of his coat and dragging him back at the risk of his own life, with the cars were in rapid motion; and he asked that the colored people of Charlotte would make up a purse for Cicero in honor of his heroic act."

"So Caesar was with him! I used to love that precious rascal; but you have always suspected him. I shudder at the idea of Mrs. DeLesline's confidence in him."

"He is thoroughly under Guelty's influence now. I know where they have gone and have sent word to them to warn them against ever making their appearance at Glyndale, as their death might be the consequence. We can do no more than try to intimidate them. I doubt, though, if they will care for my warning. They may snap their fingers at it. It would be a mockery, even if we had stronger evidence, to bring them to trial with a Party Judge and a jury composed of their own sworn Union Leaguers.—When do you go to the University?"

"I'll go down day after tomorrow to Bartonboro' and from there on to Columbia."

"We shall soon meet there, then. Do you know I have the honor of being invited to a conference with the Governor, our Northern Governor, at his earliest convenience—so his courtesy expresses it. In anticipation of the election and to arouse in a mysterious and powerful way the political adherence of the deluded blacks, he has been arming them with Winchester rifles and ball cartridges as if their liberty was at stake! They are as pleased as children are with Christmas toys. Still there is great danger in it; and I ventured, for the sake of peace, to write him a letter of remonstrance. So he has invited some of the disfranchised to confer with him. Another trick, Willie; but good-night."

The sound of his horse's hoofs on the road died away in the distance as Barton stood listening, and amusing himself with puffing out wreaths of tobacco smoke. Colonel Loyle's thoughts were these, as he went past Mrs. DeLesline's mansion: "There was a deeper design than robbery or arson. If I had evidence of it, and not mere suspicion, I would tell Willie of it, indiscreet as he is. But, Eunice, fear not. Though in your innocent heart you are incapable of conceiving your danger and Willie might fail to comprehend it, yet you shall be unharmed if it take the last drop of blood in my veins."

Was there a dream hovering about thy pillow then, Eunice—that caused thy pretty lips to part with that happy smile?

Perhaps I have forgotten to mention, because so familiar to myself, the relative positions of the dwellings we have spoken of. I shall try to give such a description as will enable any one to draw a map of the neighborhood: Glyndale village, with its horse-shoeing and blacksmith shops, was but a cluster of small houses contiguous to the state or stage road and about two miles from the Railroad Station. The villagers were gradually moving to the station for greater facility of trade and communication with other places. The Post Office too was at the station. The Episcopal Chapel of Ease was close by the village and the old stage road. North of this church, about an eighth of a mile and west of the road, was Mrs. Avery's house; then a swamp extending transversely across the road. A substantial corduroy crossing was over the swamp; then higher up the DeLesline dwelling. At this point the steep road turned nearly at a right angle, eastwardly, and brought you half a mile further on to the entrance of Oak Hill farm where Colonel Loyle lived.—After the Railroad was built (bringing its inevitable changes to the place) a wagon road was opened as a short cut to the station and Post Office which were a trifle Southwest from the village. It was generally called the Depot road and ran from the station Northeast and close by Mrs. Avery's. It joined the stage road just south of the swamp and its corduroy crossing. This saved the trouble of a new road through the swamp which at this point was five hundred feet wide; though east of it where the land was more depressed, it extended fully half a mile wide.—When the DeLeslines came up from Columbia with Commandant Nickton's wagons, they came on the old state or stage road. On the present occasion, Colonel Loyle having mounted his horse kept in waiting for him at the Depot, had ridden along the wagon road which took him past Mrs. Avery's where he had called to Barton.

If you draw the map, gentle reader, (as a novelist would say), put to the eastward of the Swamp, where it skirts the Colonel's home-place, a dot to mark the abode of a negro colony of his ex-slaves, forty in number, including both sexes. I may have occasion to mention this spot again. They called it the sittle*ment,* accenting the last syllable. Let me say here that these "sittlers" held their allotted parcels of land rent-free, and had the privilege of the swamp for hunting and the Colonel's woodlands for gathering fuel. He retained the ownership of the land and paid the taxes on it. They were prosperous and happy, and Colonel Loyle saw to it that they should continue so. They looked to him as their Judge and Court of Appeal in matters of moment; while in all minor difficulties they hearkened to their grey-haired driver, Obediah—(who was raised by the Colonel's father and was now eighty years old)—and obeyed him as they would a patriarchal chief.

After the Colonel left Barton, the latter stood a long while at Mrs. Avery's garden gate, leaning upon it, smoking a fresh cigar. At length he was roused by the approach of four negroes in the middle of the road carrying each a bunch of fowls and among them a large hog, tail foremost and feet up, which were used as handles, and with a cloth tied over the head and tightly around the snout to keep the beast from squealing.

"What's up now?" asked Barton.

"You hush up your dog-gon rebel mout or we'll bust yer insides," was the first reply he heard; and this was quickly followed by another saying in a lower voice, but loud enough for him to hear,

"He needn't hollow 'no gouging' when I gits him down;—bet I'll ramjam de eberlastin life out er dat white skin o' hisn"; to which another added, "dere won't be a God-bit left when I done tromple him." To this the former speaker rejoined, "dere's more ways to kill a cat dan choking it to death." Another said "An den de onliest way she wont come back is to hide de head far from de body" Barton laughed; what else could he do! They passed on, and he standing there busied himself again with his cigar smoke and cogitations.

Directly he heard a yell down the road, and back came flying and screaming in terror the band of thieves lately so insolent and defiant; and behind them grunting and squealing, freed from her clouts, rushed the liberated and affrighted hog. Had Satan entered the porcine clatterdasher or openly exhibited himself in sulphurous fumes? Was the hog chasing them? What could have wrought this sudden change?—The negroes, frantic with fear, leaped the fence nigh the spot where Lieutenant Barton stood. They did not wait to unlatch the gate; but crying "Sabe us! sabe us!" they bounded over or crashed through the inner paling fence of the yard and precipitated themselves into the kitchen enclosure. All they could utter in their agitation were the words "sabe us—de debbil—de Coo Cux—de sperrits from de grabes!"

The Lieutenant enjoyed a hearty laugh. He appeared to know "what was up." Soon two strange figures came down the road, clad in white, raising themselves up about ten feet, then suddenly squatting to the ground and shaking their red heads and branching horns; then bounding forward and shooting up to their superhuman height again and uttering shrill sounds as from whistles; then squatting; then bounding forward again. When they came near Barton, he cried "heigh! heigh!" as well as his laughter would allow him and the "sperrits" came to order. In the twinkling of an eye the disguises were off and two merry young men stood by the Lieutenant and saluted him.

"Jake," said one of them to the other, "leave your fixings with me and run and see that widow Cromley gets her hog. These irrepressible thieves took three from her last week. The think because old Cromley and Sam were killed in the war, she has nobody to help her. It would help her, Lieutenant, if you tell those fellows they saw the ghosts of the old man and Sam and that all dead Confederates can rise from their graves when they choose and that they know what passes on this earth. If you make them believe so I think they'll let her alone."—They conversed a short while and then he whispered in Barton's ear as he saw his comrade returning, "all hands will be wanted at the next full moon at twelve."—"All right," replied Barton and retired to the porch and through the hall towards the kitchen—a detached building—in the rear, to console the terrified new voters and aspirants, no doubt, for Legislative honors, if we are to judge from their recent divertisement in widow Cromly's stye and poultry house. The Lieutenant went towards the kitchen, but turned back, thinking it best not to make himself too well known to these fellow citizens of his, with whom he might soon come in contact under other circumstances not very agreeable to themselves.

When the hog was dropped, the bunches of fowls were dropped also. The thieves had enough to do to save themselves. As they ran pell-mell to the kitchen the cook, who had come to the door to discover what the fuss was, tried to fasten them out and had shut the door in their faces. They pleaded with her to let them in, saying they had been chased by ghosts. She too became frightened.

"Lawd o' mussy," she cried, "don't you-nah bring no ghost in yer!"

"Please let us in, aunt Sukey—jest a leedle while."

She did so and asked, "why didn't younah take off your hats and say Howdy do! Howdy do! and keep on a saying so, and de ghost wouldn't hab meddled with you?"

"Not dis kind o' ghost, Aunt Sukey," replied one; "dese hab horns and red eyes and hop like sparrers."

"And dey tall as trees," said another, "and screech and kin shet up and spread out agin like umbrillas. 'Taint no make believe; it's de gospel trute."

"And hab whips," said, in a whimpering voice, the most frightened one of the gang, "long whips wid coal o' fire stings in up. Dey touch me right yer," pointing to his shoulder and showing, not a long welt, but a bruised bump.

"Dat's a bad ting," said the first speaker, "dat ghost mark nebber come off no more, 's long you lib."

"Did de ghosts cast a shadow?" asked aunt Sukey. "We hadn't time to look for shadders," they replied.

They barred the door and hooked in the window shutters, and conversed in low tones about their experiences with ghosts of various kinds. Their greatest dread appeared to be of the last kind which one of them had seen coming out of the swamp on a horse; and the horse, he affirmed, moved along without putting its hoofs to the ground. This ghost (and he opened his eyes wide when he told of it) also had a long whip with a coal of fire at the end of the lash.

"I nebber yeddy sich a ting in my born days! What younah bin doing to-night?" asked the old cook.

"We bin going to Sister Debby to tell her dat sister Judy couldn't go to church to-night."

"Highty Tighty! It seem it take a heap of men—whole four ob you—and in de middle of de night too to tell Debby 'bout not going to Church. An den again, ghost wouldn't hab trouble you-nah for sitch a ting as dat."

"Debbil ones will, aunt Sukey," said he of the coal- of-fire bump. "Mebbe so," replied Sukey, "de debbil ones is de busiest kind of ones. I know by my own 'sperience."

After an hour or two and something to eat, they calmed down and began to boast of their valor. When day—dawn was near at hand, Aunt Sukey let them out with the advice "run home quick and nebber look behind you! And when you gits where de road bends round, you better keep your eyes shet."

The day having set in, Willie Barton, instead of packing up for his departure to Bartonboro', went gunning, ostensibly. His real object was to hunt up the thieves who had threatened him the night before and compel them to take back their threats. He had changed his mind with respect to not making himself too well known to them. He expected to meet them singly. We may well suppose that otherwise there might have been some hazard in the attempt. But that did not weigh much with him. After he had left Mrs. Avery's, Helen Clarens took it into her head to wander off too; and Mrs Avery and Mamie came over to Mrs. DeLesline's to make inquiry about her. Mamie and Eunice strolled down to Violet Spring supposing she might be there gathering more of the "pretty flowers." There indeed they found her; and after helping her gather violets and helping her arrange the bunches, the three returned to Mrs. DeLesline's.

As they drew near the house, Colonel Loyle, who had called on some matter of business either with Mrs DeLesline or Mrs Avery, was about to depart. He stood by the lower steps of the piazza, ready to mount his horse. He waited to greet the young ladies. He certainly looked attractive and, without intending it, was handsomely posed at the side of his coal-black war steed. Eunice, with a beaming face, instinctively held out her hand and advanced to him. Then while he held it, while he could not fully repress his look of admiration, she bethought herself of her manner of approach, and blushing and embarrassed, asked him "How often did you save Willie's life in Virginia—four times, was it not?"

"Oh," he replied with a smile, "you know he was very heedless and adventuresome."

He thought afterwards "How prettily she thanked me. No doubt he has been telling her some stories of my rescuing him and giving me, it is likely, more credit than I deserved."

But before he left, Mamie Avery had also approached him. She was unwilling he should go without a word from her. She had heard what Eunice said, and added "I too must thank you for cousin Willie. How many good deeds have you done?"

He became confused; a thing very unusual in him. And there was another thing not quite so unusual, he blushed.

"Let me answer you, Miss Mamie, by saying I remember only one."

"Please tell us about that one."

"An old negro woman," he replied, "had a basket of cabbages for sale at a street corner in Charleston, and was called off somewhere. I saw a cow in the act of devouring the cabbages and I drove it away and stood guard over the basket till the old woman returned."

"Ah, but we know of several other unselfish deeds of yours."

"If you do, Miss Mamie, please say nothing about them. You know not how much selfishness is hidden beneath apparent unselfishness."

Shortly after the Colonel's departure, Willie Barton hove in sight with some game he had shot, to leave a share of it for Mrs. DeLesline. He did not, of course, make known to them whether he had met with any of his dusky threateners. He accompanied his aunt and cousins Mamie and Helen back to their home. In the leave-taking at the piazza steps, the final leave-taking with Willie before his going to the University Law School, Eunice was a little coquettish (which was not characteristic of her), saying "Good-bye, brother Barton." To which he responded, with a laugh, "Good-bye sister DeLesline." Then, as if suddenly determined to study hard —O yes, he would study hard now—he turned back and said: "Do you remember when I told you of one of our old Congressmen to whom a constituent applied to get a patent for an invention, and the answer 'Leave patents for New England: go home and plant cotton'; and that you sat down and wrote some verses for me? I recollect something about Honor to manly toil, and something about ancestral pride and cynical repose.—Well, I've lost the verses and wish you to write them for me again."

"I think," she replied, "you bear in mind the gist of them. If you've lost the rest, reflect on what you have remembered.—With respect to patents and planting cotton, I've heard your friend, Colonel Loyle, say that if we get rid of the carpet-baggers and then induce the right sort of New Englanders to transplant themselves here, they would be a most valuable adjunct to our Southern civilization, and we would soon see the State blooming like a garden."

"I'm astonished at the Colonel," replied Barton, "As for me, no fraternity, if you please, with any one north of Mason and Dixon's."

"However, Willie, I'll give you for remembrance some simpler lines than those you have lost":

> Don't tell me of to-morrow; but rather let us say,
> Whene'er a good thing's to be done, we'll do the thing to-day.
> "And now to your law books and your Uncle Tim—and farewell."

—Poor Helen, holding in one hand a bird Willie had given her to carry, and in the other her bunches of violets, went submissively along with her three relatives. The violets would be strewn next day on the little grave in the church-yard.

Helen wore on this occasion a queer head-dress. It was in part made of Confederate money-notes stitched together. The story of it may not be uninteresting. The day after Eunice and her mother and aunt Alicia had found refuge in the College buildings in Columbia, the old nurse thinking they needed a stimulant roasted a little coffee, a rare article at that time. A Federal soldier on guard nearby (for the buildings full of sick soldiers were under Federal guard)—smelt the aromatic fume. When relieved from duty he went up to the room and asked if the coffee had been boiled and if he could have a cup of it. Eunice graciously answered his request. The soldier on retiring said "let me pay for it" and handed her a package containing five thousand dollars—Confederate money. He had other packages: presumably of the same kind. The fellow no doubt had stolen them on his way to Columbia or taken them while pillaging in the city and knew the bills were of no value. Still his act had a little merit in it, if meant as a tribute to her kindness and good looks. Eunice had given the package at Glyndale to Helen to amuse herself with; and she had sewn hundred dollar bills and fifty dollar bills and others, the pictures of which she fancied, upon an old bonnet of hers and appeared to take a pride in wearing it.

Seven

Pause, ere the cry of suffering pleads to Heaven
Against this fearful mockery of right.

L. S. McCord

Reconstruction agencies too powerful for us to repel had succeeded, at length, in lifting the alien adventurers into political control over us. Throughout the State the old Spirit moved to and fro whispering "Rise and strike these carpet-baggers down!" But Prudence followed close along and ceased not to say Peace—submit a while; kick not at bayonet points. See you not how the increeping host, under Federal protection, have got a firm foothold, made a sure thing of it, sent home for their brothers and cousins, their uncles and special male and female friends? See you not that the purblind wards of the Nation believe every word the new-comers tell them and vote as they direct; how the soldier-President[1] has an army at his beck and is ready, in a moment, to use effectual force in carrying out the laws of Congress as he has solemnly sworn to do?—so Prudence preached; and the majority of our people heeded her, and were submitting, waiting, pondering.

The conference to which Colonel Loyle had been invited did not take place for a long time. It was postponed by His Excellency again and again. Months had passed; a new election of State officers had been held; Guelty and Caesar had returned and had been elected to high positions. Guelty while North had renovated his facial appearance. He had entered into confidential communications with the wire-pullers there, and came back like a high priest; knew the mysteries; could dictate now with authority of a correspondent with higher powers. Through his influence Caesar, on whose intellect some negrophilists at the "theologcall Seminar" had tried experiments, was foisted into the Legislature so as to be near him, a connecting link between him and the Black Rosettes, whose secret leader, he still was. Indeed, for purposes of his own he kept the gang in his pay—a petty stipend with

---

1. Rivers refers to Ulysses S. Grant.

promise of "big money" to come—and he often harangued them at their assemblages or musters.

At length the Conference took place. Colonel Loyle and other disfranchised gentlemen were sent for, because a fresh political danger was hovering over His Excellency's head, and he had a little scheme which he thought could be effected with their help.—At the same time Mrs. DeLesline requested the Colonel to escort Eunice to Columbia. She had not been well and came to spend a few days with her friend Etta, a daughter of a Professor in the University, and she was to return with Colonel Loyle to Glyndale. Perhaps too Mrs. DeLesline thought the visit would be a gratification to her chosen son-in-law Willie Barton.

On the night with which this Chapter is concerned, there were four meetings or assemblages, disconnected with each other, yet all in some way connected with this narrative. We must therefore give our readers a glimpse at each of these assemblages, and perhaps at an irregular episodical one which was held in the dark under the trees in the Campus. If here and there a slightly satirical tone be observed, the provocation thereto should be looked for in the characters portrayed.

The Law Class had begun its weekly meeting for debate within the University buildings. It was presided over by Lieutenant Barton. As was usual, recitations of poetry constituted the first exercise. Each member of a division, the Society being divided alphabetically into six such divisions, was required to contribute at least a few verses selected from ancient or modern poets, on a subject given out at the previous meeting; and furnish a copy to the Secretary for use of any other member, if any should desire it. The recitations this evening were on patriotism and revived Horace's "O Navis, referent in mare"; Sir Wm. Jones's imitation of Alcaeus,

> What constitutes a State?
> Men—high-minded men,
> Who know their rights, and knowing dare maintain.
> Moore's
> Rebellion! foul dishonoring word!
> Whose wrongful blight so oft hath stained
> The holiest cause that tongue or sword
> Of mortal ever lost or gained.
> Dwight's
> God save the State;
> Collins'
> How sleep the brave who sink to rest,
> By all their country's wishes blest.

Then some German and French odes and chansons quoted by enthusiastic students of those languages; followed by Bryant's "Battle Field," Scott's "Breathes there a man with soul so dead," Holland's "God give us men! a time like this demands," Ryan's "Furl that banner," and other poems which may have been thought by some persons to savor of treason. None mentioned Francis Scott Key, though they had no objection to him personally.

After this exercise there came a discussion, limited to two members and to half an hour, of an historical question. The point of history for this evening was the query, Did the corruption of the Romans at the time of Caesar necessitate the change to the imperical form of government? The next question assigned was, Do revolutions always lead to political advancement?—Then followed the point in Law, with unlimited time for its discussion. But on this occasion the point to be discussed involved so much research that by request it was postponed till the ensuing meeting. It was about eight o'clock, sooner than usual, when the Society adjourned. Barton called back into the room several of his friends and proposed to serenade Miss Eunice DeLesline, who intended to return home to Glyndale on the morrow afternoon. To render the serenade more effective, he wished the aid of a musical acquaintance who lived in town; and proposed that his companions should make themselves and their instruments ready while he went to summon the absent songster.

The meeting at His Excellency's room in the Capitol was not quite so edifying and harmonious. His Excellency, a philanthropist from Elsewhere, thought his dignity warranted his keeping the "rebel" gentlemen waiting till his own perverse intellect should master, with the help of his private advisers, the programme and the points for conference.

Colonel Loyle, sauntering through the corridors, came accidentally upon a party of State Officials, all aliens, in a corner, and could not help hearing the remarks, "But the deed was signed for one hundred thirty thousand dollars—When the tract cost but eighty, and that was all you paid. To give me only five thousand dollars isn't fair. Make it ten and I'm satisfied." "But," was the reply, "you can manage the next case all by yourself. Will that suit you?"

Sauntering further he met an old colored friend, a tried friend, who had been in his regiment as an officer's servant, the amiable and courteous Sheriff Henry, as he was generally called, whom necessity had degraded to the office of usher at the State House. After shaking hands and recalling old associations the Colonel asked, "Is this another Committee room, Henry?"

"Law, yes—King David on high! one of the same sort, Sir. For refreshments, Sir. These plush sofas are where the members, especially the colored ones, take a nap when they are tired. And here is where they keep the whiskey and cigars and cards too—King David on high!"

"And how much did those gorgeous ornaments and furniture in the Hall cost, Harry?"

"Why, Colonel, as to that, you know, the General says they cost ninety thousand dollars—King David on high! But somebody who saw the true bill says it was forty thousand dollars, Sir."

"O, of course. And those porcelain cuspidors?"

"They say, Sir, eight dollars a piece. They are so pretty, Colonel, I would feel ashamed to spit in them myself and have never done so. But that's nothing alongside twenty-five dollar inkstands, considering so few members can write, whereas all spit."

"And why are not the Committee rooms carpeted like this?"

"O, they had fine Brussels carpets, Sir, but they and the mahogany arm-chairs and the tables are perquisites, as they call them, and have been carried home. Every Committee furnishes its own room every year, you know—King David on high!"

"Harry, why do you stay in a service like this?"

"Why, Sir, it pays well to do their errands and you would be astonished to see at my house the cigars and half-empty bottles and other things they have told me to take."

"What kind of errands do you go on, Harry?"

Harry laughed and said "O—what a precious set they are!" and then sadly and with a tear starting to his eye he added, "Colonel when will the like of you ever come here once more?"

Harry's imagination may have aided him in what he told Colonel Loyle; but he was certainly in a position which enabled him to know a little of what was going on at the Capitol. But perhaps the Colonel knew as much as Harry did about what was going on. In parting with him he asked,

"Well, Harry, how is your health since the fatigues of the war?"

"Poorly, Sir, poorly."

"And how's your wife?"

"Poorly, Sir, thank you; and so is the children, all poorly, Sir."

Harry looked hearty enough; but like many others of his race, rarely admitted that he was in good health.

His August Excellency was now ready to confer. Ushered into a luxurious apartment, the gentlemen were introduced to a squat, mealy-mannered, uneasy looking man named Fert and to his nephew Captain Fert; to a tall, greasy-faced citizen of pure African descent called Brigadier General Pompey Grubbs; to a candidate for gubernatorial honors, a well dressed gentlemanly person with a large nose and small eyes, both stamped with astuteness; to a colored lawyer from the North, named Rong, who by staring like an owl had acquired a reputation for wisdom; to a man named Lubb, with thin legs, broad shoulders, dissipated face and watery eyes, who acted throughout the State in the capacity of official bull-dog; and to the Honorable Mr. Troth, a name implying veracity which made His Excellency appreciate him very highly. There was also present the saintly Benjamin Isaiah.— Colonel Loyle noticed that he looked abashed and shrunk aside. He had ventured to disregard the letter he had received from Loyle and had come for a larger share of the loaves and fishes and for his own private design. He had not expected to see the Colonel to-night and seemed worried at his being in Columbia. He was scarcely recognizable, however, in his full whiskers, moustache and flowing beard, as the Reverend who with smooth sleek cheeks and hair brushed back and a white neck-tie beneath his saintly chin, had been preaching as an itinerant near Glyndale the preceding year. As if to avoid the rather inquisitive glances of Colonel Loyle, he soon made excuse for withdrawing and left the room to attend, he said, a special meeting of the Trustees at the University; a special meeting called there at his request. He had advanced a grade higher, in his estimation, by dropping Reverend and prefixing Honorable to his name. His aptitude for intrigue, his extensive influ-ence among the colored citizens, his important services to "the party," and his recent engagement as spy and confidential correspondent for the Elsewhere wire-pullers, had induced the party leaders in South Carolina to have him in a new role and to raise him at once to a lucrative position. What public position was not then lucrative by hook and by crook in the Congressionally reconstructed State?

The monthly conclave condescendingly saluted the disfranchised who entered the room in a body—men who could govern nations wisely and righteously, yet who were not allowed to supervise or control in office the lowest negro magistrate in their counties.

Upon taking their seats, the Ferts, and Grubbs, Rong, Lubb and Troth remained. Colonel Loyle arose and quietly putting back his chair, respectfully asked His Excel-lency "Does that man"—pointing to Troth—"sit here in council who lately, during the elections, paraded a band of the freedmen with loaded muskets near my dwel-ling and told them, with an evil significance, that lucifer matches cost but one cent a box? If he remains seated here as your counsellor and friend, I must beg your permission, Sir, to retire."

He continued standing, and others of the disfranchised rose also to their feet. His Excellency was perplexed—hesitated—fearing to offend the Honorable Mr. Troth who could control a large number of votes. But the Honorable relieved the embarrassment of his friend the Governor by scowlingly taking himself off.—At the time of the parade Colonel Loyle had given Troth "a piece of his mind," and Troth had harbored the thought of putting agencies at work for the Colonel's de-gradation. He had indeed done so already in a small way; and now this occurrence made him resolve to contrive more effectually to carry out his vengeful purpose.

The design of the conciliatory conference appeared to be, among other things, to secure the co-operation of the disfranchised ex-Confederate officers to suppress any attempt of the newly formed association of Ku Klux (who were imagined to be a terrible organization) against the aliens who, coming uninvited into the Prostrate

State, had manoeuvered and wriggled themselves into power by means of the colored vote, and did not wish to be disturbed in this most promising opportunity to make sure their pecuniary fortunes. They were willing to pledge themselves, in return, that the negro militia—the only armed organization permitted by the new Radical law—should be immediately disarmed; and many other promises were profusely and solemnly made, of course; O King David on high! as Harry would have exclaimed.

Colonel Loyle returned from this conference at an early hour (earlier than Guelty expected he would) and went towards the University grounds to pay a visit to Eunice. It was a very dark night. One could hardly see his hand before his face. As he entered the Campus walls he heard Eunice playing upon the harp and singing. How sweetly her voice sounded. What an agreeable change from the wrangling and discordant voices of deceitful and debauched politicians whom he had just left, to the cloistered seclusion of a seat of learning and the dulcet notes which greeted his ear. He paused to listen beneath one of the old elms in the campus.— Soon he perceived a colored gentleman with a pair of turkeys, one under each arm, stealthily moving by. Mr. Smallbits, the dusky University marshal, came upon the turkey thief. Smallbits was always dressed in black, the conventional and fashionable color of the Honorables. He was guardian of the University grounds and was forever dodging about. Detaching himself from the surrounding darkness as though he formed a part of it, he called out:

"Hy, dere! Who'se you?"

The person called to was evidently seeking to elude Smallbits and slip away behind the trees. But he perceived he was detected; so putting on a bold face, he came forward. The marshal asked:

"Wat dat you got dere, Dan?"

"I say, Mr. Smallbits," was the reply, "I hear you want some turkeys and I bin bring dese my cousin jist fetch from de country, to see if you want um." "Huccom he bring you only two?"

"He say, says he, 'Cousin Dan, I bring you de ress next week ef de Lawd spare me.'"

"How much you ax, Dan?"

"Being it's you, Mr. Smallbits, you kin hab de pair for one dollar."

"Look yere, Dan,—enty dese cum from Professor J.—'s yard?—Well, I tink seventy-five cents enough for um. Take um to my kitchen and kill um right away and pick um. We going to hab a bid supper dere to-morrow night for some gentlemen. Here—I gib you fifty cents now, and I'll owe you de balance. Go 'long, right off now."

Dan had scarcely disappeared in the darkness when the former Reverend but now stately and bearded Honorable Mr. Guelty, coming as a black cat would in a night like this, sneaked under the trees. He had sent Smallbits out (who, from his office, waited on the Trustees) from attendance at the University Library, to meet him in this spot. It will be remembered too that the special meeting of the Trustees to-night was at his solicitation. He whispered a long while with Smallbits, trying to overcome the latter's objections to some plan he seemed to have much at heart. They stood further off than Dan and the marshal had done; and all Colonel Loyle could indistinctly catch was "I'll have six of my men posted near by in case I want them. You need have nothing to do with it except to have the carriage ready. Caesar Boley is all I'll bring to the carriage with me.—O nonsense! I'll protect you! Haven't we power now to do what we please? I don't care a picayune for the danger of it."

Other expressions were lost upon the ears of Colonel Loyle. But he had reason to suspect some plot as no other listener but himself could have. Who were Guelty's six posted men but sworn fellows of his own Black Rosettes? Though he could not fathom satisfactorily the impending conspiracy, if there was one, he determined that a guard should be placed to watch the house in which Eunice was staying and to help him (if assistance were necessary) to protect her when she should be going to or returning from an entertainment at a lady's residence a half mile away in the suburbs and to which she and Miss Etta had been invited; as the Colonel knew, for he was to be their escort.—Smallbits went directly off, ill at ease; and the pious Guelty returned to the Library and the assemblage of Trustees.

It flashed through the Colonel's thoughts, "Unaided, I am not equal to this emergency. Ought I to tell Willie of my suspicions? No—not at all; for he is too rash. Yet the guardianship of Eunice should be his, if he is her destined husband by the earnest desire of his mother and her mother. I shall tell him of the probable danger and advise him to keep watch and do no more than watch and frustrate Guelty if he makes any attempt to-night."

Soon after this Barton came along whistling and was about to leave the campus to search for his musical friend, when Colonel Loyle hailed him, and they walked arm in arm a little distance up the street conversing together. "Give up the serenade, Willie, and mount guard; just to see if Guelty intends to come prowling here with any of his plots." With this they parted and returned to the campus to call on Eunice and Miss Etta. Lieutenant Barton whistled no more, but ground his teeth very unmusically together as he went off to see a gunsmith before rejoining his companions of the Debating Club and to say there would be no serenade and to thank them for their courteous willingness to aid him. He then hurried to certain parties with whom he was in some sort of alliance and who lived at a distance from the University and engaged them to meet him at his dormitory as soon as possible.

The meeting of the Honorable Board of Trustees was held in the spacious Library, which was beautifully carpeted and ornamented with busts upheld by brackets at each fluted pilaster. In recessed alcoves mohair arm chairs and mahogany desks with pen and ink were ready for all who wished to consult and take notes from the well-selected volumes which in uniform binding adorned the shelves. The

Honorables, surrounded by the assembled worthies in science and literature from Homer, Aristotle and Demosthenes to Tennyson, Hamilton, and Gladstone, felt the quickening influence of the situation and were eager for an opportunity to relieve themselves of the pressure of their pent-up eloquence.—In the absence of His Excellency, ex-officio Chairman of the Board, the Honorable Caesar Boley (*ci-devant* Bole and who said his name was Carlos Boley) the rising politician who had been at a "Theological Semnerry," was requested to preside, and the Honorable Antony Snibbs was asked to officiate as Secretary. The Honorable chairman, who had improved very much from continued association with Guelty, explained the object of the special meeting:

"Honable frens! de objeck of dis meetin will 'xplain its own self. Dis yer is 'xactly wot we gwine for to do. I say ubber race am de chosen people of God, as I larned at de Thelogcal Semnerry an we gwine for to rule. We got de power now and we gwine for to use um. Waf-fuh dis green campis aint full ob cullard boys and gals too, a-playin like lams an skippin an dancin bout in dis yer libry? Waf-fuh we no turn out ob office ebry ristocratic proud trash wot tinks it cussed mean fur wite and black to eat togedder and larn togedder? Aint we good as dem?—Turn um out is de word; an put in rale gemmen from Hio an Indanna an Maschusy an udder place where de pure libbutty is hallelujahed fur ebber!"

The Honorable Scipio Jurks interrupted the chairman who was becoming vehement and if left alone would have taken the advantage his position gave him to pour out a prolonged flood of eloquence—"Will de honable gemman 'low me to ax only dis"—

"No"—answered the chair—"I makes a pint of order dat de chair can't be stop jist yet."

Hereupon the gentle Guelty arose, softly stroking down his flowing beard and snuffing the volatilized dust—Was it from your side of the library—from your musty particles, ye old shelf-sepulchered leathery Romans, in recognition of your namesakes?

—However, while the Honorable Antony, Scipio, and Caesar replenished each his capacious jaw with a "quid" (the only Roman expression they used), the Honorable Isaiah stroked gently his patriarchal beard and said:

"Gentlemen and friends! This is a momentous moment! I come here—we all come here—to trample on conciliation! I say, to trample on conciliation!" and he smote the table with his clenched fist. "Gentlemen," he continued, "let us rise and trample on conciliation. It's been tried and tried again. Must we keep right on giving a home and two thousand dollars a year from our own treasury to ingrates who in their hearts despise us; ingrates who are nothing but democrats and associate only with detestable democrats?"

This burst of eloquence, especially the ringing and high-emphasized words Conciliation and Detestable Democrats, was responded to by groans from all the

Romans on the floor. They took fresh quids and missing the cuspidors, spat on the carpet and crossed their legs and arms defiantly.

"Aren't you," exclaimed Guelty in louder tones, "intellectually, physically, morally, socially and religiously equal to any other man on this green earth? Wasn't Severus, the Roman Emperor, one of you,—born where you came from? Wasn't Hannibal, the great general, one of you? And what about Scipio Africanus? Warn't some of the best bishops of the Church, African bishops? Look at your statesmen in the Senate and in the House; look at the Supreme State Judiciary and at Congress! Gentlemen, I love you. I acknowledge you to be my true brothers.— Now, my honorable friends, I'm going North very soon to buy books for this fine library of ours, with the money liberally appropriated for that purpose by our Legislature; and if you will pay my expenses out of the fund—which is put at our disposal—if you'll give me authority to use it—a trifle which will not count, when you consider too the trouble I'll have, I'll hunt up some good, pious, learned men to put in and strengthen our party when we turn out the miserable Democratic Professors we have here now. We must be ready to put in our own men, godly men like the two we've got now, Doctors Paunchly and Weasel. How say you, my friends? —Pay my expenses and vindicate your rights and your race!"

The Honorable Antony arose: "Dat am de trute; dat am 'xactly de purpose we yere for. Tun out dese and put our own right in. I seccunds de motion. Den when our own chillun kin play hide an seek 'bout dese old rooms as dey kin in West Point and Nappolis, an wear new sijer clothes jist like Colonel Black or Colonel Green or Colonel White eeder, dan we done got our libbutty, I says; an I seccunds de motion."

> The Chair: (looking towards Guelty) "Does my honorable fren wish de motion recorded?"
>
> Guelty replied: "Well, Mr. Chairman, we don't always record in our Land Commission Meetings, nor in our Sinking Fund Meetings nor in our Conversion Bond meetings. We don't record anything. What's the use? And sometimes in the Treasury we don't record, for fear the records may get lost. Can't we do what we please with our own? Our noble minds," said he eloquently raising his voice, standing on tiptoe, and striking his breast—"our own noble minds are our true record!"

This outburst produced enthusiastic applause. In their excitement Scipio spat by mistake on Guelty's right boot thinking it was a cuspidor, and Hannibal equally excited spat his tobacco juice on Guelty's left boot; but he merely smiled behind his beard as he thought of bonds and the cherubic Blimmilon the financier, and of his having his expenses, without limitation, paid from the Library fund.

But let us leave this circle of Honorables. In doing so we shall notice a thick set old field hand, of the Caesar Boley mold, (we have met him before under the campus trees when it was too dark to notice him well), with his nose flattened more than ever by having pressed it against the door while he listened to Guelty's harangue and peered through the key hole. This is the marshal and bursar, which at this period meant the incumbent of a large University building near the Campus kept now not so much as a "Commons" for accommodation of students as for turkey suppers for "honable gemmun." The incumbent had been prospectively elected an Honorable himself, a Representative; and hence wore broadcloth and carried a walking cane and umbrella and in warm weather, in addition to these, a palmetto fan. It would better suit his pomposity and present surroundings to say "baculum quercus vehit, umbraculum atque flabellum."[2] He was also an ardent student, having nearly learned to sign his name, while so many other members of the Legislature could only make their cross mark. This Honorable Titus Smallbits (whose station was outside the door in ready call of the Trustees) permitting us to pass out of the Library, we shall catch a glimpse on the dark staircase of the Reverend—the Paunchly, and Reverend Weasel, both D.D.s (whatever that indicated in their case), the two godly ones from the region of Great Moral Ideas. They were Professors now, the one growing fat, the other fatter. The former was vulgarly said by the spiteful and depreciatory to have in him brass enough for a full suit of armor for Goliath of Gath; and the latter, though less brazenly assertive, was said by the same depreciatory ones to be "too far away from home" when, with a child's elementary treatise in hand, he stood tremulously in his lecture room.

Let us pass these and cross over to the dwelling of the venerable chairman of the Faculty, where several Professors (exclusive of the newly inducted D.D.) not aware of the meeting of the Honorable Board (who had now adjourned & dispersed) had called to talk over the unsatisfactory prospects of the institution. They were welcomed with the easy grace and dignity inseparable from this distinguished gentleman whose truth-loving soul lighted the eye and beamed in the countenance on which a generation of pure-minded men had looked with delight.

He discussed with them the difficulties of their position and the duties which patriotism enjoined in upholding as long as possible the institution committed to their keeping by the Trustees of former years. If it must fall, he said, let the responsibility be clearly theirs who were seeking to destroy every vestige of the old regime; "quibus ego confido impendere fatum aliquod, et poenas iam diu improbitati, nequitiae, sceleri, libidini debitam, aut instare jam plane, aut certe appropinquare."[3]—Bowing down his silvery head and musing with a sadness which of late often came upon him, his friends changed the topic—for a while at least—to subjects beyond the disturbing influence of the political maelstrom in which the State

---

2. This is not classical Latin. It translates as "the oak bears a berry and a fan and an umbrella."

3. Cicero, *Cataline* 2.11.1. "I trust those whom some fate threatens, and the punishment owed for depravity, worthlessness, crime, and lust either is clearly upon already or surely approaches."

was involved; and soon his face beamed again while he forgot the "infesta virtutibus tempora."[4] Old Professor L., an excellent *raconteur*, dissipated the cloud of sadness by some amusing reminiscences, and concluding his anecdotes which introduced medical science (he himself had been many years a practicing physician) with a twinkle of the eye towards Drs. D. and T., brought these gentlemen into friendly conflict on the point presented in the story and on recent discoveries in their profession.

During their conversation the study door opened and a servant entered with refreshments. The fair Eunice, who was a favorite with the Professors, her visits to the campus being always hailed with pleasure, came gracefully in also. The gentlemen rose to receive her. She had merely a little courteous request to Professor F. to come to the parlor before he left and decide for her and Etta some point in a new German song and which they thought of rendering at the entertainment they were going to, if they should be requested to do so. He answered their summons instantly, and a few minutes later accompanied them and Colonel Loyle to the carriage in waiting for them and saw them whirled away in joyous mood.—Eunice's momentary presence was a true refreshment to minds wearied with study and care. It is not strange that after beholding her, the sedate Professors should become willing to turn for a while to poetic themes. Two of them had been sportively sending each other little effusions; and after a general interlocution whether great literary works were aggregations from trifling beginnings or were conceived in their entirety as works of art generally are; and Gibbons and Goethe, Milton and Tennyson, and some whose autobiographical confessions furnished material for a judgment, had been pressed in review; Professor X., one of the two we have referred to, mischievously took from his pocket of the last verses of his younger colleague and offered to read them. "If they are published, however," said Professor X., "they will no doubt forfeit our friend his salary." At the lines:

O heard ye not a rustling sound?—
Came it from these green graves—as though
A spirit host rose from the ground?
Or was it but the weird wind's low
Sad muttering, midst the stifled sobs
Of these bowed forms that kneel around,
Or move unwrapped in sable robes,
Whispering above each laurel'd mound,
Rest, noble warriors, rest! Jehovah reigns,
And victors fall—

4. Tacitus, *Agricola* 1.4.3. "times hostile to virtue."

the chairman frowned and interrupting the reading said "very injudicious. Cicero tells us, under circumstances similar to our own, to lay aside with our arms the 'animum armatum.'"[5]

"Well, my good mentor," responded the young Professor, the verse ends with a religious truth, 'When His just law ordains.' But let me turn you from mine to some unobjectionable Latin lines which Professor X. has written—Mitis quam primum tua lumina caerula vidi.[6]

"Pray do not," interposed Professor X. "my Latin is too limping for display."

"Permit me, however, to read the last two verses: Catullus himself would not have objected to them, if he could have thought of one on whom his affections were forever fixed":

O meae deliciae, votis precibusque sacrata,
Non tua nunc manibus sed mea fata tenes.[7]

"Very good," said the chairman, "such themes are addressed to the whole human heart; and such themes alone a true poet should select."

"But my versifying friend," replied Professor X. "has a few pieces to which I, in retaliation, desire to call your attention; and because I have long wished, Mr. Chairman to hear your opinion on the subject with which the poem is incidentally connected—that of emigrating from the State; not to Brazil or Canada or England whither some of our friends have gone—but simply away from our present distressful and apparently hopeless condition. Let me read you the poem." "Excuse me—we will hear it another time," said the chairman, and all seemed relieved by his decision. "My young friend," said he, "is apt to verge upon dangerous ground. These are times when what we consider manliness may rush to disaster if it be not curbed by prudent self restraint. While we are faultless, no one can dishonor us. This point, you remember, was settled long ago by the wisest of the Greeks. It will be no disgrace to us, if, without giving needless offence, we be ejected from our homes here. Let us therefore not think for a moment either of offending our powerful adversaries or of deserting our positions—but be wise and prudent to retain them."

"But, my good Sir," responded the sensitive and lofty spirited Dr. D. with his flashing black eyes, "Socrates was then 70 years old; about your own age, I believe; and prudence was his guide. The young, the ardent, the self-reliant, can hardly be constrained by maxims of prudence when honor beckons forward or the thought

---

5. Cicero, *pro Marcello* 31.7. "He retains nevertheless an armed spirit."

6. This is not classical Latin. It translates as "Gentle as soon as I saw your sea-blue eyes."

7. This is not classical Latin. It translates as "O my delight, consecrated in my vows and prayers, you now hold not your fate but mine in your hands."

of forfeiting the approval of those we esteem impels us to quit a position by retaining which we seem at least to acquiesce in what we ought to oppose."

Professor X. observing the Chairman rumpling up his hair and adjusting his spectacles, as it was his habit to do when roused—intervened with the remark, "Please let us hear your opinion, Sir, generally, on emigrating."—After a moment of painful silence, the chairman recovering his serenity replied:

"I cannot blame any one for going wherever he and those dear to him may be more prosperous. I am too old now to seek a new home, with some of you it is not so. The full burden of our calamities has not yet come upon us. We are powerless and I fear shall long remain so. When our slaves were liberated we submitted acquiescingly. But when the ballot was put in their hands, they having a large majority of votes, we as a people fell as no civilized people have ever fallen. Yet we are not humiliated nor dishonored. Whatever dishonor there is, attaches to those who seek an evanescent political ascendency by means which the righteous judgment of history will surely condemn. It is one thing to give the negroes equality with white men in protection of their lives, property, and freedom of action within the limits of the laws which regulate the community. But balloting is quite another thing. It is a political franchise they are not intelligent enough to use properly. Keep it from them as we do from women, children, foreigners, paupers, all whom good sense tells us should not be entrusted with governing power. Unless we do so, self-conceited negro politicians and ignorant negro voters will assuredly vitiate our Anglo Saxon republicanism. We are held down now by bands of adventurers who come here as party hirelings to control the new voters. Our condition may become even worse than it is. The future is dark before me. At present I look for but one remedy for our evils—a re-action among those now inimical to us; and when will that reaction be—against corruption and political injustice?"

At this moment all were startled to their feet by a smothered shriek from the Campus. Then they heard a cry of "Murder!"—and a chorus of unearthly laughter from a band of demons—and then the sound of tramping feet—and then all was silent once more. Rushing out with lights, the Professors beheld a figure hung up to a tree by his arms and legs and swinging to and fro like a pendulum. They soon took the nearly insensible man down and found him to be the Honorable Mr. Guelty. His face—the little his beard did not cover—was smeared with so thick a coat of soft tar that it was impossible for him to open his eyes. His mouth was filled also, and it was almost ludicrous to hear his guttural efforts to say "Ku-Klux," and "Where's Boley." The amiable Professor of modern languages thought he was speaking some foreign dialect.

"Why, Mr. Guelty, what is the meaning of all this?" inquired the Chairman; while the Professor, indignant at his cruel treatment, untied him and assisted him to his feet.

"Nothing that I know of"—was all his linguistic capability, at other times so great, could make intelligible on this occasion. His tongue was in the condition we have read of "cleaving to the roof of his mouth." Yet it may be asked what business had he on the Campus at that hour of the night? Why, on adjournment of the Trustees, had he and Caesar returned to the Campus? Did an instigation of the Evil One lead him thither, and lead his masked assailants thither, to a deed involving fateful consequences?

The valiant Caesar who had run away, as Julius never did, now returned exclaiming "Who done dis to de Honable gemman? Who dare done dis?—Come, Mr. Guilty," (he never overcame the habit of miscalling the name)—"let me lead you home." He took him off quickly, leaving the by-standers in a mystery about the transaction; and if Guelty himself did not clearly understand why he was attacked, he had at least "an inner consciousness" for a probable surmise and nursed his wrath accordingly.

Eunice and Etta having been escorted, as we have related, to the social reunion were, about half-past twelve o'clock, seen safely back to their home in the Campus. Everything was then quiet; and neither the ladies nor Colonel Loyle had the slightest knowledge of what had taken place. On his way to his hotel the Colonel noticed several groups of white and colored men in excited conversation about some event the nature of which he could not at that moment make out. Whatever it was, the news of it did not appear to have reached the late-hour merrymakers in the hall of the hotel. Sitting apart from these was Mr. Troth, in his cups as usual at that hour, who muttered to himself as the Colonel passed by to go to his room, "I'll not forget you, Loyle. You'll feel my hand upon you yet."

Yes, even so. His unpremeditated denunciation of Troth, in the Governor's conference, and soon his suspected implication in the Ku Klux event in the Campus (with which he had nothing at all to do), brought serious consequences. The why and wherefore of the animus of his prosecutors it was difficult for him at first to comprehend.[8]

---

8. A footnote in the original text states here that "In editing this long-ago written Story, the present chapter would have been withdrawn on account of its occasional acerbity, were it not that it holds the pivot on which much of the subsequent narrative turns."

Eight

Again in spite of thine unspoken woes,
Thy wilted paradise shall unfold
And blossom as the rose.

A. J. Requier

"Where is that young fellow, Willie Barton?"

This question was addressed to a group of students in the Campus the evening of the day after the occurrences narrated in the last chapter. It was asked by an old gentleman who had alighted from a buggy and was tying his horse to the railing which enclosed the grass plot within the Campus gate. It was Uncle Tim, as Barton fondly called him. He wore large spectacles and had an inquisitive, peering look from his eyes, habitual with short-sighted persons. His large-brim felt hat sat carelessly on his head. From the pockets of his rough though genteel sacque coat protruded several rolls of paper, tied around with pieces of twine. His heavy boots were unpolished. Indeed, he had returned that forenoon from an exploring jaunt towards the mountains, and after attending to some purchases in the city was on his way to his farm about four miles lower down on the Congaree. He had stopped for his young friend intending to expostulate with him on what he considered the egregious folly of his studying law instead of practical mechanics or some of the applied sciences. He hoped he might persuade Willie to change his purpose and also to become an active member of a Progress Society which he was endeavoring to form; a branch of which he wished to establish among the University students.

Without waiting for an answer to his question, he drew a handful of mineral specimens from beneath the seat of his buggy and presented them to the young men whom he appeared to be acquainted with. "You know what these are," he said, "limonites, feldspars, agates, chalcedony, pyroxene, tourmaline, corundum, and hydromica schist and quartz with a few shiny particles which may be gold. They are not what I went to hunt for; but they are pretty specimens. Accept them for your collections."—And while the students were examining them, he unfolded one of his rolls, which he took from his capacious sacque pocket, and holding up a small vial displayed a few rare insects in alcohol, remarking "Wouldn't Zimmerman my bug-friend have been delighted with these coleoptera! He had none of them; for I knew his collection. Did you ever see any like them?"

Timothy Thomleigh (generally pronounced Tomly) had been a life-long friend of Willie's father. They had been school-mates and had been graduated together in the old South Carolina College. He had been betrothed to his friend's young sister who died before their appointed marriage day. He had often dandled Willie on his knee, and the child had been taught to speak of him affectionately as of a relative. Uncle Tim was an old bachelor, with no near relatives now. For half a lifetime he had lived alone happy with his books and studies. He reciprocated the affection of the lad, supplied him with toys, then later on with books, then with philosophical apparatus; and endeavored, though in vain, to win him, as he approached manhood, to his own pursuits of experimental farming, the study of nature, and the writing of essays. He was more than ever interested in him after the death of his father (followed in a few years by the death of his mother) and often explained to him mills and evaporators for sorghum, the construction of silos, tapping cotton, the trapping of nitrogen and all about grade Jersey cows. "Now, Willie," he would say "here is an important subject; write an essay upon it." He himself was busy with these matters and wrote on them too—to clinch his convictions, he used to say.— So soon as the war ended, he organized an Agricultural Club, of which he was the moving spirit. To keep alive enthusiasm in the objects of the association, he had music and singing at the close of each discussion and elicited contributions of original songs; setting the example by writing several himself. One of these was "A Glee for our club" which I once heard sung to a lively tune; all joining in the chorus:

I.

Down streams the sunlight over the hills,
Up spreads the mist the Earth's warm bosom yields,
And soon the sweet rain will come plashing in rills
All over the fields!
Not one alone—all join to enrich
The fresh-blooming fields!

II.

The dew of the evening, the morning's soft glow
The heat of the noon-day, the breeze that springs forth
Over farmland and forest—all come to bestow
Their gifts to the Earth
Not one alone—all come to bestow
Their gifts to the Earth.

III.

A boon for the Earth comes in each lovely charm;
A boon too for us who with spirit imbued
With neighborly kindness, now join arm in arm
For all that is good!
Not one alone—all join arm in arm
For all that is good.

IV.

With nature to teach us, with reason to guide,
And justice and peace and God's help from above,
We all join to bless in her wealth and her pride,
The home that we love!
Not one alone—we all join to bless
The home that we love.

Uncle Tim had always entertained a dislike of secession, and used to add, after the singing of his Ode, "another thing, my friends, we must join hands to bring about after ousting the self-seeking carpet-baggers. I mean our fraternizing with patriotic Northerners. Eradicate sectional animosities and we'll become an unconquerable people."

"O pshaw, Tomly," they would reply, "we're that now. If a foreign war comes, there'll be no need of stretching out hands northward or southward to bring about the fraternizing although all the honors be bestowed on your patriotic Northerners."

We may add here that consequent upon his predilection for authorship and advising others to write, he made it a rule to buy a copy of every book published in the State or by a Carolinian; because if a thousand reading men should do so (which they did not do), it would be a substantial encouragement of home library efforts.

Of late years, however, he had taken hold of ingenious arrangements for house building with improvements for obviating numerous domestic servants. He had many economic theories and was always ready for an exposition of them whenever he could get an audience; as, for example, the present group of students. "A rich man," he said to them, "can build his dwelling as he chooses and eat as he chooses. Not so with those of moderate means. I can plan for such persons a dwelling and on hygienic principles and with contrivances for domestic comfort so that a family of four—reasonable ones—may live well on fifty cents a day for them all. The economy of a Frenchman could not accomplish more.—A young man who thinks a ten dollar bill represents always a chance for a 'high old time' needn't look at my plans. We need capital; and the mother and father of capital are ten dollar bills.—

Then again, come and see my new farm machinery and learn to work the machines. Your morality is improved by physical labor. I could prove this if I had time."

"But, Uncle Tim," replied a Freshman with a delicate mustache, "it isn't labor that is the mighty conqueror; we read 'Amor vincit omnia, et nos cedamus Amori.'"[1]

"Oh—the poets mislead you, young man, unless you take care to pick out their prudent aphorisms. Can you not read also 'Nil sine magno labore'; and the Ἀργὸς γὰρ οὐδεὶς in your Electra?"[2]

The Freshman so addressed stood abashed, pulling at the young growth on his lip, to which a comrade called Mr. Thomleigh's attention saying "Uncle Tim, you have an eye for nature—see the effect of the setting sun on that mustache of his"; and another, who had a little heavier growth on his own lip, said, "Freddy, they'll not vegetate by pulling, 'in occulto latent, suo succo vivrent, ros si non cadit.'"[3]

"Ah! you're with Plautus, are you?" quickly replied Uncle Tim; "you see I have not forgotten all my college studies, and some winter evenings I drop into the classics myself. And among the last things I read was a noble passage in the First Olynthiac of Demosthenes on the foundation of life-work. It begins ὥσπερ γὰρ οἰκίας οἶμαι[4]—Hunt the passage up and ponder it. I must decline, however, to argue this evening about the classics or anything else with you young dialecticians; you would keep me here too long and lead me, as Donaldson has it, through perpetual bisections of successive subdivisions.—But where is Willie Barton? I wish him to come and spend the night with me."

"He went to the depot this afternoon," was the reply, "and we have not seen him since. But we can find him, we think"

"Please do so. And as I shall not have time to visit Professor Joe, take to him this box of kaolin. I venture to predict that before many years pass, we shall make as handsome porcelain here as can be made anywhere. But here comes my young friend with satchel in hand."

The student who had gone to tell Barton that he was wanted, startled that young gentleman by the announcement. It had happened a few days before this that a sand-hiller came into town with his little home-made two wheel cart hauled by a

1. Virgil, Eclogues 10.69. "Love conquers all things; let us yield to Love."

2. "Nothing without great labor." "For no idler, [though he has the gods' names always on his lips, can gather a livelihood without hard work.]" Euripides, *Electra*, line 80. This is the first scene of the play with a dialogue between Electra and a peasant. The translation is from E. P. Coleridge, *Aeschylus, Sophocles, Euripides, Aristophanes* (Chicago: Encyclopaedia Britannica, 1952).

3. Horace, Satires 1.9.59. "Life gives nothing to mortals without great work."

4. "For a house, I take it, [or a ship or anything of that sort must have its chief strength in its substructure; and so too in affairs of state the principles and the foundations must be truth and justice.]" Demosthenes, Olynthiac 2:10, translated by J. H. Vince as *Demosthenes: Olynthiacs; Philippics; Minor Public Speeches; Speech against Leptines*, vol. 20 (Cambridge: Harvard University Press and London: Heinemann, 1962).

critter, i.e. a half grown, or rather in this case a three quarter grown bull calf in harness. His load was the usual one of bundles of lightwood; and as usual his bag for cornmeal and his jug for molasses or whiskey hung dangling from the axletree beneath the cart. Willie Barton took a fancy to the turnout; and when the bent-shouldered, lank, sallow, serious-faced sandhiller had gone into a yard to sell a bundle of lightwood to the occupants of the house which stood a rod or so from the street, Willie mounted the cart and drove off. It was nearly dark. He reached the Campus and drove the team to the rear of the North college. There he unharnessed the critter and rode him, in wild Indian style, twice around the inner campus on which the students' rooms faced, and the Professors' houses.—As night advanced and the owner of the cart had not made his appearance, Willie conceived an idea which he was not long in carrying out. He was resourceful enough in practical jokes to have conceived it, whether the same thing had been done before or not. With the help of a dozen others the load, piece by piece; then the detached wheels; then the body of the cart; then the bull-calf itself, were carried to the third story under the belfry. There they put together the cart and load as they originally stood, harnessed in the critter and tied the empty jug and bag again to the axle underneath the cart. They removed all traces of their work, sweeping down the staircase and obliterating wheel and hoof-tracks leading to the building. It was not till next midday that the sandhiller with the active assistance of the town bailiff discovered the whereabouts of the "concarn" and wondered not a little how it had been driven so nicely up under the belfry. If Willie had not ridden around the campus, he would not have been seen by a Professor and summoned to appear before the Faculty at their next meeting to explain his connection with the affair. When the student who went to call him, put his head within the door with the sudden, "Willie, you're wanted," that young aspirant for the bar replied with a frown, "Yes—about that load of lightwood!"

"No," said his summoner, "this time Uncle Tim wants you."

"Ah, that's a preferable piece of business," he cried, dashing his Blackstone's Commentaries into a corner among fishing rods and base ball bats. He was ready in a jiffy, catching up his satchel and hurrying from the dormitory.

Before he reached Uncle Tim, the satchel bearer stopped amidst a group of students saying "lend me a few dollars some of you?" They laughed at so preposterous a request, asserting that their whole class could not raise such an amount.

"Never mind about money, Willie," cried out Mr. Thomleigh, laughing, for he had overheard the request; "I have enough here for you; my sacculus is not plenus aranearum."[5]—To the group around him he added in a lower tone "you young book worms allure me into quotations."

5. Catullus 13.8 "[Catullus's] wallet is full of spider-webs."

"There you are with our lyrist of Verona, Uncle Tim," said the sprightly student who had chaffed Freddy and whose line from Plautus Uncle Tim had caught at. The old gentleman smiled upon him saying, "And where do you find, 'Venite adrura mia, juvenes; casae janua vobis semper patet?'"

With a hearty greeting Uncle Tim bade Barton seat himself in the buggy, for it was already verging to candle-light. "Take care, Willie," he said, "don't mash my bundles in there"; then taking leave of the students, they set out for the farm. But before passing through the campus gate Mr. Thomleigh was approached by a student who had been waiting an opportunity of speaking to him apart from the others; a pale young man, not over-well dressed and timid in his manner, who modestly said: "Uncle Tim, here is a rough copy of the cartoon you wished me to draw, Calhoun's Last Speech in the Senate. I have represented him seated while his speech is read for him by another Senator standing by his chair. I am not satisfied that I have made the scene impressive enough, and would like to have your criticism before I go on with the work. Did you wish me to put somewhere on the picture, Truth, Justice, and the Constitution?"[6]

"Well," said Uncle Tim with a smile, "a picture of the past should be a lesson for the future. Put Truth and Justice, but leave out Constitution. I am doubtful about that. What they have done of late with the Fundamental Law he venerated makes it such as he might not now fully approve."

After thinking awhile the student replied: "The last pen and ink picture I made for you, The Legislators conferring dictatorial power in Governor Rutledge, showed the members with muskets and swords in hand as if suddenly called to battle, and their dress and accoutrements as you had told me they should be drawn. But from an old family portrait of the time I have noticed some peculiarities in the uniform of an officer which I should like to introduce in the picture if you will bring it again when you come up."

"Very well," said Mr. Thomleigh, "but I think what you did is satisfactory. And, Jimmy, I'm conning several new subjects for you. One is the arrival of the English Colonists in South Carolina, March 17th, 1670. I mention this now—(and may St. Patrick help you)—that you may hunt up in the Library a good specimen of an English ship of that date. And you must put in the scene, (I care not about the geology of our coast), a rock twice the size of Plymouth Rock and write on it Constitutional Self Government."

This was one of Mr. Thomleigh's ways of encouraging talent and at the same time helping a poor student pay his College expenses. He represented to the needy

---

6. Cuningham, Clarence, *A History of the Calhoun Monument at Charleston, S.C.* (Charleston: Lucas, Richardson, 1888), 21. The monument to John C. Calhoun in Charleston, South Carolina, depicts Calhoun holding a scroll representing "Truth, Justice, and the Constitution." The monument was unveiled in 1887.

young artist that it was merely a whim of his own for the adornment of his parlor walls.

As Barton rode with Mr. Thomleigh past the further end of the Campus, he thought he recognized the Sheriff in close confab with several men one of whom was undoubtedly Smallbits, the college marshal. He kept his thoughts to himself. Proceeding on the road, beyond the limits of the city, they suddenly became aware of a dark diminutive object running out from the bushes in front of the horse. It proved to be a small black boy shaking a bit of paper in his hand and calling out in tones which he was evidently afraid to make too loud, "Old Massa, stop!" This he repeated several times.

"What is it, Isaac," said Mr. Thomleigh, stopping the buggy. The little fellow, about ten years old, had been strictly cautioned by his grandfather, Mr. Thomleigh's overseer, to sneak from tree to tree along a circuitous path till he reached the confines of the city; to speak to no one, but await the approach of the well known horse and buggy of Uncle Tim. He had been threatened with a whipping if he did not accomplish his errand exactly as he had been told and return as he had gone. Jupiter had said to him "Ike, you'se big enough to go arrands; and if you don't go dis one right, I'll lick you shure's you born." Bewildered by so mysterious a charge, he had successfully reached sight of the city and hidden himself in the bushes instead of going on in search of his "old massa." He was glad to meet him at last and replied to his question:

"Daddy Jupe say gib you dis"—then he skipped into the woods like an alarmed rabbit and disappeared. Holding the slip of paper close to his spectacles, Mr. Thomleigh made out the words "Come before dark and don't bring Mass Barton with you."

"But it is dark already, Willie; and I have you with me. I cannot comprehend Jupe's message. What say you, shall we turn back?"

"Not on my account, if you wish to go home to-night."

"Well, we shall drive on and see what the matter is."

A mile further on south of the city the road descended to a mill pond and near by, on the further side of the bridge over the pond, were many rugged rocks and a close clump of trees. The gloom of night obscured the road, and Willie and Uncle Tim were engaged in friendly chat, leaving the horse to pick his own way homeward, when from behind them a gun was fired and a ball whizzed through the buggy, grazing Barton's arm. As the startled horse instantaneously plunged forward, there came another report from the clump of trees further to the left, and a volley of buckshot struck the buggy and wounded the horse. The reins were jerked from Uncle Tim's hand by the frantic dashing forward of the horse which sped, uncontrolled, down the hill and onward—finally whirling the vehicle against an oak around which the road led to the entrance of the farm. The buggy was shattered and both Barton and Uncle Tim were thrown violently to the ground.

"Uncle Tim, are you hurt?" cried the Lieutenant springing to his feet. No answer was returned.—Mr. Thomleigh lay unconscious ten feet off. To hasten to him and raise him from the rocky road was Barton's instant act. As he lifted the head the warm blood oozed from a ghastly wound. "My God! Uncle Tim," he cried in anguish, and leaving the prostrate form ran swiftly to the farm house for assistance. The wounded horse, with the broken shafts, had already borne to daddy Jupe mute tidings of the disaster, and Barton met him hurrying in affright upon the road. To bear the apparently dead body to the house: to lay it upon the bed, to bid Jupe mount a horse and bring medical aid from the city, though occupying but a short time, seemed to Barton hours in duration. With tears in his eyes he sat by Uncle Tim, staunching his wounds and bathing his pallid forehead.

We draw a curtain over the sad scenes of the death and burial of the kind-hearted and accomplished friend of Lieutenant Barton. To him, almost an adopted son, was bequeathed the real estate of the deceased. But Jupe or Jupiter (so named in the will), the life-long companion and faithful co-worker in his master's plans, was to enjoy the usufruct of the farm and all that was necessary to carry it on, for five years; with an injunction to be industrious and saving during that time so as to reserve enough for his support in his declining years. The library, minerals and collections in natural history, the manuscript notes and treatises and some other things of special value, were to be transferred at once to Willie Barton. Among the effects of the deceased was a small casket marked "For Miss Eunice DeLesline."

But Willie knew nothing of all this. He was not at the funeral. So soon as Jupe returned from the city with Dr. T. and a few friends of Mr. Thomleigh, he beckoned the Lieutenant out of the chamber and taking him into the Library whispered, "Mass Barton, don't stay here. They mean to kill you."

"Tell me how you know this, Jupe?"

"Well, Sir, there came this afternoon a strange colored person I don't know; I never seen him before; and asked about old boss coming from Columbia; said he seen him there; and if you'd be coming home with him. He asked me if I was one of the Black Rosettes. I don't know what he meant by that. He said his name was Quashy. I didn't like his looks no how, nor his questions neither. I spicioned him and watched where he went. So, slipping round to the old quarry by the short cut, I seen him talking with a white man, one of them furriners that I used to hear preach about the country; though he didn't look 'xactly like the same man, because he had so much beard and it looked all stuck together like. What spicioncd me most was they took two muskets out the quarry and went off with them into the woods. One of them said, (I don't know which one), 'He shot at me once and hit me too.' What I could hear of their talk they were after you, Sir. Old boss nobody would even trouble. He too good to all. So, as he taught me to read and write, I write to him not to bring you on the road and sent the paper by my grandson to hide about and let you know.—O heavenly father! I ought to have gone myself!"—

Here Jupe sat down and cried and sobbed like a child.—"But when I see furren people prying about here, I was 'fraid to leave the house old massa left me to guard. —Now, Mass Barton, you better let me saddle a horse for you, and you go away from here."

"Jupe," replied Barton, "I don't fear any man who comes up in front of me; but I dislike to be shot in the back."

As he spoke these words aloud, one of the gentlemen from the city entered and asked "Are you in safe council here?"—"Perfectly," said Barton, "and Jupe is telling me I am in some peril."

"Yes, you are; and perhaps also in Columbia. There is a rumor there that you are supposed to have had a hand in the outrage on the Campus last night, and officers have been prowling about the University since dark to arrest you. It may go hard with you, if you cannot elude them. We will stay by your friend and our friend and do all that should be done. It is not likely he can live till morning or be conscious again; and you cannot help him."

"I leave regretfully—but it may be best to do so. Jupe, bring the horse around."

"You would better go to the stable with Jupe and ride off on the other road. The front of the house may be watched, if the officers learned you are here."

As Jupe was going out to the stable he took with him a dark colored hat and a scarf from his master's rack and at the stable saddled two horses. "Why is this?" asked Barton.—"You take this hat, mass Willie, and give me your light colored one, and muffle your face with this scarf and go on the right hand path from back of the farm till you reach the other road; I'll start first, and I'll wear your hat and ride off on the road from front of the house; and if anybody stops me I can say I'm going to Columbia for the physic the Doctor sends for."

The Lieutenant, though his heart was heavy with sadness, smiled at Jupe's precautions and did as he was requested to do. In a quarter of an hour Jupe was being shot at and pursued along the dark road, and for an old man of more than sixty years, was leading well in the chase towards the city apothecary shop; while Barton, who knew the country familiarly, was riding slowly and safely in the direction towards Glyndale.

Traveling all night by a circuitous route to avoid the environs of Columbia, he reached at sunrise a well cultivated vegetable garden near two tall chimneys blackened with smoke. They were monuments, like so many others, of the destructive march of Sherman's troops. The family whose home they had burned because the son was fighting in the Confederate army, had moved away and kindly permitted their old servants to use the grounds.—From a rude cabin constructed of scorched timbers and other debris of the mansion, issued the bent form of an aged negro who gathered some sticks from an adjacent wood-pile. Through the open door was seen a blazing fire which betokened preparation for breakfast. Barton was hungry and his horse tired. Both needed rest and refreshment. But what would be his reception from negroes irritated and incensed against the whites indiscriminately, perhaps against him especially?

However, after a respectful salutation from the old man, he ventured to ask for accommodation, offering to pay for the same. "Surely, Sir; surely, sir. Many a nice meal my old 'oman cook for de home fambly and she aint forgot it. Gib me your horse, Sir, and come in. Breakfast most ready now. Affray, old 'oman! Affray, I say! fix de table nice and gib the gemman a breakfast. Walk in, Sir; walk in; while I get 'bror Ishmael to rub down de hoss and feed um. Dis is my ole 'oman, Sir," said he, as his grey-haired wife appeared at the door. "And my name is Andy, at your service, Sir," he added, with three or four bows. His hat, which all this while he had held in his hand, he now replaced on his head and led the horse away.

The large room was oddly furnished with articles rescued from the mansion of their former owners while it was in flames; and not far from frying pans, pots and kettles was a red velvet sofa supported on rough pine legs; a comfortable lounge on which the Lieutenant felt disposed to stretch his weary limbs. The aged couple were very proud of that sofa and brushed it carefully every day.—The breakfast consisted of ham and eggs, coffee, corn-pone, potatoes, milk and butter. Conversing with Andy and his wife, Barton learned that their young master was Wash Habisham, killed in Virginia, a comrade of his; and the account of his death—as the Lieutenant minutely related it—was listened to with really sad countenances and comments. The old man and Affray appeared anxious to do everything in their power for the Lieutenant's comfort. Being told that he intended to resume his journey at midday, they pressed him to remain longer.

"Your horse is ole and e'enmost broke down; but my brodder Ishmael is a root doctor and know how to make him strong as a colt 'fore night. You see, Sir, we hab take no count in de debilment going on in other places. We stand by de ole folks. Dey always used to stand by us; and I tell de young people dey don't know their true friends. We very comfortable here; and all owing to Mass and Miss. Waffuh we do dem harm? We take no count in dat."

These honest old folks were of the gentle sort who

> In useful tasks engaged, employ their time,
> Untempted by the demagogue to crime.[7]
> Of such a one as Andy it is that Grayson has written,
> —Calm in his peaceful home, prepares
> His garden spot and plies his rustic cares;
> The comb and honey that his bees afford,
> The eggs in ample gourd compactly stored,

---

7. William Grayson, "The Hireling and the Slave," 1854.

> The pig, the poultry, with a chapman's art
> He sells or barters at the village mart.

Seeing he was weary, they quietly left Barton to himself and he slept soundly a few hours. After his nap, lighting a cigar, he strolled out among the trees. While he sat under an oak the perfect stillness of the spot induced to serious reflection. This had seldom been his mood; but the thought of Uncle Tim lying upon his death-bed made him sorrowful indeed. Uncle Tim had, during their friendly chat in the buggy the evening before, given him his purse and handed him a folded paper, bidding him examine it at his leisure. Reminded of it now, he drew it from his pocket. A part of it was in these words:

"The branch of the Progress Society which I wish you to form among the young men who are your fellow students, ought to subserve one other purpose than those intended for older men. The additional purpose is that of mutual aid in starting in life-work. Pecuniary assistance is not meant; it is emphatically excluded. What is meant is aid in securing remunerative employment for each other. There are two truths which will here occur to you: first, the praiseworthy portion of self-love, which prompts to independence in money matters and advancement in the community; and second, that we may do for a friend what we are precluded from doing for ourselves in exposition of merit or in solicitation. While a self-reliant and aggressive disposition seeks no aid of helpers, a modest, meritorious young man may find in the friendly co-operation of your Society what he needs of encouragement to action."—Then followed minute directions for forming such a Mutual Aid Club.

"Poor Uncle Tim!" mused Barton. "Alas! never again will your kindly enthusiasm be misspent on me. Wayward, indifferent, a mere loiterer! I have not rightly appreciated your fatherly interest in me"; and the tears trickled down his cheeks and fell upon the open letter in his hand. "The students call you visionary and Eccentric Tim Tom. They may learn to bless your name in a Tim Tom Club, if I can carry out your plan. And I shall earnestly endeavor to do so and make it effectual for good. Its inauguration shall perpetuate the dear name we have had so often irreverently upon our lips"—

"Here de kind o' root you want," exclaimed the root-doctor, Ishmael, coming from the woods and suddenly interrupting the Lieutenant's meditations. "You steep um for one hour and to a quart ob de essence put two pinch ob salt for good health, nine cowcumber seed for coolness in running and one pint ob beef juice dat must sure to come offer de left fore-leg of a heffer; dat's for indurance. den you make your horse drink de whole mixter, and he nebber git tired for three days. De old root gardener, name Wobers, Sir,—who teach me 'bout dis, make me promise nebber to tell nobody nothing consarning what de root do—dis one I hab in my hand now."

It would interest the reader to learn more of Isaiah's peculiar medicaments; to learn more of the experiences, comforts, pleasures and folk-lore of these old negroes in their unmolested retreats; unmolested by the party agitators who in other places were hunting up material for their purposes among those wickedly or turbulently disposed.

Barton, without the faintest smile, thanked Ishmael for his prescription and accepted the roots with payment of a larger fee than the Doctor usually received. He could not stay to test the efficacy of the prescription. At midday he resumed his solitary ride towards Glyndale.

The death of Uncle Tim was a great loss to young and old. He had but a short time before taken part in a preliminary meeting whose object was to improve the town in its rebuilding. A leading address was to be made and a discussion to follow on new streets, parks and other improvements and appointing committees to report thereon. We requested Mr. Thomleigh to prepare the opening address on general topics relating to the subject. This he did, confining himself to such topics. The meeting did not "materialize." He afterwards gave me the manuscript which he had prepared. I loved Uncle Tim, as we all did; and as a tribute to his memory I would insert the Address here; but suppose the reader dislikes episodes and prefers to go on with the story.—He was always willing to contribute to our intellectual entertainment.—We shall hear his hopeful, cheering words no more.—None of us who attended his funeral will soon forget one touching scene at the grave. The grey-haired Daddy Jupe came mournfully forward, after the grave was filled, and placed upon it a large wreath of roses. Then each of his family servants, little Isaac among them, advanced and placed a fragrant bouquet beside the wreath; and all, sobbing aloud, stood there as if bereft of their dearest friend and benefactor. Besides his kindness to them in other respects, he had not neglected their religious training. Indeed there are among his manuscripts, some of which I possess, several papers which show how carefully he studied his bible; and a sermon which I suppose he prepared when he had been requested, through mistake, to fill a pulpit—is among my mementoes of him.

I have a great mind, before taking leave forever of dear old Uncle Tim, to pick out from his manuscripts something not altogether irrelevant to what we are writing about. He was invited to take part in a course of popular lectures at the Athenæum founded by that famous orator, William C. Preston who, though he had retired from his forensic career through infirmities of old age, found pleasure in all that was useful to his fellow townsmen.

Daddy Jupe's wife who cooked for Uncle Tim at his bachelor home on the Congaree, had been bewitched. So she and her husband firmly believed. She finally died of a complication of disorders—brought on her by witchcraft, as Jupe continued to affirm. No argument of his master could drive this conviction out of him.

He knew, he told his master, both witches and wizards who inherited their mystic powers in uninterrupted transmissions from their African ancestors; and he had felt their power in his own vitals more than once. When asked if Old Pam was one of the genuine sort, Jupe shook his head as if he had no faith in that ugly old imposter.

"Pam," said he, "hab no power for to bewitch; but he's found out how to cure some dat is bewitched. Some of them. De others he never kin cure till he kin be a real witch heself. De white folks call one like him a wizid. But Dere's different sorts of witches and wizids. Pam aint got de mark on him, and can't hurt people nor fly in the air. He aint dat sort."

It was about this time Uncle Tim was invited to lecture at the Athenæum on some topic interesting to the people at large, and selected the subject of Witchcraft. Perhaps his lecture will be appended to our story, that our last page may be as it were an inscription to the memory of the dear old gentleman.

While Lieutenant Barton was pursuing his roundabout journey to his aunt's house at Glyndale, the obsequies of Uncle Tim were being attended to by his friends at the cemetery near Columbia; his pall-bearers being the Professors of the University. On a street leading to the cemetery lived St. Julian Yarkly. He and his political friends Guelty and Troth had been dining together. They watched from a window the funeral procession as it passed. They knew all about the cause of Uncle Tim's death. The Radical black sheriff and police, however, evidently (?) had no clue to the perpetrators.

"It's a pity that young scoundrel who escaped isn't in that coffin; there's where he ought to be," said Guelty, who was now clean shaved; the removal of his flowing beard being the quickest way to get rid of the tar upon it. Plenty of grease and soap had, for several days, been applied to it, but in vain. The grease however effectually cleansed the rest of his face. His cousin Yarkly pretended to sympathize with him; but could hardly keep down a malicious smile at the Honorable gentleman's unhandsome features (there was a long scar on the left cheek) exposed now to full inspection. Troth, on the other hand, was bitterly in earnest in Guelty's behalf; for Guelty's cause was his own in this particular affair; and a partnership with one so astute would be the more effectual for his own revenge.

"The young fellow," he observed, "is small game. We'll crush him easily. But I want to see that infernal Loyle brought down. We are hunting the same covey. The flushing for me may bring what you want into range; and it doesn't matter whose dog is in the bush. I'll tell you, Isaiah, how you can help me to a shot. You know all the people about Glyndale and I don't. I want a trusty man from there. Pick him out for me and send him down at my expense. Don't make any mistake about your man and I'll take care of what follows. Can you do it?"

Yarkly rose up and left them on pretense of attending to something in the next room; and Guelty sat silent and moody for a while, then nodded in acquiescence.

"Tell your man then to hand me this when he comes"; and Troth gave Guelty a small ivory-handle pen knife which he took from his vest pocket; "it's as good a credential as anything else. And here're three dollars to pay his expenses down. What name will he give?"

"I must select from two, as may be available," said Guelty receiving the knife and money, apparently with reluctance, for he was not well satisfied with engaging in anything like a joint scheme with Troth. "I can't say now which may come. But say to him 'C or P,' and his reply will show which one and that I sent him."

"Well, mister Bobolink and Monsieur Highhead would best be getting their ankles ready for the shackles.—And now for that little game you promised, so that I may win back some of my heavy loss—"

"Oh, really, my friend, I can't play to-day. I never play the same day I've seen a funeral."

Troth started angrily. He was always quarrelsome when he had been drinking. "D— your squeamishness!" he exclaimed, and followed his host into the next room. His host had heard all that passed between his guests and bore it in memory. There was a thin streak of kindliness in him—I mean in Yarkly, of course.— He was not inclined to the vindictive machinations the others were bent upon. He would plot for money, per fas et nefas,[8] but not to cut a man's throat.

What happened a few days after this, in this connection, may as well be anticipated and told at once. Troth had already and before the dinner party, suborned Lubb and set him to work against Loyle. He did not tell Guelty this. There were several other rascals in secret service for him, each on a separate beat. When the case came up in court, (if the victim should live to get into court), there was to be cumulative evidence against him from separate sources.

Guelty was not inclined to show himself much in public till his beard grew out again; and he did not care to go to Glyndale just to serve Troth. Indeed he did not like to go there at all; fearing to be recognized by the DeLeslines as the sergeant once sent to guard their house in Columbia. It happened, however, that a few cases of witchcraft, more pronounced than usual, had occurred in and near Columbia; and one of the victims was Guelty's washerwoman. He instantly thought of old Pam. He would bring him down to this witchcraft case and then send him to Troth as the most available scamp (so he falsely thought) for his purpose of espionage or whatever else was designed for the injury of Colonel Loyle. The bewitched old crone, Matilda, lived close by Guelty's house. She had snakes in her, gripings, vertigo, cramps, shooting pains in her back, her legs, arms, head and feet; she cried out strange cries in her sleep, saw scorpions on the wall, black birds fluttered about her room, her bed fell to the floor without apparent cause, her crockery and her

8. Zeno of Verona, *Tract.* 1.5.2.6. "through right and wrong."

window panes jingled, a black cat ran into her house, danced and jumped up and down and ran out again; and other incomprehensible occurrences, day and night, disturbed her peace of mind. She had lost ten pounds in weight in as many days, and at this rate would dwindle to a skeleton in the course of time.—Perhaps she had indulged too largely in fat pork and was only ailing with severe indigestion. But her neighbors, the womenfolk, were all interested in her case and alarmed about her. Every night some of her church sisters sat up with her and prayed and sang over her. Still the pains and spasms went on, notwithstanding copious doses of whiskey.

A devil can drive out a devil, if the driver be the more strongly devilish; so Guelty suggested to the women to send for Old Pam, of Glyndale; and post-haste he was sent for, and post haste he came. He had permission from his employer to delegate the care of the horse to another old man near by. The light wagon sent for Pam, was provided by Matilda's church friends, from the church funds. Pam's advent and solemn entrance into the sick chamber, where a crowd was in attendance, was indeed a memorable occasion—with his close-tied bags, every corner tied, his charms and rattles and mutterings and gibberish and variously colored mixtures in bottles. After some impressive ceremonies, he excluded everyone from the room. He and the bewitched or "conjured" alone remained. He placed mysterious things at her head and feet and on each side of her and waved a lighted candle in complicated movements. Those who peeped through a crack in the door saw her drinking something red while the exorciser sang and gesticulated over her. The result was a deep sleep. With the help of a few drastic doses the "misery" was driven out of her. It was a complete cure. Matilda never felt better in her life. Pam became a wonder and was feasted on the best the hen coops in the vicinity could furnish.

It may be told here, episodically, that Pam's turning from old time honest dealing to exorcising those suffering from witchcraft or voodooism (not the same though often used in equivalent) was in part brought about by a mirthful trick of his. When he was a boy he used to wait on a bedridden old negro over ninety years old, who had, when young, traveled with his master among the Indians of Georgia. To amuse little Pam he told him about them and their magic and their herb mixtures. He spoke many words of the Indian dialect. The deep guttural tones made little Pam's kinky hair straighten out and the whites of his eyes appear whiter than ever. He himself, Pam, had now become an old man; but he could go back to his young days and recall whatever he had heard from his decrepit old fellow servant whom he helped to nurse.—Some years before he was emancipated and employed by Guelty, he lived alone in charge of cattle on a piece of pasture belonging to his owner. An association of negro girls—the Daughters of Young Jerusalem—held a picnic at the place by Epaminondas' permission. A dozen or more of them came to his house for water; and one asked him "Uncle Pam, how old is you?"

"I'se one hundred and forty years old," he told them.

"What you 'member furrest back, Uncle Pam?"

"I 'member back," he said, "to when de Injuns been here. I was one of dem, dat time. I is changed to what I is. Changed by roots. You see, when I was a Injun, I scalpt a cullard man, which was 'gainst de rules; 'cause a cullard pusson's hair is too short for scalp. So dey hold a meeting in de wigwam, de big wigwam or de Round House, and for punishment I was changed to de very same pusson I done scalp and had to take he place on earth. Look—you see any hair on top of my head?— Well den, you know de reason why. As I was telling you, dey change me wid roots; for dey had dat time a famous medicine-man in de tribe dat could er brought down de moon from de sky, if he wanted to. Dat same squeenchy little medicine-man told me heap bout roots, but not all he knowed. He pitied me 'cause I bin his sister's child and he tell me how I kin change back to Injun again only 'cept for two minits at a time. He durs'nt do more, he say,—I hab de root now kin do it."

"O Uncle Pam, show us! let's see you change back to Injun!"

"Well—" he replied, "if you all tink you kin stand it, go fetch twelve fedders, big ones out de turkey your mammies is cooking over yonder; and dere must be wid um a silber ten cents and two large coppers, so dat if you see de Injun he won't hurt you."

After a little delay, these preliminaries were effected. Whereupon Pam stationed the negro girls in a circle behind the house, bidding them keep their eyes upon the ground, not to speak or cough or sneeze, else his transformation would be spoilt— the charm of the root would vanish like a flash. Then he retired to his room and soon re-appeared around the corner of the house, his forehead and cheeks smeared red, the twelve feathers stuck in his hair, his shoulders wrapped in a blanket, a gleaming hatchet lifted in his right hand; "O-tah-koot-le-wah," he cried, "wum-doo-thlue-co!—bau-li-so-hut-che-thal-la-pau!" and other imitated Indian talk, till shrilling into a yell and brandishing the hatchet, he pretended to leap upon them. With screams of fright they rushed away.

Some of the parents (belonging to a higher circle named "Sisters of the Evening Star") who had accompanied the Daughters of Young Jerusalem and Buds of Promise to the picnic, attracted by their screams, ran towards the house in time to see the dreadful apparition. But when they reached the house Pam was quietly pre-paring his dinner. He told them he could remember nothing of his transforma-tion; that this total oblivion was part of the magic of the root he used. He told them if he administered to them some drops of its juice, they too would change to something, maybe to cats, horses, or some wild animal—or to monkeys; for (he added) "some ob you bin dat in old times."—They were alarmed and went off to spread exaggerated reports of Pam's magic power. He became in their opinion a "cungerer"—a wizard. He was honored. He told fortunes. He made money—more than he had ever made by honest dealing and hard work. He paid attention to the effects of roots and apothecary drugs.—In his old master's time he had been chief nurse for the men on the farm; and since the physician could not attend the farm every day, Pam had been left in charge of ordinary cases, under direction, and had picked up a crude knowledge of drugs and their effects and how much of certain medicines made a dose.—He could cure such ailments as Matilda's as quickly as any one else could. He was cunning enough to know that a little humbuggery added to his reputation, and cunning enough to play magician to the full bent of super-stitious people he had to deal with. He even began to think some peculiar magic power was, in truth, inherent in himself. (Notwithstanding my making this chap-ter rather long, I may be indulged in a further exhibition of Pam's professional characteristics.)

On one occasion he enhanced his reputation in this manner. A negro woman—Silvy by name—brought her daughter to him, believing her bewitched or "cun-jured." He had heard before that they would come and had prepared himself accordingly. It would be tedious to tell all he did; his queer antics; his manipula-tions with roots, and bidding the patient touch various ones with the tip of her tongue. At length, when the bitter taste of a root caused the child to make a wry face, he broke out "Dat's de one! dat's de one!—I know 'bout it now!—I kin tell who did it.—An I see anudder ting. Aint dere anudder member in de fambly lay-ing 'bout at home—your old man Stepney? Wot he ailing?"

"Yes, Uncle Pam; Stepney bin home two days; he got de obercome. It brought on him when old Uncle Hard Times come to lib on us and sat so much. An he fren, 'Ligah Toogood, he setting by him, and he say wot wid eleben head o' chillun in de fambly, hang if he aint gitting de obercome heself. So Lige say."

"So den, so den! I knows wot a-ailing dem. But if dey tink it's de obercome, tell um I say wurk is de best physic for dat. How long dis yer child been a-ailing?"

Maum Silvy replied with tremulous tones, "She bin took tree weeks dis berry day."

"I thought so," said Pam; "dat's when I bin in de trance and see all de witches bin doing clear as de blessed light. Now's your chance; before de sun set and de tree weeks bin done gone. If you want dis chile to lib, you must make haste.—You aint bin let nobody be buried in any ob dis chile's clothes, is you?"

"Who—me!—no, dat I aint. How come you tink me sich a fool?"

"Well, den—you nebber yuddy salt bin sprinkle on your mudder grabe?"

"I don't b'lieve she ebber had a grabe. Dat's what huts me. She one of dat sort dat don't die so much as dry up like. Down where we used to lib, I nebber seed no grabe belong to her."

"Wot you bin doing for de chile?"

"Her palate bin down an I tied de hair-knot tight on top her head, yet de palate aint riz up. An dough I put beads round her neck, she's croupy as ever."

"Look here," rejoined Pam, "how long younah bin in de house you lib in?"

"Nigh on to two months," she replied.

"Did you move in on a Friday?"—"No—it was a Saturday."

"Wot was de fust ting younah carry in dere when you move?"

"I disremember, Uncle Pam."

"Was it de bible, de bag o' salt or de broom?"—"No—I'se sure it warn't none of dem;—we aint got no bible, an we keep de salt in a old teapot I carried it mong de last tings 'long wid de broom."

"An den again—when you bin a fixing and a sweeping and putting tings to rights, I spose de draffs and de dust blow in, an younah all take to sneezing?"

"Yes, Uncle Pam, I 'member I did; we all got to sneezing dat time."

"So den; an did younah say 'God bless me,' ebry time you sneeze?"

"No, we didn't—neber said it onct."

"How de debbil den you 'speck de Lawd gwine bring good luck to dat house? Tell me dat?"

Maum Silvy began to shed tears and said he made her blood run cold and that she felt all sorts of hows; but she hoped the witches, who she thought came around the house in the guise of rabbits, would let her and the child alone. Pam could make them do that. Pam was powerful enough to counteract every witch in the neighborhood. She affirmed her confidence in his help; and lowered her tones to express the awe she felt in saying

"An, Uncle Pam, I yeddy say you dig up a chile grabe and broke off de fingers ob de right hand and hab um somewhere 'bout you, and dey make you kin do whatebber de prophet Joshua kin do."

Pam was on the point of exclaiming "don't you b'lieve dat rank lic—I nebber yit trouble a grabe!"—but the idea came to him that such a report would magnify him and bring in many a quarter-dollar, and it would be best to leave the interpretation uncontradicted. While he was busy with his thoughts, he had kept his blinking eyes upon Maum Silvy. She began to tremble again and cried out piteously "don't—please don't"—and covered her face with her hands.

"Well den," spoke Pam, whatebber you bin hear 'bout me, you go right off now to de cullard people grabe yard. Dere's a bottle in dere wid a green mixter I seen de witch put dere. De bottle aint got no cork in um. It was a old man witch; and if you spicion him, don't you ebber name him, for de Lawd's sake; else he worry younah worse. He kin change de obercome in de fambly to a choking misery in all you-nah insides. So quick to de gate, turn to de right along de fence nine steps, den face round an walk nine steps, den hunt behind de hard boards and see if nary bottle bin dere. Dat bottle bin put so a rabbit kin upset um. If dat bottle turn ober so a drap of de green mixter spill on dat grabe yard ground—your daughter bleege to bin done dead dis same day. Go git it; hold it so it can't spill; cork um, tie de cork on tight;—here, I gib you dis string on dis rag to make de cork; cork um tight— den go where no eyes kin see you and bury um deep in de ground wid de bottom downwards. And see here"—(and Pam began to whisper)—"lem me see your leff hand."—she held it out to him.—"So den; cross de second finger ober de fust finger. Jist so; dat's right. Keep dem fingers crossed jist so when you go arter de bottle an no witch kin tak you. Go right now, before de rabbits begin to play 'bout. Carry de chile wid you. Den come back here to me for de physic for de gal, and tell me if I aint speak de trute to you."

Old Pam had put the bottle with the green mixture there himself and knew she would find it. When she was out of hearing, he said, with a broad grin, "dat's worth two silber quarters. Deys poor folks—so I charge only one quarter dis time; I guess dey hab dat much. Gee-ma-netly! aint she scared!" said he with another broad grin.

Everything turned out as he expected. And Doctor Pam was in greater request than ever. Such cases as Matilda's, to which he was now called (fits of indigestion) were common to him.

But to return to our story. Later on in the same night he was in close confab with the Honorable Mr. Guelty whose stable at Glyndale he was guardian of; and was sent by appointment, at nine o'clock to Troth's room at a suburban boarding house. "But wait a minute, Pam," said Guelty, "there're some ferocious dogs about, if you miss your way. I'd better go a distance with you and see you safe there"; which he accordingly did, and enjoined on the old witch-doctor to be faithful to him in all circumstances and not to any other man. "Let me alone for dat," replied Pam, and swore a great oath of eternal fealty to him and no other.

Troth was waiting to receive him. Pam entered the room with his head wrapped up in a red handkerchief, his ugly visage protruding from its folds, and with a show of mystery handed Troth the penknife, and to the query "C or P"? he answered P, as he had been instructed to do. The two looked at each other steadily for a few minutes. Then Troth asked, Can you lie?—Pam's head moved negatively, as if he had never done such a thing in his life. Can you steal?—Pam's head moved negatively again. Can you kill?—Pam's mouth grinned and showed his projecting teeth, like an old rat's. Do you love every white man you know?—The mouth grinned wider.—Troth took out a handful of silver coins and spread them on the table. Pam's blinking eyes were fixed eagerly upon them. Do you love money?—Again the mouth widened, but never a word came from it. Troth gathered the coins and put them back in his pocket and said—"Let's take a walk."

Pam was not a reticent negro, but rather a talkative one. He, however, feared eavesdroppers (for he was one himself) and did not intend to utter a word to bring himself into trouble. And besides, he had not yet "caught on" to the kind of business he was wanted for. Troth, so far, was inclined to think him a fool, and wondered why Guelty had sent him such a fellow. While they walked along a by-street, Troth asked him How did you get to Columbia? "The colored folks sent a wagon for me."—"Who paid expenses?" "Don't know, 'cept they did."—"How'll you go back?"—"Walk." "Didn't Mr. Guelty give you some money?"—"Not a cent."—

Troth whistled. He was thinking, "fleeced again, even in so pitiful a scam as three dollars!"

When they reached a secluded place, Troth explained what he wished done and concluded a bargain with Pam, who swore an outlandish oath to do as he was instructed, and to be faithful to Troth and to no other man on earth.

When the oath-bound Epaminondas got back to the negro domicile where he was staying, a small house of three rooms, he desired to be left to himself a while "to tink ober a ting" he said; and they respectfully—with a feeling akin to awe—closed him in a room and retired to the outside of the house. There he laughed heartily, but so as not to be heard, and counted his money several times, by quarters (his way of reckoning)—"seben quarters and dese five makes eleben quarters, and Matilda give me two quarters—so I hab a dozen of dem in all;—'nough to buy a sow, if it warn't I kin git a pig wheneber I feel hongry for one. Dey tink old Pam a fool; but you see, you see!" and he chuckled to himself and tied his cash in a canvas bag which hung to his waist by a leather string; then buttoned his clothes over it. In putting away his money his hand touched something suspended from his neck. He took it out and smiled at it, saying "Luck follow me sure. 'Taint ebbry nigger got de charm of sitch a grabe-yard buck rabbit foot as dish er one." Then he carefully tucked it in again.

While Troth went to his gambling saloon and midnight potations, Pam was in request by members of the Rising Sons of Ham, a few of whom lived in Columbia. Delegates from the Daughters of the Golden Chariot called on him at the same time. One purpose of their visit was to solicit a contribution towards the celebration, in grand style, of the next Emancipation Day.[9] Pam said "If I had any money, you be sure I'd give you some; but I aint got a single red cent; and I bin studying how I kin git back home. But lem me tell you-nah one thing—dat Celebration got to be paid for by de buckra people!" and he put his thumb to his nose and winked. "Dat's so, sure 'nough!" they all responded with broad grins; and one of the buxom delegates from the Golden Chariot sidled up to him and said "we hab a table sot for you new, and it's been paid for dat way, and we come to take you dere." And thither they went. It was a plentiful spread. "We bound to git a libbing. We de chosen people of de Lord." And they sung Marching on to Canaan; the gurgling from a quart bottle reminding them of the bubbling from the Rock in the wilderness.

During the repast one of the sisters inquired of Pam

"Why didn't you bring your wife wid you?"

"Who—dat gal!" said Pam, "she done gone.—I'se too ugly, so she say. But she find out fust where I hide my money (I usen to hab money den, but I aint got none

---

9. A celebration of emancipation, typically observed on June 17 and also known as "Juneteenth."

now), and she bin took more'n half; more'n four dollars.—Good ridrance ob bad rubbidge—I mean de gal when I says rubbidge."

"Taking only half de money show she was well brought up," said a youthful daughter of the Golden Chariot.

"Maybe so—maybe so" rejoined Pam doubtfully. "I married de gal to be muched, as I'se getting old; and dat's all de muching she gib me."

"But you mought er tried one ob us down here; we don't run 'way," said the Chariot's daughter.—Then Pam and all of them laughed and went on enjoying their feast.

But there were other late meetings elsewhere, secret ones, not so innocent in intention. Columbia was a special rendezvous place. Union League aspirants for the Legislature or for political recognition, were conversant with ideas about holding together for race supremacy and for upholding those who had liberated them and following their lead even to devastation of all else. Such fidelity, it is believed, was implied in their oath of membership. Caesar, or rather the Honorable C. Boley, was at one of the League meetings, in a second-hand broadcloth suit, and was plied with questions about his heroic rescue of Guelty on the campus. He was supposed to know, moreover, all government secrets. He communicated little. The truth is he knew very little; but his ominous nods and enigmatical expressions enhanced his reputation for confidential participation in political intrigues. "It'll come out," he said, "you must wait. You seen de President in Washington—dat old warryer—haint you?"—"No, but we hearn of him."—"Well, I seen him. He know ebbry thing, don't he?"—"No, not things down here."—"Well, den, he got de guns and de amnition and kin do things down here, can't he?"—"Yes, if you pull he coat tail right."—"And aint he coat tail pulled right? Ax de gubner dat. Where's you all's gumption gone to?—I tell you we got de power and we gwine to use um. You know what an oath is—a court oath?"—"Yes, it mean pull down what's to be pulled down."—"Den you get your oaths ready, dat's all."

It was well they had not (could they have?) an able-brained impetuous leader of their own race. The river Ganges may whirl and splash and foam here and there in its course—may even be an object to swear by—but it spreads out at last in marshes and oozy impotence.

When Pam was setting out on his tramp home next morning, he was waited on by a young negro woman who, with gushing tears, told him there was another case of witchcraft for which his services were desired. It was on the road five miles up, and she would take him there, and he could spend the day there and be provided for. As it was on the line of his way home, he consented; and they reached the clearing and group of shanties in time for dinner. The victim in this case had both legs drawn up and could not straighten them out. He had been so for three days. The buckra doctor who had visited him pronounced it rheumatism; but the sufferer thought he knew better. His wife said, "he wear de eel skin an besides dat he bin carry de potato in his pocket—nine of um, one after tudder, till dey shribble up; yet de ailment still on him; so it couldn't be rheumatism."

Pam asked her in an undertone "What de full and true name of dis yer man?"

"Nem mind what my name is," said he to Pam's inquiry, which he had overheard; "you cure me, dat's what you yere for. I'se willing to pay for it."

"Look here," said Pam, "what de Lord do, I can't undo. If a witch trouble you, den let me lone for dat. Tell me how you fust come so, and don't tell a lie or else I can't help you. A man like me don't lie and don't wait for to hear a lie."

"Why not do de 'chantments widout dat?"

"Cause I can't, less I know de truth."

"Wait den till after dinner. I don't feel like tell you now."

The difficulty was that he feared to tell his true name or to tell what Pam desired to know. Even after dinner the patient, once a strong able-bodied fellow, now sadly emaciated, was averse from telling how he came to his present condition. But finally he told of his running away from his owners after a thrashing for gross misdemeanor, and that he had joined a company of colored soldiers following along with the Federals just after the surrender; and that he was one of a crowd who had helped to kill and mutilate a young white man at Newberry. "And wherebber I mute-alate him, dere de pains strike me now. His speerit is a-doing it. I kin see him a-coming at me when de pain strike me most. I know he doing it. Kin you dribe him off—dribe him off?"

"He aint no witch," said Pam, and shook his head up and down, frowning and muttering to himself.

"Who he den?—I tell you he strike hard," said the alarmed patient.

"De sperrits comes, de sperrits goes; who kin hold em; who kin beg um stop? dey comes, dey goes like de wind!" and Pam's head went up and down again for a minute or more. The victim on the bed trembled and shrieked "He on me now! Strike me dead, O Lawd, O Lawd!" His wife ran in to him, but he waved her off. "Don't tech me! He on me now! Just where I slashed his limbs, he slash me now ober and ober, O Kingdom come—Kingdom come!"

"De sperrits comes, de sperrits goes; who kin stop um!" repeated the witch-doctor. "Yet, besides de sperrits, der may be a witch troubling you; maybe two of um. I kin dribe dem off. Lem me lone for dat."—When he first saw the patient, he judged the buckra doctor had made the correct diagnosis. What Pam wanted now was an opiate. He knew about opiates; had used them before. Unfortunately he had none with him. Matilda had swallowed all he had brought from home. He was studying out a pretext to get an anodyne from the city. His eyes had been busy (as usual with him) when he came to the group of shanties. He knew he could obtain what he hinted at in saying, "Dere is a root to get, and I might hab to go far to find it, and it kin only be got on a hoss wid white hoofs."

"Why, dere's just dat sort of hoss next door and I kin borrow him" exclaimed the sobbing woman, "I kin git him right now!"

"But" said Pam, "four silver quarters must be put ober de root to bring um to de surface of de ground; and I must hab three hairs from de man's head to put wid de quarters."

"I hab two quarters and I kin borrow two from Uncle Jerry if you'll get de root and sabe us." She ran out to Uncle Jerry and brought the coins. Then she went to the bed and returned with the three hairs, which the exorciser tied together with a black thread and placed with the coins, folding them in a piece of brown paper which he carefully examined first, saying it must not have a stain upon it.

Within half an hour Pam had skirted through the woods on the white hoofed horse and was well on his way to procure the drug he wanted and some other medicaments for his decoctions. He got them at Schwomm's shop. After leaving the apothecary's he was hastening through the suburbs when he was met by some women coming from Maum Matilda. They recognized him, although he had his red cotton handkerchief tied over his face as if he had toothache.

"Is dat you, Uncle Epaminondas? Huccom you here? I thought you bin gone home?"

"I bin and come back. What if I kin fly?"

"I believe you kin, if you want to," the woman reverently replied. A crowd began to gather, and Pam put his horse with the white hoofs to its quickest pace and sped up the road, his coat skirt streaming and the ends of the red handkerchief flapping like wings. Up and up he went, up a sandy hillock in the road, and disappeared in a cloud of dust. The dumfounded group of women cried out in amazement as if he had gone up out of sight, and one exclaimed

"I wouldn't like dat Paminondas for to stay at my house. Wonder if he eat little chillun! Dat man's a witch!"

"How kin man be witch?" another asked.

"Course he kin," the first speaker replied, "if he got de mark on him. What mark, you say? Why, where de debil put it, when he swear to de debil."

Pam having surmounted the sandy hill top, turned his horse aside into the woods. The spectators failed to see him re-appear on the road beyond. He did this for effect; and he was also shortening his course back to the rheumatic sufferer. He stopped in an obscure spot in the woods thinking he might be watched and that it would be better to act a little. He dismounted and stooped at a trickling streamlet. He took out the brown paper parcel, pocketed the coins and buried the three hairs, smiling and talking to himself; then scratched the ground here and there, picked up something, perhaps a root, and put it in his coat pocket. At length he mounted the horse and pursued his way. On his return to the house he noticed the patient's paroxysm of pain was nearly over for this attack; and he administered an opiate with magic accompaniments. By supper time the bewitched mutilator was in a profound slumber.

Early next day Pam set out on foot, and met after an hour or so, a squad of the Governor's constabulary or negro police on horseback; and along with them was a wagon with a tent and a supply of provisions. They had come by a cross road into the one Pam was following. "Where bound to?" they asked of him. They were going towards Glyndale themselves, they informed him, and offered to give him a lift. He got up on the wagon. They put many questions to him about the people around Glyndale, which Pam answered to suit himself, and proved to their satisfaction that he was "a no account old fool and didn't know nothing." At the next long hill-rise they put him off the wagon with little ceremony, saying the horses had load enough to carry. One of the negro constabulary, in pretending to help him down, tripped him and he came nigh falling. He looked keenly at him and said, "I knows you. You needn't grin like Chessy Cat. I knows you, Gus Doings, if you has got sojer clothes on. And lemme tell you, Gus, if I is a hard looking man, I'se got good feelings; and I shan't forget dis. De sperrits 'scribe you and say If you see on de road such-an-such a man, shake de pestilence to him"; and he menacingly shook his fore-finger at him nine times, counting aloud and pausing with every three menacing motions of his finger. Augustus Doings did not appear to relish the mysterious imprecations. They were soon out of sight and Pam trudged along, falling at times into that silly habit of his, talking to himself. "You after de Coo-Cux; and de sojers 'll come nex, den de Court, den de Jail. I bin hear tings. De debil'll let he whole witch flock loose bimeby, and fly 'long wid 'um heself!"

Soon Pam began to get tired and hungry and turned into the woods and sat down near a spring under the shade of the trees. He took from his bundle chicken, pork-pie, biscuits and cake, which his female friends had put up for him. He stopped eating "every now and then" and talked to himself. After a slight repast (considering the quantity he had in his bundle) he, strange to say, held a chicken leg near his mouth, while one might count a hundred, without taking a bite of it. A sudden thought or recollection had seized him. He was looking up vacantly and appeared unaware that he had raised the chicken leg to his mouth; so absorbed was he. Then a grin began to crinkle and broaden away from his projecting teeth; then he laughed; then, as it were, he came to himself, and put the chicken leg back into his bundle and tied it up, and sat musing. "To tink" he said to himself, "dat a man like him would be after a ting like dat! To actily ax an old nigger like me if I kin bewitch a woman for him! Well—well—well!—But he wouldn't say who. He too cunning for dat just now. But bimebi, you see! Only he say, kin you do it, Pam? Kin you gib something to change de 'fections (he call it) and make de woman lub where no lub is now? I tell him de only witch doing ob dat sort is wid plenty of money. Money kin do it wid most ob dem. Yet wid som, a world full ob money can't move

de heart a single speck.—Maybe I know what he after. Pam aint de fool dey tink
he is. He didn't like what I told him. I could see dat. So hoping he mought trust
me and keep me to mind de hoss and not turn me off, I say Let me study 'bout dat,
Sir; maybe I kin do it. Lemme see, Sir. Dere is a root I know hab lots ob power in
um; a strange root; I know where 'tis; and, sir, dat root kin make a mouse lub a cat.
I hab done dat much wid it; and, Sir, de cat, she turn and lub de mouse. An dey is
lubbing one anoder to dis day.—I'se a man wot don't tell a lie; wot I do, Sir, I kin
do.—If he bin fool me, den I fool him. He wasn't drunk needer. He was in yearnest;
in dead yearnest."—

    "Well," he say, "'tink of it old Pam, my friend'; dat's what he say to me; 'don't tell
a single soul 'bout it; and here's a quarter dollar for you.'—A quarter dollar! Did
you ebber!—He couldn't 'ford more dan dat!—But he lub money. I tell you he
does. An he kin keep wat he kin lay his finger on; he kin dat!—If he want Pam's
help, a quarter dollar won't get it. How much he 'speck Pam to do for a quarter
dollar?—A old man hug he money, 'cause if it's gone, he can't work for more. But
a young man is free-handed; not mean like dis yer one.—A quarter dollar! Indeedy!
Dog my cat!—He must tink ebryting gwine turn jess his way; he's so sure-footed.
But I hear say even de monkey kin fall from a tree."—Then Pam laughed a quiet
laugh, stretched himself, took up his staff and bundle, and trudged on along the
road which led to Guelty's stable near Glyndale.

Nine

Young ones, what do ye here, . . .
Why have your footsteps hitherward been led?

A. G. Mackey

The painter of a landscape passes by many objects within his view and groups together others to form his picture. We have delineated some devastations of the large and irresistible army of invaders who swept through the State at the close of the war; our subsequent discomfiture; the return of our footsore veterans to their impoverished homes; the hoisting up, under force of Congressional Reconstruction, the bottom rail to the top and the simultaneous disfranchisement of nearly every influential white man who had taken part in the Confederate contest for Constitutional rights. All this has been merely ancillary to a love story, the threads of which we designed to pass through these troublous incidents. We have had to omit from our picture a most important object because it was too far in the background. It would have had its prominence, had we been nigher to it. It is this:

Throughout the length and breadth of the State tens of thousands of returned Confederates were quietly attending to their farms or their merchandise, and were watching the thievish aliens at Columbia who seemed, to themselves at least, securely seated high up on the tree limbs and, like Pam's monkey, not conscious they could have a fall. But scrutinizing eyes were upon them; the eyes of the quiet men in faded gray uniforms—indistinctly visible in the background of our picture. They were awaiting the disavowal at Washington of the wrongs done in the name of Federal authority. The agents of that authority, having gained political control in the State had already gone on from peculation to undisguised spoilation, and it was reasonable to anticipate that, sooner or later, armed interference in their behalf would be withdrawn and we would see the Federal bayonets no more. The countenances of a few of the wrong-doers began to show they were uneasy at heart. Their cozened dupes, the Republican "wards"—state officials, judges, legislators, college trustees, Lunatic Asylum regents, city councillors, constabulary captains, militia Generals, and a host of civic magistrates, all of them with very little money in pocket—perceiving those few above them beginning to become anxious, began also with one accord to roll their eyes and whisper "for de Lawd sake don't leeb us."

It would be but repetition to depict affecting scenes elsewhere than in one or two localities to which the denouement of our story leads us. The poetic young man who lived near the home of Eunice said to me: "Sir, to form a conception, a deficient one at best, let the flickerings of petty tyranny radiating from the central Radical misrule at the Capital, be focused on Glyndale. Then take an image there and stamp it on every square mile within the State borders.—O, I tell you, Sir, intimations are gathering fast of a retribution from on high—and, Sir, in this same life of ours!"

Let us return to our story and to Glyndale; begging permission, however, to linger a little longer in sight of the University at Columbia.

Material enough for a chapter may be gathered from a school-marm's satchel; the one Willie Barton and his chum, the law student Harper Dillon, found in the swamp, far from the road-side in the thickest of the swamp, when once they were out gunning in the neighborhood of Columbia—before the recent occurrences. How it came where it was found is a matter of conjecture. Willie and his friend took it to their room in the college, along with their string of doves and robins which they intended as a present to an invalid Professor. After keeping the satchel a week and trying to find its owner, they brought it to me. It was not locked. The lock had been broken and the satchel was gaping open when found in the swamp. The contents were rumpled and in disorder and stained by moisture. It is likely that the satchel had been stolen, taken to the swamp, broken open, searched and rifled, and then flung into the bushes where it was found. The lady's name, if we are to determine about it from the papers and letters in the satchel, was Sallie T. Wxxx. But no such lady was known in the city; nor, so far as the young men could discover, had ever lived there. Yet undoubtedly the writer of the papers had lived in the city and for as long a time as three or four years. Could she have borne two names, her real one and a fictitious one? It is probable such was the case; and what had been written and preserved for her own use belonged to a girl or rather young lady whose identity had been made ingeniously unrevealable by any tell-tale of pen and ink. It was evident that some of the memoranda were designedly enigmatical. She alone could interpret them.

As there were in the open satchel no valuables nor papers of pecuniary importance, I did not consider it necessary to do more than have the matter mentioned in the newspapers with the hope that the owner would come for it, prove property, and take it away. This was never done. The owner may have long ago left the State. She may even have seen the newspaper article about it and preferred to relinquish rather than claim it. I would beg pardon for making use of it, in case she has any objection to my doing so; though really there ought to be (to me) no more compunction in this regard, than one would have in using an Enemy's dispatches picked up on the battlefield.—Yet in making known some of the contents I shall obscure the identification of persons discernible here and there where the writer had not, through inadvertence, completely obscured them; or I shall only hint at them under the characters assumed in this Story. Let us call the lady Miss Sallie and begin with extracts from her private Diary. The tiny little volume, the diary, had been secured in a leather case with a clasp-lock. But whoever had gotten hold of it (perhaps some negro boys), not having knowledge of the combination fastening and thinking it contained jewelry, had ripped open the leather casing.

"XXX. It is nigh on to New Year's day and I am still in this dratted place. Hope to be out of it before this time next year. Those rubicund alms-gatherers with their professions of sanctification—have bothered me to day for a contribution. Don't they know they are among the exempt? I gave them $1 when they came the second time. After all my teaching of these dinkie brats, I've sent home to Ma only $2,675. —The Committee vexed me so with their jabber and flattery I nearly forgot the bag of gold XZ brought; in behalf of a friend, of course. I must ship it for him by express tomorrow to the bank in. . . . where I sent the three other ones. Don't think it safe to keep it, even if the rumpus is over; for those little demons rummaged my desk last week and stole my breastpin—and just after I had had evening prayer with them and they had sung so sweetly. It was a darling keepsake from one who loved me and I was anxious to recover it. I had thought of keeping Z's bag in that very desk, as the least likely place for a search.

"XXXX. They couldn't trace me however they fussed about it. It was my bundle of clothes and nothing inside.—It's worth jotting down the date, for a big quarrel is going to break out between us—K and me—that there was 'sutthin purty—it shine like fire'; that's enough to hang a tale on.—Well, the sanctified ones came for another dollar to-day and invited me to a picnic. I'll go for the fun of it and my money's worth, as the school boys and girls are to be excluded this time.

"XXXX. Did you ever! the G. chucked me under the chin before I had been an hour at the picnic. What next?—I must have looked my best to-day; for I had not got from the shade of the last clump of trees when the oleaginous Rev. Dr. D.— insisted on kissing—one of his holy salutations.—XZ brought another bag, the heaviest yet. I've locked it in my portmanteau and locked that in my drawer and run big nails into the holes over the window sashes and bolted in the blinds and locked the door of my room and hooked it besides, and yet don't consider it safe. I'll slip off to Charleston in the 10 P.M. train and express it from there; the sooner, the better. And with it I'll carry his friend's 30,000 of State B's for his confidential agent in N.Y. who will send them back here to be converted into other B's. I believe this is the third time this same batch have been redeemed. I know the secret of his first getting them. They are to come in from a different quarter this time. Wonder what part XZ gets. I secured my own commission in advance. That's o.k. Ma thinks what I send her is all her poor, hardworking child can save from her salary, denying herself every comfort and risking her life! She'll be surprised some day.

"XXXX. Have recovered my breastpin. Was expostulating to the school about it, when one of the ebony brood, with plenty of white in his eyes, held up his chubby hand. 'Speak out, Trip,' I said.—'Old Miss Beemailer kin find de teef,' he cried emphatically, shaking his head sideways—a sort of horse motion—in assurance of his opinion. 'Who's she?' I asked.—'Lib up de road,' a half dozen of them sang out; and one excitedly added 'She find out wid a bible and a key, Ma'am!'

"I began to be interested and wrote a polite note to the old woman with the Germanic name and sent it by Trip. She came back with him, her sleeves rolled up and her apron covered with soapsuds, and bringing her divination implements. She said to me, 'I can do it by the shears and sieve or by making the bible turn with the key on the 18th verse of the 50th Psalm; but shall I use a shorter way.' She winked at me, then called out 'Now, you young thieves, I've no time to lose; stand round in a circle!' They all appeared mortally afraid of her. She moved deliberately around, facing them, holding the bible in front of her and a key hitched lightly on the edge of it; and muttered over and over

> By St. Peter, by St. Paul—
> By the Lord who made us all
> Fall, key, fall—O fall, key, fall!
> Thou the thief if it fall to thee,
> Thou the thief and we all free.

"I am not sure I caught her words aright. She, I thought, made the words for the occasion.—She eyed the black faces steadily as she moved, and in gazing around the second time the key dropped in front of a thirteen year old girl, a moody ill-looking specimen with a kinky mop of hair. Mrs. Beemeiler may have given the book a sleight of hand tilt. I don't know. She was full of the experiment, enjoyed the evident alarm of the pickaninnies, and said to me 'You don't know these imps, Ma'am; they all lie and steal; that one there (pointing her finger at the culprit) has your breastpin; good-day, Ma'am.' And with a laugh she went back to her washtubs.

"It was now my turn. 'Here, you Susannah Euphemia Almedia Huckins, stand before me! Where's my breastpin?'—Her eyes rolled, but her lips were pressed together as if they would never open again. I took the rod to her and at the third cut she said defiantly, 'I nebber took it—I nebber seed it—I nebber knowed you had a breastpin.'—'What,' said I, 'I've been wearing it in this room over six months and you never saw it, you abominable liar! When it was so hot the other day, didn't you see me take my collar and breastpin off and lay them on the desk? Didn't the bible and key show you took it?—Now sit in this corner till after school and I'll attend to you; see if I don't.'

"'Yes, ma'am,' sang out one of the larger boy pupils, 'dat bible is a sure thing; it bin carried three times round de grabes.'—And the key? I asked. 'Dat's sure too; it once bin a church door key, ma'am; no udder kind'll do it sure like hit will' he replied. Then twenty or thirty vociferated in confirmation of the statement, and that Mrs. Beemeiler had found out many a thief. 'Yes'm' said one of the larger girls. 'Phemy Huckins is bad, ma'am. She make it rain yisterday so we uns couldn't go and play buzzard. She not only kill a toady to bring a drizzle-drozzle, but to make it rain hebby, she hunged up a dead blacksnake onto a bush, ma'am. An if she had-der hung'd up two of um, thunder would er come wid de rain.' Again the majority joined in denunciation of the culprit, so glad they were to have suspicion shifted from themselves.

"After school when Euphemia and I were alone, I called her up. 'Susy Euphemia, where's my breastpin?' she had had time for reflection and penitence, and looking piteous said, 'Miss Sallie, come wid me.' I put on my hat and gloves and went with her, thinking she would take me to the hiding place of the breastpin, near by. But she led me to the suburbs, then through a lane, then across a field, then over two fences (and not being expert at this, I tore my dress on a splinter), then through another field to an old unused well which was covered with boards. The sun had shrunk the boards and you could see through the chinks.—'You see dat well?' she asked. 'Of course I do,' I said. 'It tumble down dat well,' was her answer as she pointed her finger at the chinks.

"'You little wretch!' I cried, seizing her by her two arms. 'Don't, Miss Sallie,' she exclaimed, 'I'se ticklish.' Then I caught hold of her mop of hair and gave her a good shaking. 'Did you bring me all the way here and make me tear my dress, just for this?' Grabbing her harder I said 'Come to Mrs. Beemeiler; she knows your lies!' I was roused now and determined to see the case out, if it took three hours.

"'Don't, please don't, ma'am, and I'll tell de trute; 'clare to gracious, I will, Miss Sallie!'—'Did it fall down this well?'—'No'm'—'Say Hope you may die'—'Hope I may die, ma'am!'—'The truth now?' 'Yes'm.'—'Come along, then; I'll try you the last time.' 'I'll take you to de breastpin, ma'am, 'clare I will.'

"So we returned by the way we came and she led me to the school house, all the way back to where we had started from. She took me to the outside of the building, to a crack in the weather-boarding, and with a thin stick she fished my breast-pin out. In order to get it into the crack this spat of the Evil One had mashed the breastpin flat! It was so angry, I marched her to her home and told her people she must not come to my school any more.

"I'm told her mother switched her; so did her father; then her uncle, a Methodist exhorter; he also prayed over her; then she stole 25 cents from a neighbor's and had a nice time on cakes and lemonade.—O, well! It's getting to be with these blacks as I know it to be with some of my white acquaintances in power here: I do wrong, you do wrong, he, she, and it do wrong; I won't tell, you won't tell, he, she, and it won't tell. And the 'it' is not herein an unimportant personal pronoun.

"XXXX. These Othelloes (O Katie, aren't you jealous?) want me to prayer meeting. I'll be jiggered if I dance that tune! I wish none of their bowing and scraping if they do wear soldier clothes and brass buttons.—The Gov. invited me to a cozy tea. Two men called and would have immediate conference with him, in the hall. I heard some talk about Ku Klux and Colonel Edmund Loyle.—I've seen that handsome fellow and would like to set my cap for him. They say he's terrible; but to me he'd coo like a dove. I first saw him at an up-country town. A rabble of yelling negroes with muskets, pistols, razors, bludgeons, were rushing to kill a man, when he came forward unarmed and faced them. They stopped still and looked at him. He raised his hand and said softly Go home! and they instantly dispersed. I could have run up and hugged that man!—I heard too that, before his lovely brown mustache began to grow, he saved from drowning a pretty school-girl whom a blundering boy had shoved off in a bateau on the Congaree river, during a picnic on its banks near the Falls. The bateau was whirling among the rocks when he swam out and, though he had no paddle, brought her safe to the bank quarter of a mile away. That's the man for me!

"XXXX. Editor of 'Christian Purity' sent ck. for last two letters. Wants a more stirring one and offers $20 if it comes up to his view. I'll get items from gov. and my old buddy Lubb, and see what horrors they can rake up for me. XXXX. Well, that's dispatched, and I told Editor I must have $25 for it or I'll hand it over to 'The Vineyard of the Lord.' That'll bring him.

"XXXX. A pretty howd'ye do! And my pet pupil in the bargain—the little mulatto with lustrous eyes—Amarilla Surcilla Sarah Ann Jane Jackson is her full name on my book—tells me she is to leave school and go as chambermaid to the Hon. Mrs. S—. I know the design of it—to send her North to Mrs. S's sister to be made a very slave of. It's downright kidnapping. I went to remonstrate and was offered $50 to say nothing about it. I took it, of course; and have kept the girl to wait on me.—A lady here asked me the other day where was my home. I told her 'When I was young, home was where mother lived; now home is wherever I can gather in most money.'

"XXX. Edith T., who has been appealing to benevolent old ladies and Church leaders petticoated and otherwise, wants me to help her write letters; says I have a knack that way. I'll keep my name out and do it if my share is secure and out of first funds to hand. Mary M.. having come into a snug little sum by her letters, started Edith on the track. She can't manipulate the sympathies; so I claim full half and leave all the responsibility to her. That Katie, thirty and a flirt!—has lost the office she expected to get. So much for calling me last year 'a red head keener.' She sees very well my hair is a delicate auburn. And I never drank too much wine by mistake walked away arm-in-arm with a brass-button constabulary, as she did, the scrawny ninkum! What brought her down South anyhow! Her kind of brains ought to stay home.

"XXX. Mem. To the Hon. the Com. tee, Miss Susan B, Mrs. L, and others of the 153d. Branch of the Female Moral Idean and Philanthropic Association: Not opportune to agitate Women's Rights here. Ladies hold to their ancestral femininity. We may start a Mothers-at-Home society and gradually work up to elective franchise. True, as you hint, most of them would remain in-doors, while every colored woman would rush to the polls.

"XX. Well, I had to—just had to; and he paid well too. The information by itself was worth it. If he will have the honor of heading epistles U.S.S., the price is fixed. To think! G. and Witt and Snibb and Truthy and John, without counting the Saint (O goody!)—and with them all I had to endure not a little impertinence; but gathered in 500. I washed off the candidate's dratted paroxysmal lip-touch (seal of solidarity, he called it) so soon as I got home. Confound his impudence! Maybe he thought he had paid for it. Edith's cousin may come here now as quick as she likes; and I'll surrender my place in the school to her for half her first year's salary, in advance. Trust nobody, is a good rule. There's something higher before me with more spondulies and less drudgery.

"XXX. I'm glad, real glad, to know Katie sprained her ankle yesterday. Would show off, with rollers, how to skate on ice. She did it on a long entry floor— holding back her gown so prettily! The remark has been made by some cynic that combined with our sympathy there is within us something not altogether unpleasurable when we hear of the calamities of our friends.—I agree to that; with no appeal to reason about the misapplied name of friendship or a lesser sort of calamities. What I say is, it'll do her good to have plenty time for reflection while she is nursing that ankle of hers into shape for another show-off. I'm a red head keener, did you say?

"XXX. I declare it's too bad! Received ck. for $40 for that big lie sent to the Vineyard of the Lord. Even Lubb laughed at my rendering of 'The Bloody Atrocity.' He knew there was no truth in it, and 'Christian Purity' wants one like it. I'm glad I didn't put in the insinuations against Colonel Loyle; so my heart has less burden upon it. I don't mind a lie or two when one doesn't see distinctly the damage done; but that man is worth a dozen Lubbs. Heigh ho!—What if that haughty Columbia lady did say of me 'she lacks indignation.' My face burned and I buried it in my hands when I heard of that cutting remark. The keeness of it is in its truthfulness. But tut-tut! My barque is launched and such insults won't check the flowing of the stream.

"XXX. Home to-night in a glow; and juged my pen into the inkstand (as I sit over my diary) till the nib is split. See the scrawl it makes!—Well, if Katie put that audacious blackamoor up to a thing like that, she'll rue it pretty soon. I know a trick for that, and have power where she least expects.—I feel like bundling up and going back; and brother would better come along with me. Something here must topple over, and we would best stand from under while we can lay claim to honesty and fair dealing. I can induce him to go after one or two good hauls. And, meanwhile, should I accept the secret offer of the Carolina patriot in N.Y. for a paper of official facts and figures?"

I could go on with pages more of these extracts; but sufficient has been given to exhibit the interesting character of the Diary. The satchel also contained letters and newspaper clippings; among the latter some amusing and some malicious "correspondence from South Carolina." The sprightliness of style in a few of these indicates Miss Sallie's authorship. What she did with letters received from others, I cannot say; kept them somewhere else? sent them home? destroyed them? she knows.

Those I examined were all from herself (copies) with enigmatical indications to whom addressed—interpretable by herself alone. I should like to see what the political intriguers said to her; but communications from them (if there were any) she did not have in the satchel. Some girls keep diaries of heart-experiences and carefully preserve all their gushing love letters. But this one meant business and was sharp enough to be piquantly pleasing both in her diary and letters. A pack of her letters, as she could write them out for us, would throw much light on Radical transactions (within her ken) during the Reconstruction period. One of the pieces under the heading "Correspondence" I shall introduce here as a specimen of the information about us sent to the North by irresponsible parties and calculated to retard the restoration of harmony between the North and the South. If editors and their correspondents wish to get to Heaven—but, pshaw!—here's the piece:

"Education, hand in hand with religion, is making rapid strides among the down-trodden here; still from this Macedon comes the cry to you, noble women of the North, to send, of your abundant means, kindly blessings which, like bread cast upon the waters, will return with refreshing to your souls. The thoughtful Editor of this Heavenly Instrument, 'Christian Purity,' will remit your benevolent donations to safe hands; and many a fervent maiden, self-expatriated to make effectual your moral mission, will extend your beaming influences to the benighted ones in this dark region of our land. How you would all rejoice to see, as I saw today, the beautiful luster of their upturned eyes;—to hear, as I heard to-day, the chorus of their sweet juvenile voices chanting anthems of Plymouth Rock and melodious Emancipation strains. No doubt your imagination catches the refrain 'Wait for the wagon, and we'll all take a ride.' Yet if I could give better frocks to the girls and have the breeches of the boys mended, it would indeed be gratifying. If a Sabbath contribution be taken up in only half a dozen churches and sent to me, the generous in-flow would be judiciously managed. The National Freedman's Bureau does not reach our needs in this particular.

"For the older ones, also, help is sadly wanting. The wicked Ku Klux raids have deprived many an aged colored friend—our friends—of daily sustenance. And shall it be said 'For them no sheltering roof; for them no hearth-stone; for them no humble couch? shall the peltings of the pitiless storm come over them, and torrents of rain and lightning flashes—and not a shingle to avert the engulfing deluge?'—No, friends of humanity, No! To you we appeal not in vain! Even here, so far off here, I seem to turn my ear to your charitable response and the resonance of unmeasured gifts into the Missionary Box, the coins drop one by one.

"There was a distressing case in this neighborhood, some seventeen miles from the Capitol. You may well say, with England's favorite poet,

> Drops of compassion tremble on my eyelids,
> Ready to fall, as soon as you have told your
> Pitiful Story.[1]

"Not a grey-haired sire, but yet an ignorant one, if he was sturdy; and why ignorant? Because he had never had the advantages of instruction—pressed by gnawing hunger, had taken from a rebel farmer a sheep and a pig;—and who, under the circumstances, would not?—and with a couple of friends (dear name of friendship!) had gone into the forest to feast upon them. They were pursued and the half-eaten viands ruthlessly snatched from them. They swiftly escaped. That very night the brutal Ku Klux surrounded their rural cabins, dragged them forth and whipped them; and because a colored woman, staying with one of the victims, cursed the attacking monsters and fired a gun at them whilst inflicting the stripes, they whipped her too! She of the gentler sex! Where is Whittier, to write a poem against these Southern monsters! Had they no thought of their own sisters and mothers? Should not the entire force of our army and navy be invoked to put a stop to such outrages?

"The Governor's Constabulary, an imposing body of mounted negro police—and those colored men, dressed in bright regimentals, do look handsome on horseback—arrested fifty-seven of the white farmers, and as there was no lack of sworn testimony to prove that fifty-three of the miscreants were in the Ku Klux band, they were put in prison and will be tried in the United States Court. They had men on their side to swear that the three citizens they whipped did more than help themselves to food;—they had (they swore) set a dwelling house on fire; but, of course, not one of our magistrates would give credence to so malicious a falsehood. The house which was burnt was merely a rebel's house. Your correspondent would be happy to have at least one hundred fifty dollars sent through the Editor

---

1. George Canning, "The Friend of Humanity and the Knife-Grinder," 1797.

for presents to the suffering martyrs of so foul a conspiracy against the sacred rights of our common citizenship.

"Another case—but shall I go on? Hath not the sympathetic heart bled enough to-day? What says the inspired Whittier—

> And when the bondman's chain is riven,
> And swells from all our guilty coasts
> The anthem of the free.

Yes, from this specially guilty coast, every rock and sandhill of it, made guilty by two centuries of serfdom! And how can that anthem swell as it ought to swell, unless their stomachs be full,—those you yourselves have set free? Unless the backs be covered with raiment; those you yourselves have saved from the lash? Unless the soul be soothed to raise its Ebenezer?—And money alone can do that. Talking of whipping; why, I've heard that in slavetimes they lashed grown men if they refused to pick cotton; and when remonstrated with had the audacity to sing that British abomination

> If I had a donkey what wouldn't go,
> Don't you think I'd wallop him? No, no, no!

We wheedled them however out of the advantages of the cotton. That's a consolation. We knew how to make the right thing happen!—But I was going to tell of another case of inhumanity.

"This other case I refer to is frightful, perhaps more so than the last. It was told to me by Lubb himself, and I give it on his authority. Would you believe it—two colored citizens were accused (erroneously, mind you)—were even said to have been caught in the act, of kidnapping a little white boy; one of the poor buckra class, whose dad and uncles and all his male relatives old enough to go to war (oh, they were a vicious set!) had shot many a cursed bullet against us, perhaps killed some of our men—these two colored citizens, as I said, were accused of voodooism; of worshipping a serpent. (They may have been Obi-Men as they call them in the West Indies.) It was declared they were taking the child, as a calf without horns, to be sacrificed on an altar in an almost inpenetrable recess of a swamp (Hell Hole Swamp is the name of it, I am told), to dance and howl around him in this almost inaccessible spot, then to stick the child's neck with a knife and mix his blood with rum or whisky, which they would drink till frenzy seized them—women as well as men. All this while a muffled drum would be beating. The calf without horns was then to be cooked and devoured with frantic howls and rushing about and horrid debauch of cannibalism. Well—the two men did have the little boy and he was crying bitterly; they were caught in the woods with him. But they declared he had wandered out there and became lost, and they intended to carry him to his home. This must have been the truth. Yet the Ku Klux demons came upon these benevolent creatures that night, took them to the woods, tied them up to trees, and forced them to confess they were voodoos and were going to eat the child, and had eaten one that was missing the year before. What is a confession worth, that was forced from them? Then they whipped them unmercifully and undertook to make them leave the State, under escort of their own fellow conspirators; concealing them by day and passing them by night from Ku Klux band to Ku Klux band. But the Constabulary was on the lookout and came upon the Ku Klux who, by this time, had got their poor victims a hundred miles up the country. A conflict ensued. Three of the mounted negro constables were badly wounded, Lubb tells me; and the voodoo men having been given weapons by the constables and told to fight for their liberty, began to do so, and were both killed. Some say the negro constables, being a little confused and firing wildly about at the Ku Klux (who could make themselves invisible, so Lubb says) accidentally killed the voodoos. Others say that the Ku Klux did it; and this I believe. The fight was, you may say, in the dark; except for the glimmering starlight; and when it ended (I mean the fight) not a Ku Klux was there; nor any sign or sound of them. The only sound was the dismal hooting of owls; and the hooting seemed to come from every tree. The constabulary fled,— for they thought a thousand witches were in the forest—and did not go back to get their wounded comrades till sun-rise next morning.

"And now what do you think? Why, the old Carolinians, the ex-rebels, (if there can be any ex in the case), are going to call a Convention of their own. To put down the diabolical Ku Klux, do you ask?—Not a bit of it—but to show by facts and figures (when they meet 3 months hence) that the Northerners now in power here, have been systematically pilfering and cheating, and playing havoc with the State credit under cover of legislation. They have suggested an Investigating Committee on Public Printing; an Investigating Committee on State Bank Bills; an Investigating Committee on Rail Road Bonds; an Investigating Committee on Taxes and on other special matters, and on Republican rascality in general; and expect to send a grand Special Committee to General Grant to show him what is doing here. I'm willing to bet he'll kick them out, or very near it, if they intrude their dirty hoofs within the honored threshhold of our White House at Washington.

"Now, as I said, we philanthropists have much to do in teaching the dear colored children and elevating the national wards to their exalted level of intelligent manhood suffrage—the grandest work the sun shines on—and we need money. If within twenty days a thousand or two, (the more, the better), could be placed in my hands, I would know what to do with it. In the meanwhile, let our gifted writers, to home continue to make negro characters, dear Uncle Toms and the like, prominent in literature; let them be, as they have been, examples of virtue, noble martyrs, courageous heroes. We and some few English people are the only ones on earth to give them their true representation. We'll reap the benefit of it in their allegiance to us when it comes to National politics." (Signed S-).

It would fatigue my readers, were I to extend further this compilation from the satchel. So I shall follow up the half-hidden vestigia of only one other subject, in so far as it has a bearing on the Story we are telling; and put what I find, or think I find, in my own words; reconstructing the disjoined memoranda and interpreting what is enigmatical, according to my conception.—It appears that the Honorable Mr. Guelty attempted to secure Miss Sallie's services in a scheme of his own. She was known to more than her brother in the XXX office, and to the head of that department and to the governor and honest John and the astute speaker of the House and other officials; for she was an active, shrewd little diplomatist, with finesse and strategy lurking in smiles and dimples. She retained, however, one spot of her heart true to its womanly excellence. She was a bright one among the School Marms (as they were generally called), a heterogeneous swarm; a few of whom, we must honestly say, were hard-working and sincere agents of a spasmodic philanthropy, the intention of which was good, but its task far greater than it could possibly accomplish.

The Honorable Mr. Guelty had met her at some semi-official "tea parties," and admired her talents, and supposed he could purchase their use at his own paltry terms of remuneration. "Miss Sallie," he said to her, in an undertone, at one of these coterie entertainments, "if your valuable time could be spared to do The Party a service in missionary work, to whom would you look for direction and emolument?"

"Not to the party with a capital T," she replied; "the Association which first sent me here is the only Abstraction I have dealt with—abstraction of that kind, I mean; and my connection with it is in name and nothing more. I have learned to look for direction and emolument to personal embodiments engaging my services—to the substantial, producing substantials. What sort of mission is it?"

"Educational and religious and akin to your useful labors here."

"Fudge!" she said, "tell me the real business."

"That must come in as a consequence; preparations must be made for it. At present it is solely as I have stated it."

"Then," said she, "I can give you a week, if it pays. And prepayment is my rule; with the reserved right to stop short of success, wherever the visible success indicates an augmented value to my part in the performance; and I'll hold the prospective issue in abeyance, to modify, retard, or render it nugatory, if the terms I then dictate are not instantly complied with. I'm frank and exacting too—am I not?— I've won success sometimes where others reaped all the benefit."

"Even so, Miss Sallie," replied Guelty, "and I shall be equally candid and tell you the whole gist of the scheme. Surely, it will serve the party, with or without your capital T, to have a foothold for observation or, if you choose the expression, for surveillance, if a school for colored children be established at Glyndale; and if one so circumspect as you are shall take up temporary residence there to inaugurate the school."

"What sort of place is Glyndale and who lives there?" asked the "red head keener," as Miss Katie offensively dubbed her.

Guelty was puzzled by the sudden question, and his unreadiness—his mental hesitancy—to answer it was instantly detected by the young lady who, so soon as he had broached the subject had conceived that the benevolent mission he hinted at covered up some secret design of his own. But he replied within ten seconds:

"The place is in the country; and if I must tell you my hidden motive, Colonel Loyle lives there, and we would like to watch him. Mr. Troth says he is a leader of the Ku Klux and we wish to prove it."

She had not removed her penetrating look from his face, and asked "Who else?"

"Well—" he replied, "the Peltons, Fairbanks, Norants, Gillespie, Averys, and others live there; and a blustering young fellow named Barton is often there; and there is, I believe, a widow with something like a French name which escapes me at present."

"And who else?" she persisted.

"O, as to that, the rest are chiefly negroes," he replied.

She thought to herself "The jaunt will be a recreation, furnish matter for a newspaper letter, and show that I am alive in the good work." Then she responded:

"I have no objection to go there, Mr. Guelty, and examine the suitableness of the place for an extension of the charity of one of the special church associations with which I am *en rapport* as you French people express it—you who can't remember French names; and isn't your own name, Guelty, a French name?—However, I will give a week to the examination you wish for two hundred dollars—and my expenses and an honorarium (say ten dollars) to my temporary substitute in the school here; and I go only because there is no pressing extra business in my charge at this particular time"

"Very well," said Guelty although his soul sank within him at the mention of so much more than he was willing to give—"tomorrow morning at eight o'clock I shall call at your house. The afternoon's train takes you to Glyndale in a few hours; and I will give you a letter which will assure you accommodation at the Post Master's, who is a friend of mine and at whose house I have a furnished room for myself or any one bearing a letter from me. His house is near the Depot, which will be convenient for you and he keeps a buggy in which his son can drive you about in your investigations."

Though Guelty was worth fully fifty thousand dollars, yet to pay Miss Sallie the two hundred she demanded sent a thrill of anguish through his whole system. He could not, however, gain her services otherwise. When he left her he said to himself, "I shall have to make this up in the next transaction with my friends."

Miss Sallie reached Glyndale; and she was not at all squeamish as to making her temporary home in the domicile of a negro, nor as to sitting at meals with him and his family. She came South to do such things. If a thing "didn't pay" she wouldn't do it; if it did, she would. The first question she put to the Post Master, after having refreshed herself, was "Who lives here?" The ready answer was "The DeLeslines."

"Are they the most prominent people?"—"Yes, Ma'am, dey rank on de top."

The Post Master's wife added "de vary tip-top, Miss; everybody knows dem."

It seemed strange to Miss Sallie that Guelty had forgotten their name. "Does Mr. Guelty know them?" she asked the Post Master.

"I tink he ought to, Ma'am," responded the Post Master. Then checking himself in a matter relating to his patron's affairs, he appended to his hasty response the words, "but I can't say, Ma'am, because I disremember dat he ever speak to me about dem." He may know them very well, for all that, Miss Sallie thought; but she said nothing.

She did not spend the whole week at Glyndale. She examined, however, into the feasibility of establishing a new mission school. She concluded it was not worth the trouble and expense. The population was too sparse; the whites as well as blacks too poor. A ten cent piece was a big coin to the negroes there. They held out their hands to her for pennies. She disliked that; always did. No gold or silver jutted up from that soil; no greenbacks floated in that atmosphere. All this she saw at once, and was disappointed; but she got in the buggy and went to work; called openly on all the families; made known her object and discussed it with them. She was courteously treated, and the benevolent feature of the Mission commended. No one had any objection to the education of the negroes, young or old.—She was more than once at the DeLeslines' and at the Parsonage. She listened with apparent interest to Mrs. DeLesline's rehearsal of genealogies. She had long talks with Eunice and fell in love with her. She mentioned Mr. Guelty's name, but Eunice did not know him; had heard of him as a preacher to the negroes, but had never seen him.

Miss Sallie was so charmed with Eunice that on her return she could not sufficiently praise her to Mr. Guelty. She noticed his confusion and thought she understood it, and that his ulterior object was to establish the Mission school at Glyndale, in which Eunice would be sure to take an interest; and he, being its promoter, would visit it at times, and might in this way be brought into pleasant acquaintance with her. This was Miss Sallie's conception of his scheme and his willingness to pay for the trip she had made to Glyndale. The police espionage on Colonel Loyle may have had a modicum of truth in it—but it was not the main underlying design. The putting it forward as Guelty had done, was in keeping with his usual "candid" confession of his motives.

Miss Sallie's interpretation, though in the right direction, was still off the track; and it was off the track even when, shortly after this, he consulted her about her writing to Eunice to invite her to take a ride (by a route he would mark out) to an adjacent out-of-the-way country place under her (Miss Sallie's) care, to help found a school there; inasmuch as her (Eunice's) advice and guidance would be of great value towards the realization of so benevolent an object. But Guelty tried without success to induce Miss Sallie to write to Eunice on this subject. "No," said she, "I cannot see my way clear in any such project as that."

She understood her own position in the State; that she was regarded as an adventuress "lacking indignation"; that many of her class of Northern School marms had made themselves obnoxious to the Carolinian ladies; and she could not be persuaded to write a letter on a benevolent or any other subject to Miss Eunice DeLesline.

If Miss Sallie's valuable time had not been taken up with other demands upon it, she would have probed Guelty's plans, however shrewdly he covered them up. Her astuteness was fully a match for his;—his was like an owl's, hers was like a needle's. But her proclivities were not in the direction of his. There was no viciousness nor vindictiveness in her heart, and if she had been "caught young" and brought down to live among us, her brightness of intellect would have made her one of the foremost of our many ardent and loveable Southern women of Northern birth. She was not of the Benjamin Isaiah stamp nor of the Miss Katie stamp. She had already seen through Isaiah's pretensions to piety and philanthropy; and would soon have unraveled his plot so far as Glyndale was concerned. His last proposal to take Eunice with her in that benevolent founding of another school for colored children and to go on a route of his selection, excited her curiosity; and it was fortunate for Guelty that Miss Sallie was immediately and completely engaged in steering a high official's leaky little boat through the billows of a threatening storm and for a remuneration far above the paltry pay of so stingy a fellow as the Honorable Benjamin Isaiah. She had asked herself, What meant that glimpse of suppressed subtlety when he spoke about Eunice? How could that selected route through the woods with Eunice, implicate Colonel Loyle or have any reference to him or bring any disaster to him, supposing him to be the chief object aimed at in that quarter? Yet that he is the chief object to others, I know from intimations of a conspiracy which I have gathered up by indirect questionings of some leaders in The Party?

Guelty miscalculated when he thought of engaging such a young woman as Miss Sallie to aid him in any such scheme as was lurking in his heart. He miscalculated also in thinking he could hire any such young lady for espionage on a gentleman like Edmund Loyle.—Miss Sallie had recently met in Columbia her "handsome Colonel," as she called him, and would have liked to speak with him if she could have done so without the knowledge of those in whose service she was; a service well paid for and promising still greater pay. She contented herself, therefore, with a secret determination to write to him anonymously, if she should find out any positive peril with which he should be environed, and to give him timely warning to take care of himself.

Having put down some words in commendation of Miss Sallie, I shall close this chapter with a few more kindly words by saying that among my most valued friends were one from Massachusetts and one from Vermont; and I still cherish their memories. One of them must have had a father from whom he inherited his own probity and practical usefulness. In speaking of him once he said "My father lived in a small town, and lived there all his life, and had an enemy or rather an un-friend who lived near by him; a rich man, with whom he had not spoken for twenty years. They passed each other as perfect strangers. Yet when that enemy or un-friend died, he left my father sole executor of his estate." Such men as my Northern friends we could get along harmoniously with for a thousand years. But save us from the sort that flocked down upon us so soon as we lay prostrate; and bayonets were held at our throats! In speaking against some of this class, we have in our hearts no diminution of respect and admiration for the noble men of the North who would, I have no particle of doubt, denounce these fellows worse than I have done.

The finding of Miss Sallie's satchel by Willie Barton and his friend, had preceded by some weeks the Ku Klux occurrence in the University Campus, and its sad issue to Uncle Tim; which was one of the "fateful consequences" of that injudicious frolic.

The conspiracy against Barton and Colonel Loyle, begun in St. Julian's dining room, was not left to weaken through inaction. Troth was by nature more strenuous in revenge than Guelty. The latter's policy was to watch and wait. He would catch a fly as a spider does. The former would dart at it like a lizard. The sod was still fresh on the Thomleigh grave; old Pam had not yet reached his home; when Guelty was sought out by Troth for a second consultation.

"What does the governor say," inquired Troth, "of Federal help?"

"Everything satisfactory. We'll soon have troops to do our bidding." responded Guelty, "you may prepare your scheme accordingly. My own private plans have been formed. I don't inquire into your ulterior designs. You'll not inquire into mine. We'll do nothing to thwart each other. You can't expect our agreement to go further than that."

"If chance favors," said Troth a little impatiently, "you'll help my plans with as much strength as if they were your own and shield me from any judicial consequences with all your influence?"

"Yes—if you refund any pecuniary outlay or any damage occasioned on your behalf."

Troth walked up and down the room they were in, thinking whether such reparation might not empty his entire pocket into Guelty's. Either would cheat the other at the first opportunity. Both knew this. Their hatred of Loyle and Barton was their only bond of union in their nefarious scheming. Each had already, before this union, been carrying out his own separate scheme. Guelty had admitted the less powerful partner into a seemingly common hunt for vengeance, because he supposed he could make some money for himself out of Troth. If money did not come of the alliance, he would abandon his colleague as quick as wink. The occurrence in the Campus, the dreadful tarring and swinging up of Guelty (charged against Ku Klux, whether the genuine Klan was in it or not) formed a pivot on which to wheel their ordnance and direct their shot.—Let us now go back to the time of this occurrence, or a little later, to the time when Eunice was to return from her visit in Columbia to her home at Glyndale.

Already the counties had been penetrated in every direction by emissaries of the party in power. In many places the emotional nature of the ignorant freedmen had been acted upon regardless of the danger which might spring out of their irrational excitement. What cared the carpetbag rulers?—all they cared for was to remain some years longer with their hands in the State treasury.—Yes, all the counties had been penetrated; from the island-studded seacoast of Beaufort, Charleston and Georgetown, up through the lowland plains to the cascade ridges of the interior and onward still to the piedmont hills of Greenville and Oconee. And the object in every direction was to control the negro vote in favor of the carpetbaggers and scalawags.

Ten

Like some fair barque, whose prow hath wooed the wave
Which leaps in maddening surges on the shore
Where foam-crowned eddies lure her to her grave—
Yet still hath borne her proudly on her way
Though tempests rage and billows roar and swell.

G. H. Sass

In the attempt to reconstruct the State by Congressional interference and military force, the plain truth was ignored that it requires a long time, a life-time or more, to reverse established habits of thought and action throughout a community. The interference, irritating in itself, involved the instantaneous lifting up of an unqualified inferior race to the political level of a proud superior race. And this we looked upon as a premeditated degradation of ourselves. Our conquerors, moreover, were actuated by the motive of permanent party supremacy for an indefinite period; and that meant the unimpeded power of taxation for sectional aggrandisement. We believed they covered these designs under the humanitarian—or rather pseudo-philanthropic—pretenses for which they claimed the world's admiration; an admiration they are still claiming in newspapers, magazines, sermons, addresses and gilt-edged volumes of poetry and in monumental inscriptions. Their claims need indeed this incessant bolstering up. We simply say "Truth crushed to earth will rise again; the eternal years of God are hers,"[1] as one of their own poets was inspired to write as to the judgment of impartial history; the judgment respecting the requirements enjoined by the National legislature for the re-admission of the seceding states into the Union and respecting the gathering in of "the results" of "the rebellion." We are presenting in this story but a small part of all this and we come now to a deplorable portion of that small part, slightly connected with the suppression

---

1. William Cullen Bryant, "The Battlefield."

of the so-called Ku Klux Klan. It is not wonderful that the stimulating of the newly enfranchised black voters to continuous political activity for party purposes, stimulated also sentiments and sporadic outbreaks of race hostility; the wonder is that is did not end in worse effects. It was only by the admirable endurance of the white citizens and through the mercy of God that utter desolation was averted.

So far as the ensuing chapters touch upon the subjects here referred to, they present but a semblance of realities. We are painting a picture, not compiling a history. And we are conscious that the picture is painted with splenetic dashes here and there; for the shadow of a raven flock seems hovering overhead. A raven flock? —nay, vultures—harpies—"pedibus circumvolant uncis."[2]

Winchester rifles of the best pattern had been purchased by those foisted into authority, and several quotas of state arms furnished by the U.S. (to wit, "10,000 Springfield muskets") were repaired and renewed as a job with pecuniary gain to the unscrupulous contrivers of the plot, who seemed not to care if the result should be the bitter irritation of one part of the people against the other; a condition of affairs which had brought Colonel Loyle to the conference with the State officials. The only good the deluded "citizens of African descent" derived from the pretty weapons and distribution of cartridges was a holiday parade to the music of battered drums and some wild practice at the target. The cotton fields were left to take care of themselves. The new "milish," some without shoes, could stand at the fence —O what a delight!—and grin at the quiet ex-Confederates and their sons toiling to keep the crops from grass. Meanwhile all had to live; and all were not industrious nor honest. Nightly depredations continued on sheep, hogs, poultry, barns and store-houses. If the owners took justice into their own hands (the laws being ineffective), they imperiled the lives of their families. In one instance, the unjust demand of a "ward of the Nation" not being complied with, he deliberately walked to the pasture and shot down a valuable Durham bull; and the ex-Confederate thought it prudent to submit to the outrage. No doubt a Winchester cartridge had come into use in this case.

In many localities as well as at Glyndale, reckless bands, excited for political ends, paraded with weapons furnished them by the party in power. Sometimes with foul-mouthed oaths they stopped carriages on the highways. They even threatened to "kill from de cradle to de grabe." In several parts of the State collisions between the Whites and negroes occurred notwithstanding our self-repression; for it was our policy as well as natural inclination to keep on friendly terms with our former slaves. So soon as counter organizations began to be formed for self protection, the cry of Ku Klux was raised; the general government at Washington was (perhaps) deceived in respect to them; the aliens in possession of the State called for Federal

2. Virgil, *Aeneid* 3.233. "The Harpies fly around with their barbed feet."

aid; the aid came; horsemen were sent rushing with clanking sabres among the poor farmers, breaking up peaceful households, surrounding farmhouses with cordons of sentries and letting the mean minions of injustice search through every chamber and under every bed for the "disloyal" whom a spiteful Scipio or Hannibal chose to hint "mought be one of dem Coo-Cux." No country can furnish a more detestable picture of oppressive tyranny than was endured at this time in the Prostrate State. Many and many a good citizen preferred the re-establishment of military rule to this Reconstruction tyranny; preferred to go back into a "Military District No 2."

The valorous Fert was authorized to ferret out the Ku Klux and crush out incipient rebellion. With the help of gubernatorial constabulary and having at his beck the bright sabres of soldiers who were obliged to obey but who blushed to let the sun glitter upon them in a cause like this—he scoured the region about Glyndale. Rewards were offered by the colored legislators to harrow up the disloyal, which designation pointed in some instances to their former masters. In many places crops lay neglected in the fields, the owners being imprisoned under heavy charges. Disloyalty (disloyalty to what?) must be eradicated. Martial law prevailed. We submitted—what else could we do?—There was at Glyndale a strange stillness—as of desolation. White men walked about with compressed lips. A half-heathenish gibberish of the "man and brother" was all which greeted the conquering marshal and his nephew and deputy on many a weed-encumbered farm which had formerly bloomed like a garden. Strong men who had braved death as soldiers on dozens of battle fields and who could have wrung the neck of Fert and his deputy as if they were chickens, submitted to all this for the sake of peace. They knew that in the political and social fabric black threads crossed white threads everywhere. Defenceless women and children, their natural defenders slain, were living all around them. The men therefore submitted, lest the upper and nether millstones should begin to grind: and they should be brought again in conflict with the Government to which they had recently laid down their arms. Some few—and can we be astonished at it?—being of the class threatened with the Penitentiary if they formed any unauthorized military association—were roused to retaliation and may have formed associations simply as a means of defence, to ward off or intimidate the more reckless and incendiary negroes by frightening them or taking away the loaded weapons hid in their huts—those weapons the alien party furnished them to overcome the humble white people. If any but inconsiderate young men were engaged in these so called Ku Klux raids—think you they would have pursued a course of such mummery as this? What was it but a frolic devoid of wise foresight, when recently the Winchester rifles were gathered in near Glyndale—when the moon was full—the time at which Barton had been summoned to be present? Some terrified "wards of the Nation" fled with woful appeals for safety, to the Chief Magistrate; who thinking his time might come next, ("the wicked flee when no man pursueth"),[3] had a company of Federal soldiers at bivouac close by his mansion, that his precious eyelids might not be distressingly open, but sweet dreams might continue to hover over his soft couch—dreams of Five-twenties and of oceans of floating greenbacks. With the tramp of soldiers and the clattering of arms the "harrowing" was thoroughly begun and arrests were made in every direction. The President (Grant) had proclaimed martial law over nine counties of the state. Six hundred citizens were arrested and put in jail. Then followed the Judiciary machinery to arraign and send the victims to their doom. A crushing out of the little bugbear was achieved and Cuffee went on eating stolen sheep and hogs; his wrongs redressed and his hunger eased, his old master in jail and philanthropy pleased.

But we must take our readers back to a point of time before all these consequences had come to pass, when the fermentation of them had just set in. We must go back to the day after the swinging up of Benjamin Isaiah and which brought alarm to the Governor and his associates. What happened then to the Lieutenant in sequence of that escapade, we have already told about. Let us now return to that time and tell of the happenings to his Glyndale friends.—The night of Guelty's ignominious treatment had not quite changed to daylight and he was still smarting under his injuries, when two of his Black Rosettes were detailed to hurry towards Glyndale, watch for Barton whom he suspected, and keep him under surveillance. These emissaries carried with them a flask of whiskey and partook thereof and became pugnacious; and meeting some young white men on the road threatened obstreperously to "kill from de cradle to de grabe." The pugnacious ones were roughly handled, and being let go, ran off to stir up their malevolent confreres in the neighborhood to help them wreak their revenge.

Colonel Loyle was of course ignorant of this occurrence—in fact it had not all been accomplished—when he set out homeward with Eunice by the afternoon train. Barton had met them at the Railroad Station and, as we narrated, had returned to the University and gone home with Uncle Tim southward.—The cars, northward bound, having proceeded some fifty miles, stopping now and then for wood fuel and water and to take in passengers in the usual slow way of Southern trains—began at length to encounter groups of the excited malcontents. At times stones were thrown against the cars. At last a pistol or rifle ball (a Winchester?) smashed the glass of the ladies' coach and passed through the other side. When within ten miles of the station near Glyndale, about twilight, at a curve of the road, three rapid shrill whistles from the engine startled the ear; then followed instantly the crash of the engine and of the forward cars and a vibration, thumping and wrenching aside of the car in which Eunice and Colonel Loyle were seated; the lady passengers uttered shriek after shriek; the car lurched and was evidently going over the embankment. The Colonel comprehending the situation in a second, said in a

3. Proverbs 28:1.

calm voice "cling firmly to my arm, Eunice," and placing his left arm around her waist he rose steadily with the upheaving car and grasping with his right hand the bench on which he had been seated, lifted her and placed his feet upon the ceiling of the car just as it settled down the embankment. To force open the door and bear Eunice to the grassy hillside beyond the reach of further danger was the work of a moment. With a quiet smile he placed in her hand a bouquet which Lieutenant Barton had brought to the cars for her that afternoon.—"This fell from your hand, Eunice," he said. "And dropped into my bosom in our sudden pirouette. Stay here while I render help yonder. Wait for me, Eunice, till I come to you."—Composed, yet blushing deeply, with more than thanks in her look and with a tone he had never heard in her voice before she answered "I will wait till you come to me." In an instant he had plunged amidst the debris and the confused, struggling mass of human beings, directing, encouraging, extricating children and ladies or bearing the wounded tenderly to beds formed of the cushions from the cars. We need not enter into a minute description of the disastrous scene. The imagination of the reader can form a picture of the horrors and distresses of the sudden catastrophe.

Lubb now made his appearance, all right. He had a knack of coming up in that condition whatever wrong he was engaged in. Being all right himself in the disaster, he was not making any exertion to set others so. He appeared a little dazed and kept looking at Eunice who stood alone and serene where Colonel Loyle had placed her; serene as a statue excepting the changing color of her cheek while she watched her deliverer in his benevolent ministrations to the helpless and wounded.

Lubb had closely dogged both Barton and Colonel Loyle before the train started from Columbia that afternoon. He had "shadowed" them about the platform and the ticket office and appeared to glance ever and anon at Barton's hands. Colonel Loyle was led to do the same and observing some tar on Barton's wrist, took an opportunity (while Lubb was talking aside to another detective) to caution him to draw on his gloves; for Barton had told him of the last night's deed and had been sternly reproved for engaging in it. While Barton was left in Columbia to the management of Guelty and of Lubb's subordinates in the city, he himself had followed Colonel Loyle. He watched him and all with whom he conversed at the various stations on the road. He had been, as we before said, secretly hired by Troth for this special espionage of the Colonel. But his eyes, during the journey, were always wandering from him to Eunice; back of whom he was sitting in the corner of the car.— Can we fall in love at first sight? Unaccountably, involuntarily, *fall* in love, as from an unobserved precipice down to Elysian plains? Or has Cupid golden-tipped arrows, in truth, which transfix the heart in the twinkling of an eye and then, alas! "haeret lateri letalis harundo."[4] Can such a nature as Lubb's be susceptible to tender

4. Virgil, *Aeneid* 4.73. Dido is portrayed as a deer wounded by the arrow of her passion for Aeneas. "The lethal arrow [Dido's passion for Aeneas] sticks in her side."

impressions or kindle with ecstatic emotions that he should dare look upon so pure loveliness and not retire abashed? Pan and his crew may fall down and worship the laughter-loving Venus; dare they offer incense to Diana? Would not Belial flee from a Cecilia or Catharine where beauty, though it fascinate the eye, is ever illumed with beams of angelic innocence? Without analyzing the emotions of Lubb, certain it is that he was infatuated as much as Guelty had long continued to be. He now could watch nobody else. He had even the courage—it was not strictly speaking, impudence, impertinence, effrontery, it was a kind of respectful courage—to come and stand before her. Her bouquet had fallen at her feet, the expression on her face as her gaze followed Colonel Loyle was one of rapture, the disorder of her hair and robes giving her even an additional charm; and she stood at that moment the impersonation of a loveliness rarely seen. Lubb scarcely knowing what he was doing approached nearer and nearer as if irresistibly drawn to converse with her. Colonel Loyle whose glance seemed everywhere, came up at this moment and said to Lubb, "just as the cars were thrown from the track I noticed two men, both wearing slouch hats, in the forest over there, making off. I took them to be negroes. Summon some men from this crowd and pursue them without delay. The first house you will reach is Captain Logan's; tell him your purpose; give him my name; he will furnish you guides and assist you. It is your public duty. Go at once."—With a bow of acquiescence which he could not but make and a curse in his heart which he durst not utter, Lubb obeyed.

By the time assistance arrived from the nearest stations Captain Logan had come to the scene of disaster with his buggy. Colonel Loyle anticipating the anxiety of Mrs. DeLesline who was expecting her daughter, accepted the offer of Captain Logan's buggy to convey Eunice home directly across the country. This might be done in an hour. He left the care of the baggage to his friend till he could send to his house for it next morning.

Being apprised by Logan, when out of Eunice's hearing, of the excitement against the so-called Ku Klux and the afternoon's disturbance in the neighborhood (instigated by certain negroes who had come up from Columbia); and being convinced that the obstructions placed upon the Railroad track were due to the exasperation of the colored people, he willingly accepted the pair of revolvers which Captain Logan offered him.

With pleasant and encouraging chat the Colonel and Eunice soon entered the forest road. After riding about five miles familiar scene after familiar scene came to Eunice's view in the dim and darkening landscape. At a turn in the road she at length perceived the lighted dwellings at Glyndale and near at hand the shadowy outline of a little Gothic chapel.—Was that a scream which dismally reached her ear?—"Colonel—stop!" she whispered.—"Was that the voice of poor Helen? From the direction of the grave-yard. Listen!"—Yes, again a scream as if from one whose mouth was being gagged or whose breath was been stopped by some one's hand.

"Eunice, remain here a moment. Take the reins and—this pistol. Keep it cocked —so—and if you need me, fire it."

It was indeed poor cousin Helen. She had come at an untimely hour, as she often did, to strew fresh roses which she had been gathering till twilight, upon "her Robert's" grave. A band of the turbulent freedmen ready for infliction of any insult and injury upon the whites, had been consulting about their grievances near by the graveyard and had followed her and laid hold upon her. Colonel Loyle leaped in among them. At his command "Scoundrels, let go!"—three or four strapping fellows rushed upon him. The others fled, but unfortunately in the direction where Eunice was waiting. Felled to the earth among the graves by an unexpected blow which hit him at disadvantage, Colonel Loyle at the same time heard the report of Eunice's pistol and saw uplifted clubs over him. "Knock his brains out and bury him right here!" his assailants cried. Two of them struck together at his head as he lay upon the ground near a tombstone. In the dim light of the graveyard and their own confusion and the turning of one of the clubs by the tombstone, the simulta- neous blows failed of their object—one club smiting against the other; the weaker one splintering and flying from the hand of the would-be murderer. Before the other's club could again descend Colonel Loyle had raised his pistol and shattered the arm that wielded it and sprung to his feet. The assailants startled by the shot and the scream of the man who was hit, fled and clambered over the brick wall of the graveyard. Without delay the Colonel was at the side of the distracted and moaning Helen. Gently assisting her he said "Helen, follow me—come, follow me!" She did. But as he jumped the wall in the direction in which he had left Eunice and eager to reach her, his leg was caught by a muscular hand and he was beset by half a dozen furious and yelling negroes. The attack was renewed upon him with clubs and razors; and one who appeared the leader pointed a musket at him. Placing himself against the brick wall, he fired upon the leader and he fell—his musket exploding as he touched the ground. Notwithstanding this the crowd still pressed upon him.

But what of Eunice? Scarcely had she been left seated in the buggy when the horse's head was seized by one of those who had run from the graveyard. The dis- charge of her pistol which Colonel Loyle had heard, had been aimed at the hand which grabbed the bridle, and the horse dashing forward the buggy which struck her assailant to the ground. The horse being an old army horse was not so much affrighted as excited to a nerve power which propelled him whithersoever the intel- ligent hand that guided him willed him to go. Eunice had no thought of deserting the scene of conflict. The horse had carried her several hundred paces from the spot where she had been left. Skillfully turning the Church corner she wheeled the buggy into the path she was familiar with, round the Church enclosure and to the spot where Colonel Loyle was defending himself. Like Bellona in her war chariot she thundered with the impetuous horse and rattling buggy abruptly down upon the dark group facing Colonel Loyle, firing into them as she approached. At this moment Helen, who had in her excitement managed to climb upon the graveyard wall, rose erect upon it, her white robes and long black hair fluttering round her, and with an unearthly maniac scream clapped her hands again and again, then leaping up from the wall sank fainting to the earth.

"Lawd hab mercy! Lawd sabe us! De Coo-Cux! De sperrits from de grabes!" burst from the swarthy horde; and dropping their weapons they broke into precipitate flight.

The horse was guided by Eunice to the spot where Helen lay insensible. He was firmly reined in, snorting and pawing the ground, while Colonel Loyle lifted the dead-like form in his arms and placed it in the buggy. "Take hold of Helen and give me the reins, my brave Eunice" he said.—They soon passed the church and gained the main road—the stage road leading up to the Avery and DeLesline dwellings. "It is over now," said the Colonel, "and, Eunice, you deserve promotion on the field for your masterly movement to the rear, thundering in like a re-inforcement and deciding the action."

With a tremor in her soft voice she asked "Have you been hurt?"

"Fortunately I am unhurt; and I tried not too much to hurt these deluded fellows. I hope none are killed. If so it would bring me into miserable trouble. Had I been killed, though, there would be a great jubilee. And how did you fare, my calm goddess? Not even alarmed I will venture to assert?"

Before she could answer a figure moved from behind a tree crying heigh! heigh! (as it approached the middle of the road) and halt! as the buggy came nigh. Logan's old warhorse stopped of its own accord and stood motionless, champing the bit.

"Gillespie," said Colonel Loyle recognizing him, "is all safe at Mrs. DeLesline's and Mrs. Avery's?—Yes?—I am glad to hear it."

"There is great excitement in the neighborhood but no actual disturbance in our immediate vicinity. We have guards however at every house" replied Gillespie. "I was going down to find out something about the firing and noise at the church."

"Some fellows wished to stop us there and a few shots were fired. Poor Helen Clarens was in their clutches and we rescued her. She must not be allowed to wander about if it is in the power of the good people at Mrs. Avery's to prevent it without keeping her shut up. Has Mrs. DeLesline heard of the accident on the Rail Road?"

"No, indeed; what accident?—Though I should have known something had happened by the delay of the train and now by your bringing Miss Eunice home in Captain Logan's buggy."

"Scoundrels placed a log upon the rails and threw the train off. Come back with us, Gillespie; for we must take Helen who is still insensible to Mrs. Avery's as soon as possible."

"Mrs. DeLesline's carriage is close at hand," replied Gillespie. "As there is so much disturbance to-night, Carlisle and myself were driving down to the station for Miss Eunice, when we heard the pistol shots near the church; and he is guarding the carriage while I came around to find out what was going on. Your mother, Miss Eunice, is at Mrs. Avery's where we were to call for her on our return from the station. Colonel, would it not be better to take you all in the carriage? It is more comfortable for Miss Helen."

They were soon by the side of the large old fashioned family carriage, into which Helen was tenderly placed, still in charge of Eunice. "She breathes well," said Eunice "though apparently in a deep swoon—and it may be for her good. Do you know both Mamie and I think her reason is returning—and Mr. Fairbanks agrees with us. This may be the crisis of her mental ailment."

The horse and buggy were turned over to Mr. Carlisle, a friendly neighbor of the family, and Gillespie mounted the box of the carriage, adjusting his revolver in his belt as he did so. Colonel Loyle entering the carriage assisted in supporting the apparently sleeping form of Helen Clarens.

On parting with Eunice in her mother's portico, after their return from Mrs. Avery's, Colonel Loyle said "Eunice, you need rest now. I shall see that your trunks are brought over to-morrow; at least as much of them as we can find. But where is the bouquet? That was certainly saved?"

"I left it; I was thinking only of my preserver"; and while she took the hand he offered in bidding adieu, she added "how can I adequately thank you? Twice within the last few hours you have saved my life."

"Nay—the last time 't was you who saved me. And how shall I adequately thank *you*?" He still held her hand. She drooped her head to conceal her face. Rousing himself as from a dream, he hurriedly said good-night and hastened away. He walked alone along the road. It was as quiet as on a Sabbath noonday.

A little later he was at his own dwelling at Oakhill, pacing up and down his broad piazza. He recalled to mind all that had so unexpectedly happened on the journey from Columbia and at the Church yard and at the parting with Eunice. If we be permitted to interpret his thoughts on this last topic, their import was saddening to his heart. "Never have I observed in her the hauteur of many of those whose name she bears nor boastfulness on that account. Her mother, though, cherishes the memory of the family's ancestry and would feel miserably humbled by association or relationship with me; nor will she ever consent to be separated from her daughter. Then why have I allowed—no, it is not that—I have struggled against it—it is involuntary. My admiration has become intertwined with a fondness so idolizing that I am happiest when nigh Eunice or doing something which may please her. Is she another's? I dare not ask her. She would die before her delicacy and dignity would permit her to speak a word about that to me. O, if I could but ask her Are you engaged to Willie? O, if I could but find out—from her own lips—

if she feels—hath ever felt—even a kindly consideration for me! Have I so far forgotten the allegiance I owe to my own soul and to friendship and the promise to
her father to give a helping hand to Barton—as even to let word or deed or look
of mine indicate to her the love I determined to hide from every eye?—There is, I
am inclined to believe no fixed engagement between her and Willie Barton. Yet
what I have heard to that effect leaves me under an impression that some entanglement, some implied engagement exists. Her mother talks of it. Everybody about
here talks of it. Barton acts up to it. She is mute. She has never admitted it, so far as
I know. I have no right to speak a word or seek further knowledge on the subject.
—Yet Heaven knows how I love her and have loved her for years. It is a part of my
being." Her mother, though of Northern birth, is now transformed, heart and soul,
and believes it to be her sacred duty to uphold the DeLesline name and to trans-
mit it to whomsoever her daughter shall marry. She has often said so. My father's
name, humble as it is, is good enough for me. Then let me think all that has
occurred but an enchanting episode in my lonely life."

Here he paused and folded his arms upon his breast, lost in reverie, while his
eyes looked up at the far off stars. How many beautiful things, like the lights of
heaven, are far off from us!—Then he resumed his walk more rapidly, saying to
himself, "When these political harassments have passed, I must leave her to Willie
and hie me back to wild western scenes, the home of my future days."

Going into the yard, he loosened the chains of his lionlike dogs. They yelped
and almost fondled him and placed their paws upon his breast and looked affectionately into his face. "You love me, don't you, Ponce?" and he patted the monstrous dog's head and playfully pulled his ears. But Leo pushed Ponce aside to
receive a kindly recognition for himself, and Lu, not to be overlooked whined her
plaint and nestled her head upon her master's arm. "Now all of you keep good
watch to-night and wake me if any danger comes." The intelligent and faithful
guards skirted around the premises in various directions, snuffing the ground;
then, as their master retired within the house and barred his door, they stretched
themselves out with their heads between their paws, the starlight glittering in their
wakeful eyes. It may be remarked of Ponce and Leo that they came of an abnormal
Columbia mixed breed, Great Danes or mastiffs which had been killed off on account of the strength and fierceness they developed; qualities undesirable in a city.
Sancho had two pups of the breed and thinking they might share the fate of the
others, gave them to Colonel Loyle at the time he brought from Virginia the corpse
of young Lieutenant DeLesline. The Colonel had trained them to obedience and
they were very serviceable guardians of his house.

The house was an old two-story dwelling, built shortly after the Revolution-
ary war. It was, however, in good preservation and had been renovated within
and beautified without by Colonel Loyle's father. It crowned the summit of a gently sloping hill; and like many plantation houses in this climate, was shaded by a

magnificent growth of oaks—(whence its name Oakhill)—and approached by a long avenue of stately trees. A pretty cottage near by was occupied by a German farmer and his large family of sons, who were placed in charge of the fruitful fields which stretched away from the mansion. The Colonel's sole companion in his library, at his table and everywhere in his house was a one-armed delicate young man who invariably wore on his head a close-fitting velvet cap without a rim; and when he went outdoors he used to put on his straw hat or felt hat over this cap. The Colonel called him "Johnny." His story must be postponed for another time.—The farmer's good-natured Frau kept the house in order and supplied the meals when the Colonel was at home. In his absence Johnny took meals with her at the cottage, kept the farm accounts, tended the poultry and stock belonging to himself, had charge of the dogs, and studied such books as his patron advised him to study.— The Colonel, an only son, left alone in the world, had early learned to rely upon himself. He had lived so much a solitary life before and since the war, that his friends wondered when he took a long journey to the West (where he had once been in stirring adventures) to bring home this delicate and maimed youth. The report was that he had promised to take care of him, if the child recovered from almost fatal injuries inflicted upon him by hostile Indians who had killed the rest of the family.

However, let us change the scene.—All were fast asleep at Mrs. DeLesline's house. But the excitement had not died away in the kitchen, in which a brisk con-versation was going on. The kitchen was, as usual in the South, a detached build-ing. A window in it was open. The light from the window fell upon two men; one black (christened Lucius but called Luke or Luky); the other white (at least on the outside); and the two were standing at the fence which separated the inner garden enclosure from the fields beyond.

"I'se glad to hear, Mass Lubb, dat brudder Caesar send me huddy. He great man now."

"Yes, Luke, and we'll make you a great man too, if you tell me all you know and find out all you can for us. Remember you must swear against Colonel Loyle and Lieutenant Barton."

"But, Mass Lubb, dey no bin dere!"

"That's nothing; you must swear you saw them there. We'll pay you and make it all right."

"But dey no bin dere. How Luky gwine swear he seed um?"

"Here—you want a drink of this?—Good, ain't it?—Do you like it? Drink some more.—Here's a dollar, Luke,—real silver. Mr. Guelty'll send you another. This one came from Mr. Troth. Both great men and able to protect you if you swear as we want you to. Look here, Luky; your old master was in the Legislature, wasn't he? Well, we'll put you there to fill his place and make laws."

"Waf-fuh, Mass Lubb?"

"To secure your rights."

"I'se got rights 'nuff now."

"Your white friends at the North think you ought to have more. Remember you must swear against Loyle and Barton. I was told to consult old Pam, but he is such a fool I can get nothing out of him; pretends he is too old to follow the Colonel up who is here and there, then not here nor there, all the time; and Mr. Troth must get a younger man to follow him up. Now take me in to Supper and then shew me the bed you say Calline will give up to me; for I'm real tired."

There was one servant in the corner of the kitchen—an old woman—Eunice's old nurse, Maum Patty—who listened rather than talked, and was often dozing. When Lubb came swaggering in with his oily speech and his whispering to Luke, Maum Patty's eyes were fixed upon his face. While he eat and drank and winked at Caroline and lit his cigar at Luke's and cursed the gentlemen of the neighborhood and threatened their destruction—she quietly but intently watched him. Being under the influence of liquor he was the less guarded in concealment of himself. Suddenly the old woman arose, tottered towards him and pointing her skinny finger in his face cried out, "Where's Sancho?—Where's my husband, my good husband Sancho? When I found his bones, there was a bullet in his skull. Who did that, Mr. Jailey?"

Lubb started; but declared he knew nothing about it, nor had any knowledge of anything she was talking about.

"You say you're named Lubb? Didn't I see you in old Master's house and in the yard and in the kitchen when your men burned the house down? Didn't they call you Jailey then? You think I can forget that night?"

"Luky—I must go out of here. The old woman is crazy. I can't stay here and be abused so. The white people abuse me enough. If you colored people whose liberty I'm protecting, don't be my friends, I must go and leave the democrats to put you back into slavery."

"I wish I was back, Mr. Jailey, and never to see the like of you again. Where's Mr. Hawks? Where's the Sargent? Who of you killed my good husband Sancho?"

"I swear to you, Ma'am, I was not there. I swear it solemnly; and you must call me by my right name, Lubb."

"Come, aunt Patty," interposed Caroline, "come to your little room near old Missis' house, and let dese people be I'm going to stay with you to-night." And she coaxed away the faithful old wife of the murdered Sancho, endeavoring to divert her thoughts by telling her something of her pet Miss Eunice. But the old nurse refused to be pacified and murmured of it even in her sleep. It was Jailey. Maum Patty was right.—Guelty who had remained at his old home longer than Yarkly had done at his, when the Northern volunteer troops were disbanded, and had thereby lost all his share of the contents in the black trunk had brought Jailey, a fellow townsman, to the Prostrate state that he might, among other things, ferret out for him the truth about the trunk. He could not well do it himself. It was to his interest, politically, to keep on good terms with his cousin St. Julian Yarkly (who from infancy had lived in a town far distant from Guelty's). He knew this cousin of his to be a man of more than ordinary ability. He advised his chosen ally to change his name and as far as possible his facial appearance. His next step was to obtain for this ally a subordinate position in Yarkly's office; for Yarkly had risen to a responsible state employment. Jailey (or Lubb) was personally unknown or but slightly— if at all—known to Yarkly. He had been transferred only towards the close of the war to the regiment to which Guelty and Yarkly belonged. Jailey's altered facial appearance and his assuming the name of Lubb and hailing from a far distant place, with a concocted story of a previous life, would very likely prevent recognition even if while in the regiment he had been casually seen by Yarkly. And so it came to pass that Lubb succeeded in deceiving Yarkly.—His secret agreement with Guelty was to act as a spy on the Honorable St. Julian. He indeed spied out all he wished to spy. He found out the jeweller in New York who had bought the contents of the black trunk for ten thousand dollars—Then Jailey or rather Lubb had a private revenge of his own to gratify against Guelty. He had never forgotten the tearful complaint of his only sister whose engagement of marriage at home with an estimable and wealthy neighbor Guelty had broken off through his pretended admiration and interference. It was kept a family secret and Guelty continued friendly with them—more friendly than ever, to make amends for his conduct. But the brother swore in his heart that some day he would get even with him. He thought himself strong enough now, and that an opportunity had come, for his long cherished purpose of revenge. He revealed the secret of his coming south to St. Julian, told him his true history and what he had found out about the trunk. St. Julian bought Lubb's tongue and the oaths lying in a black cluster beneath every papilla of that tongue for five hundred dollars cash and a better paying office. And so Lubb had two friends, one paying him to find out, and the other paying him because he had found out.—But more than this had he lately found out. Isaiah, not aware of all his treachery, still relied on him, (as much as one rogue relies on another) and needed his assistance in his long cherished plot. To make the assistance effectual, he was compelled to divulge a part of it to him—deceiving him of course as to his ultimate design in so strange an adventure; but imparting his intention of using the searching of houses in the Ku Klux raids to effect his purpose of seizing upon and marrying Eunice at any and every hazard. He promised Lubb one thousand dollars—if he helped him to success in doing so.

"Aye—help you, cunning villain! Katy Jailey would help you too, were she here, I bet! No, by heaven, this fair lady shall not be yours! She can't be mine—but she shall never be yours! Those eyes of hers! O, never have I seen such eyes as hers!"— And so the maudlin Lubb fell asleep at last with his empty whiskey bottle on the bed; while the waning stars of the faint dawn sank, one by one, before the eyes of many a poor farmer rising to his early task; before the eyes of many an anxious mother praying for her sons in prison.

With regard to Lubb's hidden enmity against Guelty we must quote—though it be from memory—the lines,

> And if we do but watch the hour,
> We'll find there is no human power
> That can evade, if unforgiven,
> The patient search and vigil long
> Of him who treasures up a wrong,[5]

and ask ourselves Is there in truth a Nemesis to help revenge in a case like this?

The next day there appeared in a partisan newspaper the following notice, which had been also telegraphed Northward:

"Horrible Ku Klux outrage in a Graveyard!!"

"While a small number of devout colored people were peacefully returning from a prayer meeting near Glyndale about ten o'clock last night, they were set upon by more than fifty armed Ku Klux in disguise, who suddenly sprang from the grave-yard of the Episcopal church and wantonly struck down with muskets the alarmed citizens, and basely shot at them while lying defenceless on the ground and begging for mercy. One of their muskets was found near the spot and is kept in evidence against them. It is said Colonel Edmund Loyle was ringleader of the diabolical crowd in their dastardly attack. Sixteen of our colored fellow citizens were severely wounded. How long are we to witness such outbreaks of the old rebel spirit?"

This was but one of the numerous newspaper attacks upon the inoffensive young Colonel; some of them inspired, no doubt, by the vindictive Mr. Troth. But the Colonel was not without his host of friends from whom every mail brought assurances of adherence and assistance. There was talk of his quitting the State to avoid the persecution of his clandestine enemies. Some of his best friends advised him to this course.

A young admirer living near Oakhill and whom he took pleasure in listening to because of his innocent and poetic remarks, sent him some lines a portion of which we shall here put down—to be perused or skipped by our "gentle readers."

For Colonel XXX: a hint of protest when it was rumored that he intended to emigrate Westward.

> Traveling alone through all a winter's day
> The east wind in his face, young Sanford reached
> A hillock from whose bosky groves were seen
> A city's far off lights, like twinkling stars.

5. William Cullen Bryant, "Mazeppa," stanza 10.

A thousand miles and more, with cheerful heart,
Scripless and oft afoot had he trudged back
Homeward, still facing homeward; resolute
To toil where neighbor help and cheering words
Make toil a pastime; and where love's sweet smile
More blessing hath than mines of wealth can win.
Screened from the chilling gusts, near by the road,
A camp-fire blazed Self-exiled gray-clad men
Were busy with their bivouac for the night.
Yet not the sparkling blaze nor laugh nor song
Nor savory meal, had made the traveler stay
His weary steps—but that a voice he knew,
Long, long unheard, trilled forth a well known song,
An old home song. And Sanford paused, spell-bound,
And hallooed through the frosty air the name
Of his old friend.—Laughter and gleeful song
Were in an instant hushed.—Who in this place,
They wondering asked, named any of their group?
Yet Belton shouted back; and soon rough hands
Were clasped in friendship; and the crackling fire
Shot brighter up while in its flickering light
All courteous rose and cordial welcome gave.
And long debate they held, he to his home
Returning—they, on other lands intent,
To rule, as they had ruled, in dominance of
law-enacting wisdom and by right
Of Saxon inexterminable power.

But we have quoted enough. The young poet pursued the theme through arguments for and against emigrating, till Belton was induced to turn back "o'er the froze and icy roads" to the genial clime they had not sufficiently prized; because they had a continent to rove in, and all its rich western lands to partake of and to appropriate some lovely spot of it to themselves whensoever it pleased them to settle down.

In the preceding chapter we told of Miss Sallie's intention to communicate to Colonel Loyle any project against him which she might become aware of. There were other sources from which he occasionally learned of what was transpiring in the councils of his enemies. I recall to mind one of these and shall conclude this chapter by introducing to the reader a queer friend of mine; a native of the state; age fifty, head bald, stature short, nose long, eyes blue, features vivacious, limbs nimble, and so was his tongue, and so were his fingers.

Theophilus Diedrich Munnikhuysen Schwomm was of German descent as his name implies. Though advanced in years he was an indefatigable worker in whatsoever he undertook, and it was hard to say what he did not undertake to do. He was liked because always ready to work for others, not for remuneration but for the pleasure of it. What was a trouble or bother to his neighbors was a nut for his ingenuity to crack. His success was his reward. He plumed himself for doing what they failed in. He was "a born mechanic" and delighted to get at contrivances requiring the use of tools; from mending a clock to constructing a roof or repairing a steam engine; but his regular business was keeping a drug store. Somehow he had learned to scarify and cup, and had the necessary implements for that operation. He claimed to be a specialist in fitting on trusses; but his whole system experienced a joyousness when his cupping apparatus was in requisition. He alertly went long distances to cup old or young, man or woman, white or black, and would abandon any work he had on hand, not excepting his drug business and his meals, to hurry off anywhere to cup a person. Such performance was then talked about with the utmost relish until his next case of cupping supplied a fresh subject of conversation. So it came to pass that his hard name was dropped by many of his English-tongued acquaintances, and some called him Doctor, some Cupper, and some who knew not his real name spoke of him as Dr. Cooper, which appellation he humorously answered to, inasmuch as there had been another and celebrated Dr. Cooper in the same city. He cared not how he was called, he said, if he was not called too late for dinner. The colored folks knew his place of business as "Cupper's Potekerry" or simply as "Cuppy's." He however advertised it as the Homeopathic and Pharmaceutical Depository and Thompsonian Medical Emporium. Whatever its name, these folks came long distances to buy physic there. In many shops a trifle more than the quantity purchased was added as an inducement to such people to come again. This could not well be done with medicines; so Dr. Cuppy kept on his shelf mint-drops or under his counter a bag of parched pindars for "brottus" (brought us?) to bring customers back for other purchases. Little negroes sent to him for no more than a dose of Epsom salts, would hold out a hand and say "aint you gwine gib brottus?"

Mr. Schwomm was fond of telling how he recovered Pam from a swoon. It happened at the close of the war that an assistant army surgeon, returning homeward and suffering from a swollen limb, stopped at Schwomm's drug store and was taken in, put to bed, assiduously nursed and cured. The surgeon having nothing wherewith to repay these kind attentions—indeed Schwomm would not have taken pay—presented him as a keepsake a few dulled surgical instruments. These Schwomm had long itched to try. He had sharpened and burnished them—It may be mentioned here that one of his hobbies was the collecting of odds and ends which he thought might come in use one of these days. He had at home a tight and dry room for keeping such odds and ends; brass nobs, halves of scissors, knife blades, horns, ornamental bits of wood or iron, screws, nails, pieces of wire—everything which could possibly come in use one of these days. Even from a discarded hoop-skirt picked up in the suburbs he extracted the bands of steel and laid them by to come in use one of these days. The surgical instruments were considered too valuable to be stored away in his Omnium-Gatherum room. He kept them near at hand among his drugs. His anatomical knowledge was very limited; but that would not have deterred him from cutting anywhere into the human body, should he ever get a chance to cut into it.

He had cupped round about Glyndale,—his birth-place—and Pam knew him and concluded to go down to Columbia and have his finger cupped. His middle finger of the right hand which had been struck by a briar, was sore and inflamed and swollen to twice its natural size and hindered his attending to Mr. Guelty's horse. He had used bread poultices on it, and when he showed it to Schwomm it was caked all over with hardened bits of the poultice. "I can lance it for you, Pam, a finger is too small for cupping. I have some genuine surgeon's instruments here. Let me first cleanse the finger and scrape off this bread stuff which is on it." Pam submitted inasmuch as he had come so far to have his finger cured. Schwomm, intent on his job, scraped as though he was scraping a piece of iron. The pain from scraping was intense, in the inflamed condition of the finger, and Pam fainted dead away. Schwomm's clerk cried out "throw water in his face—put a pillow under his head—unbutton his clothes."—"Don't do that," cried Schwomm, "don't rouse him. Now's my chance. Hand me that Surgeon's knife."

Taking advantage of Pam's unconsciousness he laid the finger flat on the floor —upon which Pam lay stretched out—and ripped it open to the bone. With one bound Pam was on his feet. Within a week his finger was quite well again. When an old acquaintance remarked "Schwomm, I believe you put Pam in a fainting fit purposely to suit the operation," he answered with a knowing look, "it was neatly done, Sir—neatly done. I know how to rouse a negro from a swoon."

Had he given up Pharmacy, there is one Government position he might have aspired to. He should have been in the United States Weather Bureau. O yes, he knew about weather! When a party of young men wished to go fishing, they would consult him. "Doctor, will it rain today?"—"Let me see," he would answer, and with some remarks about thermometrical conditions and an area of high pressure, would go out in front of his Emporium and look up at the sky and scan the horizon carefully. If his forecast was such as this, "you may expect a heavy shower at half past eleven to-day," then they would be pretty sure there would be no rain, and go a-fishing accordingly. If he had said it would be fair weather, they would perhaps have staid at home.

A few more words about the Doctor. He had been a Lutheran, a Baptist, a Methodist, and was now an Episcopalian. He said if he ever left the Episcopal Church he would embrace Mohammedanism, for he admired its tenets. He was anxious for notoriety in political as well as religious matters. Therefore he professed himself Reconstructed. He addressed a negro as Sir, and a negress as Madam, and a group of the sexes as Ladies and Gentlemen. This brought business to his Emporium. He argued, too, in favor of reconstruction. Some evenings he declaimed to those collected in his store, "For me, no North, no South. I know only a united Country and its glories. After a few years your Confederate wrath will cool down and you'll all think and feel as I do."

I hardly wish to let the idea remain with me that there was in Schwomm's mental make-up some faint resemblance to that of an aged man I heard of in the upper part of the state and who was reputed to have been in the Revolution. Two patriotic writers of historical sketches for a Monthly Magazine once traveled a tedious day's journey to see and converse with the aged survivor, and took with them note books to record his reminiscences. They found his talk incoherent and unsatisfactory, and one asked him "On which side were you, anyhow?"—"Well," said he, "sometimes with the Whigs and sometimes with the Tories, just as they happened to be uppermost in my part of the country."—Schwomm, however, professed to be Reconstructed on principle, not because the Radical party happened to be uppermost in his part of the country. They, consequently favored him. Bought his drugs. His business flourished.

He was not so wedded to the uppermost party as to forget what was due to old friends. If he became aware of a scheme detrimental to any of them, he could not forbear giving a hint to them about it; but with a strict injunction of secrecy as to the source from which the hint was received. It was to his Depository and Medical Emporium Pam had come for his opiates for the rheumatic sufferer. "Pam," said Schwomm on that occasion, "I saw you and Troth together. Look here; you and I must let our own people be. If I'm reconstructed, it's mostly on the outside. Inside is the same soft spot where I love my people; and that spot will never grow hard. And I don't betray any confidence, Pam, in telling you your Cousin, Caesar Bowleg, has a swelled head, and I should like to cup him."

Not far from Glyndale was a small farm once owned by the Schwomms. There, in a secluded corner, Theophilus's father and mother were buried. The farm had been taken for a long standing debt of his father's and Theophilus went to Columbia to seek a living. He always hankered after that farm and the recovery of the (to him) sacred spot in the corner overgrown now with cedar and cypress. In the days of his druggist apprenticeship he had begun to set aside every year a little of his salary towards the repurchase of the old homestead whenever there should be a chance to repurchase it. His admiration for the Loyles and other good residents at and near Glyndale was not abated by his becoming "reconstructed." He was entirely sincere in his warning to Pam to let such persons be. His advocacy of Reconstruction brought him into confidential relations with the smaller fry of the Radical leadership, and thus he found out some points of their policy, and points, too, which worried him because he perceived the Glyndale section would be harrowed unmercifully.

Schwomm spoke German, after a fashion, and it was a pleasure (perhaps an amusement) to old man Hennchen and his sons, whenever they brought to Columbia farm produce for sale, to stop at the little corner shop—rather let me say The Medical Emporium—and chat with the proprietor and drink beer with him. He engaged them to keep an eye on those paternal acres which he desired to repurchase. With father Hennchen (Colonel Loyle's trusted and trustworthy overseer) he entered into a secret compact to receive from him, Schwomm, and to deliver into no other hand but Colonel Loyle's, certain packages of medicine labeled "Sure Remedy for Pleuresy and Pneumonia. To be taken internally," and which he cautiously committed to him in the inner office of the shop. This was done from time to time. In each enwrapped package or parcel was a blue phial carefully secured with sealing wax, and in the phial a paper giving information of political machinations, in order that the Colonel might be on his guard against the same. There was nothing on the bottle or on the paper enwrapping it, to indicate from whom it had come.—All this is narrated here to disclose another source of the knowledge the Colonel had as to what was being concocted by the Radical leaders.

Eleven

I woke and saw the mournful stars
Go slowly trooping o'er the plain,
Bearing the grand old hero Mars
Upon his crimson shield. . . .
But look across the azure plain—
Look back—and tell me once again—
Is my brave hero dead?

C. V. Dargan

Scarcely had a fortnight elapsed since Colonel Loyle escorted Eunice to her home, when he returned to Columbia for a few hours. Let us anticipate him and transport ourselves thither to meet him.

Here and there in the gray dawning sky above the city a faint star appeared, growing fainter every minute. Here and there in suburban yards crowing cocks challenged other lusty crowings far and nigh. Watch-dogs, their watching done, curved themselves up in their beds of straw. Here and there early milk-carts were hitched up in farm enclosures, the horses' fetlocks wet from the dewy grass and the wheel-rims looking as if they had been soaked overnight. Shops and stores were still bolted and barred. Lower shutters of dwelling houses were closed tight, though bed-room windows were open. Some of those lying quietly on the beds were half awake conning over the duties of the day and some, many more, were still buried in slumber. Peacefulness was over the farms, over the city, over the houses, gardens and streets;—peacefulness as of the olden times.—Excepting a drowsy driver from the dairies entering the suburbs; excepting a few weary policemen returning from their rounds, no human being was a-stir. Not yet were seen the briskly stepping carriers distributing the daily papers. Yes—a few boys, breakfastless, had begun their work—a few and far between. They had come out since we took our first peep at the dawn. But not yet were seen the day-laborers with dinner pails in hand, solitary or in couples, thumping echoes of their steps out of the pavements, echoes audible far away. They were still at home waiting for breakfast which their wives were busily preparing. Not yet the market wagons had begun to rumble in with loads of meats and vegetables, coops of chickens, baskets of eggs and buckets of blackberries. They were getting ready and would soon be coming in.—The night had gone; the day not fully come, but the promise of it was here. Its incipience was discernible in the sky and the fields, in the streets, in the curling smoke from one kitchen chimney, then from two; then from a dozen or more chimney tops. At last, servants, rubbing their eyes, sauntered out from hotels and houses to wipe off the front steps. Factory whistles began to signal for their workmen, and minute after minute, now, brought forth on every side indications of awakened activity.

The scourer of the Hotel steps on Main Street looked up from his work and stood, scrubbing brush in hand, while a horseman slowly rode towards him and dismounted. It was Colonel Loyle; and the horse was his favorite Selim; both as cool and calm as the dawning day. The Colonel had stayed with one of his army comrades five miles away, and was here at this early hour in order to attend to some business perhaps requiring his signature and he expected to be on his way homeward before midday.

An hour before this, in Guelty's house, a dim light had glimmered between the slats of the window blinds in the sitting room. The street door had been unlocked and Guelty had stood there taking leave of Troth and Lubb. These two walked away together, Troth saying "I'll soon pay you the five hundred I borrowed tonight." "Yes," replied Lubb, "I must have it to-day; it was not mine, but some of Yarkly's I had in hand."—They separated at the next corner. Troth, after a few paces, sat down on a door-step and took from his breast pocket a parcel of papers and began to figure up with a stub of pencil an account of his losses in the cardplaying at which he had been engaged and at which he had been fleeced by Guelty and Lubb. There may have been a confidential understanding between these two. Lubb may have calculated on an even share of the winnings. Guelty may have calculated that all winnings should be his own. Troth was calculating—there was no "may have" about his case—what he had to pay; and wondered how his luck turned out to be so bad. He fumblingly (for he was sleepy and not over sober) put back his papers into his pocket and dropped one of them. This paper was picked up soon after by a young newspaper distributor, Phil Gaston, who came to put a newspaper at this door. He examined the manuscript and seeing the name of Colonel Loyle among the memoranda, said to himself "Why, father knows him. He may have dropped this. I saw him myself riding into town a moment ago. I'll give this to father to send to him. He and father used to be in the army together."

Old Mr. Gaston, maimed in the war, was soon hobbling to the hotel. The picked up paper came into the hand of the Colonel before he had finished his breakfast. He puzzled over it and endeavored to comprehend its contents; which he failed to do except in one particular. In regard to this particular point, he thought it incumbent on him to devote a part of the morning in tracing out the author of the memoranda; for they bore unmistakable evidence of the instigating and suborning of certain despicable fellows against himself. He knew enough before and from other sources to divine the meaning of these items in the memoranda. The nature of the plot, the precise end to be attained, was not manifest at least to every one, in the cabalistic annotations mixed, as they were, with gambling and speculative money matters. A more sober plotter would have been more careful even of such annotations of his.

The place and time of finding the paper being known; and the statement of a policeman who had seen Troth then and there on the house steps with a parcel of papers in his hand, having been obtained; these things added to testimony as to Troth's hand-writing—proved beyond doubt that he was the man to whom the memoranda belonged. During the day Loyle showed the memoranda about; and meeting a friend of his, the Professor of Moral Philosophy in a College not a hundred miles away, said to him:

"Let me put to you, Professor, a hypothetical case: Mr. B. is inimical to Mr. A. and plots to ruin him. He drops a paper containing evidence of such plot. The paper is picked up in the street by a friend of Mr. A. and comes into A.'s possession. Is he justified in retaining possession of it?"

> Professor: I should say, yes, as a means of self-defence.
> Colonel Loyle: Suppose such evidence of a plot to injure Mr. A. is mixed up with other and business memoranda which may be of importance to the owner of the paper?
> Professor: When two duties or expediencies conflict, the greater supercedes the less, the more important the less important. Reasoning from this principle I would say Let A. keep the criminating evidence, whatever else is conjoined with it, for his own vindication of subsequent action requires it. This is permitted him, indeed it is obligatory on him. Still further, I would say A. and B. are not only inimical but in active hostility to each other. Would you hand over a loaded pistol to an enemy, because it is his, knowing that you will instantly be shot with it?—To my mind the relation of Mr. A. to Mr. B. is identical with that of two men in battle, where rules of morality and equity give way; inter arma leges silent.[1] In a struggle for life—whether by a direct blow in the face or by a tripping up of your enemy's foot by your foot, you bring him to subjection—whether your agility or strength or your subtlety averted your death— is not a question for a Court of Honor.

"Ah, yes," interrupted Colonel Loyle, "honor—my honor—is the point in question."

1. "In times of war, the law falls silent" (Cicero, *Pro Milone*).

"Well, look at it in that light," continued the Professor, "What is honor? is it not truthfulness and integrity and justice to all in every station of life—and it involves courtesy to all except scoundrels and criminals. Honor has nothing to do with them. They are beyond the outmost margin of it. If you have documentary evidence of such men plotting your destruction, retain that evidence for reasons already given, leaving out considerations of honor.—Look at it in another light: as you know, the same mental power is in Cunning as in Wisdom; the same discernment in adapting means to attain an object; they differ only as to good or bad objects aimed at. Now I say Wisdom verges into folly,—if it be squeamish; if it perks itself up in sentimental fastidiousness, and thusly allows Cunning to gain its end. The wisely masterful mind never bedims itself with such fastidiousness when the contest is with unprincipled rascality.—We are speaking, of course, not according to the Golden Rule, which is inapplicable here, but as to the hypothetical case before us." Colonel Loyle smiled at the earnestness of the Professor whose eyes began to have an abstracted look and whose voice had run into the tone habitual to him in lecturing in his class room. However, after parting from the moralist, he said to himself, "If any friend of mine were in danger, I might act differently. But as the case stands, and I alone seem aimed at, I'll give Troth back his memoranda. They are his, not mine."

He immediately enclosed the paper to him with a few words telling how it had come into his possession. Troth cast his eyes upon the ground as if abashed; but the diabolical expression of his countenance was in no degree relaxed.

Another week had passed. Colonel Loyle had gone to an upper District and had again returned to Oakhill. His enemies in Columbia had seized upon the incident in the graveyard and were fomenting an excitement about it, as they did about the lawless occurrence in the Campus. They had for some time been desirous of arresting him as a leader of the Ku Klux. Though they had some fear of his resisting arrest (for in their hearts they knew he was innocent), and fear too of his friends rising in his support, yet they thought resistance, even if bloodshed came of it (provided it was not their own blood) would be so much the better for themselves and the Republican party. It was important to implicate some prominent ex-Confederate in the Ku Klux disorders, to justify the State authorities in having appealed for Federal troops, and in harrowing the Counties (Grant's nine court-martialed ones) and humiliating the outspoken denouncers of legislative malversations.— Guelty had infused into Troth some of his own timidity in this instance; had brought him to be cautious in order to keep their own skins unharmed; to enter upon the policy of taking Colonel Loyle unawares and his friend Willie Barton at the same time. The proof of Barton's Ku Klux misdeeds could be made manifest and would spread over Colonel Loyle. This ensnaring policy was finally adopted. The report of Loyle's intention to quit the State had reached their ears. They were anxious to capture him before he could go away. Their emissaries had been lurking nigh his home and watching his movements and reporting them to their leaders.

Colonel Loyle had just closed his door when the growling of his dogs arrested his attention, and he heard the voice of young Carl Hennchen; who, being sent by his mother Kunigunda, had come to report that three gentlemen of the neighborhood were at the Cottage, and had sent him to say they wished to speak with him and desired he would call his dogs in; that the gentlemen were Major Norant, Mr. Pelton and Mr. Crosnahan. After the faithful night-watchers had been called in and placed in the study where Johnny was reading, the late callers rode up to the house and were received in the dining room. They were old companions in arms of the Colonel's, and excused their untimely visit with the remark that they thought it important to confer with him without delay. During his brief absence from Oakhill, they told him, spies had been sent from Columbia and were still busy in the country around; and it had been noticed that they had been watching Colonel Loyle's premises and holding private conversations with the colored farmhands at Mrs. DeLesline's. There were rumors, originating from what had leaked out from these farm-hands, that all the Ku Klux in this section would soon be marched off to jail.

The conversation of the visitors became, after awhile, more desultory. Fragments of it may throw additional light on the condition of affairs at Glyndale.

> Mr. Pelton: (who occasionally, when excited or vexed uses "big words" instead of profane ones, and they seem to do him as much good, especially when enforced with a sprinkling of Latin)[2]—I am still floundering through indetermined conflusterations of the *jus vagum et incertum*[3] of our reconstructionary regime; but my overseer, Joe, noticing my perplexity and wishing to console me, says all things have to be onnatural before they can be natural? Our hereditary notions and methods, however, I shall not depart from. The "onnaturalness" is all on the other side.
>
> Colonel Loyle: May we not avoid friction by parallelism, instead of crossing lines at all angles? I mean by parallelism that we, the white people, will help the black race develop themselves on their own separate line of betterment, mental

---

2. Fondness for the classics was not uncommon among gentlemen in South Carolina. An English traveler and scholar who stopped fortuitously at a plantation residence found his host well acquainted with such literature, so much so as to astonish the traveler. "I once visited a merchant in Charleston and saw on his table, at his home, a Greek Tragedy which he had been perusing—in the original of course. I could mention lawyers also who kept up habitually their knowledge of the ancient languages. French was understood by so many of the educated people that it was an exception to find one of them altogether ignorant of it" (WJR).

3. Rivers means by this "the vague and uncertain laws."

and material; hoping that their estrangement and incipient hostility engendered and fostered by our political adversaries, will weaken and sink away with the subsidence of their sudden and foolish ambition to govern their former masters. I am trying the experiment in farming; and so far, it is merely an experiment. The colored people have already adopted a sort of parallelism of their own accord in religious matters; and I think will be inclined to submit to it, without much demur, educationally. It is chiefly in politics that the "onnaturalness" occurs; and we may help in the quickest way to remove that, if our large farmers would try my experiment and thereby add to the percentage of our white population.

Major Norant: (an active practical farmer and influential in the neighborhood as the intimate friend of the Colonel)—Our poverty stands in the way of our bringing white laborers here at present. And, besides, many farmers prefer negro labor. So soon as you returned from Virginia, you divided off your spare land on the other side of the swamp and settled your old slaves on it and helped build their cabins, and gave them provisions and an outfit of farming utensils; and then established your non-political German and his sons in charge of your own home place, men who know how to mind their own business. You did wisely for yourself and generously too for your negroes. You set them up for life, charged no rent for the land, and enabled them to support their families. Consequently they all like you and don't trouble your farm or steal what they know belongs to you. We didn't follow your example and have had to bargain for negro labor; and no matter what the bargain is, no matter how favorable to them, there lurks a suspicion that we are cheating them. So we have pilferers and disaffected workers to contend with.

Colonel Loyle: Your laborers are not all disaffected, are they?

Major Norant: No—some of the older ones we believe to be faithful. The younger we cannot trust; especially if they have been inveigled to Columbia on pretense of Excursions, and have seen there the complete mastery of their party. When a negro of mine has once been there, I put no more faith in him.

Mr. Pelton: Yes, and Lubb and his spies corrupt them here as thoroughly as Guelty and Yarkly and Grubbs and that detestable Caesar Bowlegs and other informal nabobical slubberdegullions corrupt them in Columbia. I've been in contact with the gang. Opportunity, it is said, makes many a man a rascal. But these fellows' rascality is inborn and goes about in search of opportunities. I've known some persons a jot or two religious and solicitous to repress their unrighteousness; and they were more or less successful. These fellows we are speaking of have no conscience at all. Their accumulated innate diabolism oozes from the very pores. Why, Sir, you can tell when they are nigh you, even in the dark; from their exhalation of a brimstony empyreuma.

Major Norant: (who knows Pelton's point of irritation and his proclivity to abuse the new-fledged magnates who had once treated him shabbily, remarked with a mischievous smile)—You are hard on them, Pelton.

Pelton: I ought to be. I've been among the *hesterni Quirites*[4] and their riff-raff, runnion, thimble-rigging leaders with fair promises on their lips while their fingers are itching to rummage in your pockets. I saw the red-head Senator who openly bought his office and who said there's five years more of good stealing here; and the streperous rodomontadist who declared "damn principle; it's money we want and don't you forget it." As to the judiciary—well—I've read that when it was the fad to make New Year presents of gloves, an English judge received from a lady who had won a case under him a hand-some pair full of gold coins. He retained the gloves through etiquette, but returned the gold. Need I ask if any of our Radical judiciary would have done that either before or after a decision?

Crosnahan: He would say, I bet you can't do that again!

Pelton: You're right, Cros.—O yes; I went to them in a case so plain a booby would see the justice of it. I went, as you know, for redress; and, for three weeks, thought every hour I'd get it; and came away, cozened, flimflammed, diddled, jockied, hocus-pocused and bamboozled, because I didn't slip money into their hands. They hanker after it with irrepressible costermongering insatiableness. It makes me almost sick to think of that batch of extortionate upstarts whose champagne guzzling—they scorn whiskey now—inebriates every particle of their corporality except the one foul spot of their thievish acuteness. That spot has Argus eyes all over it, and is, never entirely asleep. As to the "man and brother" imitators and hangers-on in their gang, all I have to say in appertainment to their specific Simian genealogy, is that I believe in paleontological uniformitarianism.—and then, because I expressed myself rather freely in the office there in the State House, a sleek little clerk from a Lake State, no doubt with his last month's salary in his pocket in good jingling gold wrung from us by their onerous taxation,—said, yea Sirs, he said I was an old rebel against his country's flag—*his* country, forsooth!—and as we had been whipped into subjection, we would be kept there till we penitentially acknowledged our transgressions. I doubt if he or his father or his uncle or brother or cousin ever smelt the smoke of a battle field. Confound him!— He said too that I was still suffering with Confederacy on the brain and that my remarks indicated, intellectually, phenomenal abnormality. When he

---

4. Persius, *Satires* 3.106. "Citizens only yesterday approach with veiled heads." The full phrase is "hesterni capite induto subire Quirites." Literally, this is "citizens of twenty-four hours stand-ing," and it refers to slaves who were freed at their master's death. Their heads are covered with the cap of liberty.

noticed my frown and the doubling of my fist, the unruffled whippersnapper with exasperating affrontery interrogated me as to isothermals and the meteorological condition of the atmosphere; and informed me his father had patented a self-acting cooling sprinkler with its gyrating circumferential extremity perforated with minute apertures. –

"I heard, Pelton," said Crosnahan, "that you posed the Ohio black lawyer they made Judge down there?"

"Yes, Cros," replied Pelton, wiping his brow, "I had a little confab with that ornament of the Supreme Bench. I met him in the State House, fuddled, though it was several hours before dinner time. A few bottles must have been left over from the Champagne supper in the Committee room the night before; at least he came from that room. He began to talk of the purity and wisdom of Congress (to which I demurred not) and the immaculate righteousness of Thad the Statesman[5] (which also I did not dispute). My posing of him was on this wise:

"'When the war was over there were thirty-six states in the Union, counting West Virginia and Nevada with its sixty-two thousand or such like small amount of people?'—'Yes,' he said.

"'Is twenty-five three fourths of thirty-six?'—'Of course not,' he said.

"'Is twenty-seven three fourths of it?'—'Yes,' he said after a little calculation.

"'If eleven states were out of the Union as Thad's Congress declared, there were twenty-five left which you agree is not two thirds of the thirty-six states. But being anxious to adopt the Thirteenth Amendment without Constitutional defeat, you got the number up to what you wanted by counting in some of the seceding states as full members of the Union, in January '65, before the war was over. That Amendment being so fixed, Congress then counted the seceding States out of the Union, "dead" so far as being in the Union is concerned, and said they could not get back, except by first adopting the Fourteenth Amendment. Now, passing by the hocus-pocus of the Thirteenth Amendment, let me ask you about the adoption of the Fourteenth. Ought not the States to have been in the Union before they could vote for its ratification? And anyhow, did Ohio (your own State) and New Jersey actually vote to ratify it?'

"'You seem to be a little too keen,' the Judge replied, 'but I doubt if you can make out your facts. You don't understand the case.'

"'Well,' said I, 'let me put a case which both of us understand. In our system of government the States control suffrage and define by their Constitutions the right to vote?'

"'Yes,' he said, 'I acknowledge that.'

---

5. Rivers refers again to Thaddeus Stevens.

"'Our State Constitution of 1868 confers on our former slaves the right to vote; I mean they had not that right before the adoption of that Constitution. Is that so?'

"'You're right there,' he answered 'they had no right till that Constitution gave it.'

"'But was it not by their votes that that Constitution was adopted?'

"'Right again. Their votes adopted it; it couldn't have been done otherwise.'

"'And yet,' I said, 'you've just admitted that they had no right to vote till after that Constitution had been adopted. Was not their voting then, to adopt it even if it came about through Congressional and military legerdemain, usurpation?'

"'Oh, chugh!' he answered, 'Oh, chugh! don't bother yourself about Congress! She's all right! Usurpation or no usurpation, She won the case.'

"'Yes,' I said, 'won it by the help of Federal bayonets. But don't move off, Judge —(for I saw him moving away)—One more question. Why did not your party in Congress let the Supreme Court decide whether or not the Reconstruction laws were in accordance with the Federal Constitution? Why, when they feared—perhaps knew—what the decision would be, did they hastily take from the Court jurisdiction in the matter?'

"'Congress,' said he, 'is supreme; you can't get behind her.'

"I replied, somewhat tartly perhaps—'You overestimate her, as you style it. Can't the wisdom and might of the people back her down and turn her out?'

"But the guzzling curmudgeon walked off uttering a string of profanity unbecoming the dignity of a Supreme Judge of South Carolina, even if the dignity was undeserved and foisted upon him."

After this narration, which was calm enough, Mr. Pelton suddenly boiled up into a passion and vented himself in his own peculiar string of profanity especially as to the boast of the party in power that the Constitution was inviolable. But growing calmer after a while, he muttered "latrones, peculatores flagitiosissimi, ad poenam sempiternam damnati—ignes infer-r-nos";[6] trilling on the last word. His countenance showed that his anger was relieved by this peculiar style of execration.

"We try," continued Major Norant turning (with a pleasant smile from listening to the irate Pelton and again addressing Colonel Loyle)—"we try to keep the older freedmen in our interest. My man, Cato, who was always faithful to my father, has been proof against all corruption. He tells me whatever he sees or hears. 'Massa,' said he last night, coming to my bed room, 'tell Colonel Loyle to look sharp. That vagabond, Pete Rooney, who was drummed out the army for his no-account-ness, and was lashed by the Coo-Cux a week ago for lying against his neighbors, swears the Colonel was one of the crowd the last full moon and took the guns belonging to the State, when you know he was gone to Columbia at that same time. A white man, I don't know who he is, (some say he came from Mr. Troth) has been

---

6. By this Rivers means "bandits, the infamous embezzlers, condemned to the eternal punishment of hellfires."

to see Pete and has given him money to go to Columbia to Mr. Guelty. So, my good Massa, you tell de Colonel to look sharp!'—Besides what Cato says, we ourselves know that Pete is the only worthless white man within ten miles of Glyndale and that they have won him over to their side by promising to do something for him after the next election. He'll swear to anything they want. Cato told me of the spies about your farm; he saw them prowling at night as nigh as your dogs would let them come. Strange negroes, many with muskets, have been stealthily gathering in the swamp, three miles off, where our friend here, Crosnahan, saw them; about fifty of them at the least, weren't they?"

Here the major looked towards Mr. Crosnahan, who was a silent kind of person, and who nodded a corroboration of the statement.

"Well," continued Major Norant, "Cato, at my request, went down there. They were cooking poultry. Of course they brought no such food with them, nor did they expect to buy any. They wanted Cato to bring them some of my geese. How did they know I had any up at my dwelling house? Five of the geese are missing, anyhow; but it's not worth while to go into the swamp to look for their feathers. Cato asked what they came here for? and was told it was an Excursion. What company? he enquired. They said 'a few Rosettes, some of The Sons of Elijah and the rest mongrel.'"

The major's last remark (about the Rosettes), casual as it was to the speaker, brought to Colonel Loyle the recollection of his talk with the Federal soldier, Tom Chiltree; the recollection of the kidnapping attempt on the road through the swamp; and the occurrence in the College Campus. He became absorbed in thoughts like these: What mystery is hanging around that scoundrel's plots? I am aware she fascinates almost to bewilderment those who look upon her loveliness. He's become a monomaniac, no doubt; and such are oft-times dangerous. I have had secret information of some of his designs; not all of them. Tom was correct, indeed, and more than he thought when he told me Guelty would bear watching. But he can hardly be at or near Glyndale at this time unless his pursuit of Willie is ended; and Willie is in or near by Columbia. A boyish and hazardous business was that. I myself may have been seen in the Campus or seen talking privately to Willie on the street.—Rousing himself (for his visitors had respected his abstraction and downcast eyes), he asked "Have you heard anything lately of Willie Barton?"

"Not very lately," replied Mr. Pelton, "but I heard something of him a few weeks ago when I was at Bartonboro'. It was just like him. Before he went to Law School, he was at Bartonboro' to say goodbye to his young friends and to make a night of it; and they had a parting frolic at McKeegan's tavern. Willie took on a little more than was good for him; and after his companions had said farewell, nothing would satisfy him but to bid goodbye to Bob who used to drive his father's carriage. Bob had gone to a League meeting half a mile away; and Willie went after him, with a fresh flask of whisky in his pocket. He insisted on going in and attending the

League. An altercation and tussle ensued; he lost his hat, was cut slightly in the arm with a razor, and his coat was ripped down the back. Bob, who told me of it, said Willie had a narrow escape with his life; for, as he put his hand in his pocket, one of the League drew a pistol and was about to fire, when fortunately Willie's hand returned to sight with the flask of whisky, and he insisted on their taking a drink under penalty of being Ku-kluxed for refusal. They inquired if he was a Ku Klux, and he told them he was Head Centre, the middle of the whizzing spokes when the sparks flew round. It was well that some of them who knew him from infancy took his part and saved him from being mobbed. After considerable wrangling, Bob succeeded in leading him back to McKeegan's.—He is exhausting pretty fast the little his father bequeathed him; and I'm glad he's gone to study Law and to make a man of himself. I fear however the League has reported him as a Ku Klux on his own confession."

The Colonel frowned, but made a friendly excuse for Willie. Mr. Crosnahan overcoming his habitual reticence, remarked: "It's foolhardy to bring one's self into Court while affidavits are selling at fifty cents a piece. I've a mind to write to him tomorrow, having been his tent-mate, and tell him to keep always within the limits of the Law he's gone to study."

"Do so, Crosnahan," said the Colonel, "tell him equity wears the crown. However, if they oppress us wrongfully, I hold myself justified in defending, as I can, both myself and those dear to me; and I prefer to do it openly—at noonday. They say they will have my heart's blood, as I am informed. You tell me I am threatened now; with what? arrest on perjured evidence—mockery of trial—imprisonment. I have done no wrong. But because the kindness of my neighbors has made me somewhat prominent in their service here and elsewhere, the aliens at Columbia would shout in victory to see me manacled and imprisoned. By God's help, I may thwart their iniquitous game. If in order to compass my degradation they are trying to drive me to some overt act—well, let them try it. We have forty men within easy call, old companions in many a danger, who need no drill. You will stand by me if I need you"—

The three approached him and in turn, with lips compressed, grasped his hand. Then Colonel Loyle spoke, with altered tone, "I thank you most heartily my friends —I have for some time thought that while our survivors' association for benevolent purposes remains unaltered, we may yet branch off and be a Rifle Club. Should a time ever come for instantaneous action, a hundred such organizations might be pulled as by a single string. There need be no secrecy. Such clubs, not drilling, would not contravene the Militia Laws of the interlopers at Columbia. There will be power in the very showing that we possess power. There is great moral effect in the conception of a body of resolute men moved by one mental impulse. In that lies the secret of martial supremacy. You know very well the physical effects of such bodies of men in action—say of well mounted cavalrymen, hurtling down upon a line or square of blanched cheeks and trembling knees; even though the line or square be in military array, they are very nervous in awaiting the on-coming and crushing impact. A mob, however large, will instinctively flee before the fire-eyed horses, above each head a flashing sabre, the reverberation of their coming not rising from the trodden earth alone, but also from the sweep of the rushing mass itself, hurled directly on them;—it is in truth the irresistible thunderbolt of war."

There was a burst of merry laughter, in which the Colonel joined, as Major Norant, clapping his hands, exclaimed "The same old Loyle!"

But it would hardly have been the same old Loyle, if his thoughts had not reverted to the welfare of the survivors of his regiment and of their families; especially those decrepit through wounds and struggling for subsistence. Crosnahan had told him of the destitution of the Simlins, widow and daughter; the husband killed in battle, the brother in prison on trumped up Ku Klux charges; and the little they had to live on stolen from them, except a sack of corn.

"Have they no meat?" asked Loyle.

"None at all. Old Mrs. Simlin says she can live very nicely on the corn."

"I shall see to that; Johnny will send her a flitch to-morrow," and so saying he stepped out and called to Johnny who was reading aloud in the Library with Ponce and Leo and Lu sitting around as his audience; and the visitors in the dining room heard Johnny's voice—"You, Ponce—look at me, Sir, and hear what the book says," and then the Colonel's voice "make a note of it, Johnny."—During his brief absence, his friends whispered to one another and Pelton said "don't tell him about that. Calm as he usually is, I fear to see him roused to anything like impetuous action." On his return the Major asked, "Is it true, Loyle, that we may look for Government troops along this way? They have been up and down about thirty miles from here."

"I have not heard positively yet," he answered, "but if they be United States troops, they will be welcome. We can trust them for manliness and fair dealing. Every United States soldier will be glad to see us regain our home rule from those who would rule us for their own rascally purposes."

Major Norant: Yes, we can trust them. The North is full of good people. I have lived among them, and have tried to overcome their prejudices.

Pelton: I know that's your favorite theme. Have you been excogitating another new plan of fraternization?

After a moment's pause the Major replied: "We often have aversions which pass away after a little intercourse or end in mutual friendliness. Sometimes impressions turn into opinions not easily changed and which, although not well founded, remain with us throughout our lives. Of this kind are the opinions entertained of our people by very many men and women of the North. Indeed these opinions have been cherished till they have become convictions almost ineradicable; having been fostered during several generations and made subservient to personal interests by prejudiced traveling investigators, falsely so called with Northern school histories in their satchels; who come South intent on gathering material for a lecture and predetermined to have material as interesting as it would be if gathered in the Soudan or on the Congo. Such 'investigators' are aiming for positions at home which will put money in their pockets. Their lectures are to please a special audience. The material is often gathered by looking through car windows. We should not think their distorted views of the South and its people spring from malignity. They spring mostly from a desire to make money. They are encouraged by smart business men who see abuse of the South diverting emigration westward to enhance their investments there. That being done they'll turn their millions to develop Southern resources; unless some more promising enterprise opens up in the Pacific islands. Moral and mental betterment of negroes is not their ultimate aim here or elsewhere. The tourists, encouraged by these money makers, are shrewd enough to know that the more imaginatively picturesque or piquant and abusive their views and expressions, the more money they get, the more lucrative the educational or political position they obtain among their fellow townsmen. Their journeys had been meant for business and to provide well for themselves. The Southern people laugh at their exaggerations and misrepresentations and at the Northern newspaper descriptions of our barbarism and cruel oppression of innocent citizens of African descent.

"Laughing, however, does not cure a stab. If we seriously inquire how this ill-repute of us may be checked, the most rapid and convincing plan is to bring the whole North to the South to see for themselves. This being impracticable, we must use means similar to the means used for our defamation. The North has its gigantic printing presses working day and night; issuing books, newspapers, periodicals; pictures in all of them. If we pay the printers, they will issue the same kind of publications for our vindication. As with the exploring tourists and lecturers and Magazine story-tellers, so with the owners of printing establishments; it is a matter of dollars. The South, unfortunately, has not habituated herself to producing books nor to buying books; the North has. The South is not a profitable field for authorship; the North is. Its intelligent men, intelligent women, intelligent boys and girls, buy books and read them.

"The conclusion is that the most feasible method of reversing and annulling their misrepresentations of us, is to encourage our own writers and help them gain the attention of this vast host of Northern readers; thinkers they are also; and energetic actors. From East to West the very climate seems to stimulate to mental and corporeal activity. Let us not, in our turn, indulge in vituperation. Let us speak of them as we believe them to be—well educated, wide awake, adventuresome, resourceful; disposed to be just and generous; that is, the better class, omitting the meddlesome negrophilists and theoretic sociologists."

Pelton: O, stop there, Norant, and mark it Caetera Desunt;[7] else you may soon fritter away your encomium. It sounds strange to hear you talk so now, you who fought so strenuously through the four years war.

Colonel Loyle: Well, I for one agree with the Major's estimate of the better class of Northerners; quite different they are from such as we have around us now.

Pelton: The Major forgot to say that up yonder, whoever has a trumpet of his own, blows it. Excuse me, however, for interrupting my friend; but we have, Colonel, already too far prolonged our visit, and with thanks for your courtesy must bid you good-night.

When his friends left him, he set his dogs on watch again, barred his door, and was busy till late at night writing letters.—Mr. Crosnahan's residence being in the opposite direction from Oakhill—towards Switchy Creek—he bade the Major and Mr. Pelton adieu. These two continued together and, as a volunteer patrol, rode around for several miles and to the village. All was still. Though it was a midsummer night and the moon had now risen, no human prowler seemed a-stir. A rabbit leaped from her covert and hopped along in front of the horses; then sat in the road till they approached; and this the sportive "cotton tail" repeated till it was her pleasure to jump into a field of tasseled and crepitating corn. The crickets chirped; and from a cluster of plum trees in the middle of the corn field, a wakeful mocking bird, harlequin of the feathered tribe, trilled melodiously, dropping at intervals into fantastic imitations of beast or bird.

The Major: What we desire is peace like this and security at home; security on the farms, the roads, and everywhere. We desire the recurrence of the time when a person, of either sex, might walk alone through the length and breadth of the State and be free from molestation. If this be hindered, remove the hindrance. If we can't excauterize the leopard's spots, get rid of the leopard.

Mr. Pelton: Fairbanks and perhaps all the churchmen would rather keep our leopard. They think his spots are comparatively few and may wear away under the efficacy of internal remedies.

The Major: Caustic is better. However, I hope they'll not become disheartened at the failure of their moral-suasion treatment and go away from the leopard while the leopard is here. Especially do we need Fairbanks and preachers such as he is. There was a preacher who had two calls (one with a small salary and one with a large salary), and asked his colored sexton which he should accept. The answer was, "you'se called to be where de most debbil is." If our Reverend friend be of the same opinion, we shall not soon lose his services at Glyndale.

---

7. A common phrase meaning "the rest is missing."

—Well, I suppose, Pelton, we may go home now and seek our rests. In a scene like this I can hardly credit the tales we hear of marauding bands and hurtful deeds. So good night; your road home leads, I believe, straight off from this by-way.

The major's horse quickened its step of its own accord, knowing apparently what was in its rider's mind and that ahead were stables and pegs to hang the saddle on and stalls filled with fragrant hay.

As he drew near Mrs. DeLesline's, the Major thought he saw a man sitting on the fence of her vegetable garden close by a dense patch of sugar corn, and a female form leaning on the railing a few feet from him. In a twinkling the man was gone. If he had dropped into the ground he could not have become more suddenly invisible. There was not time to notice his color nor style of dress. A patch of full grown corn is a perfect hiding place even in broad day-light.

"Is that you, Caroline?" asked the Major riding up.

"How d'ye, Mr. Norant," said she smiling; her white teeth glistening as the moonlight fell on her face.

"Who was that man?"—(He would have had no occasion to ask if the man had not disappeared so quickly).

"Oh, he's all right," responded her musical tongue through a ripple of laughter.

"You're out late to-night, Caroline."

"O, I don't know, Sir; our folks are all abed and this is my holiday; and to-night's really too warm for sleep. Don't you think so, Sir; and that makes you come out to take a ride?"

Caroline, without deliberate attention to it; merely from long association with her young mistress; had acquired a little of Eunice's gracefulness of movement. Her associates would say she had become "lady-fied" and finical. Her language, too, was grammatical, and her dresses as nearly fashionable as she could make them. Her comely figure, light-brown complexion, coquettish eyes, hair adorned with a rose or two, her easy pose and smiling face—presented a pretty picture in the moonlight.

"Ah, Caroline, I'm afraid it's not the sultry night keeps you awake; you're after some mischief"

She laughed with such hilarity—perhaps she knew her lover (if such he were) was crouched nearby—that she could easily have been heard at her mistress' house; and this assured Major Norant that the mischief was not of the insidious kind. He then inquired if she knew of the gathering of men in the swamp and country around. She said yes—but the strange people must have all gone away again, as everything was so quiet.

"Do you know any of them?"—Two of them, she said, she had known in Columbia.

"What are they here for, Caroline?"

"I asked them that, Sir, and they told me that whatever it was, none of the men knew; the leaders kept their intentions to themselves. They tried to find out; but confessed they couldn't."

"I believe you, Caroline.—Take good care of your Mistress' house; and tell the ladies not to go around on their charitable errands, till this commotion is over. You, too, would better be at home; good-night."

"Good-night, Sir; I'll be at home in a minute."

Surely, mused he riding off, everything is unusually quiet. I shouldn't wonder if after all it was only a feint on Glyndale and the whole posse comitatus has already gone to take by surprise the real point they are aiming at.—The mocking bird he had heard half an hour before, appeared to have followed him; for it trilled out lustily, near by, its imitations of jays, canary birds and squealing pigs, as if for his special benefit.

When the major reached home he had to attend, himself, to his horse. He was unwilling to rouse the aged Cato. His hostler—a frolicsome young buck whom Cato had long "'spicioned"—could not be found. He said next morning that he had been (as usual) to a sitting up prayer meeting. But if Caroline had been asked about it, she would perhaps have told more truthfully where the young buck had been that night; hiding in that batch of corn and listening to all his master said.

In the stillness of early morning Major Norant heard, before he fell asleep, the distant whistle of the night train from Columbia as it reached Glyndale station. Before breakfast the mail (about a dozen letters) was distributed to the inquiring recipients. One letter was directed in a handwriting different from that of the contents. This may have been purposely done by the party sending it, or the envelope may have been injured in opening it for espionage at the Columbia post-office and replaced by another envelope to preclude detection of the injury; or the Glyndale postmaster, Guelty's appointee, may have had something to do with it. Some letters confidently expected failed to come to hand. Such as were received were so uncertain in statement and contradictory of each other that nothing positive could be gleaned from them as to any constabulatory movement on Glyndale. Even private communications in a roundabout way from Schwomm and others had ceased to come to the Colonel's hand.

Friends further down the road gave information, later in the day, that at least thirty men, chiefly colored, had gotten off two miles below the Station, but had immediately gone in a direction opposite to that which led to Glyndale. Major Norant and others with him, were confirmed in the opinion that only a feint was intended at this point. But Colonel Loyle was too acute to be thrown off his guard by such manoeuvres. He was not apt to be outwitted even if, at that juncture, his private intelligence from Columbia had been to some extent cut off. In his campaigns he had often referred to the Palmetto motto his men wore on their buttons and used to tell them "parati" applied as much to "opibusque" as it did to "animis";[8] that "forewarned" bore with it the essential accompaniment of "fore-armed," which was the practical part of the adage.

The silent Crosnahan had done some scouting in his time, and successful scouting too, and before he left Colonel Loyle's house, had been requested to be on the look-out. He therefore, after a short sleep, had set out on foot ostensibly to hunt up his strayed stock. His first report, written in pencil, was left with Carl Hennchen to give to Johnny if the Colonel was not at home. It was as follows: "6:30 A.M. All the negroes have decamped from the swamp and gone down towards the Railroad track, saying they would stay there and take the down train to-night. A squad of soldiers with a motley following have, however, come up on the old state road and are going into camp this side the church. One whom I met out chopping wood said they were aiding the civil authorities to arrest Ku Klux: Who got you men into this mess? I asked, He said he 'supposed it was some of the carpet-bag scrubs who rule things about here.'—I'll go further round after breakfast, and report again †."

A further incident of the interview with the Federal soldier was this: Though the old scout, Crosnahan, was a reticent man, he had a habit of whistling when he knew there was no danger in it. On parting with the soldier referred to he began to whistle

> Way down in old Virginny,
> Not many months ago,
> McClellan made a movement,
> And he made it very slow.

"O—John!" cried the soldier, resting on his axe-handle—"where did you get that tune?"

"Across the line," was the reply.

"Locked up?"

Crosnahan turned and faced him saying "See here now—cast your eye over me; do I look like a man such a thing could happen to?" then he turned and continued to walk slowly away, still whistling the tune.

"I say, John"—sang out the soldier, "don't hunt your strayed cattle over yonder"; pointing to the swamp in the direction of Mrs. Avery's.

"Why not?" asked Crosnahan, coming back some steps and pausing as one willing to hear more.

"The devil's there."

"I've seen him before" said he turning and walking away. But he stopped again to ask, as if on a sudden, and irrelevantly, "Where did he come from this time?"

---

8. A reference to the motto ANIMIS OPIBUSQUE PARATI (prepared in mind and resources).

"From below—from that steaming hot-hole, old Charleston," was the response.

"Look here," said the scout, "you must not talk that way. I came from there. Old Charleston!—I know the place—crowned with beams from glinting ocean billows —city of nobles; not here and there a gentleman or a lady, in the highest meaning of the words; but hundreds upon hundreds, to purest honor formed and courteous mien and soft-toned speech.—I know the place. Goodness has made her dwelling there; and all her children, far and nigh, cease not their praises of her honored name.—Don't tell me he came from there, unless he merely passed there on his circuit."

"Poetic"—said the wood-chopper.

"Truth often takes that form," replied Crosnahan, turning off and whistling.

"But look here; wait a bit," said the chopper, coming up closer and wiping the sweat from his face; for the day was growing sultry already; "I'd like to know how you men down South are going to get quit of these overswarming darkies that are crowding you?"

"Remove them."

"How will you do that?"

"By your help. Your grandfathers brought them here." "How, if they're naturally on the increase instead of decrease?"

"Isn't there naturally more of *de*crease than increase in de-pellation, de-migration, de-portation, de-out-the-nation? Hunt that up in your Webster Spelling Book."

The private in blue thought awhile; then nodded his head up and down several times to the ex-private in grey; and turned back to his chopping, humming

> The rebels they soon found it out,
> And pitched into our rear—

Perhaps these men of few words had come to as clear a solution of the Race Problem as political philosophers in their fine-spun disquisitions.

Besides the letters brought by mail that morning to Glyndale Post Office for the negro postmaster to distribute, one came for Colonel Loyle by private conveyance. A gentleman stepped from the cars among the small assemblage on the platform at that early hour, and selecting out an intelligent looking lad, about sixteen years of age accosted him as follows: "What is your name?"—"Jim Brearly, Sir."—"Were you in the war?"—"No, Sir; I was too young. My father was."—

"Where is he now?"—"He was killed in Virginia."—"What Regiment?"

"Loyle's, Sir."—"Do you know Colonel Loyle?"—"O yes, Sir—we all know him." —"He's still alive then?"—"Oh yes, he's as well as ever. He rode past our house only half an hour ago, just before the train came in sight."

"Could you take a letter to him and put it as soon as you can into his hand, if I give you half a dollar?"

"Certainly, Sir, you can surely trust me for that?" "It may be of service to him. Goodbye, my lad—I must catch the train now or be left behind."

This letter the youth would not part with nor let any one even look at the envelope; but went direct to Hennchen's cottage and sat there till he had the opportunity to see Colonel Loyle about midday and deliver it as he was instructed to do. It contained these words among others: "a faithful colored friend of yours (Sheriff) overheard a high official say last night 'then Colonel Loyle is dead.' His anxiety brought him to me to inquire if such was the fact. From the secret conclave whence the utterance came, I thought if you were not really dead, perhaps a plot which they consider sure is formed against you; and I send you this information by a friend of yours who will pass Glyndale to-morrow; and shall beg him to have this letter conveyed promptly to you, if you are alive as I verily believe you are. It will be a sad day for us when the truth shall be, Colonel Loyle is dead!"

When the scout Crosnahan went through part of the swamp in his exploration he came across a quaint or rather uncommon enclosure; at which had recently occurred an event interesting enough to be mentioned.

There had never been eradicated from Caesar's mind certain superstitions imbibed in infancy. Whatever he was now to engage in for Guelty's purposes, worried him. He was not so obtuse as to fail to discover a little part of these purposes. He could not repress misgivings of hazard and disaster to himself in connection with them. It may be that he felt too a little uncomfortable for being in a plot against those who had befriended him in his slave days. So he bethought him of Old Pam known to all Black Rosettes for his communications with mysterious agencies. Caesar determined to visit his relatives at Glyndale and to have a secret confab with Pam. Guelty allowed him to go and enjoined upon him to make a thorough reconnaissance of his old home place. He did not take much money with him nor his best clothes. He laid aside even the appearance of a proud demeanor. He came among his former fellow slaves as "old Caesar," not as a Legislator and Trustee of a University.

Pam, since he had been dissociated from active work with the Rosettes had become famous as a an exorciser and curer of those "cunjured," which brought him more money than if he had set up to be a conjuror and nothing more. He encouraged the ignorant of his own race, far and wide, to believe in his power over all sorts of witches and wizards.—We described in a former chapter his Professional characteristics; but he had developed them in an imposing style. The ridicule which his natural ugliness; his protruding teeth, the constant blinking of his small eyes; had brought upon him, was offset by making these facial defects subservient to his assumption of supernatural influence. Weak-minded plantation negroes, men and women, attached importance to consultations with him about their bodily ailments, and fancied sufferings from witches who had stealthily come upon them as owls, bats, snakes, or other nocturnal dwellers in the forests. Many a negro carried little "voodoo" bags brought from Pam. Some had them tied around their waists next to the skin. "Wear dis," he would tell them, "and don't look in 'um, don't untie any ob de seven knots; else de charm be gone." Money—"fourpennies," "sebenpennies" and quarters had come to his pocket, payments in provisions had come to him, obedience to his commands, domination, and the satisfaction of being esteemed wise and powerful. He had cunning enough to secure every advantage possible from his reputation of having sealed with his blood (deny it as he would) a compact with the Evil One, in propria persona, horned, hoofed, and barb-tailed.

Caesar had heard of this blood-sealed compact; he believed it; and when now he felt himself overshadowed by impending danger determined to seek, in secret, the help of Pam; to seek some glimmer of light through his envelopment of darkness and doubt.

There were numerous narrow paths through the swamp made by those who hunted rabbits and shot doves and robins. In a dense covert in this swamp, a little distant from the stable which he took care of for Guelty, Pam had constructed a hut (the one Crosnahan had come across) in which he kept skeletons of lizards, rabbits, squirrels, and of other animals which, in the opinion of his dupes, contained enchantment in their bones. Pendent dead and shriveled frogs and snakes hung from the bushy covering of the gloomy enclosure. Dangling among them were dry calabashes with pebbles in them, two or three of which he rattled in each hand during his incantations. The door of the hut was simply a thorn bush. The approach to the door was along a narrow foot path through the underbrush; and this path was also made to circle round the hut, close to it.

To this retreat he betook himself when he pretended he felt need of necromantic re-inforcement, or whatever force it was he needed to counteract witch-power. No colored person, old or young, dared intrude upon this sacred hut. He still lived in the log-house adjoining Guelty's stable, but he carried some of his devotees to the hut intending they should spread reports of its awfulness. Those who wished to consult him at the hut approached near to the spot with their gifts and left them in a box with a heavy oaken lid; but were not to intrude beyond this box, which marked the boundary at which, in cases of appointment with him, they must stand till he called them to approach nearer. There was a red pole stuck in the path where the box stood. To consult him, one must bespeak an appointment and be punctual or forfeit his oracular response or pay another honorarium. He knew that to continue powerful he must hedge himself about with ceremonies.

Caesar had an engagement with Pam at this hut, when the stars began to shine. For this special visitant the weird insignia were arranged to the best effect and empty flasks filled with phosphorescent fire-flies were hung among the pendent frogs and snakes. As darkness drew on Caesar entered the swamp and soon heard dismal howlings and now and then the noise of rattles from the hut.—With the revival of his childhood superstitions, he strangely ceased to be the half or rather the one one-hundreth-educated man Guelty had made him and fell back in thought and language almost to the level at which we found him at the beginning of this Story—when he was pulled out the wagon by his heels. His old nature re-asserted itself.—The stars began to glitter overhead while he stood at the box and red pole and called out "O Pam! O Pam!" The witch-doctor came into sight, his fore-head bound around, with a white fillet and a large snake skin around his neck. He was mumbling cabalistic gibberish and shaking a bottle containing a bright blue liquid. He called on Caesar to approach and handing him the bottle bade him drink instantly and spill not a drop. Caesar obeyed. What had been put in the bottle was known to Pam alone; perhaps a concoction of roots or berries the effects of which he had tested. The drink instantly acted on Caesar, confusing his brain; Pam, the while humming a dismal chant, seized his arm and marched him round and round the hut. Then he hurried him inside, closed the bush door and bade him lie down on his back and watch the scintillations from the flasks. After a few moments of silence Pam said in a low tone "Speak!"

"O Pam"—ejaculated the frightened Caesar, "What gwine come to me?"

"Don't ax," said Pam—"Speak!"

"O Pam! Mossa Guilty, he pick me for do I don't know what.—O Pam! it 'pears some trouble gwine come! Blood—blood! Whose blood?"

"Don't ax," replied Pam in an almost menacing tone, "Speak! Pam yearry you. Dat's nuff for Pam. De Sperrit in Pam say Speak! Pam say Speak!"

Caesar's oath to divulge nothing concerning Guelty and the Black Rosettes recurred to his confused mind and he remained silent. At last he said,

"I'se come to hear you speak."

"What you put in de box?" asked Pam.

"A silver half dollar, and a quarter dollar."

"How much in your pocket now?" inquired the exorciser, "I kin see tru you. In dis here place you's only a mere man, de old-time Caesar, not Mister Honable Boley. I kin see ebbry ting about you."

"I hab only two greenback dollars for de Church" muttered Caesar still lying on the ground and watching the flickering of the fire-flies and the tremulous dried toads and snakes.

"Hand dat out and don't go for to deceeb de Sperrits"; and Caesar obeyed the imperative order. When Pam had transferred the greenbacks to his own pocket, he took a bottle of another colored decoction and handed it to Caesar. "Sit up and Drink dis; and mind you don't spill a drap, else de world turn round and de clouds fall on us."

Caesar sat up more frightened than before and drank as he was ordered and began to experience increase confusion of intellect. "O Pam," he asked in a whisper "what'll happen if a lady be kidnap?"—Then his eyes swam and his head rolled from side to side. "Git on your back again and shut your eyes" cried Pam eagerly and stooping over him asked "Who?" and heard the faint response "you know what he know—sojers—house—missis—," then his utterance failed him. Pam with a higher tone of voice cried into Caesar's ear "blood—blood—your blood—if you don't speak, and tell me all you know!" He shook him. It was of no avail. Then he said to himself "he fall 'sleep too soon. I gib him too much. I'se sorry for dat; but nem mind!"

When Pam saw he was insensible, and there was no remedy for it, he dragged him from the hut and then carried him on his shoulders to a distant spot in the swamp and set him down against the trunk of a tree. He sat opposite to him and chuckled and made faces at him and mocked and chuckled again. A moment after, as if a new idea struck him, he frowned and pointed his finger at the insensible form—"traitor to your old Miss—traitor to your young Miss!—From de fust time dat Mister Isaiah preach pisen into you! You tink he make you great man; and for dat you sell your berry soul, till de hell gate gap open for you. And you aint far from dat gate now."

Then he left him there with his back against the tree and his head drooping, and returned to the box with the oaken lid. He took out Caesar's propitiatory offering of money, counted it and put it into his pocket; saying, as he walked off with a grin on his face "I tell him ebbryting what gwine to happen! When he wake up, he'll know ebbryting jiss as he wish to know um! He tink old Pam too fool; not worth-while to stay wid de Rosettes. He say so heself. He bin de chiefest one to hab a hand to git me out de Siety. Bimeby he find out he more fool dan Pam is. He turn me out, did he?—he and de preacher-politishun? I'se too fool, is I?"

As the mocking and now half vicious and vindictive old fellow left the swamp, nursing his wrath at his exclusion from the Black Rosette lodge, and ever and anon prompted by the Evil One to return to Caesar and do him mortal injury; as he came upon the road leading from the swamp up to Glyndale, and was inclined to go back and wound Caesar, he saw at a distance a mild illumination of the pathway and the wandering carpenter walking as in the effulgence of the moon; although there was no moon overhead at that time. Indeed the illumination seemed to come from the apparition itself. Instant fear unnerved the bedeviling exorcist. He could not tell why. He thought a fleeting moment of his temptation to do bodily harm to the unconscious man at the root of the tree. His knees trembled and smote together. He staggered back a little way into the swamp, crouched in a hiding place, then sank upon the earth face downward, and quivering in every limb.

Immediately after this a change took place in Pam's disposition; the beginning of a change. It may be unjust to say that under the influence of political agitators he had become thoroughly vicious. Before it came to that he had been turned out of their councils as an unmanageable fool. Some remnant of his better nature remained in him and was now reviving. He thought of his former contented life with his old owners. He thought of their good friend and neighbor, Colonel Loyle's father, and of old Mr. DeLesline. Whether it was a vision or a reality he had seen after his diabolical worrying and drugging of Caesar, it certainly led him to his present reflective state of mind.

It was the evening after that occurrence, the evening when at a later hour the three gentlemen called on Colonel Loyle. The horse belonging to Guelty had been exercised, curried down and provided for. The nailed up horseshoes were prominently on duty. The stable door had been locked and the key hung up in its place in the log house near by. Pam had sauntered to his secluded hut; for he had received a fee, two "sebenpences," in a case submitted to him by a domestic of Mrs. DeLesline's household. He had undertaken to find out by his magic art who had been robbing not only the mistress but the servants themselves. He wished to be by himself to think out who the thief could be.—No one to his knowledge had ever ventured unbidden to his enclosure; and when he was there he felt entirely alone, and was in the habit of talking to himself. It helped his reasoning. He even mimicked the voices of those he imagined himself speaking with. He went through pantomimes. Sometimes he yelled. On several occasions he had vociferated so shrilly as to be heard by some negroes passing by on the road, and they had reported that "sperrits" conversed with him. One negro girl even saw a spirit flying out from the enchanted leaf-covered hut. She could not say what it looked like, except that it had wings; for she had taken to her heels at the first glimpse of it.

A peculiar habit of his may have led ignorant people to believe that invisible beings conversed with him on the road, in his garden, in the stable and elsewhere. In talking he frequently left out the personal pronoun, substituting his own name for it. For example, he would say to himself "When Pam gets home, the fire for cooking Pam's supper will be out. How will old Pam like that?" He not only talked aloud with no one present, but asked himself questions, and laughed with himself. It would confuse our narrative to adopt this style of his. We must leave out his "Pam" and replace the pronoun.

On the present occasion his thoughts were only expressed now and then in an emphatic utterance. His cogitations, after disposing of the theft business were like these: "Dey all call me ugly; and even when I was too leetle to work, dey all say I was a fool; I look like one and I act like one. But de Colonel's good old fadder—for sure he was good—he say to me one day 'Come here, Pam; you'se a smart boy; I bin notice you for some time; you work well, and kin behave well; so here's a dollar for you.' He actilly gib me a silver dollar. De fust dollar I ebber had! Yet dey call me fool now. Caesar, he knows I is."—Here he laughed, laughed aloud, and rocked himself about with merriment. "When he done git back to his brudder Luky after sleeping in de swamp, he wouldn't tell whar he'd bin all night. Didn't know who he talked to nor anyting he said, so I hear." Then he renewed his laughing and rocked himself till he nearly fell off his little bench.—"I'se so ugly, too, dat some run from me, and say I'se de debil. Maybe I is, maybe I aint. I'se not de debil dis minute, purty

sure I aint, for I tink of doing a good ting. Nem mind; I kin make tings happen, ugly
as I is. Now den, now den! I got a cough mixter, powerful to cure. 'Aunt Patty,' says
I," (and he changed his voice to a whining tone)—"'I hear you hab a bad cough,
and I bring you dis. But de way to take it is a secret. Step one side, Aunt Patty, so
nobody kin hear it.' 'Yes, brudder Pam'" (here he imitated old Patty's voice). "Den
I say soft like, 'Aint Miss Eunik too young and too purty to hab trouble?'—Den she
listen; for she lub Miss Eunik. Den I say 'Look sharp!'—'How?' says she.—'Look
sharp again,' says I—and again I say 'Look sharp!'" (Here he rose from his seat and
walked round and round outside the small enclosure, busy with his thoughts; then
came in and sat down again, pondering)—"I wish I could find out edzackly. Dey
don't trust me in de Lodge. I'se too fool for dem. I thought I'd find out more last
night. But Caesar don't know much; and he fall 'sleep too soon; but *he tell something.* He say kidnap, he say sojers, he say house, he say Missis. Dat's something.
Dere was anodder of de Lodge come here—O Cracky! how fine he was dress up!
Seems to me a nigger dress up like dat, oughtn't to hab no trouble in his mind. Yet
he 'fraid bout something. I couldn't find out nothing from him. He like Caesar and
more so; kin keep his jaw more muzzled up. He carry a pistol too; but was just as
troubled as a rabbit could be. If he'd swaller two grains of gunpowder ebbry morning, he'd git braver, maybe.—I'se a old fool—is I? What dey come to me for, den?—
De new boss, de preacher politishun, when he buy dis piece of land and put me here
to keep his stable and his horse and buggy—to keep um right here;—what he want
horse and buggy here for? He don't use um. He say he might have to, some day,
sudden. What for, now? Gwine run 'way?—Shucks!—de rail road would take um
quicker and furder. What he mean by spying out Miss Eunik? I'se a spy on her, is
I? I know bout some things, let 'lone de lub root." (Pam reflected a minute or two
and continued) "He aint say a weenchy word more 'bout dat lub root. Maybe I
habn't gumption 'nough for him. Maybe he 'spicion me. Nem mind.—What he
and de other Honable—Truth, dey call him—I'se got his money now" (here Pam
giggled and rocked himself on his little bench)—"What dey want de Colonel shut
up for? I says to myself, says I, old Paminondas, what's you keeping dis horse and
buggy here for; you old ugly Debil, you too fool to ebber find out! yaw, yaw! Maybe
so, maybe so! I'se too fool to be in de Rosettes; is I, Mass Caesar Honable Boleg—
is I, Mass Honable Benjmin Isaiah?—I aint forgit; I tell you dat much!—Now lem
me go fix up dat cough mixter for Aunt Patty.—Dey aint going to be cotched, not
troo me, no how dey fix it. Eebin if ebbry one chuck me a quarter dollar it aint
gwine fetch me to do it.—I knowed dat smiling brown-eye one ebber since she bin
a baby—bless her purty soul! And I knowed de Colonel since he high on my knee,
den higher and higher till he reach my shoulder. When he was a boy didn't he take
de blame on hisself 'bout dat calf wat got drownded? And after dat, didn't he sabe
me from being sold to dat savage-face red-whisker trader from Awleens? And didn't

he let me hab corn when de craps failed, and nebber charged me?—But, my goody! I needn't do nothing for him. Dey can't catch him if dey was a dozen Mass Guelty and a dozen Mass Troths and a dozen Honable Bowlegs and a dozen Saint Lubbs and a dozen more of um. He too smart for de most cunningest of de lot! And he spunky too; chock full! I done tell him all I know and spicioned; and what leaked out of Mr. Boleg. My new boss, de preacher politishun, dat pays me for staying here mayn't tell anybody what's in his head for to do; but I bet he aint fooling dat double-jinted sharp-eye one in de old house over yonder on de oakhill.—I hope some more of dem worried Lodge members would come here to be cunjured wid or to be uncunjured. If dey know anything, fool as I is, I'll make um tell de news, if I hab to keep um fast, right here in dis hut, for a whole day and howl round um till deir liver and lights draps down to de sole of deir feet—to de very toes—dam if I don't!"

It took considerable provocation to bring that word out of Pam's lips. He appeared to be a little bit astonished to hear it. Then he laughed to himself, re-arranging his dried toads and lizards and snakes. At last he began to prepare the cough mixture for Eunice's old nurse. While mixing it, he muttered "And he used to preach too! Jist like a godly saint wid long hair down to de very shoulders! Hardy Eddards, if he is a nigger, is good enough preacher for Pam. He don't meddle wid dese long hair furriners. When Pam wants to git to heaven, he'll follow Hardy."

Tom Chiltree had come back to the State on a visit. He had been so enthusiastic about a beautiful spot of farm land near Glyndale (which he fell in love with while hunting up United States mules just after the war) that a relative of his in Tennessee had advanced him money to purchase it. Tom had just succeeded in securing his deeds and renting out the farm till at some future day he should return to live upon it. He did not think himself entitled to call on Colonel Loyle as a visitor, but soon met him and had a long talk with him. A part of it was this:

> Tom: One class of new-comers are here on legitimate business, moneyed men, unconnected with politics. Another class are mere adventurers, turning a penny, lukewarm as to who shall control the offices. These may be here to-day and gone to-morrow. The war has made them tramps. The third class are the bold, unscrupulous, political fellows united for public plunder. These have cajoled the negro voters to favor their schemes, promising their leaders a share of the spoils.
>
> Colonel Loyle: What would you suggest respecting them?
>
> Tom: Combine against them. Your good men appear to me too much scattered. They should unite by all lawful means, despite the hostility of party power at Washington. The victory will, at the last, be on the side of the good and honest men, although their antagonists have, at present, the Federal authority to back them. The bad fellows cannot get that backing much longer. Their rascality will become so rank that all decent public men at the North

must abandon them. Colonel Loyle: I hope, Tom, you and many more like you will come among us and help forward whatever contra force we shall be able to put in motion against them.

Tom: O—I'll come; and others too, in battations, when you need help for home rule and white supremacy.—Do you know, Mr. Guelty sent Lubb to me in Columbia when I had my deeds recorded? He offered me twenty-five dollars for my bargain. A big inducement, that! He said he had long had his eye on that farm. Such might be the case; but it seemed to me he wished to find out what I knew about Glyndale and its people and about Barton and yourself. When Lubb approached me and unexpectedly offered me his hand, I extended mine with the customary Pray, Excuse my glove, for you give me no time to remove it; he said "I reckon it's as honest as anything I could touch." What did he mean?

"A compliment, no doubt," replied the Colonel, with a smile. "Well—Lubb took me to his room to taste his extra-fine whisky. The more he drank, the more impenetrable he became as to his designs. When I descanted on your virtues, he laughed and bade me discuss that point with Troth. And when I inquired if Guelty was friendly with you, he laughed again and filled another bumper. I appeared to amuse him very much. I never knew a man who could be so drunk and yet as cunningly keep his secrets to himself. In pumping each other it was a drawn game. I should suppose, however, they would all like to see some misfortune befall you; and it is well to be on your guard. We know that men have been put in jail in other counties of the state for mere spite; though it is done under cloak of suppressing the lawless Ku Klux; and the same thing may be attempted here in this County.—By the way, Lubb was once drawn from under cover. We were talking about his mother and sister when with no apparent reason He became suddenly excited, grumbled about his insufficient pay and cursed Guelty as if he hated him. It sounded strange to me. He said he had been cheated by Guelty—He said too, when I took leave of him that he would like to live up here and die up here and would steal a farm here if he could get his deeds recorded."

"His deeds are recorded, and the deeds of those he serves," were the parting words of Colonel Loyle.

After Eleven

Two Letters from the Lieutenant.

Eunice had in her early years corresponded with Willie; but learning that he showed her letters to his friends, she told him he might continue writing to her, whenever he pleased, with the understanding that no more letters would go from her to him.[1] The correspondence was replaced on his part by bouquets, presents on birthdays and other tokens of remembrance. Sometimes she sent similar presents in return for his, at the solicitation of her mother.

She and her friend and neighbor, Mamie Avery, and Dupont Gillespie were accustomed to take long walks; at times ministering to the poor and sick; at times simply for exercise. After one of these strolls they were resting on the benches at Violet Spring, when Mamie took from her pocket the last letter she had received from her cousin, Lieutenant Barton, and which he had written two weeks before the tarring of Guelty in the College Campus. Gillespie had received one also at the same time; and he and Mamie proposed to read them to Eunice if she wished to hear them. She, of course, readily assented; and Mamie read as follows.

"My course of Law studies here is preposterous. Why not teach us what the law is now, and leave us to trace at leisure its development from the time of Adam? I am already heartily tired of all this rigmarole and am inclined to give the study up. I know how to write a Will; and when you come to that, consult me.

"Let me tell you something more amusing. Our class took supper, a few nights ago with the Professor. When we were near the conclusion of that agreeable academical performance, the aged cook, Clarindy by name, ran from the kitchen into the yard, wringing her hands and crying out in her feeble and squeaky voice 'Please somebody holler fire! Please somebody holler fire!'—The soot in the chimney was burning. The men servants clambered to the roof with tin pans of salt and a wet blanket; while we went in and pulled the stove aside and stopped up the hole where the smoke pipe enters the flue. All danger was averted. The frightened Clarindy, as

---

1. This section was inserted between chapters 11 and 12 of the manuscript and does not appear to belong to either.

if deprecating a scolding for carelessness, sang out 'I nebber know dat hole bin dere, so help de Lawd, else I wouldn't hab started de fire in de stobe.'

"What is life, Mamie, if we have no fun? Therefore, a party of students, and some blooming maidens with us, went down the river in a boat to a spot where the late freshet had washed away the bank and exposed part of an old Indian burial place. We obtained fragments of pottery and a few stone spear heads. A grey-haired darky living there sold us specimens of arrow points; two of them obsidian. He called them thunder-bolts; and in proof of this, affirmed that once while cutting timber, he had found one imbedded in the tree beneath the bank. 'I found dat tunder-bolt,' said he, 'de same year Gineral Laff-yett bin come here. How time do fly!'—When I come home, cousin, I'll bring you what I bought for your collection. The Professor had much to tell us about archaeology, urn burial, embalmment with powdered roots mixed with bear grease, the sitting posture of corpses, et cetera. We found no human remains; but certain dark chunks of earth may have been the residuum thereof. The preservation of bones depends very much on the soil in which they are buried.

"The old man's daughter had found a perfect dark-stone Indian axe or tom-ahawk, and gave it as a present to one of the young ladies with us. Her dad thinking it worth half a dollar made angry remarks about her giving it away for nothing. 'I don't care a drat!' cried the damsel; 'I don't care, I tell you;—twenty times I don't care!—there now!'—'Look yere, you chile,' said he, 'Don't Care come to bad end, and 'fore dat—ginerally—she hab no house to lib in.'

"I don't know if I have reached the funny part yet; but it'll come in, Cousin Mamie, if you be my proxy and kiss

"Euny for me."

"Eunice, shall I do it?" asked Mamie in a merry mood. Eunice shook her head negatively.

Then Dupont produced his letter and began to read, skipping parts of it here and there. Perhaps Willie would have prefered his reading the whole of it, for avoidance of inferences.

"I borrowed a hundred dollars from good Uncle Tim a month ago—and wanted to give him my note for it, which he refused to accept. Out of his generous gift I had a high old time in suppers to the Law Class. Have only ten dollars left; will borrow when I get round to Bartonboro'. I've always thought Uncle Tim intended to leave his farm to me. So when I settle down, I'll sell the farm and call in my promissory notes.

"When a certain event takes place for you and another similar event takes place for me, we'll be neighbors then, Old Gill,—with plenty of fun ahead."

Gillespie suddenly thought that he had read too much and blushed and stopped, folding up the letter and slipping it into his pocket. Mamie laughed. Gillespie blushed again. The pensive Eunice appeared to be very little interested in the letters she had listened to.

Twelve

And so I masked my secret well;
The very love within my breast
Became the strange, the potent spell,
By which I forced it into rest.
Yet there were times, I scarce knew how
These eager lips refrained to speak;
Some kindly smile would light thy brow,
And I grew passionate and weak;
The secret sparkled in my eyes,
And love but half repressed its sighs.

H. Timrod

Eunice was but thirteen years old when the war began. In the State's upheaval and turmoil of four consecutive years; in the afflictions and bereavements of her own family and of the families of her friends, it was seldom that she had taken part in reunions and entertainments such as contribute to the enjoyment of maidens at her time of life and of her social station. Then again there was scarcely a young gentleman at home. They were on the battle fields. During these years her sedate white-haired grandfather had been so much her companion that she was unaccustomed to frivolous gossip, and had no relish for it. She had grown up amidst plaudits of courageous deeds and of patriotic sacrifices.

Among those whom she knew personally, but one ideal of manly comeliness conjoined with nobleness of character had strongly impressed her imagination. That image came before her in her dreams and whenever she thought of heroism. In her scrap-book of Confederate victories the printed accounts of her father's regiment had a conspicuous place; and the name of the gallant young Lieutenant Colonel had become to her a household word. In that scrap-book she had used her artistic skill in drawings of battle scenes and he had always a prominent place in the pictures. His features and bearing were accurately represented too. It was, perhaps, in a slight degree more than simple admiration of gallantry; but it was not yet that which it was destined to become. She followed his achievements with a flush of pride and cherished her remembrances of his gentle tone of voice, his almost loving glances, and even his blushes when he held her hand or turned from her own look of admiration which sometimes she could not altogether repress. There was not much difference in their ages. There was nothing we would call reverence in her feeling for him; we have already called it admiration; but—well, if any young lady reads this, she'll know all about Eunice's heart. I do not profess to know all about it myself.

Often a fire lies smoldering and imperceptible to all around till some occurrence starts it into an upward blaze. It has been truly said that in the life of many a maiden a time occurs—a day, an hour—when the whole current of her existence is suddenly changed. Such a time now occurred to Eunice; in the evening a beautiful bud—in the morning a blooming rose; in the evening a gentle, affectionate, dutiful child—in the morning, with the full strength of womanhood developed in her heart, she looked with steady gaze upon her chosen pathway in life; upon her pathway opening directly in front of her, from which neither adders nor ravening beasts should ever turn her feet away. Strong will was in her nature and was now in this matter fully fixed, to remain fixed. She clearly realized her soul's determination, her life-devotion. Too long had she walked in paths leading to dim, distant shrines on which she had no heart offering to lay. Too long had she brooded over what she kept in secret and which seemed ever drawing her to one side, while on the other her footsteps had strayed amid thorns and briars. When, early the day before, Colonel Loyle had been passing the Brearly house, as Jim said, who received the letter for him at the Station, he had with him well-filled saddlebags; and the report was spread that he had gone off. But he was only conveying his important papers and documents to a friend's for safe keeping in case his own dwelling should be ransacked by official hirelings. He had returned home in the forenoon. Eunice knew nothing of this. But she had long divined—her heart had found out for her—that if he left the State it would be because he loved her and because he believed she was engaged to his friend Willie. He was too honorable to say aught which could possibly lead to a weakening or non-fulfilment of such engagement or to an appearance of his coming between Willie and his happiness or her happiness. —She had heard the general rumor, and thought it probable, that he would soon leave the State to return no more; and she had whispered to herself "O that I had the wings of a dove that I might follow him in his troubles and be near him forever!"

At early dawn she rose from her couch beside her mother's and retired to her dressing room. She stopped not to notice the flowing robe and disheveled tresses and burning cheek reflected from the mirror as she passed—a flitting vision of beauty. Entering the little room, which was also her study and library she closed the door and advanced to the window that looked out towards Oakhill, and softly repeated, blushing while she spoke, "'courageous helper,' 'dauntless heart,' did you call me? And when you said 'wait till I come,' did my foot move more than a statue's would have moved, till you came? And must you go again into the wilderness and far away forever, because the faint image of another love comes between us? Am I deceiving you, and still more deceiving Willie, because I must wait till your lips declare your love? O maidenly reticence and self-repression! O love—love! O speak to me heart; go not away from me, far away from me forever!" And then she pressed her hands upon her forehead, as if to check and allay her lovelorn anguish; then calmly stood looking towards Oakhill and gazing into the brightening clouds which heralded the approaching sun.

Mrs. DeLesline, missing her, came into the room unheeded by Eunice. She looked upon her daughter with her usual affectionate admiration, yet not without instinctively perceiving an altered mien and altered spirit in the dreamy, longing eye, and altered tone in the very attitude of her child—a child no more—a woman now, and such a woman in the purity of her soul and fascinating power of her loveliness, that her mother falteringly said "Eunice, dear, what hath changed you?"

"The love of a noble soul hath kindled love in mine, and if there be a change in me, it is the change it hath wrought"—she replied, but looked not away from the golden clouds. "I can no longer resist it. Why must he go far away to the West and leave me forever? Would he not stay if he knew his staying would make me happy?"

Mrs. DeLesline paused ere she asked, "Whose love, my Eunice?"

"The love of Edmund Loyle," she quietly responded, but ceased not to keep her eyes fixed upon the golden clouds.

Directly the sun rose up and diffused his glowing rays upon her fair face and around her silken tresses. Mrs. DeLesline put her arm around her and said, "Come, tell me all; for there has never been any concealment between us."

"I fear, mother, I have been too long concealing from you what my heart has felt."

"But what will become of Willie, if you love him not? Come, sit on this sofa, Eunice, and let us talk together. Have you not always loved Willie?"

"As children we loved, mother; but the full soul yearns for more than children's love or liking, for it is not really what I now know love to be. Long ago I felt how weak and trivial and defective my regard for him had become in comparison with my admiration for the generous spirit that watched over his feebleness, guarded him, and raised him up to honor for my sake. I could not but know this. My heart would have been blind indeed, if it perceived not that I was loved, though the lips uttered no word of affection."

"Has he, then, my daughter, told you of his love?"

"No—mother; but I know he loves me even as I love him."

"Eunice—beware, my child! Colonel Loyle is too stern and manly a character to admire a maiden who turns from a life-long affection or liking as you have borne to Willie, to give her heart to one who asks not for it."

With a deep blush she responded, "if he knows that I love him, it is only as I know that he loves me. The mystery of our mutual affection has been as Heaven has ordained it. And I thank Heaven for the ennobling joy it has wrought in my soul. Although he should never tell his love to me, nor I tell mine to him, I shall go down to the grave, his alone. If Willie be deceived, let me deceive him no longer. I have never said to him that I loved him—never felt for him the affection you speak of. In this, dear mother, you can give me counsel and aid as you have ever done through all my life. He shall be to me a brother always; I may still like him with the old child-liking—but my heart and my hand are not mine to give him. His disenchantment may come more kindly through you, who have encouraged him. Therefore I have spoken."

She arose; kissed her mother's cheek and smoothed the hair from her forehead, and took her hand, leading her back to her chamber and toilet, smiling upon her and caressing her;—she, the strong in purpose, leading the mother feeble and faltering now;—the strong in purpose, because a love that knows no turning nor abatement hath entered into her heart forever; because she had confessed it; because she felt confident her love was returned as ardently as her own heart's love was given.

While Mrs. DeLesline, irresolute and with sad thoughtfulness remained in her chamber, Eunice a half hour later, was busy among her dewy, fragrant flowers. The tramp of a horse upon a by-road which led through the woods and the sportive barking of dogs reached her ear. She felt, before she raised her eyes, that Edmund Loyle was approaching. Handsome, graceful—to look upon him, was to have always afterwards in the mind the image of one of whom we could say

> his life was gentle and the elements
> So mixed in him, that Nature might stand up
> And say to all the world, This is a Man![1]

His father, born of humble parentage, had struggled with poverty and risen to comparative wealth. By his elevation of character he had won the recognition of the aristocratic circles of the neighborhood, while the poor never ceased to utter their gratitude for his benefactions. On the other hand Lieutenant Barton's claims to the hand of Miss DeLesline were supported by a long line of ancestry on his side. Not that any one of them had ever distinguished himself—but were not their names on the genealogical tree! Was that not enough? Besides this, Mrs. DeLesline

---

1. William Shakespeare, *Julius Caesar*, V.v.

preferred an alliance with him because he was the only son of her dearest friend, and Eunice her only daughter; and the two mothers had fondly looked forward to their union. She had never dreamt that it could be otherwise. The disclosure she had heard from Eunice, the resolute purpose avowed, the transformation which she had just witnessed, made her suddenly recognize and feel that Eunice was no longer her child as she had been her child. Bowed down from her slate bearing of yesterday, with her head drooping she sat in her chamber oblivious of her household duties. At length she paced the floor saying aloud, "What would her dear grandfather have said? Fortunate is it that he is in his grave! Descended, distantly though it may be, from a younger branch of a royal family, now to stoop so low— to marry one whose genealogy goes no further back than to his father—and he a nobody! Alas the times indeed are changed, when such men rise to equality with the highest in the State! To give up the noble name of DeLesline for that of Loyle! May God forgive us!"

She forgot that she had been simply Miss Vanderkoop of New York—distinguished only for her grace and beauty—that her personal charms gained her the love of Colonel DeLesline, when she was on a visit to friends and schoolmates in South Carolina. Five others then bore that family name; and she little thought it would eventually fall to her to perpetuate it. She loved her husband devotedly. And it was distressful to think his name would be utterly gone when she died. This family pride had not been abated by poverty. It was like a matter of principle with her. It was more than this. It was like a fixed thing—a bright-colored coat of arms hung up conspicuously before her; and she conceived it to be her duty to up hold and preserve it. With this view she had thought of requesting Willie, when he should marry Eunice, to change his name of Barton to DeLesline, or to unite them. It would sound so well to be called Mrs. Barton-DeLesline. Her own individuality had been completely merged into her husband's family, and she would die with composure if through her the aristocratic name survived. Willie's soft-heartedness, she doubted not, would yield to her desire that he should adopt the family name; but she durst not hope for such concession from Colonel Loyle.

The distinguished virtues of the DeLeslines for several generations had endeared the name to all who knew it; and she was justly proud of it; the whole State honored it. The passing away of it was like the reversal of hope into a barren reminiscence. Not altogether so. We embalm such names in History which is philosophy teaching by examples. How much more desirable is the presence of the example— it is philosophy personified, leading by eye and voice to rectitude and nobleness of life. Happy the community recognizing and honoring such living examples! If the old South Carolina gives place to the new, remnants of the old will linger longest where men like these have lived.

But Mrs. DeLesline did not philosophize about the family name. She was proud of it because it was patrician and her husband's and hers; and she wished, through a spirit of fidelity to its old *prestige,* to perpetuate it. She often lisped to herself, Mrs. Eunice Barton-DeLesline! It was a sentiment with her—this pretty conjunction of family names.—Yet one other sentiment of her heart was potent still—her devoted love to her only child; a love strengthened now by their bereavements and impoverishment. Though bowed down to as The Mrs. DeLesline, and proud to be so bowed down to she was not altogether supercilious nor unreasonable. At this supreme moment of her heart's trial, she felt that her pride in the family name ought not to displace maternal love and the promotion of her daughter's happiness. She felt, if she did not say it "thy people shall be my people; whithersoever thou goest, I will go."[2] But her aristocratic attachments were not giving way with her entire consent. She was, as it were, involuntarily slipping down from her husband's inherited social position and from the level of the exclusive class with which she had been connected. That exclusive class had been biblically characterized: "they themselves measuring themselves by themselves and comparing themselves with themselves."[3]—For a moment or two, when her pride was touched, her thoughts verged to antagonism: "How can I give up the settled expectation of so many years? Ought I not to object; to utter some word of protest? Is not Eunice throwing herself away?" —Then her motherly affection warmed up and prevailed and she would say, "No, No—there must be no estrangement between us. To live apart from Eunice would be misery indeed!"

Many pages would be needed to portray the conflict of Mrs. DeLesline's emotions. The few sentences here put down will enable the reader to understand the full nature of her alternating culminations of family pride and of maternal affection.

She too had heard the approach of Edmund Loyle. Stepping to her window and turning aside the curtain, she looked out upon him as he rode Selim, his coal-black steed with the white star in his forehead, she watched him emerging from the shadow of the trees and approaching the garden. As he courteously removed his hat in the presence of Eunice, she too could not restrain her admiration; but mournfully said "Noble in bearing and in character; yes, as a monarch! I believe he has never done anything mean, cruel or false; and on the positive side, has been studious, beneficent and measuring up fully in duty to himself, his neighbor and his God. And yet I would not have him allied to the DeLesline's; for who was his grandfather? Where is his genealogical record? Marriage should go by blood. But Eunice, darling—your happiness shall be my happiness, if God gives me grace to bear my great disappointment."

Then with an outburst of grief she cried, "My heart is bereaved—bereaved— and my soul is sick within me! O Eunice, beautiful daughter—take not all thy love from me!" She sank again upon her chair and covered her face with her hands. She

2. Ruth 1:16.
3. II Corinthians 10:12.

had never felt that Eunice could be other than her own Eunice still, if Willie Barton married her—Eunice Barton-DeLesline!—but now—now—she had seen the sole lord of her daughter's heart ride from the shadows into the sun-light.—

"I am glad to see you so well this morning" said Colonel Loyle, as he dismounted and entered the garden, bringing in with him Leo and Ponce—"and, Eunice, while Willie Barton is away, you must permit me to protect you if you need protection; will you not?"

The blushes on her cheeks made her in truth a queen of the roses. Ponce and Leo, powerful and savage as they were, came of their own accord and lay down at her feet, looking affectionately to her face and whining for her notice and caress.

"And I have brought these friends of mine," continued Colonel Loyle, "to be your friends. Feed them with your own hand and let them know your voice. They will guard you as no other watchers can. Mr. Gillespie is busy on the farm and need not be told to stay at the house for your protection. And should you want me at any hour, unchain Ponce and say 'Ponce—to Oakhill!'—and he will come to me. You may confidently trust him with a letter, if you wish to send one. He has been so trained that if I chance not to be at home he will deliver it to no one but Johnny."

She raised her inspiring, love-lit eyes to his, and placing her hand in his, replied "You always guard me; therefore I feel no fear."

He had never seen her so lovely. There seemed to emanate from her eyes and to pervade his whole being thrilling rays, as it were, which caused his frame to quiver as he strove to appear calm and indifferent. Had he mastered himself when his lips moved but uttered no speech? When he lingeringly resigned her hand and turned his face—when he silently rode back beneath the trees—when reigning in his horse, he turned and looked upon her gazing abstractedly after him from among the roses, with Ponce and Leo at her feet—when he bowed adieu; and sighed when she could not hear, then plunged into the thick forest? He who for years believed he had completely mastered himself—what sudden power was there in Eunice to-day —what mysterious emanation from her spirit to his—that he could not control his heart nor dare stay in her presence?

When the gloom of the forest enveloped his retreating form, the color drained away on Eunice's cheeks and she thought again deep down in her heart "O, what shall I do if you go away from me forever!"

We must follow Colonel Loyle. Chagrined, displeased with his frail nature, because he had not more completely kept under control the love within him; he debated with himself the question of remaining to help his neighbors in the difficulties and dangers surrounding them or of departing immediately to the West that he might be blameless of intervening between his friend and the fair Eunice, whose power over him had become, as he now for the first time felt, magically irresistible. If possible, he would see her no more. Let sorrow be his lot; that he could bear; but not the never-ceasing self-condemnation of having dishonored the claims of friendship. Further and further into the forest he penetrated, pondering his duties in this eventful crisis both of his own affairs and in those of the State, and of Eunice too; for though he had no sure reason for it, no proof of it, yet he felt that harm was hovering near her.

At length, following one of the hunters' paths through the swamp, he came within a short distance of the encampment of soldiers who had been brought into the court-martialled county to suppress the Ku-Klux and arrest the men who were supposed to belong to such organizations; and he was aware, from secret information, that he himself was particularly aimed at. As he slowly traversed a narrow path which covered the end of a gorge beyond the swamp and between two hills overgrown with trees, he heard voices as of men wrangling and quarreling. Stopping and listening, he distinctly heard the voices again deep down the gully or ravine between the hills, and could see the disputants close by an old tree on the side of the declivity; a civil officer of the arresting force and an aged negro man.

This officer, Captain Fert—not the chief marshal, who was operating elsewhere; but his nephew and deputy—had been one of those Northerners who had adroitly kept away from danger whenever danger was to be faced; and who became most loud-mouthed and valiantly oppressive of the South, when the war was ended. He was now partly in control of the special constables in the pay of the alarmed State authorities to hunt down and arrest all the unfortunate old Carolinians who were in ill-favor with the ruling power or with any of their own former slaves. It was easy to frame charges of disloyalty, as they called it, or, which amounted to the same thing, of being connected with any concerted effort, especially in the nine court-martialled Counties, to defend their families from insult or their property from spoliation. All husbands, fathers, and brothers so disposed were liable to be arrested, tried and imprisoned as bloody Ku Klux.

Fert usually hunted with his uncle, like a couple of beagles; but preferred to act separately as he made more money by it. He had managed to get under his direction or the chief magistrate had gotten for him from higher authority, a detachment of cavalry whom he brought into this neighborhood to assist him in making arrests. They were encamped a short distance off. Colonel Loyle's attention being called to the loud and angry wrangling borne up from the ravine as through a tunnel, he easily heard every word uttered by the disputants.

"Wish I may die if 'taint so. I tell you, 'fore you arrest um, de old man say, Bud, we must hide de money. Dere's two tousand dollars for de farm and de house. We can't git off now; and if dey catch us wid de money, dey'll jist take it from us. De best plan is to hide it Bud, till we come back. They mustn't ketch us wid de money on us. We've done nothing wrong and dey can't keep us in jail long. You see, Mass Fert, when you bin ketching all dere relations in de udder deestrict, 20 miles from here, dey sell out to quit and go away. But you too quick wid de cabberly. I neber heer of more dan de two tousand dollars, I tell you. My massa, Jim Corday, always speak de trute. I down-face any man 'bout dat."

"You lie! There was more, you cunning rascal, and you stole it. And now you claim half of this. I'll be hanged if you'll get round me that way."

"I 'clare to God, Mass Fert, dat's all I see um hide under de root of dis old pine tree. I bin 'fraid to take um. But I say, if you take um and gib me half, den it's all right and nobody kin eber trouble old Sye. Now you got um and put um in your pocket, you say you won't gib me none. Dat's cheating."

"Cheating—did you say!" and Fert seized the old man's throat. Colonel Loyle was on the point of rushing down upon him and dismounted to do so. But Fert had struck the old negro several blows in the mouth and on the head with the barrel of his pistol and kicked him down a steep cleft of the gully. He fell, and was motionless. As Colonel Loyle after tying his bridle to a bough, clambered down, (the declivity being somewhat abrupt where he was attempting to descend), Fert fled from sight. The poor old man was dead indeed, his head lying on the rocks and bent from the body, and blood trickling from his mouth. "Such your fate, poor deluded fellows! But perhaps, old Sye, you deserved your end. After all your master's kindness to be traitor to him at the last, when trouble came upon him. When he and Bud had gone away, it was your duty to guard what they left concealed. Is there any gratitude in your race? Even if your rascally conduct is due to the influence of others, still, Old Sye, that excuse does not cleanse the soul." Climbing up from the ravine and Remounting his horse, the Colonel rode forward to the camp. Frying pans, tin kettles, empty bottles, potatoes, ham bones, chicken feathers, smoking embers, were here and there in confusion. Black men, mulattoes, white men, were lying down or strolling about. Among the white men was Lubb, half drunk even at this early hour. Was that the Honorable Mr. Guelty yonder?—he who slunk just now under that tent? What means he here?—And was that the Honorable Caesar Boley, who hid behind that tree yonder? What means he here?

The small squad of cavalrymen and the manly looking lieutenant commanding them were at a little distance, as if they loathed the association of such a motley crowd of spies, informers and thieves. Colonel Loyle rode through the camp up to the cavalrymen and received and acknowledged the respectful salute of their officers. "May I inquire sir, where is Captain Fert," he asked as he bowed to the Lieutenant.

"He went off about an hour ago"—"Can you inform me in which direction, sir?"—"Over the hill yonder."

"Pray excuse me—but I wish to find him. Did he go alone?"

"No, sir—he went off with an old man named Sye. Will you leave your name, sir?"

"Loyle is my name."

The Lieutenant started; for he knew there was a plot there formed for the capture of Colonel Loyle and Lieutenant Barton, and he was here to aid especially in their arrest as dangerous leaders in the Ku Klux outrages. He was impressed with the courteous bearing of his visitor and said in his heart "Heaven defend this gentleman from the clutches of these fellows. Before I will arrest a man like this, I'll break my sword and smash that rascal Fert's head with the hilt." As the Colonel rode off, he met special constable Fert coming into camp.

Having met before in Columbia, they needed no introduction; and Colonel Loyle began: "Captain, I come to inquire how the distressing calamities under which this neighborhood is suffering may be mitigated—and to offer my counsel and my services if they be acceptable in any measure looking to the amelioration of our present distress."

"Things have gone too far, Mr. Loyle. I am but obeying orders," was Fert's reply; and he turned abruptly away, confused under the steady eye of Colonel Loyle. The latter observed blood-stains on Fert's hand, and his lip instinctively curled with contempt as he turned his horse towards his quiet home at Oakhill. Fert beckoned to the Lieutenant in command of the troopers quartered near by and pointed to Colonel Loyle as he rode off; but the Lieutenant took no notice of the beckoning and pointing nor moved from the spot where Colonel Loyle had left him standing.

The Colonel, upon his arrival home, found Norant, Pelton and other friends awaiting him. They apprised him of what they had discovered of the plot to arrest him. The alien rulers of the State were anxious to magnify the importance of what they called the Ku Klux conspiracy against the lives of themselves and the elective franchise of the new colored citizens, by implicating in the movement some of the prominent ex-Confederate officers and this one especially. After his friends departed Johnny placed in his hand a letter from Lieutenant Barton.

"My dear Colonel—I made my way home from Columbia to my aunt's and arrived last night, by a round about route; because I heard they were going to arrest me at the University on suspicion, so soon as I returned from the Thomleigh farm. And I did not wish to bring disrepute on your *alma mater,* so I skirted round from Columbia. I stayed several weeks with a friend to enjoy the good fishing in that vicinity. I fear I did not put on my gloves soon enough at the Depot when you noticed the tar on my wrist. The Reverend Honorable Guelty is at the bottom of this persecution of me. Perhaps you know of the attempt to shoot me (about which I don't care the snap of a finger) and of the melancholy death of dear old Uncle Tim. I send you also a newspaper report about yourself, which, no doubt, you have already seen and laughed at. As you never belonged to any Ku Klux order and fear nothing, and I unfortunately do, I shall leave to you any movement I should make, or the selection of any time and place to confer with me. I shall keep close to my aunt's house till I hear from you. You have not been here since you brought cousin Helen home; and Aunt Mary, who will take this to Mrs. DeLesline's and get it sent to you from there, wishes me to say how much we thank you for the timely rescue of cousin Helen. You are so accustomed to do brave deeds and forget them that perhaps our thanks may take you by surprise. But there has been a wonderful change in her. She seems to be recovering her reason. The Reverend Mr. Fairbanks—a cousin you know of 'her Robert,' came over from the rectory as soon as he heard of her seizure, violent excitement and subsequent swoon; and he has been carefully attending her with Dr. Kloan. They think favorably of her condition. She woke from her stupor about noon, looked serenely around, recognized us all, asked if she had been sick, and when had she left home to visit us. Then she went off into a quiet sleep again. Mamie is planning diversions for cousin Helen and visits to Mrs. De-Lesline's, to yourself at Oakhill, and to the Reverend bachelor at the Rectory. Of course Eunice will be of the party and Gillespie comes in for another 'of course,' while poor me must stay in concealment. I think I'll go anyhow.

"Yours most sincerely W.B.—"

Colonel Loyle struck a match and burned this letter. Much that it contained he already knew, but not Willie's foolish coming to Glyndale. Walking up and down his piazza awhile, he said to himself, "It will be harder to get Willie out of this scrape than any I ever had to help him out of. He has run right into their net. They know where he is, I'm sure. It seems impossible for him to get away from Glyndale before night—if even then. I can help him now only at great risk to myself. But we shall see." He called Johnny and said, with a smile, "Johnny, I know you can clean and load pistols and rifles with your one hand"—"O yes, Colonel, and use them too. Don't you remember?"—"Well, Johnny, fix all our arms immediately. But I will load my own pistols myself."

Johnny retired to his task and the Colonel continued to walk to and fro in the piazza. After awhile he carefully prepared his pistols and strapped them to his waist beneath his coat and went out to mount Selim again. It was very seldom that he carried a weapon; only when absolutely necessary.

"But, Colonel, don't go out again till you have had your dinner. It has just been placed upon the table. I am sure you ate a mere morsel at breakfast and have been in the saddle since daylight."

"Thank you, Johnny my boy,—but let Frau Hennchen have a plenty of hot coffee at nine o'clock to night. I may bring company with me. Just at dark, Johnny, take Lu into the house and you yourself keep watch in the yard and don't forget to keep our arms secure"—and he rode off.

The day was exceedingly sultry and portended one of those violent summer storms which at times desolate field and forest. Johnny, having been much alone, was in the habit of talking aloud to himself. He looked at the threatening sky and then towards his patron as he disappeared down the long road of oaks and remarked, as if talking to a friend, "When you see him look that way, and his eyes shine that way and he sits on his saddle that way, something more than usual is the matter. Whatever it be that rouses him now, I know he is right and will come back conqueror." And Johnny, with a firm faith in this matter which the whole world could not have abated if it tried—turned whistling into the house and to his dinner, as gleeful as if his revered friend had gone to bring home a bride; though it would seriously have puzzled Johnny to conjecture who could move that steady heart to the folly of woman's love or what the Colonel's "way" would be under circumstances so foreign to all those in which he had seen his gallant chieftain act.

When at seven o'clock he galloped up the avenue he was alone, and proceeded directly to the stable and carefully attended to Selim's needs and made him comfortable before he entered his house to refresh himself. Buoyant and ready for action, he appeared; joyous rather than thoughtful; as though his plans were complete, whatever those plans were. He laughed with Johnny and played with Lu and sipped his coffee. Soon several of his old soldiers came into the hall and took a cup of coffee and spoke apart with him and retired. Again and again this occurred, and the "down, Lu!" with which the large dog was kept quiet by her master convinced Johnny that he understood why Lu had been brought into the house and Ponce and Leo carried off in the morning. The men who silently came in, armed and with spurs on heel, though now horses appeared near—convinced him that active reconnoitering was going on in various directions. Scarcely had the last scout retired, when Ponce bounded into the room and placed his paws on his master's breast, holding in his mouth a letter which he had brought. Patting the faithful and intrepid dog, he gave him food from the table and eagerly took the letter open and read:

"Nurse has discovered a dreadful scheme against me, so soon as your capture is certain. What capture? The swamp is full of armed negroes to intercept Willie (Nurse says) We know Willie was at his aunt's an hour ago, six P.M. Old Pam was in our kitchen last night and talked with her. He told her to tell me 'The net is set to catch the bird.'—Also a note addressed to me (dated yesterday) has been mysteriously left at the house. It is written in a feminine hand and says Mother and I should immediately leave Glyndale and take you with us. Gillespie assures me I am safe. We would feel more safe if you were nearer to us.—Eunice"

Colonel Loyle knit his brow; compressed his lips to a thin line; looked at his watch; and then hastily left the room and went to the stable, taking Ponce with him. "There is time to find out more of this double or treble plot. I see now why Guelty and his tool Caesar were hiding in the camp this morning. The simultaneous attack here on me and at the Avery house is set down for twelve o'clock, as my scouts have found out, and their gang of detectives are keeping close and are not likely to show themselves on the main road before that hour. I can still venture upon it and carry Ponce back. There is imperative need now that Ponce should be there.—But why did not Willie do what I told him to do in the letter I sent him? He should be twenty miles away at this moment. His staying can only be understood by supposing his own trusted negro messenger (from the DeLesline farmhands) whom I sent back to him has played traitor to him and given my letter to Fert or Guelty. But perhaps every colored man about Glyndale has been tampered with and will play traitor to us."—Leaving no orders, he rode alone along the road towards Mrs. DeLesline's.

Guelty, who was dead-sure of catching Barton, had privately agreed with Deputy Fert to give him five hundred dollars if after the capture of Colonel Loyle at his home at Oakhill, he would postpone going to the Avery house for one hour and take the cavalry to Mrs. DeLesline's, capture and carry off on any pretext the men guarding her house, if he should find any there as was likely; and then proceed to Mrs. Avery's after Barton; leaving Mrs. DeLesline's house and its inmates in Guelty's power.

This disarranged slightly the original plan for the simultaneous capture; but Guelty's money offer prevailed. His marriage (the runaway scheme for which he partly communicated to Fert as the object of the new arrangement) and whatever awaited the consummation of it known to himself alone—he was determined upon now, once for all. He had ordered out his Black Rosettes and had sent Lubb down to pay liberally, for him, as many other negroes as he could rely upon to aid his scheme and to suborn them to testify afterwards against Loyle and Barton, so as to make sure their ruin or a life-long imprisonment; if they were not, one or both, killed to-night. Then, he thought, Eunice would be all his own. Even the Reverend Hezekiah (who was established in "little Africa" as successor in the Reverend Isaiah's missionary work) was to keep himself in readiness nigh Bartonboro' to officiate at the marriage; and Pam was to have the horse harnessed to the buggy, in case they should be needed.

But with his inborn intriguing spirit, Guelty perceived that if he could steal a march and carry off his prize without waiting for the performance of all Fert had agreed to execute, he could evade the payment of the promised reward, and there would be that much saved in his own pocket. He had therefore secretly slipped from Fert's camp and was watching his chances near Mrs. DeLesline's house, when Colonel Loyle—seen from their hiding place—rode down in that direction, carrying Ponce along with him. Judging that he would soon repass on the dark road, he, with the aid of Lubb and his special squad of twenty Black Rosettes (sworn to do his bidding) placed obstructions upon the road, tying a rope across it from tree to tree, to balk or trip the horse, while he and his allies from their ambush should pounce upon the fallen rider. Guelty with the spirit of intrigue which had guided him from his early youth, had not neglected to have still another string for his bow. He had obtained secretly from his friend the Governor who hated Colonel Loyle a promise of special reward from the Contingent Fund if, from his intimate knowledge of the environs of Glyndale he should capture Loyle or Barton through his own artifice. He assured the Governor of this intimate knowledge which he had of every by-path and that if circumstances were favorable the capture might be effected in this way more readily than by a body of cavalry and without any bloody collision. The Governor cared not how it might be effected, provided the deed was done. Whether Guelty's shrewd counterplotting made him a marplot, remains to be seen. He had not so much personal grudge to gratify against Loyle as against Barton. Loyle was the Governor's aim and also Troth's. But both the ex-Confederates were here in the same net; and he smiled to himself in thinking how he would fleece Troth for his services to-night in helping him to his revenge on the Colonel. He had the game in his own hand—all around. Above all, he hoped in his heart that this night's success would be a triumph for him in making Eunice his wife.

Whether or not he should have kept to one cunning scheme instead of mingling other cunning schemes with it, remains also to be seen. His inordinate love of money led him to think he was shrewd enough to avoid paying Fert that five hundred dollars and at the same time gather in a large award from the Contingent service fund and from his friend Troth. But while he sat in a clump of bushes by the dark road-side, ruminating on these things, he could not but shudder at the thought that Loyle whom he awaited was dangerous to grapple with, and the dog too, carried along as Loyle's body guard; so he supposed.

After a brief conference with Eunice (whom he advised to keep her pistol ready to hand) and with Mrs. DeLesline and Gillespie, and leaving Ponce again with them, Colonel Loyle was riding rapidly back to his own house, when Selim in the darkness of the night—for storm clouds were gathering over head—plunged his breast against the rope, reeled back and fell. Guelty, hidden in the bushes, fired at Colonel Loyle who was freeing himself from the fallen horse. The ball struck Selim in the head as he suddenly reared himself at the side of his master, saving that master's life. Guelty's idea was to wound and disable Loyle rather than to kill him. The Party wanted him for trial. At the same instant Lubb, less of a coward than Guelty, rushed up behind and tripped Colonel Loyle, and the band of Black Rosettes jumped on him and pinioned his arms.

"It is your game, is it, Mr. Guelty!" who came up now, pistol in hand, "and you, Mr. Lubb,—what mean you by a trick like this?"

"Mum's the word to-night. Lead him this way, men!" said Guelty, quite elated at their success.

He was lead further off into the woodlands, over a fence, to the oak grove, and thence around to Violet Spring as to a completely secluded spot, and there bound securely to a tree and gagged. They did not know or rather did not take time to think that this their hiding spot was familiar ground to those against whom they were acting.

There Guelty left him under guard, for the present, of all except Lubb and Caesar. These two he took with him to reconnoitre nearer Mrs. DeLesline's residence. He would summon more aid if he needed it. Fortune appeared to smile at last upon his nefarious designs. He sent Lubb to watch at the east of the house while he and Caesar watched the other side, keeping within the border of the woods. Caesar was his guide in the intricacies of the environs of the house.

Selim, crazed by the bullet in his brain, had turned and run frantically down the road past Mrs. Avery's, then turned confusedly again and run towards the house he had just left. He bounded directly against the front garden fence, the blood streaming into his eyes and dripping from his face; and neighing piteously; he fell, crushing down a panel of the fence in his fall. The inmates of the house, hearing the neighing and the crash, hastened to the front piazza. Ponce and Leo leapt to Selim's side and whined as they recognized their old stable companion in his death struggle. Eunice and her mother, and Mr. Gillespie with a lantern, came out to the garden fence and bent over the dying steed. Gillespie, after a slight examination, remarked "Colonel Loyle's Selim, saddled and bridled, and a bullet through the head."

Eunice stepped forward in a moment, shook her curls from her blanched face, and laying her hand upon Ponce's collar, said, "Come, Ponce!" They darted away into the woods, heedless of Mrs. DeLesline's impassioned entreaties to return. "Shall I follow her and leave you here alone?"

"Yes, Dupont; Leo will be with me; lose not a minute; save her, no matter what becomes of me.—Go, take the lantern with you."

Gillespie shut down the slides of the lantern and hastened in the direction Eunice had taken.

Thirteen

As thickly fall the twilight shades around,
And night begins her gloomy sceptre sway,
From yon old ruined pine with ivy bound,
The lonely owl hoots forth his nightly lay;
With rapid sweep the night-hawk seeks his prey.

Russell's Magazine

It had been a breezeless, sultry noon. The leaves of the forest had begun to shrivel in the baking heat. The shingles on house roofs appeared to undulate in the quivering hot air. When the blood-red sun sank slowly down, the twilight brought no abatement of the sultriness. Clouds were banking in the west where sheet-lighting glistened in fitful flashes. The moon was to rise at nine o'clock. So it was laid down in the almanack. But it was not likely any eye at Glyndale would see her in the eastern sky; for there two clouds had begun their billowy heaping up, mounting over each other toward the darkening zenith. Nature appeared to be gathering up her latent forces for some deadly conflict.

The storm clouds were still gathering overhead, and peals of thunder began to shake the air, when Eunice entered the forest. She was hastening in the direction of Oakhill, her first impulse leading her there and by the shortest path. She had just entered the forest when she heard a voice from a tree, saying, "This way, if you seek Colonel Loyle." It was Lubb or Jailey who, seeing the dog with Eunice, had leaped up upon a low branch of an oak to avoid his terrible teeth. He knew no flattery or pretended goodwill could deceive that incorruptible guardian.

"O show me where! Is he killed?" she quickly responded.

"No, not quite. I will lead you to him if you keep that dog from me. I am Colonel Loyle's friend."

"Come, quickly then," she imploringly cried.

Jailey's brain, so often fuddled, was never very clear. It was not clear in this sudden emergency. There seems to come over an erring man whose doom is nigh, a fate-ful confusion of thought and purpose. The shadow of Death's uplifted dart falls upon his soul and paralyzes it.—To frustrate Guelty was now Jailey's chief design, without calculating his further course and without regard to consequences. To balk the man against whom he had long harbored ill-will on his sister's account; an ill-will made rancorous by recent discovery that he himself had been systemati-cally cheated by that same scoundrel—was the only clear determination he had. He cared nothing for Loyle. He led Eunice whom he would not have willingly harmed rapidly in a direction off from Guelty and Caesar—away from Violet Spring where the Colonel was tied—away from the west side of the house which side led to that Spring and on which side he knew Guelty and Caesar had gone to watch. His design was to lead her away from them. But they were not in that place. Guelty had sneaked nearer Mrs. DeLesline's house, to assure himself that Eunice was at home. He had witnessed what occurred at the garden fence and hearing Mrs. DeLesline's screams to Eunice to return, had hurried back to his first watching place to call Caesar, then skirted the woods around in the opposite direction (the same in which Jailey had been put on guard) to intercept or follow her, taking Caesar with him. He was exultant now in the apparent certainty of his success; a double success, captur-ing Loyle and capturing the still greater prize he aimed at. He had no time to sum-mon part of his gang from Violet Spring. It was a fatal error for himself to leave them all there to guard Colonel Loyle. But he was excited and bent only on reach-ing Eunice.

Jailey had, by hurrying Eunice so quickly away into the pathless woods saved her from the interception of Caesar and Guelty. That was his main object, traitor-ous though it was to his employer. And lucky for her was the haste he had used; for he knew not Caesar and Guelty had left their position and were hurrying towards his.

Jailey thought of taking her by a circuitous rout back to her home or some other place of safety, if he could find such a place. But so soon as he had lead her astray in the entanglement of the forest, the intricacies of which he was not acquainted with he became irresolute, confused as to the direction he should take, and seized with a strange and mortal dread of the powerful lion-like dog whose collar she held. The dog had been growling at him ever and anon, despite the chiding of Eunice. The thought struck him, he must get rid of that dog whose growling kept his nerves in a tremor. It was a quickly conceived, a half crazy, almost suicidal act on his part. For some weeks past his drunken habits had unstrung him. When put upon his solitary watch, he had made free use of his whisky flask to steady his nerves; but it had not produced that effect. Slipping his pistol from his pocket behind him, he put the barrel, with a shaky hand, in contact with Ponce's head and fired. But Ponce winced from the touch of the pistol and the bullet, slightly wound-ing him, buried itself in the earth. Eunice, in her alarm, let go his collar. With an ominous yelp the fierce dog seized him by the throat, dragging him down, and tearing open veins and arteries held him as a tiger would hold a struggling jackal. —Jailey, more confused than ever, seemed to have lost the ability of resistance.

Guided by the pistol shot and Jailey's gurgled curses Guelty hurried up. Eunice, her pistol in her hand (which, and her stiletto, she carried as Colonel Loyle had advised her to do) stood gazing in astonishment at the fury of Ponce and the writhing of her treacherous conductor. "Stand back," she cried, pointing her pistol at the breast of Guelty as he broke through the bushes. Caesar stood aghast (and purposely in concealment) a few feet behind his master in iniquity. But Guelty with a cry "at last!" leapt for his prey and had almost laid hands upon Eunice when Ponce, letting go the throat of Jailey, unexpectedly flew at that of Guelty who, taken unawares, rolled upon the ground faintly screaming at the impetuous onset and the sudden sinking of Ponce's teeth through his nose and cheek. He fell near Jailey. With blood-shot eyes and failing strength, Jailey, incoherently uttering something about his sister at home and his being cheated here, raised himself to his elbow and with the pistol which he still grasped almost touching Guelty's breast, fired directly into his heart.—It was the last ball the weapon held.—With his face crushed in Ponce's jaws Guelty half sprang up, lifting the dog with him, then his limbs relaxed and quivered and he lay motionless—dead!

(Have we not said that Ponce came originally from the hands of the aged and faithful Sancho, whom Guelty revengefully killed, as narrated at the close of our first chapter? The thought flashes upon us. Was the spirit of the murdered old man present in this dismal spot, summoned, as it were, by the rumbling thunder of the sky to look on at the fearful retribution of the crime which had brought bloody death to himself?)

With increased fury, Ponce sprang again upon Jailey and renewed the gashing of his throat. There was but feeble struggling now; for Jailey was dying.—Caesar, without daring to help or even show himself, frightened as he had never been in all his life, climbed the nearest pine tree and climbed to the very top, and would have gone higher up if he could.—All this happened, we may truly say, in less time than it takes to tell it.

Gillespie, bewildered by the first report of Jailey's pistol (when he fired at the head of Ponce), but put, by the second and louder report, upon the direction to the dense thicket of undergrowth; then guided by the vicious growling of the dog, reached the scene of conflict and opened his lantern. Astounded by the awful sight he could only ejaculate, when he saw Eunice standing with her ready pistol in hand, "Thank God, I have found you!"—Two mangled and bloody men, one still in the throes of death; the furious dog rending them both by turns—the dead and the dying; Eunice, with pale firm face, holding her pistol at Gillespie's approaching form; the flickering beams from his lantern; the occasional flashes of lightning, and sullen booming from the black clouds above; the sighing of the fitful storm-wind through the trees around;—all brought a shudder even to the veteran Gillespie. "Come away, Miss Eunice, from this horrid spot!" he cried.

"Now to Colonel Loyle—guide me or follow me!—Brave Ponce, my hero,— come!" she said. The dog, giving his last tearing gash to the dead Jailey, alias Lubb, placed himself at her side with evident token of satisfaction, the gore of her enemies dripping from his jaws. How admirable the instinct in him to discover latent enmity, to yield willing obedience in the service of genuine friendliness!—With her left hand on his collar and her little silver-mounted pistol in her right (as if that pistol could do wonders!—and it might too, for she was a skillful marksman), "On to Colonel Loyle!" she cried and led the way.

They were hastening they knew not whither, when Ponce snuffing the ground, exhibited signs of joy and suddenly turned to the right, whining and yelping, his nose still to the ground. "Let us follow where Ponce leads us, Miss Eunice," whispered Gillespie. They soon came to the fence over which the pinioned Colonel Loyle had been carried and which separated the DeLesline estate from the woodlands. Over this fence Ponce leapt and following the trail guided them first into the grove where once they practiced at the target. It was in sight of the Spring.—The continuous rumbling of thunder rendered inaudible to the guard at the Spring the sound of their coming and the low growling of the dog. Eunice could with difficulty hold him back. Yet he seemed to know, as though he was a human being, the object of the business they were engaged upon, and the method they thought best to attain that object. The flashes of lightning disclosed to them the group of negroes at the Spring. "He must be there, Miss Eunice," whispered Gillespie. "Stay here with Ponce and let me examine nearer."—"No, No—we will go together," she replied.— The Black Rosettes guard joking and passing to each other their bottles of liquor, sat or lay near the Spring and at a little distance from the tree to which Colonel Loyle was securely bound. Knowing he was gagged and tied as strong as knots can tie, they thought as little of him as they would of any other arrested "buckra"; for they were not cognizant of the secret designs of their leaders and were all "furriners" in fact to this locality and its people. At a glance Eunice determined her plan of action. She was familiar with every foot of ground around the Spring. "Stay here with Ponce, Mr. Gillespie, till you hear my pistol fired behind Colonel Loyle. I see where he is. I know how to reach him. When you hear my pistol, then let Ponce loose and shout and fire your own pistol. If we scatter the guard and rescue the Colonel, we will then all get to the house as quickly as possible."

Leaving Ponce with a few caressing pats on his head, she made her way around the guard and safely reached the rear of the tree; though she feared—notwithstanding the dark dress she wore—that she might be seen while lightning flashed from time to time. "Colonel Loyle," she said close to his ear, "I will cut these cords and then fire my pistol as a signal to Mr. Gillespie who will fire from the opposite side and let Ponce loose."

Colonel Loyle nodded his head in response. With her sharp stiletto the cords were cut, the gag removed, his arms and feet untied. The pistol was fired, quickly answered by Gillespie's, who raised the old war yell and rushed with Ponce to the attack. Colonel Loyle too bounded into the midst of the guard, striking right and left. "Coo-cux! Coo-cux! Lord hab mercy!" broke from the guard as they scattered through the forest.

With fervid thanks to Eunice, Colonel Loyle conducted her without delay to the house. If they had not tied him where they did, she could not so readily have succored and rescued him. The excitement and rapid movements of the past hour—now that her purpose was achieved—began to show their effect in her almost exhausted power of endurance. She was forced to lean almost fainting on the arm to which she clung. The back windows and doors of the house had been barred. They were obliged to go through the front garden. The stopped a moment over the fallen Selim. The Colonel sadly said "shot to death—and by a lurking murderer! Through how many battle perils may you not have passed unhurt, to fall so ingloriously now! But it may be my fate also.—Gillespie, it is necessary that you make your way to Oakhill and as quickly as possible, and bring me my roan horse. Tell the men of the obstruction across the main road. It may be still there. And tell"—He took Gillespie aside and communicated his further commands. Finally he said "if you are not back here in thirty minutes I must seek the men myself on foot."

Placing Eunice's arm again in his own he led her into the piazza, saying, while they awaited the unlocking of the door, "You have released me in good time, my heroine, to save Willie for you, if it may be done—whatever happens to myself. May his restoration to you repay in part my debt of gratitude."

She sighed; and as a glittering flash from the sky momentarily made visible the fair face uplifted to his, he saw a look of love in it which she would never have shown him in the garish light of day. O what an effort to restrain his arms from holding her for one minute to his heart!

Mrs. DeLesline received Eunice with fervent demonstrations of joy and chided her rashness in venturing into the forest. With a happy smile Eunice retired to her apartments up stairs; while her mother conducted Colonel Loyle to the supper room and spread refreshments before him.

"They will be hunting for me in an hour's time, Mrs. DeLesline; but with your permission I shall let them find me here; I mean near by.—I regret it, if I shall be bringing any disturbance to your household. Yet, to be some protection to you, if need be, and to be close to Mrs. Avery's in order to help Lieutenant Barton, who it appears has not gone away as I wished him to go this morning—I have abandoned the plan I had first formed for frustrating the schemes of the banded villains to-night. Tomorrow better counsels may prevail."

"I heartily thank you, Colonel. We shall certainly be more secure with you here. Though hundreds of men are in the neighborhood of Glyndale, on you alone the whole community relies. I really believe that were we in a desert or on some separate isle away from any government to protect us, you would be by nature our ruler or our king."

Her voice was unsteady as she thought of her morning's conference with Eunice. Despite her motherly regard and preference for Willie Barton, she could not but feel convinced that her daughter would have indeed a most loveable consort and guardian in the unpretending young Colonel before her—serene and smiling, though he knew two bands were then centering near at hand, one to capture, bind, degrade if they could, perhaps slay him; the other, with friendly zeal to involve themselves and their families in trouble by espousing his cause, and Barton's too at his request, in whatever manner he should bid them do it. He much preferred to face the raiding band alone and spare his friends the ignominious consequences of trial and imprisonment which they could easily avoid by abstaining from mixing themselves up, by implication, with young Barton's Ku Klux proclivities.

"My dear Madame," replied Colonel Loyle, "you flatter me. I value most highly your esteem, and the regard of my neighbors and old comrades. And yet, do you know, I am almost ready to quit this once happy home, perchance to see it no more. I remain now only because I cannot bear the thought of leaving my friends in their present circumstances of political oppression. So soon as quiet shall have been restored, I purpose to sell my lands and go far West to a beautiful spot I once explored and purchased. Did I ever describe it to you, Mrs. DeLesline?"

"No—Colonel—but what will become of Eunice if you leave us?"

His voice quavered now as he answered "If I could serve her—if she should desire me to stay—But the mention of her recalls me to her service now in helping Willie. What I am about to venture for him a few minutes hence, is based on the condition or rather certainty of his being at Mrs. Avery's. A change of position on his part may defeat my effort in his behalf. He is so impulsive, that unless he remains where I expect to find him, my plan will be defeated. My force to help me is so small and the number of our assailants so great, that to act efficiently I must act at one place at a time and move expeditiously to the next point. Many negroes too are here armed and goaded on by base instigators to do harm to him and others in this neighborhood. An attempt on Willie's part to escape to-night, may end in his death. If they seize him in such attempt I'm sure he will resist. To save him I must now get possession of him. Having a force of my own I can refuse to give him up and thus find time to send him away in safety. At this hour I must surprise those who expect to surprise him. I must get him off from them, and at the same time protect this house; that is to say, if they come here also in search of him."

"Colonel, he is so thoughtlessly venturesome that I can only hope he may not defeat your disinterested efforts for his safety. We know how much trouble and anxiety he has caused you by coming home and now by not escaping as you had devised. I regard him as my son, Colonel Loyle; and long hoped he would become more a son to me than he is, and as his own dear mother wished him to be. It will nearly break his heart to know that Eunice declares her hand is not destined for him. Perhaps his buoyant, careless spirit may bear it better than I suppose. Eunice says there has been no betrothal and can be none. I never dreamt that in her heart another idol was enthroned."

A flush spread over the face of Colonel Loyle. No doubt the gallant soldier would have been embarrassed to frame a reply to Mrs. DeLesline's remarks, had not Gillespie luckily entered the room. "Your horse is without—here is the bugle—the men have set out to their new post in the Indian graveyard. Was that precisely what you wished? for there was some hesitancy about it as I had no written order? and it contravened your previous plan of operation.—" The Indian graveyard, as it was called, was quarter of a mile from Mrs. DeLesline's, between her house and Oakhill. It was a spot reputed to be haunted. It was just visible from the roadside.

Colonel Loyle replied "Perfectly right, Gillespie. I know no spy, no negro spy, will venture near that graveyard so late at night, even if it were to save his life. The change of post going through the swamp may baffle all spies—and I am closer to my men. You know this vicinity perhaps as well as I do. Do you agree with me that a bugle call can be heard so far a night like this—if I blow it, say, in the piazza here? There must be no mistake about it?"

"Distinctly—if you blow between the thunder rolls."

"Mrs. DeLesline, you have no objection to my leaving a sure guard with you, in case I shall take Mr. Gillespie and a part of my men and dash through the negroes in the shortest way to Mrs. Avery's house and give Willie a chance of escape? Having sent him off under an escort, I can then cut my way back to this point while the chief body of the enemy are perhaps searching my house at Oakhill. If the cavalry men come here, you ladies will have nothing to fear. I wish they would come for I can leave you entirely to their guardianship. But the dastardly cunning wretches who have managed to employ them have schemes of their own to carry out and may ransack every chamber in this house, if they gain an entrance. My favorite dogs are equal to half-a-dozen men in defending yourself and Eunice. Will you allow them to be in the house—in your chamber—in your company till I return here and the onset on me here shall terminate? I shall feel relieved of much anxiety if you have them with you?"

"Whatever you desire, Colonel Loyle, shall be done," replied Mrs. DeLesline.

"Then it is time—Gillespie, bring in Leo and Ponce from the hall-way. Please call Eunice down, Mrs. DeLesline; the dogs are devoted to her already."

As Gillespie brought them in, Eunice entered by another door. The monstrous animals came to her caress and stretched themselves at her feet. "My courageous Ponce!" she said, patting his head.

"But Eunice," asked Colonel Loyle, "whence these blood-stains on his face and paws! Indeed, his whole breast is stained with gore; more than this slight wound I see on his head would produce"—and he stooped down to examine the wound.

"It is the blood of two men who waylaid us when we were seeking you. Mr. Gillespie will tell you about it tomorrow," she replied without raising her head and gently smoothing Ponce's strong neck.—The dogs were given food from the table and like gentle lambs crouched again at the feet of their new mistress whose presence, from the first sight of her, appeared to exercise a magical charm upon them.

The Colonel looked inquiringly to Gillespie and beckoned to him. He bent to the Colonel's ear, who had again seated himself, and whispered. "Ponce tore Lubb's throat because he tried to kill him in the woods and Lubb while dying shot Guelty through the heart who had come up and who was also pulled down by Ponce. They both lie dead in the forest."

"Thank God! Most glad I am to hear that!—You must try to get the bodies before they are discovered and bring me whatever letters and papers you find upon them." Then he said aloud "My greatest fear for to-night is removed. The hand of the Almighty was in this righteous penalty. Ponce—well done, old friend! No higher reward can be bestowed on you than to be always near your new mistress— if she will receive you into her service."

His glance to Eunice was acknowledged by her smiling and laying her hand upon the faithful Ponce's head. Bidding adieu to the ladies and telling them Gillespie,—as matters were now simplified, would stay and attend to bolting the doors, he passed with him through the sitting room into the hall, and there examined and adjusted his pistols. Closing the door after their exit, he requested Gillespie to remain a while there in the piazza and was about to go out into the rain and storm, when a strange figure bounded into the piazza and against him. He seized the violent intruder by the throat and drawing a pistol demanded "Who are you?"

"Me, Colonel—Willie Barton!"

"Why, man alive, how came you here and in this plight?"

From head to foot bespattered with mud, dripping with rain, without a hat on his head, his hair matted over his face—his whole figure was most grotesque, as it was lighted up by the quickly recurring flashes of lightning. But his merry laugh showed his old recklessness in perils when his scouting continually brought him into "tight places."

"I judged these fellows, Colonel, were stealing a march on us and closing around before their promised time. A colored friend told cousin Mamie something of their manoeuvres. The storm, maybe, hurried them into action in order to arrest me. So I sneaked away from my aunt's and threaded my way through the swamp, where I lost my hat in some bushes; I just blackened my face by smearing a little mud over it and over my hair; and tripped some half dozen of them into the swampy mire as I passed. You know I can talk their lingo to perfection and laugh like them. They're as thick as blackberries in the swamp and half frightened at nothing at all.—By the way, I saw Crosnahan down there tied to a tree. He'll work himself loose."

"That accounts for his sending in no more reports. But I'm glad you are here. What will you do with yourself now? Can I get you off from here? The whole crowd will be after you and me directly—in ten or fifteen minutes, it may be?"

"O—I know a nice hiding place on the roof of this house, which was fixed while we were repairing it; and I'll just go up and lie quiet there. It was good foresight to fix that place—wasn't it? I thought I might have use for it some day. I can get to it without the knowledge of the family; and if the devils search for me here, the family can conscientiously asseverate that I am not here. Just let Gillespie help me to reach the sky-light and the roof. They shall never arrest me and jail me. I'll die first."

There was a sound as of trampling feet from the direction of the swamp, heard through the pelting rain. The darkness was intense and the storm increasing in violence. "Willie, be quick—slip indoors—and avoid going near Mrs. DeLesline's rooms up stairs. My dogs are there and will rend you in pieces in your present disfigurement."

Barton slipped in and was helped to gain the roof through a part of the house away from the chambers. The Colonel then bade Gillespie remain inside and barricade the doors. "I think now you'd better stay here as special guard to the ladies" he said to him.

Scarcely had Willie entered the door when scout Crosnahan appeared, saying in his usual calm tone "The rascals tied such hard knots it took a long time to get my hands loose. They're still keeping watch around the Avery house. A part have drawn in closer to it and a part are coming here. Barton, in guise of a darkey, passed me in the swamp; but it was policy not to speak to him."

> Colonel Loyle: He is safe here. Get, soon as you can, to your horse, Cros, which no doubt has been taken for you to the Indian graveyard over yonder.

The murmuring and trampling from the direction of Mrs. Avery's and the swamp became more audible—and could it have been heard there would have been a similar sound from Oakhill, for the main body of raiders were busy there. The Colonel stood a while in the dark near his horse. In the lighting up of the scene by the flashes from the sky, a crowd of dusky forms were observed gathered about the barn and another crowd about some outbuildings a thousand feet distant, but nearer the dwelling house than the barn was. The smell of smoke began to fill the murky, humid air. A crackling was heard and dark figures moved stealthily around the outbuildings. "These," thought Loyle, "are Black Rosettes, and acting under instructions from Guelty before he met his fate." Soon the buildings emitted from windows and from chinks in the weather boarding the light of the fires burning within. Then through the shingled roofs shot up tongues of flame hissing in the rain.—The domestic servants, roused by the fire, were caught as they emerged from their quarters and put under guard.

Colonel Loyle who had watched all this, mounted his horse and rode through the front garden to an elevation in the road towards the Indian burial ground. He paused till a moment of stillness prevailed. Then rang out the old time bugle call—then rang the shrill response—bugle echoing back to bugle—and Colonel Loyle dashed forward on the splashy road to meet his coming band.

The heart of Eunice throbbed quicker and her eyes flashed as the bugle call told her Colonel Loyle was in action. She prayed for his safety. Ponce and Leo rose to their feet and then lay down again. Willie Barton stood up near the chimney on the house-top, peered down the dark road and said to himself "Would to heaven, I could be in the saddle when that bugle blows—though we all may be hanged for it!"

The crowd of Guelty's negro henchmen around the burning out-buildings shrank back with the cry "Wot dat!" and rolled the whites of their eyes at each other in alarm. "All we had to do" said one of them, "was to burn de barns; so I'se going to quit before de Coo-Cux debbil gits here. I don't like de sound of dat bugle no how. I nebber hear one sound like dat."

The thirty ex-Confederate cavalrymen in the Indian graveyard leapt to their saddles and with the old yell which they could not keep down, sprang into the road and made their rapid way to their leader's call.

On the road he heard their approach and awaited them. They checked up and saluted. Without a word he put himself at their head. They rode more slowly then and came in sight of Mrs. DeLesline's mansion; and there he turned them from the road under the branching oaks opposite the house and halted them.

"All keep quiet, men, and listen for Fert and his cavalry coming from Oakhill." They had not long to listen. The clanking of the sabres and the splashing in the rainpools along the road could now be heard, for there was an intermission of the storm. In addition to the buildings already fired, other buildings had caught and the environs of the mansion were lighted up. Colonel Loyle could distinctly see deputy-marshal Fert as he passed along with the troop; and heard him remark— "that infernal rebel Colonel should have staid at his own house, if he is as brave as they say he is. He is hiding here, no doubt. But, by heaven! I'll shake every sheet and blanket in the house till I find the skunk."

He conducted the troop into the yard and had them drawn up in line near the house. He called to some of the civilian informers and spies, white and black, and posted them around in proximity to the house. He inquired particularly for Guelty and Lubb. No one could tell him where they were. He swore terribly when he learned from some of the barn-burners that Barton was not at the widow Avery's, whither he was next to direct his raid.

"We know this fellow Barton was there after sunset. That's positive. How the h-l could he get through your lines?"

Willie laughed on the housetop and had a mind to call out something in response. It was mere good luck that he did not do so. He regarded the whole affair a high-style "lark," one of the best he had ever been on.

Fert expected Guelty to appear every minute and wondered that he did not see him. But no time could be lost; so he dismounted and running up the steps into the back piazza, hammered against the door with the butt of his pistol. No response came. "We'll break it in then," he cried;—"come, twenty of you darkies—search any crack and corner—pull out every bed and shake every blanket—till you find the cowards. Destruction seize the Honorable Mr. Benjamin Isaiah if he isn't here to gather his own roses!"

"It is time to stop this outrage—even if a conflict comes. It is rash; but the venture must be made. For myself, it is a good enough cause to perish in." So spoke Colonel Loyle under the oak trees. At his command his men slowly and quietly filed into the yard and halted in front of the troopers and saluted them in a friendly manner. No word was spoken. The officer of the troop recognized Colonel Loyle and smiled, and gave no orders to his men. All sat like statues on horseback.

"My God—my God—what is this!" exclaimed Fert, springing from the piazza and mounting his horse. "Draw your swords!" he shouted in alarm, while slinking behind the cavalry. "Lieutenant Andrews! I have authority to give you orders, Sir!"

"My sword shall be drawn," replied Lieutenant Andrews (the same young officer whom Colonel Loyle met in the camp), "in any honorable cause; not in one like this, nor at your command. The war against the South is over. I understand my duty here and when to draw my sword. I obey my official superiors in that, not hirelings of thievish adventurers."

Fert, for all his bluster, felt this insult (which he had brought on himself) as keenly as one of his nature could. He saw himself deserted at the last moment by the help he had relied on, to enable him to ride roughshod on and over whatsoever he wished.—"I shall have you, Sir, reported and under arrest!" he replied.—Colonel Loyle and his men continued silent. So did the amused troopers.

At length, advancing alone, again saluting Lieutenant Andrews (whose action or rather non-action was a great relief to him), Colonel Loyle said, "by the kindness and noble forbearance of this honorable officer I am emboldened to say to Mr. Fert in behalf of those whom he is seeking to oppress, that against him alone we thus appeared in self-defence.—Mr. Fert, come forward, Sir. You are a dead man the instant you succeed in forcing hostilities. Order these incendiary fires to be extinguished. I myself saw your men set those houses on fire."

"Who are you—who give me orders?"

"I, as you know, am Edmund Loyle," then turning to his men and pointing to Fert, he gave the command "Take aim!"

Lieutenant Andrews gave no orders against this. He only smiled and looked on. "Stop, Colonel, for God's sake, stop!" cried Fert to Loyle, "I'll have the fires put out." He turned and ordered the awe-stricken negroes, who had stood with wide eyes and open mouths a little distance off, to extinguish the flames. "Now, Sir, a word with yourself. Come nearer unless you wish all ears to hear." The deputy marshal crest-fallen and sullen, drew nearer—under that peculiar spell which Loyle appeared to exercise when he willed to do so. He then uttered in a solemn low tone "At the root of the old pine tree, in the ravine, where you put the two thousand dollars in the breast of your coat—"

"For God's sake, Colonel Loyle! What do you mean? Come further off."

"This spot suits me, Sir; and I have but to say that I alone was witness, and that unless you instantly draw off your men—as you have power to do, however it was delegated to you—and promise never more to hunt me up or Lieutenant Barton or disturb this dwelling—the rest which I have to say shall be openly said. Shall I proclaim it now?"

"I promise—here is my hand upon it."

"Keep your hand to yourself, Sir, and wash that old negro's blood from it if you can—and the blood of Guelty and of Lubb, who have lost their lives partly through your association in their schemes."

Colonel Loyle then gave orders in a quiet tone to his men and they left him and filed from the yard and formed again under the oaks. Fert, terrified at what he had heard, requested Lieutenant Andrews to send his men back to camp, and hastily followed them himself. The Lieutenant more amused than astonished at this running away of the valorous Fert, remained a moment to give some directions to the negroes in their work of extinguishing the fires; then approaching Colonel Loyle, extended his hand and received a warm grasp in return.

Fert, stung to the quick and maddened by the disclosure of his crime, halted his horse near the house as if to wait for Lieutenant Andrews; while the troopers laughing rode on to camp by the longer route along the broad State road. Secretly vowing revenge, Fert gritted his teeth and cursed the scoundrel Guelty, as he thought of the unpaid bribe of five hundred dollars which had disarranged his plans and brought him to this discomfiture. At this moment Willie Barton unable to restrain himself longer, mounted upon the chimney and shouted "Hurrah for Colonel Loyle!"

Fert looked up quickly and called back with an oath "hurrah for the skunk and yourself too!" and raising his pistol fired as Barton began to clamber down the roof to the eaves of the house. He fell head forward from the roof to the front piazza shed and then rolled off to the ground among the blooming garden flowers. At this moment the storm which for a while had relaxed its fury and seemed to be passing away, came down again in all its wrath and with a sound as if of wailing from the murky sky. A crash of thunder shook the house as Barton fell.

Gillespie who was watching within the house from a partly closed entry window, exclaimed aloud "they have killed Willie Barton!"

Mrs. DeLesline and Eunice heard the exclamation and came in haste from their chamber—"Where—Oh! where is he?" cried Mrs. DeLesline, "Fallen into the front garden!" he replied; and he ran down stairs and through the other door at the rear of the hall, to make known the disaster to Colonel Loyle.

"I saw Fert shoot him," he exclaimed.

"Run him down!—let the dogs out!" shouted Colonel Loyle, now for the first time to-night fully excited, as he and his men from under the oaks darted in pursuit. "Yonder he is!" he cried, pointing to the fleeing Fert, whose horse splashing through the puddles of the miry road, goaded with a spurring which made the blood trickle from his sides, flew as if to outstrip the lightning which again was flashing along the road and through the forest. For many, many years, no such storm had raged at Glyndale.—In the forest, not very far away, from a tall pine tree which, moaning with the wind, swayed to and fro over two ghastly corpses, Caesar Boleg had just fallen; and the bolt from heaven which struck him lifeless to the earth, had split the tall pine from top to bottom—standing yet blasted—a monument to the dead who lay among the blood-stained leaves near its roots.—But this was not known while the other and last companion in their guilty conspiracy was spurring as for his life along the drenched and muddy road.

Leo and Ponce, set loose by Eunice, hearing the cry of Colonel Loyle to his men, had leaped forward yelping in the pursuit of Fert. The blinding rain poured in his face, and the thunder appeared to crash close above his head, while the savage yaps of the dogs and the yells of his pursuers and the hoof-strokes of their horses came nearer and nearer behind him. He knew imperfectly the way to the camp. While the Federal troopers, with their commander, Lieutenant Andrews, who had rejoined them, had merrily retired by the main road, he had taken a shorter path through the woods and swamp. Bewildered and fleeing at full speed, he came out of the swamp to the higher ground and near the ravine. He mistook the path; and as a flash again lighted up the forest and the thunder claps reverberated over him—horse and rider leaped down the steep descent. A cry of terror burst from Fert's frightened soul. With a heavy thud and a splash he was precipitated dead and bleeding near by the cold stiff body of the old man which had lain there since the morning.

His pursuers who knew well the forest paths, halted as they approached the spot; except Ponce and Leo. They leaped down and standing over the corpse of old Sye, lifted up their heads and howled mournfully to the scattering black clouds in the sky.—The storm had suddenly ceased; and the moon, long obscured, now poured her light upon the dismal scene.—The silvery beams were intercepted ever and anon by spectral shadows of cloudlets; drifting ravelings from the edge of the storm gone by.

"The transgressors shall be destroyed together." Psalm 37.

"Is not destruction to the wicked? And a strange punishment to the workers of iniquity?" Job 31.

Before Loyle's men left the spot he said, "Some of you go down and search Fert's pockets for letters and papers. I dislike to do it; but it is self-defence and our only way to obtain what may be of importance for our justification."

Three of them did so. "Here," exclaimed one of them, "is a large package of money with 'James Corday' written on it."—"Keep that for the right owner," said Colonel Loyle, "it's the money Corday sold his farm for. And if you look by the roots of that old pine tree, you'll find the box it was in."

"Here are letters and other papers"—the men called out, bringing them up to the Colonel; who, after a hasty examination in the newly restored moonlight, remarked, "Yes, and two of them from a high official; and in the batch evidence, no doubt, to exonerate us and to spatter with infamous blotches our hypocritical oppressors."

The horsemen then rode back to Mrs. DeLesline's.

Gillespie, who had remained there, learning of the capture of Fert's papers and the importance of them, was reminded of the Colonel's request for any documentary proof that might be found on Lubb and Guelty; and he hastened to the forest near by to make search. Lubb was too cunning, perhaps, to carry criminating papers about with him. All that was found on him was a little money, and a little whisky was still in the flask. These things were allowed to remain in his pockets. But Guelty's corpse gave up damning evidence of "wickedness in high places."[1] These Gillespie took, and a phial of chloroform from his inner vest pocket; and one other article—the medallion with Eunice's miniature which Guelty wore about his neck. When Colonel Loyle saw this he exclaimed "How did the villain get this?—When last my eyes rested on it, it was in the hand of Colonel DeLesline the night before he fell at Sharpsburg. He had gazed a long while upon it, and lifting his eyes to me requested that I would be friendly to Willie Barton. I have been friendly to him; and at the last have witnessed the avengement of his death. At present, however, I will retain this and see that it is restored to those to whom it belongs. Say nothing about this medallion to the ladies who are now overwhelmed with affliction. The papers we will also keep in safety. We do wisely to secure them for the vindication and protection of our friends who have imperiled themselves by acting with us to-night."

What is to be recorded now in this connection is indeed astounding—so wicked is it in design. There was afterwards found among the papers taken from the corpse of Guelty an intended communication to the partisan "Daily—." It was written in

---

1. Ephesians 6:12.

pencil, with the date omitted and to be supplied if occasion should require it; which could readily be done. The pencilled words were these: "The Honorable Mr. Guelty being in the neighborhood of Glyndale in the public interests, happened to take a stroll from the Railroad Station towards a little farm which he owns near by. On a sudden he saw his own horse and buggy which were kept at the farm, the horse coming at a galloping rate towards him on an unused drive-way through the woods. He advanced boldly in front of the vehicle and caught the reins of the horse. Who should leap from the buggy and rush away into the forest, but the very man whom he had left in charge of his farm—an old man—a poor fellow Mr. Guelty was charitably helping by employing him as above stated. He is named Epami-nondas, and appears to be at times a little demented. On his disappearance—for he ran with the swiftness of a demoniac—what was the surprise of the Honorable Mr. Guelty to find in the buggy the recumbent and insensible form of a fair young lady who lives with her widowed mother at Glyndale! How came she there? Had old Pam frightened her and she swooned? Had he in one of his crazy fits, picked her up and placed her in the buggy and then she swooned?—It was fortunate that the Honorable Mr. Guelty was near at hand and came so promptly to her rescue. So soon as we shall see the hero who saved her and learn more particulars of the affair, we shall send the information to you."

So poor old Pam was to bear the guilt in case Guelty was foiled in his plot at the last moment! How cunning he had been in keeping old Pam at the stable. Was this story to be told if he himself should be caught with the insensible Eunice (made so by that phial in his vest pocket)—and before he could get to the Reverend Heze-kiah, with Caesar and maybe others of his Black Rosettes to witness a certain quickly performed ceremony and testify to the bride's acquiescence therein?

During the occurrence of these events, the settlement east of the swamp was contributing its help for the preservation of Colonel Loyle's property at Oakhill. Just before he had set out towards Mrs. DeLesline's, the old driver Obediah, already spoken of in this Story, had come to him and said:

"Master, I hurry here to tell you dat cousin Pam is in de sittle*ment*. He bin larn something 'bout de Rosettes by one of dem who was witched coming to him to be onwitched and he say Mr. Guelty find out he, Paminondas, aint bin true to him and he gwine to send de Rosettes for to kill him after Mr. Guelty done wid him; so he run to us for to sabe hisself. He say plots is set for you and the Lesline fambly, and all your own houses here is to be burn down to-night."

"Well, Obadiah," said the Colonel, "I'll take care of myself, and you will take care of the houses. You and the men used to be drilled by my father in bucket prac-tice so as to save the houses in case of fire. Johnny will help you. Bring the whole force from the settlement, each man and woman with a bucket and do the best you can. And one thing more: I'm going off now, and if Lieutenant Andrews comes here with his cavalry, tell him what you have just told me."

When Lieutenant Andrews, accompanied by Fert and his gang of constabularies, came to Oakhill, the Lieutenant was secretly informed of the purpose to burn the property. On leaving he detailed one of his troopers to remain there on guard. This guard and Johnny stationed themselves, with the dog Lu, in the front piazza, and two of Obediah's men, the Colonel's faithful ex-slaves, kept watch at the rear corners of the house. Obediah and his bucket squad took their position near the big barn where there was a copious spring which emptied its water into the swamp —though at that time the storm was surely pouring down rain enough to quench any fire.

The aged German, Hennchen, and his younger sons guarded their cottage and its out-buildings; while the eldest son, Carl, was posted at the Colonel's stables, and another, Rudolph, at the cattle sheds. All the whites were armed with pistols and some also with shot guns; and a discharge of a pistol was to be their signal for calling assistance.—About an hour after these arrangements were made, and while the Colonel and others were busy at Mrs. DeLesline's, the dog in the piazza began to growl and Johnny and the soldier saw by the lightning flashes a crouching figure sneaking from the roadside bushes towards the front piazza. They let the dog loose and hurrying after her easily captured a young fellow whom Lu had hold of. They brought him to the piazza. On searching him they found several bolls of cotton steeped in turpentine and a box of matches. He confessed his purpose and that he was under orders of the leader of the Black Rosettes. He said there was another man out under the same orders to burn these houses, and that he had gone around to the opposite side of the enclosure. They tied the prisoner securely to a piazza post and then settled down to continue their watch.

Soon after, a pistol shot was heard and a blaze was noticed at the barn and the fire began to spread. They left the prisoner doubly tied and hastened to Obadiah's assistance. The bucket squad was quickly at work and the fire extinguished and the barn saved; the heavy rain helping materially to put the fire out. The dog, with Johnny and the trooper was put on the track of the incendiary who had fired the barn. He was soon captured. He refused to surrender to Johnny but readily did so to the Federal soldier. He was brought in to keep company with the other henchmen of Guelty. They were both "furriners" or negroes unknown to the neighborhood.—When handed over to Colonel Loyle next day, he took down their depositions in presence of witnesses, and let them go. They promised to behave better in future, with protestations of gratitude for his clemency.—As they and their associates were in the special service and pay of Guelty, his death caused the disbandment of their League.

It may be set down here that Pam was, soon after these events, taken care of by Colonel Loyle, and given a house and piece of farmland at the "sittle*ment*." It was for him a re-union with his old acquaintances; and it was by their assent first obtained that the Colonel permitted him to live among them. He toted his few articles of furniture from Guelty's log-house piece by piece; and his pots and pans and all that was his. One thing he closely buttoned up in his bosom, and that was his canvas bag of money, containing forty-seven dollars, nearly all in quarters. He had kept it buried, which may have been his reason for preferring silver coin to greenbacks. He professed to have turned religious and said he had consequently lost his exorcising endowments and effective management of witches. But he still practiced medicine and claimed special ability to diagnose between the deceased and the "cunjurd." His first religious impulse was to build a Church at the Sittle-*ment* with his accumulated treasure. But as it was not enough for that purpose, he bought a mule.

From the "Daily —," the "official organ" of The Party.
"Terrible storm and Lamentable Loss of Life at Glyndale!!"

"A thunder storm of unprecedented violence burst over Glyndale last Friday night. Deputy Marshal Fert, our exalted compatriot was riding with the cavalry under Lieutenant Andrews in pursuit of the Ku Klux, when some of the horses of the troop affrighted by the blinding lightning, became unmanageable. In endeavoring to restore order, the Deputy Marshal's horse fell with him down a precipitous gully and he was mortally injured and died the next morning. His body was brought here yesterday draped in the flag of the Nation and with an imposing military escort of our colored Constabulary. They were met by the handsomely uniformed and equipped colored militia under command of Brigadier General Grubbs. The Stars and Stripes on the Capitol were at half mast, and the Governor and State officers acted as pall bearers to the virtuous and valorous deceased.

"But we have to mourn other irreparable losses. The lightning set on fire the home of a poor widow named DeLesline. The Honorable Mr. Guelty, the Honorable C. Boley, and the Honorable Mr. Lubb, being in the neighborhood at a religious assembly to advise in building a new house of worship for our colored fellow citizens—ran immediately to save the home of the poor widow. Just as they came in sight of the house a terrific lightning bolt prostrated them all and with most fatal effect. In our bereavement it is some consolation to know they died in the performance of a noble charity.—In our next issue we shall speak more at length of the estimable character of these patriots whom we ought all to emulate. It is proposed to erect a monument at Glyndale or on some conspicuous spot in this city to commemorate their services to the State and their noble self-sacrifice. Truly, as Saint Paul says, 'in the midst of life we are in death.'

"It is reported that the notorious Edmund Loyle, the so-called Colonel, the leader of the Ku Klux in the Glyndale section of the outlawed County, has fled to Canada."

This report had as much truth in it as the Editor's other partisan misrepresentations; and those in power were aware of it. Nothing more was said of Colonel Loyle in the Official Organ after Lieutenant Andrews had conferred with the Governor. The Lieutenant had read over with Loyle the papers found on Fert and Guelty; and two of the letters bore the signature of a high official; one indeed for whom the Governor had, even from childhood, entertained a cordial affection.

Fourteen

I love him well; how much—how much!
And I will die!—Why must he go?

H. H. Caldwell

The magnates at the Capitol enjoyed themselves regardless of the impoverishment throughout the State. They were not willing to spend their own money without some selfish object. They were, at present, anxious to please the Federal government; and the expenses could be paid out of the Contingent fund. The rumbling of muffled drums at the burial of Fert and Guelty had scarcely died away when a centrally located structure was flashing with variously colored lights. The high officials of the State, the presiding officers of the Senate and of the House of Representatives, the judges of the Supreme Court, Brigadier General Grubb and Staff, and others in authority, were, we can suppose, assembled to entertain the United States officers who had been sent to hunt down the disloyal Carolinians. A band of music was stationed on the lawn; but softer music within guided the merry dancers. In the refreshment rooms foreign and domestic viands, delicately seasoned, tempted the appetite; flanked as they were with champagne and other delectable beverages.—And so in many other mansions and public halls—habitually —carousels and gambling extravagance beguiled the late hours of night. There was no thought of the poor mothers, in every direction, who could barely furnish food to their fatherless and half-starved children. Some, it was true, were a little better off; but their small residue of worldly goods was but a prey for the relentless tax-gatherer. Could not the manipulation of the public finances suffice your greed, ye rulers of the prostrate State?—But let us return to our Story.

Mrs. Avery had no aptitude for business, particularly if it required a ceremonious function. She, too, was poor in comparison with Mrs. DeLesline; and the latter had therefore requested the privilege of superintending the obsequies of her almost foster-son, Willie Barton, who was lying a corpse at her house; and did so, regardless of expenditure, that the funeral might accord in all respects with the old aristocratic status of his family. She had also ordered a monument which she intended should be the handsomest in the burial ground of Bartonborough. She was actuated not only by the love he had cherished for her daughter, but felt a melancholy pleasure in all she did for him, as though his mother stood at her side as she remembered her in former days when they were together at school in New York, and whispered her grateful acknowledgment and smiled upon her with the old beaming look of devoted friendship.

But Fortune had not been dispersing favors at Glyndale for the past year or two. And Eunice, aware of her mother's straitened resources, brought to her the little casket bequeathed to her by kind old Timothy Thomleigh, saying, "Take these jewels, mother, which the executors of Mr. Thomleigh sent me. They were intended, no doubt, for a bridal gift, if his favorite had married me. Let them be now used to help place upon the grave the monument you have designed."—Mrs. DeLesline was at first disinclined to accept them. But Eunice earnestly desired that the jewels should be devoted to the erection of the monument. And inasmuch as they materially contributed to the immediate fulfilment of her mother's purpose, they were accepted with the remark, "his mother joins with your mother, my daughter, in blessing you for this affectionate remembrance of poor Willie." And Eunice, with tears in her eyes, retired to her room.

They were poor indeed now though they were loth to acknowledge it. Wealth in slaves and stocks and bonds had vanished like smoke, along with patriotic investments in Confederate securities; and Mr. DeLesline and his family had retired to the country to live on the small proceeds of the sale of their property in Columbia.

The repairing of the burned dwelling house, the year's salary of Dupont as overseer on the farm, the recent destruction of her barn and out-buildings, the partial failure of crops during several consecutive seasons, the disappearance, on the night of the attack on her place, of her horses and mules which had been stolen and driven off beyond recovery—all these depletions of her purse had resulted in pecuniary embarrassment, and she found it necessary to confer with her daughter as to stricter economy in their domestic management. Old Mr. DeLesline had, for many years of his life, when he was wealthier than the farmers at Glyndale, paid half the salary of the rector of the parish; and Mrs. DeLesline, his daughter-in-law, regarded it as a religious obligation to sustain the Church, and to keep up, now that the people of the neighborhood were poorer than ever, this annual subscription. So sadly sunk in poverty were the numerous old men, women and children, that a streamlet of kindly benefactions had been constantly flowing from her house to theirs. Many a pair of little eyes brightened up when they saw Eunice or her mother approaching; and the Reverend Mr. Fairbanks knew where to go for assistance in his ministration to the sick and distressed. This year the DeLesline subscription to his salary could be met only by borrowing money or selling some of the few articles of jewelry which Eunice and her mother still possessed, and which had fortunately been in a small trunk Aunt Patty saved for them when they fled from the burning mansion in Columbia. This means of meeting their obligations was decided upon. They visited Columbia ostensibly for other purposes and disposed of all their trinkets (except a few heirlooms precious only to themselves) for less than half their value; and on their return home paid the money to Mr. Fairbanks with a courtesy which left the impression on his mind that it was a trivial contribution from never-failing stores of wealth.

The summer had passed and winter had set in bringing with it to Glyndale more than ordinary gloominess. Mrs. Avery was always timid; and now, since the death of Willie Barton and re-iterated threats against her for having had in her house a leader of the Ku Klux, she was continually apprehensive of harm to her household and was seeking some gentlemanly person to take Willie's place in her family. Mrs. DeLesline was aware of this and desired to approach Dupont on the subject in order to reduce her own expenses. She knew that he was to some extent cognizant of her difficulties. At length, with considerable mortification of her pride, she confidentially apprised him more fully of her pecuniary embarrassment and proposed that instead of a yearly payment, he should take a third of the income from the farm, and board at Mrs. Avery's as a protector to her and Mamie and Helen Clarens. This would be better, she said, than having a stranger there in Willie's place. Dupont's love-making to Mamie was just in such a stage of progress as to render it desirable to be near her and to protect the household from threatened molestation. He therefore assented willingly to Mrs. DeLesline's proposal if it should be agreeable to Mrs. Avery. Poor Eunice, while this negotiation was proceeding at the breakfast table, was in her room above with head bent down and eyes bedimmed with tears.

Troubles often come in groups. The faithfulness of Luky or Lucius, Caesar's so-called "brudder," and the dutifulness of the coquettish Caroline began to be undermined by seducing and vitiating appeals of their colored friends. An entanglement of the affections decoyed the maid to associations where her fealty to her old mistress was impaired. The influence of colored political aspirants drew off Luky (now answering to his full title Mr. Lucius DeLesline) to haunts of corruption. He did not yet steal from his old owners, who liberally supplied his wants; but he no longer defended at all hazards their property from theft by others. He had been notified by his religious fraternity that for his adherence to the interests of democrats, it was in contemplation to expel him from Church membership; and that the "Lig" would see to it that some dark night he should receive thirty nine lashes on his bare back. Now, when a pig disappeared or a dozen fowls were missing, Lucius knew nothing about it, and took no effectual means to find out the thief or prevent a recurrence of depredations. His demoralization made him worthless as a guardian of Mrs. DeLesline's out-door interests. His sleep was not even disturbed the night her meathouse was stripped of all its contents. Old Maum Patty was incorruptible, but was too infirm to be more than an apparent protector of the house and its sorrowful inmates. She did her best to keep the table supplied with eggs and butter; but even these had now to be economically used. One cow and a half dozen fowls represented but poorly the former abundant source of daily culinary luxuries.

Yes—the winter had come and was nearly gone. And Mrs. DeLesline's difficulties were by no means lessened by the flight of time. Without horses and mules the farm could not be cultivated. She had not money to buy any to replace those of which she had been robbed. She made an inventory of part of her furniture. But the furniture at this country seat had always been made up of superfluous remnants from the town mansion, and unless Eunice's piano and harp were included, all that could possibly be spared would but purchase a single mule. If she did purchase one, it might soon be stolen from her. After deliberation and repeated struggles with herself, she consulted Mr. Gillespie about hiring from time to time such animals as should be needed. He promised to consider what could be done, for it was near time to prepare for the crop. To her surprise and delight he informed her next day that inasmuch as he would share the crop, he would contribute the working force. He soon had horses and mules on hand and extra workmen turning the soil for planting. The secret was that Colonel Loyle, who had left the vicinity after the death of Barton, had returned to Oakhill the preceding evening and Dupont had visited him. How the animals were obtained was never known to Mrs. DeLesline nor to Eunice.

But their pleasure in surmounting this difficulty was not of long continuance. Next afternoon an execution was levied on the dwelling and farm for unpaid taxes. Their property, as was all property in land throughout the State, was assessed far beyond its real value. The party rulers at Columbia were bound to gather in all the money which could be exacted from everything to which valuation could be ascribed. Even clergymen—unexempted (perhaps by mistake) from the Professions —had to pay a license tax of ten dollars for preaching the gospel. The law required that the Receipt should be conspicuously displayed at each one's place of business. The Episcopal clergymen at Columbia came to me in a quandary asking if he should tack his receipt to the pulpit, for that, he said, was his place of "business."— The rising of the sun was not more certain in those days than the coming of the tax-gatherer.

While many things in this Story are mere shadows, there was reality and to spare in the change of the State tax. Before the war it was three hundred ninety-two thousand on property valued at four hundred ninety million. It was now two million—on that property reduced in value to one hundred eighty-four million.[1]

---

1. James S. Pike, *The Prostrate State: South Carolina under Negro Government* (1874; republished New York: Harper & Row, 1968), 252. Rivers drew these figures from the first edition of *The Prostrate State.*

It was even worse than this. The President of the Tax-payers Convention, an ex-Lieutenant Governor of the State, said to them—about the time of Mrs. DeLesline's difficulties—"not only is the annual tax increase manifold, but by act of the late session of the Legislature, two tax levies are required to be paid within the limits of one year. This is an intolerable burden and is calculated, even if it be not intended, to bring about a wide-spread confiscation of property. And the worse feature of the matter is the curious and anomalous fact without parallel in the history of any representative government, that they who lay the taxes do not pay them, and that they who are to pay them have no voice in the laying of them."

I happen to have a photograph of a cluster of the "representatives" and shall quote what is printed thereupon. It was spread at the time it was made among those acquainted with the facts and must be historically true: "These are the photographs of sixty-three members of the reconstructed South Carolina Legislature, fifty of whom are negroes or mulattoes and thirteen white; twenty-two read and write (eight grammatically); the remainder (forty-one) make their mark with the aid of an amanuensis; nineteen are taxpayers to an aggregate amount of one hundred forty-six dollars and ten cents; the rest (forty-four) pay no taxes, and the body levies on the white people of the State for four million dollars."—Perhaps this last sum refers to the double levy for one year.

Since I have given two quotations I may as well give another; from a gentleman of New York (formerly a resident in Charleston) who was in the same Convention. After speaking of the enormous appropriation of four hundred thousand dollars for "Legislative expenses," he continues "Last winter, a committee of both branches of the Legislature was appointed to investigate the frauds and blackmailing connected with the Blue Ridge Railroad legislation of the previous session. The Governor, the main witness, appeared before this Committee and accused the former Legislature of all sorts of villainy. Alluding to the Bill granting aid to the Road, the Governor says, 'When the Bill came up, a member of the House came to one of the parties and said "the report can't go through until I get five hundred dollars"'—And when an injunction was served on the fiscal officers of the State to prevent an endorsement of the bonds, the Governor alleges that the parties procuring the injunction proposed to withdraw the same if twenty-five thousand dollars would be paid. After many clear and explicit charges of fraud and corruption, the Governor, with an honest burst of indignation against this corrupt body, says 'I know of the fact, or have been told so by a hundred different persons, that money had been paid to get a certain Report through at the last session. I want to say: do you suppose that if our Savior would come here with a Bill ever so good, and want to get it through, or it was thought best to get up a Committee to investigate Him, do you suppose He wouldn't be crucified again if He didn't pay something to prevent it?'"

Yet from what I heard, I would observe poetically; that this high functionary had no more music in his soul nor was he "moved by concord of sweet sounds," and continued to enjoy the undiminished confidence of his party who understood, no doubt, his meteoric "burst of indignation." Let us return to the saddened home of our friends, soon to be as desolate as thousands of other homes around, unless a heavenly blessing bring to its rescue wisdom and energy and unfaltering courage.

"Eunice, my daughter, what shall we do," said Mrs. DeLesline, sobbing, "unless we can raise two hundred fifty dollars, this shelter may be taken from us. I cannot appeal to Mr. Gillespie again. Would we not better sell half of the farm?"

Eunice silently paced up and down the floor, looking on the faded carpet, and thinking poverty was indeed nigh at hand. At length she stood before her mother. "Madame, do not fret so. I can teach. Let me seek a position in some school. My earnings may support you and myself; for we have learned now to live on a little."

"God help us, my child," was the only response from the humiliated heart and quivering lips of Mrs. DeLesline. But Eunice still stood before her, erect and hopeful.

"Why repine, dear mother? The proudest in the State have set to work. Many, very many, have far less than we still possess. We can sell, of course, not only half the farm, but all we have here, and seek employment in some city—far away, if you wish—but not until our present engagement with Mr. Gillespie has terminated. With better crops this year we may even escape the necessity of selling the farm at all. To meet these taxes, sell now the piano and harp; and as they are old and may not bring much, let us add our silks and satins and the presents Uncle Richard sent me from California; Such of them, I mean, as Maum Patty saved for me—and pay the taxes demanded of us."

"Ah! Richard—Richard!" exclaimed her mother with an outburst of emotion— a paroxysm of grief such as Eunice had never witnessed in her and which she could not comprehend; some old remembrance of his love for her or her love for him? What ever it was, she flung herself on the floor and wept as if her heart would break. And so Eunice, unable to comfort her, left her, and softly withdrew from the room to search upstairs in her trunks and drawers for whatever might be sold to meet the emergency confronting them. On her knees before a large trunk, her hands were busy with her repertoire of valuable dresses many of them inherited and of old-time style—useless now; a plain calico would suit her best, such as she was then wearing; yes, sell them all; mamma must not weep so again. The thought of her mother's agony caused the tears restrained till now to trickle down her cheeks. She was weak, too, from privation and worrying and began to weep sorrowfully; when of a sudden Ponce's joyous yelping in the front garden, which was now his home, caused her to suppose Colonel Loyle, whom she was least expecting, was nigh at hand. She felt assured Ponce would have been so joyous at the approach of no one else.

Is it unreasonable to believe that close to the body's heat-producing vitality there may be in the dark a faint luminous emanation perceptible to vision keener than ours? However this may be in the dark, certain it is—in light or darkness—that to our sense of smell, dull as it is, there is a perceptible corporeal effluvium, and it is possible to distinguish some races of men by it. In lower animals which have not our means of obtaining sustenance nor our safeguards for self protection, there is a subtler and stronger sensitive ability to detect and recognize such effluvia, and at a considerable distance; and perhaps to hear sounds farther than our ears can hear them. And so it may have been that Ponce became aware of the coming of Colonel Loyle, the one he knew of old by all his senses and with all his affection.

Eunice was unwilling to be met in her present distress; and hastily replacing in the trunk the brilliant robes, descended the stairs without going to her mother. Throwing a shawl about her head, she hurried from the house towards Mrs. Avery's. But the Colonel, walking through the woods to Mrs. DeLesline's had seen her departure and quickened his step to overtake her; for the shades of evening would soon settle over fields and woods. She had already reached the spot near the dense swamp where Guelty and Caesar had endeavored once to carry her off—the recollection of which always filled her with horror. A tremor seized her limbs; for she was weak and faint. How foolish, she thought, to flee from him; and how foolish, too, to come on this spot alone at this twilight hour!—But Colonel Loyle had come up with her now, and turning to him she had taken his hand in greeting. She shivered and looked so pale, that he asked:

"Why do you tremble, Eunice? Have I returned to you before your grief admits my presence near you?"

"O, no—no!—but the remembrance of that night—that dreadful night—and the thought of those who met me here to wrong me (as I have since been told) the same who would have wronged you too,—their bodies torn by lightning or mangled and now in bloody graves!"

"They met their just deserts; think of them no more."

The traces of suffering which the sorrowful day she had just passed through had impressed upon her face, touched the heart of Colonel Loyle. He still had her hand and while he looked upon her there was that in the look which quickly changed the pallor of her cheek to a roseate tint. She softly said "welcome home again." He gently drew her to him and bending over her whispered "would that you would let me be always near you. I have loved you—through all my life! Give me, Eunice, some place in your heart."

She raised her face to his, her answer in her love-lit eyes; he kissed her blushing cheek; she put her arms around his neck; he kissed her rosy lips (they had come so close his own). They spoke no word; but the caroling birds seemed to sing in blither strain ere they nestled in the shady trees around.

They did not go to Mrs. Avery's, but with loitering step and hand clasped in hand, returned to her mother's. The Evening Star, the one of beauty and of love, shed her first fair rays upon them as, happy now, they passed through the garden to her home once more. When they entered the hall, Eunice was disengaging her hand to go upstairs; but he held it saying

"I cannot stay longer now than to make my respects to your mother;—so, good night." She leaned over from the baluster, pausing on the steps she had begun to ascend and—well, she said "good night"—then tripped to her room and looked upon the tumbled silks and satins in the unclosed trunk, with thoughts how changed! and eyes all tearless now. Mrs. DeLesline, taken unawares, had scarcely risen from the posture in which Eunice had left her, when Colonel Loyle entered the room. She could not conceal from him all indications of her recent affliction; and the Colonel sought to cheer her in what he supposed to be her continued grief at the untimely fate of Willie Barton.

Since the funeral, Loyle had been to Columbia, to several cities at the North and West and to Washington; making known to influential friends the truth of the late occurrences at Glyndale, and had in spite of many obstructions and vexatious delays succeeded in causing an abandonment of proceedings against himself and his neighbors, for Ku Kluxism and thwarting the Fert and Guelty raid, the true "inwardness" of which the public, generally, had no notion of. He had put aside his own private interests till he had secured exoneration for his friends. Colonel Nickton and Lieutenant Andrews and other Federal officers, some high in rank, and even Tom Chiltree from Tennessee, could hardly do enough to satisfy themselves in their efforts in his behalf in Washington. The proceedings were finally abandoned not on Loyle's account, but to shield "the party" from the damaging exposure of their own misdeeds.—His unexplained long absence from Glyndale, for nearly six months, had added to Eunice's distress. She began to suppose the rumor correct that he had fled to Canada or had taken refuge from prosecution in his western lands nigh the Rocky Mountains and she would not see him for several years—perhaps never.

His sudden appearance at home again; Eunice's leaving the house; the fact that they had met; were all unknown to Mrs. DeLesline. So soon as she saw him enter the room, there was awakened in her the old indescribable reverence for his controlling wisdom. She felt some alleviation of her troubles in the very light of his countenance. She really forgot for the moment her pride in the DeLesline name. Here is a source of help, she thought, if help can come from any human source; and she did not hesitate to place her grievance immediately before him.

"It is not about Willie I am worried, Colonel Loyle; but can they take this house from us in default of paying the onerous taxes imposed upon us?" and she handed him the papers served upon her that afternoon. Happy as he was in her daughter's love, he perceived in a moment that he must postpone any reference to it in her mother's present absorbing trouble; and replied:

"There is no telling, my dear Madame, what our rulers may do; but these proceedings need not be pressed. The undisguised and unaccountable friendship which St. Julian Yarkly exhibited for me in my last visit to Columbia may enable me to secure his influence for a stay of proceedings in this case also till arrangements can be made to pay what is claimed. Shall I say three months or six months?"

"It will be the greatest kindness to us, Colonel, if six months can be allowed us. It may prevent Eunice from going off to teach school."

The Colonel smiled and said "That may not be necessary. I shall keep these papers if you do not object, and attend to them day after tomorrow. I am here this evening to ask if yourself and Eunice will do me the honor to ride with me to-morrow morning. I met with a new style of carriage while away at the North. I brought one home with me, and should like your opinion of it. So may I come for you at nine o'clock?"

Mrs. DeLesline assented. She as well as Eunice had become feeble from depress-ing anxieties and long detention at home. Even before her horses had been lost, the family carriage was so shabby in appearance that it had not been used. A brisk ride in the invigorating air would help to bring a tinge of color to Eunice's pale cheek. After Loyle's departure she called to Eunice to let her know that he had come home again and had merely stopped to invite them to ride in the morning. Eunice laughed merrily at the news; and when old Patty brought in tea and a happier evening had been spent than they had long known, Mrs. DeLesline said repeatedly to herself "how joyous Eunice is to hear that Colonel Loyle has returned."

The Collector of the Glyndale region, through a plea of insecurity there, kept his office in Columbia. He was a rabid anti-Southern politician and inimical to Colonel Loyle; and the latter preferred to have no intercourse with him, and cer-tainly not to solicit a favor from him. The alternative was to make an appeal to Yarkly who had a controlling influence upon the collector.—The interview with St. Julian in Columbia was to the Colonel surprising and eventful. He had sent a note to that magnate requesting a brief conference with him at one o'clock, with refer-ence to the tax-execution on Mrs. DeLesline, with a view to its postponement for some months till she could obtain the means of payment. With the note were sent the papers in the case. St. Julian had in the unfinished granite State House an inner office or private room approached through the larger office where his clerks were employed. When Colonel Loyle's note was received and a clerk dispatched to say the appointment was acceded to for the hour designated—St Julian shut himself in his inner office, locking the door. Pacing backward and forward as a wild ani-mal in a cage might do, he bit his lip till the blood came and clenched his hands till the nails sank into his flesh. In agony he groaned "Ah, yes! DeLesline!—ah, yes —ah, yes! Isaiah in his grave and Lubb rotting at his side! The widow ruined and her few paltry acres threatened!—Good God!—one twentieth of what that trunk contained would be to her in her poverty a boon from Heaven! Struggling for food, while my wife is arrayed in gorgeous robes and flashing diamonds!—I ought to be rotting along with cousin Isaiah. I cheated him too!—How long, O God, how long thy heavy hand stays poised above my head? When will the blow descend? Why spare me still?—Last night my nephew was brought home drunk. He squandered what I gave, then stole my purse. What dared I say? Let him steal it all—steal it all —steal it all—and curse me and spit upon me. He knows I am a thief!—I'd give ten times my wealth to be a man like Loyle.—Reparation?—Hah! tell me not of that. You mean my degradation, ye fiends from hell!"

He sat down, pale and exhausted, staring on the floor, oblivious to repeated knocking at the door. At length he rose and unlocked the door and called his confidential clerk; and sent him to the proper office with a record of the DeLesline delinquency; bidding him pay all demands and have the Collector notified that no further action be taken with the distress warrant. The clerk went out and did as he was ordered, placing in the corner of his vest pocket a twenty dollar bill as his perquisite in the transaction. The receipt, when brought to St. Julian, he folded in an envelope directed to Mrs. DeLesline. He crushed in his hand the remaining money bills the clerk brought back and tossed them into his drawer, and sat in moody silence awaiting the arrival of Colonel Loyle.

When so many flocked to the Prostrate State for spoliation, it would have been strange if a few had not had a lingering spark of conscience in them. Already there had been defections from the horde of unscrupulous peculators. The deeds of the entire gang, are they not recorded in the Book of Investigations?—Yet there were some among them whose early lessons at their mothers' knee revived at times to startle and check them in their hurrying course of iniquity. St. Julian's remorse was awakened no less by the debauchery of his favorite nephew (he had no children of his own) than by the terrible fate of those whom he named in his frantic outburst in his private office. Years after, when broken in fortune, his repentance no doubt would have led him to make restitution of his ill-gotten gains, if he had had the ability to do so. His weakening at this moment was not yet down to that repentance point; but it was gradually coming upon him and with indications enough to be apparent to "the party." He was consequently fleeced by his associates, when turned out of office for a more available follower. They spoke of him derisively by his old nickname, Saint Yarkly.

"Allow me to shake hands with you, if you please," he said with a touch of humility when Colonel Loyle was ushered into the inner room at one o'clock. From long habit he had learned to repress his emotions; and had now almost completely curbed himself as he continued: "the case of Mrs. DeLesline has already been attended to by a friend of hers. I have but to hand you the receipt for the taxes, and to request as a favor to that friend, that it be given to the widow."—Who her friend was, he could not conscientiously make known.—The Colonel who knew nothing of the antecedents of St. Julian Yarkly in connection with the black trunk, was as much surprised at this termination of the case, as Mrs. DeLesline and Eunice were, subsequently, at the arrival from time to time of valuable gifts from the same unknown friend, sent to them in ways through which it was impossible that the giver could be traced.

"Allow me to lock this door, Colonel Loyle, to avoid intrusion; for I wish our conference to be private." After sitting in deep thought awhile, his visitor silent too and wondering what topic St. Julian could broach worthy of so much precaution and secrecy—he asked:

"Colonel, did you ever meet with Richard DeLesline or know of him?"

"I knew him many years ago, and I met him once on the Rocky Mountains during a snow storm and we traveled some days together. But your question is a very strange one, Mr. Yarkly."

After silence again, as if he were weaving together scattered threads of reflection or hesitating to utter what was passing in his thoughts, he continued: "Of course you knew my cousin, Benjamin Isaiah Guelty?"

"Was he your cousin?" responded Colonel Loyle in some astonishment.

"My mother's sister's son; though we never met in boyhood, living as we did, far apart." After a further reflective spell, he added:

"I know your character well, Colonel Loyle, and can entrust you with what I am going to say. They are both in their graves—Lubb and Isaiah. There was once a transaction or two connecting the one with the other; and in some way Lubb discovered that Isaiah had superintended the burial of Richard DeLesline; when, I know not; where, I cannot exactly say.—Mr. Lubb was in my secret service and was watching Isaiah for me; why, I need not tell you. Some things he found out for me; but such was his inborn villainy that I would not, without further evidence, vouch for the truth of any information he imparted to me. His espionage on my cousin was not directed specially to these matters; but Lubb had his suspicions that some mystery was attached to the dealings Isaiah had had with Richard DeLesline, one of the sons of old Mr. DeLesline who lived in this city before and during the war." —Again he was lost in reverie and a look of agony flickered on his face, which, remarkable to say, he did not attempt to conceal.

"Can you tell me, Mr. Yarkly," inquired Colonel Loyle, "where your cousin had the dealings which you refer to, with Mr. Richard DeLesline?"

"I cannot; except that Isaiah when he left home, and was quite a young man, practiced law in several towns along the western border of Missouri. If I knew more I would tell you. I have said this much that Mrs. DeLesline may consider whether or not it may be advantageous to her to investigate the matter. I do not know the lady. You come here as her friend, do you not?"

"Especially so; you could not commit her interests now or hereafter to a more friendly guardian. And I thank you, Mr. Yarkly, for the information you have imparted to me in her behalf. I hope it may lead to her pecuniary benefit."

"The family are poor, are they not?"

"We are all poor now; and unless these harassments at Glyndale are discontinued, many will be obliged to quit their farms and seek a living elsewhere. Let me entreat you to use your influence to alleviate our burden in all directions."

"Would to God, I had never set foot in this State. While I am here, however, I shall be honored, Colonel, if you will permit me to aid you in anything which shall bring advantage to the family of Mrs. DeLesline."

As Colonel Loyle passed into the outer office he encountered the confidential clerk in altercation with a dissipated-looking young man with his hands manacled, and in charge of an officer. It was Yarkly's nephew (or rather his wife's petted nephew) who had dangerously stabbed a negro in a quarrel over a game of cards in a place of low repute; and who had begged permission from the magistrate to be brought here that he might plead with his uncle to become bail for him.

Pondering all he had heard from St. Julian, Colonel Loyle with head bent down walked on through the corridor of the State House, and almost walked into the arms of the Governor.—His excellency was a man of decidedly low-caste ideas; but he was subject to fits of grandeur. He had such a fit in him to-day.

"Hah! Colonel Loyle," said His Excellency holding his head high up, "can't say I'm glad to see you, Sir; but since we've met, I must assure you we'll harrow Glyndale and every d— spot where the Ku Klux hide; and show no mercy on all we catch, Sir. We've got the authorities at Washington to back us, Sir."

"Do you remember the reasons for your promise to Lieutenant Andrews?" was Loyle's reply.

His Excellency looked above and then down, hesitated, and said "I shall keep my promise so far as you are concerned."

"That will not suffice. My friends were included. What say you as to them?"

"Yes—yes—" was the reluctant reply, "your friends too, if they are not Ku Klux. Your friends were listed and their immunity, I remember now, was stipulated for."

Colonel Loyle bowed and passed on. He went directly to his old army associate, the Law professor at the University, and had the necessary papers drawn to be signed by Mrs. DeLesline and Eunice to enable him to take charge of any property left by Richard DeLesline in Missouri, California, or elsewhere. He knew no harm could come from his going to make inquiries; and he thought he could do so without exciting too highly the expectations of Mrs. DeLesline. He hoped also to be able to unravel more satisfactorily to himself Guelty's crafty and persistent machinations so far as Eunice had been their object. Did it not accord with the sordid nature of the base fellow to have some ulterior motive for entrapping her; some pecuniary gain commensurate with his risk for its attainment? "Yes," he concluded, "I must go at once and investigate this matter."

Ere sunset he was once more at the Glyndale Station. He had left his carriage and horses in care of Dupont, or rather at his disposal, for the service of the ladies during his absence; and was delighted to see him drive up with Eunice and Helen Clarens to meet him. "Mamma," said Eunice blushing, "sent us to bring you home; and to tell you she has a cup of tea ready for you, as you may not find one awaiting you in your bachelor quarters at Oakhill."

Before concluding this chapter, it may not be irrelevant with the preceding events of the Story to set down an incident which occurred before the Colonel took the cars for his return to Glyndale. He then saw plainly, for the first and only time, the carpenter Noel.

Having nothing to do for a few hours, he obtained a horse from his friend the Law Professor, and was riding out partly to reflect on what Yarkly had told him and partly to revisit some scenes in the neighborhood with which, in old times, he had been familiar. In the forest groves south of the city he came upon a bevy of boys, and asked them who they were. "The coming generation," one of them replied. "What are you all doing here?"—"Playing," responded the frolicsome group. Then one of them questioned him, "Have you seen the carpenter, Sir?—the one they are going to kill?"

"No," he replied, full of interest in this subject, "where is he?"

"He was here a little while ago talking to us."

"What did he talk about?" asked the Colonel.

Then they conferred with each other; some holding their heads down, as if recalling to mind what they had heard the carpenter tell them. At length one said "things changeable and things permanent forever."—"There is a way of life and there is a way of death," said another. "Right prevails over might," said the largest of the boys. "I suppose he means," spoke out a little rosy fellow, "when we grow up."

"I hope before then, my lad," replied Colonel Loyle. "But where is Noel the carpenter now?"

They could not tell which way he went. Some pointed in one direction and some in another. The Colonel was aware that the Radical rulers of the State were hounding Noel down; the humbler people having spread the report that he prophesied the speedy destruction of the iniquitous party in power.—Loyle had never seen him except at a mere glance, and had long been anxious to meet him. He was the more anxious now; for he believed that what the carpenter had predicted, if really he had predicted it, would assuredly come to pass. And he believed, further, that the teachings ascribed to him would work their way to a blessed realization in the near future.

He was riding along with eyes upon the ground and thinking of these matters, when he noticed a tremor in his horse, and lifting his head, was startled to see standing beneath a spreading oak near by, a vision, as it were, of a well known face and form often seen by him in pictures; before which he reverently bowed his uncovered head. And when he looked again, he beheld only Noel the carpenter in his workman garb moving off from beneath the oak.

Colonel Loyle spoke no word. But he thought "This is unquestionably a devout man, bent on a peculiar and benevolent mission. Whence the occasional gleam, as is reported, in him and around him? Did I see something of the kind just now? Is it more than imagination? Is it not this and this alone in those who have perchance seen the glitter of his saw and other tools he carries with him, or at night the glare of a lantern to illume his path?—However, he is a remarkable, almost a saintly personage. And his calm courage leads him even into the midst of his enemies."

And so the Colonel began to think also of Him who was once on Earth in the midst of enemies, yet kindly disposed towards all; whose gentle life exemplified for us mutual forbearance and forgiveness.—The meeting with Noel made a deep impression upon him. He told his friends, after this, "If I live to see these present troubles over, I shall give all the aid in my power to permanent reconciliation of ourselves and our Northern brethren."

Fifteen

Postscript.—Epistolary

My dear XXX.

I have found among the papers entrusted to me, the story entitled "Eunice" which you have inquired about and which I now send you. When it was, in part, read to me by the author, I was told whom he had intended to represent by some of the characters in the story. But you must permit me to keep that information to myself.

It appears that the older brother of Colonel DeLesline—the Richard referred to in the preceding chapters,—had gone beyond the Rocky Mountains and had amassed a fortune in gold-mine discoveries. This brother was naturally reticent even to the point of seeming morose; and on account of some estrangement had determined, when in his early manhood he left home, not to write to any of the family or any of his former friends. Some said his self-banishment was caused by sensitiveness with regard to an uncontrollable admiration for the handsome lady who had bestowed her hand upon his more fortunate brother. This may be merely conjecture. However, his only communication with his family consisted in valuable gifts which came by Express from time to time for her daughter and only child, Eunice, to whom he seemed much devoted and who resembled her mother in attractiveness of form and feature. At his request Eunice's likeness taken every year as she grew up, was sent to him in return for his rich gifts.

After the breaking out of the war, he was on his way to his native State to cast in his lot with his fellow citizens. It was in February, 1862, that he reached a small town some little distance from the border of Missouri.—What I am now telling you was learned from Colonel Loyle after his marriage and from investigations which led to the finding of the Will where it had been deposited by Guelty for safe keeping and which consequently led to the recovery of the fortune bequeathed to Miss Eunice DeLesline.— Her uncle was bringing with him a favorite horse whose attachment to him was extraordinary and almost equal to that which the most sagacious dog exhibits for his master. Desiring to inure himself to hardships which he knew would be required in camp life, and to keep in exercise alertness and self-reliance, he journeyed alone and exposed himself unnecessarily to the severities of mid-winter. He had, during a terrible snow-storm, such as is called a "blizzard," arrived at the town spoken of. Drenched to the skin in fording the icy cold water of a swollen stream, and travelling many hours in this condition through an unfrequented stretch of country, he contracted acute pneumonia and was nearly helpless when, about midnight, he reached the outskirts of town. The extreme cold and the fast falling snow had driven the inhabitants within doors. He knew not where a hotel could be found. One solitary light was seen. This was in the office of a young lawyer (he said he was a lawyer) from one of the Eastern states. He was no other than the man named Guelty in the Story.

The office fronted on the street. Behind the office was his sleeping apartment, and beyond this were several rooms extended into the yard and rented to a poor Swedish family who had charge of the premises whenever Mr. Guelty was absent. The lawyer boarded at an adjacent tavern around the corner in the next street, but spent most of the time at his office with plodding industry which sometimes kept him at work till late at night, as on this occasion. He had had but a common school education and was resolutely studying to supplement it with further acquisitions.

Mr. DeLesline rode upon the pavement and tapped at the door. When it was opened by the startled student, the snow-covered horseman could barely say with a voice scarcely audible from hoarseness, "Will you care for me; I am exceedingly sick," and dismounting he placed the bridle in the young lawyer's hand and entering the office sank exhausted on the chair from which Mr. Guelty had just risen. After leading the horse to the stable and calling the Swede to attend to it, the lawyer hastened back, placed more wood upon the fire, assisted Mr. DeLesline in divesting himself of his wraps, and administered such stimulants as he had at hand. The delicate and refined features of the invalid were in striking contrast with the almost repellant coarseness of the lawyer who, though but about thirty years old, had a settled hardness of face which might have belonged to a legal intriguer of double his age.—All that occurred need not be related. It is enough to know that Guelty was soon assured of Richard DeLesline's ability to repay whatever kindness and service he could render; that the sufferer appeared to appreciate the good fortune of being in a lawyer's office; that he declined till daylight the attendance of a physician and was very anxious to have at once a Will drawn up. "After that," said he, "let the Doctor come." The Will consisted simply of a statement of his property in land and mining shares and bank deposits—all which (estimated by Guelty at half a million dollars), with everything else he possessed, he bequeathed unconditionally to Eunice, his niece. Nor would the testator rest till Mr. Guelty had summoned from the rooms in the yard and from the adjoining tavern, the requisite number of witnesses to the execution of the will. Perhaps he had a premonition that his clearness of mind would be of short duration. Guelty obtained for him a comfortable room at the tavern, and Long before sunrise a physician was in attendance. But not-withstanding medical skill, the progress of disease soon brought the patient to a comatose prostration ending in death in less than forty-eight hours.

As a client of Guelty, in whose hands the deceased had left his will and placed his affairs, all that appertained to the disposal of his effects and to his burial was directed by the lawyer, with no question raised as to his right of administration; especially since he made it known that he was carrying out the directions of the deceased. He could well afford even lavish expenditure on the obsequies or in send-ing the body to the family in South Carolina, instead of giving the corpse barely decent sepulture. For he had found on the person and in the traveling-bags of his client sufficient to make a little fortune for himself. He told no one what he had found. But It became known subsequently that shortly after this time Mr. Guelty's father in ——, an impecunious farmer, had purchased for cash two valuable farms in his neighborhood. The family of the DeLeslines never heard of the death of Richard nor of the Will. Guelty's malfeasance as to Richard DeLesline's effects was thoroughly concealed, not only by the disruption of mail facilities on account of war, but by his own departure from Missouri. He returned to the East and finally entered military service in the Union army and was present at the battle of Sharps-burg where—as we have seen—he was not too squeamish in appropriating articles of value from the bodies of the slain.

When, by the strange discovery mentioned in the first chapter, he found Eunice to be the same with the heiress of the will, and the original of his idolized minia-ture, there was a commingling of love—such as his nature was capable of—with his selfish avarice; and he determined to make her his wife and at the same time secure to himself a title to the wealth bequeathed to her. His sole chance of accom-plishing this, he knew, was to kidnap her and by threats or otherwise gain sufficient expression of consent to legalize his marriage. The death of the testator and the will in her favor were secrets which he intended should never be divulged till he had succeeded in his design.

The writer of the Story said Guelty was a combination rather than a single per-sonage. There was abundant material in the carpetbaggers from which to make up such a character; including the disposition ascribed by Xenophon to Menon the Thessalian; who did not persistently attempt to cheat his enemies, being aware they would be suspicious of him and on their guard. He found it easier, as Guelty did, to take advantage of those whom he called his friends. One of these "friends" was Mr. Troth. The last time I saw him—after he had gambled away all his money and had become poor—he was staggering along a by-street in Columbia towards a low groggery; and it was yet early in the forenoon. I have heard that Colonel Loyle often responded liberally to Troth's applications for pecuniary assistance. I mention this to you because it has not been told in the story nor what became of this influen-tial colleague of the carpet-baggers.

Other circumstances were related to me which occurred after those here have been mentioned, both concerning the marriage of the Colonel and the unostentatious and noble Eunice; and interesting details of the recovery of the Will and of the property; and the story of Johnny's romantic life in the Indian territory; and also concerning the part taken by Colonel Loyle in the restoration of kindly feeling between the whites in South Carolina and their former slaves, after the rescue of the State from those whose power had been built on the delusion of the ignorant freedmen and by fomenting hostility between them and the excellent gentlemen who have since benefited them and their children with a generosity as conspicuous as their heroic endurance—for the sake of peace—of carpet-bag and scalawag supremacy and misrule.

You are familiar with the fact that such unscrupulous domination was terminated after eight years by a peaceful revolution in 1876. We wish the Story had been continued to the stirring scenes of that epoch to the Red-Shirt March, to the gathering at which a trumpet sound would have called forth the Angel of Death, to the leveled bayonets of Federal soldiers keeping the duly elected Democrat members from entering the Legislative Hall; but, no doubt, the writer was following the fortunes of Eunice and a small part of those of Colonel Loyle, and put down his pen when he had exhibited the happy blending of their lives. He said the union of these two adumbrated the quiet patricianism of the Past arm in arm with the progressive energy of the Present.

One remark of the author I should tell you of: that there was no intention of personal attack in anything he had written; though with so recent a theme he felt he was treading on warm ashes, like Pollio,[1] and no telling when his foot might be burnt. I think, too, he was inclined to portray in a "Part the Second" the brightening scenes of material prosperity which followed the disastrous period of Reconstruction, from a note he made where this little story ends abruptly. His bitter remembrances were apparently merging into kindlier feelings towards all parties. —At your request I send the manuscript to you. Perhaps, from its crude form, he did not purpose to publish it unless his health should enable him thoroughly to revise it.—I send also along with it a couple of Uncle Tim's essays which I found tied up with the Story.

When you visit me again, you can look over the other papers, some in prose and some in verse, the writing of which was doubtless more than a simple amusement; it wiped away worries—"molestias abstersit,"[2] as the Roman orator expressed it. Indeed his occupation with the pen was like that orator's, who, being debarred from

---

1. Rivers refers to the martyr Saint Pollio, who was burnt alive during the persecutions of Diocletian in 304.

2. Cicero, *De Senectute* 2.7. The full quotation is "non modo omnes abstersit senectitus molestias," and it translates as "It erased not only all the anxieties of old age."

participation in public affairs, had sought at Tusculum to banish from his thoughts the altered political condition of his country by busying his mind with literary work.

On the occasion of Eunice's marriage, the young man who lived near Oakhill and was addicted to composing verses, made up the following:

> Love for love glows in their hearts,
> His happy looks confess;
> And she—a radiance she imparts
> To grace his manliness.
> To her a king he is, I ween,
> And she to him a queen.
>
> Yet but the poor her subjects be,
> 'Tis so she wills; and he,
> Her king, approves; for far and near
> The old, and children dear,
> The sick, the maimed, await to see
> The smiling queen appear.
>
> With gifts she comes, in simple dress;
> Nor homage seeks; but who—
> Again I ask—who would not press
> To pay her homage due
> For goodness' sake? And reverence make
> To her rare beauty too!

Whoever has become interested in the story may like to be told that after the lapse of a few years Mrs. DeLesline died and was buried at the side of her husband. She requested that the family name on the monument should be in very large letters. And she hoped, in case of its obliteration here or its being forgotten, that it would be revived at the resurrection.—Eunice preferred to reside on her inherited Glyndale farm; and the Colonel caused the dwelling there to be renovated and the grounds tastefully adorned. Besides this farm he superintended his own at Oakhill, riding thither very frequently.—Johnny espoused (the truth is she did it) the young daughter of the German Hennchen, named for her mother, Kunigunda. Her husband's pet name for her was "Leebstie D"—the D for darling; but she led him a tough life. At times he dreamed the Comanches were again at hand. She was devoted—besides her attention to him—to instrumental music and became organist in the Reverend Fairbank's church. They all, except Carl and Rudolph, lived together in the Colonel's house at Oakhill and took good care of it.— Schwomm, proprietor of the Pharmaceutical Emporium in Columbia, bought back his paternal acres near Glyndale and placed them in charge of Carl and

Rudolph Hennchen.—Miss Mamie Avery was married to Lieutenant Gillespie and lived with her mother. Mrs. Loyle and Mrs. Gillespie visited each other almost as often as they did in their girlhood days; happy days, but not more so than those which came with blessings for them now.—When Ponce died of old age, at Glyndale farm, a grave was made for him and also a headstone, the inscription thereon being prepared by Eunice, his indulgent mistress.

About the Authors

WILLIAM JAMES RIVERS (1822–1909) was one of South Carolina's first professional historians and a founder of the South Carolina Historical Society. Also a noted novelist and poet, Rivers was professor of classical languages at South Carolina College and the College of Charleston.

A native of Greenville, South Carolina, TARA COURTNEY MCKINNEY holds a B.A. in history from the South Carolina Honors College at the University of South Carolina in Columbia.